A STRONG HAND TO HOLD

When Jenny O'Leary's dearest and closest younger brother Anthony is killed in action in 1940, grief threatens to engulf her. Then, working as an ARP warden tending to Birmingham's injured in the worst of the raids, she saves a girl whose loss is far greater than her own. Linda Prosser is just twelve and running back into her house for her brother's teddy she is crushed beneath the debris. It's Jenny who offers Linda not just a hand to hold, but a home and friendship that lasts through the years. Until Linda falls in love...

A STRONG
HAND TO HOLD

by

Anne Bennett

Magna Large Print Books
Long Preston, North Yorkshire,
BD23 4ND, England.

British Library Cataloguing in Publication Data.

Bennett, Anne
    A strong hand to hold.

    A catalogue record of this book is
    available from the British Library

    ISBN   0-7505-1715-8

First published in Great Britain 1999 by Headline Book Publishing

Copyright © 1999 Anne Bennett

Cover illustration © Angelo Rinaldi by arrangement with
Headline Book Publishing Ltd.

Published in Large Print 2001 by arrangement with
Headline Book Publishing Ltd.

Magna Large Print is an imprint of Library Magna Books Ltd.

Printed and bound in Great Britain by
T.J. (International) Ltd., Cornwall, PL28 8RW

All characters in this publication are fictitious and any resemblance to real persons, living or dead, is purely coincidental.

Acknowledgement

I would like to thank the following people who helped me write this book: Lorraine Michaelson-Yeates, Ruth Adshead, Josie Miery and Mr Chris Harvey of the Ocean Liner Society and my late father John Flanagan for his tales of Northern Ireland in the early 1900s. Heartfelt gratitude to my family for their unfailing encouragement, my editor Andi Sisodia for her constructive criticism and advice and to Denis my husband for his immeasurable support.

Chapter One

Birmingham, October 1940

'Now are you all right, Mother?' Jenny O'Leary asked, placing the breakfast tray with the pot of tea and toast spread with the last of the jam ration across her mother's knees as she sat before the fire.

Norah looked at her daughter with a pained expression – the one Jenny was well used to. The older woman's furrowed brow caused deep lines to run down her face; the bun into which she had made Jenny scrape her grey hair appeared tighter than ever; and her mouth was set in a thin line. Ignoring the question, she whined, 'The house is perishing. Put some more coal on the fire.'

Jenny suppressed a sigh, knowing she'd be late for work if she didn't get going soon. 'It won't help to put more coal on, Mother,' she said, tucking the blanket around Norah's legs as she spoke. 'What's there will burn up in a minute and warm the place, and you know we have to be careful with it.'

She knew her mother wouldn't believe her. The war was now fourteen months old, and despite Norah having four sons and a son-in-law in the fighting line, she still seemed to think a world war shouldn't affect her life at all. Before Norah was able to make a reply, Jenny's grandmother Eileen

Gillespie came in from the kitchen.

'Shouldn't you be on your way?' she snapped at Jenny. 'Go on, I'll see to your mother.'

But suddenly there was a knock on the door. Jenny raised her eyes to the ceiling. Who on earth would call at this hour? They weren't expecting any parcels.

When Jenny saw the telegraph boy with the buff telegram in his outstretched hand, for a moment she couldn't move. Her head swam and she fought against the nausea that rose in her throat. She had the urge to thrust it back at the boy, refuse to accept it, as if *not* to read that one of her brothers was killed or missing would mean it was untrue – a mistake.

Instead, she found herself not only taking it from him, but thanking him before she shut the door. She stood with the thing in her hand, shaking so much she couldn't open it. Her grandmother, coming into the hall to see who'd knocked, found Jenny sitting on the stairs, arms around her legs while shudders ran through her whole body.

Eileen's face blanched white at the sight of the crumpled telegram in Jenny's hand and she grasped the door jamb for support as she said, almost in a whisper. 'Who?'

Jenny shook her head mutely and Eileen grabbed the telegram from her and ripped it open. 'Dear God!' she wailed. 'It's Anthony!'

'Missing?' Jenny asked, and she cried out to the Almighty to give her some vestige of hope.

But her grandmother shook her head and went into the living room to break the news to her daughter. A howl of agony escaped from Jenny. A hard knot settled in her heart and sent spasms of pain through every part of her body; and although she cried out at the acuteness of it, her eyes stayed dry and she wondered, bleakly, how she'd get through the rest of her life without her beloved brother.

She hardly felt the cold of the hall seeping into her as she sat on the stairs, hugging her knees and listening to her mother's sobs from the living room and trying to come to terms with the devastating news. Anthony had been in the RAF for just five months, as he'd joined on his eighteenth birthday in mid-June. By then, the true cost of lives lost in Dunkirk was common knowledge and most people knew that just a small stretch of water separated the UK from German armies, and for the first time in many years, the British faced the possibility of invasion and subsequent defeat.

Anthony had been desperate to join up. Knowing the fight to protect Britain would come from the air, he'd soon tired of the Home Guard which he'd joined when war was declared, and where he'd trained with broomsticks, with just a black armband to show he was in any official capacity at all.

Jenny remembered it so well, the day he'd got his wish; he'd stood before her in Air Force blue, his hat at a jaunty angle and the light of excitement dancing in his eyes. And though Jenny was bursting with pride, her stomach had contracted in fear for his safety.

For just a few short weeks, all the time the RAF

could spare to train their fighter pilots, Anthony was stationed with the 605 Squadron in Castle Bromwich, not so far away. Meanwhile 'The Battle of Britain' had raged in the skies. Jenny read all the news reports. The papers used the number of enemy planes lost in comparison to the British as if it were a score at rugby. Nineteen to four, or fifteen to seven, they'd claim. She doubted the accuracy of the British losses and presumed it was done to boost morale, which she found distasteful. War was no game and every pilot lost belonged to someone.

And far, far too soon, Anthony had become a part of it, stationed in a unspecified airfield in the South. Now Jenny began to pray in earnest for her youngest brother, for while she worried and prayed about the rest of her family, she knew that her younger brother in particular faced mortal danger on a daily basis.

However, by the end of September, 'The Battle of Britain' was over, the Allies were victorious and Britain safe once more from invasion. Anthony had been home on leave for a few days. Now, just two short months later, he was dead. Jenny let out a long, shuddering groan.

She got to her feet, shivering, and went into the living room, where her mother seemed awash with tears; Eileen Gillespie held her daughter pressed to her breast. Jenny would have welcomed comforting arms around her, but she knew that would never happen. Anyway, there were practical things to do, and she seemed the only one able to deal with them. She first had to phone the Dunlop where she worked as a typist,

10

and then see her sister Geraldine and her sister-in-law Jan, the wife of her eldest brother Seamus, to tell them the tragic news.

She didn't want to see the priest – she felt God had let her down – but her grandmother said Norah needed him to visit and so she made herself go that afternoon. Geraldine and her small son Jamie were installed in the house by then, for Geraldine said she was worried how the news of Anthony's death would affect Mother with her delicate state of health.

As Jenny went down Holly Lane to the priest's house, she wondered for the thousandth time why the whole family went on with the pretence that her mother was some sort of invalid. Norah O'Leary was nothing of the sort, and if *she* knew so must they – but Jenny had only ever spoken about it with Anthony. For years it had been the same, and Norah had kept her husband Dermot dancing attendance on her because of it.

When he'd breathed his last, in the spring of 1939, Jenny had known with fearful trepidation that she, as the only unmarried daughter, would be expected to take over from her father. The prospect filled her with dread, for she knew her mother didn't like her that much – and to be truthful, she wasn't that keen on her mother either!

She had hoped the war might postpone the grim prospect she saw before her, but when she suggested giving up her job and joining the WAAFs, the family were loud in their condemnation. Only Anthony told her to go for it. More than once, he and Jenny had glimpsed their mother through the window walking around with no apparent stiffness and without her sticks, and yet when they entered the house later, they would see her sitting in her chair, covered with a blanket, complaining of the agony she was in.

Norah O'Leary was a fraud, and both her younger children knew it. Jenny remembered how Anthony had told her to drop the charade the others practised. 'For God's sake,' he'd said, 'stand up to Mother before it's too late.'

'Oh, it's all right for you,' Jenny had cried. 'You're a man. You'll soon be out of it.'

'So could you be,' Anthony had pointed out. 'Join up, if that's what you want. Mother's not helpless and Geraldine only lives up the road.'

But it had been no good. Jenny had been unable to withstand them all telling her how selfish and inconsiderate she was and how she should know where her duty lay. She supposed she'd scored a minor victory though in refusing to give up her job when Geraldine had suggested it.

'How will you cope?' her elder sister had asked.

True, in the beginning it *had* been hard dealing with her mother and the housework as well as her job. Previously her father had seen to many of Norah's needs; now there was just Jenny to do everything. She'd been glad Anthony was too young to join up with his elder brothers straight away, for she'd depended on him a lot and they'd grown closer still. Yet however hard it had been, and still was, Jenny knew that if she'd been with her mother day in, day out, she'd not have been able to stand it.

And how in God's name was she to stand this latest blow? she thought, as she turned up the garden path of the Presbytery. Who would she confide in now and tell her hopes and dreams to? Who now would deflect her mother's anger and comfort Jenny when Norah had reduced her to tears yet again. Jenny's eyes misted over with misery, but she refused to let any tears fall. She had an idea that once she began crying, she'd never stop – and she had to talk to the priest.

Father O'Malley was very sorry to hear about Anthony. Jenny was not the only one of his parishioners to come to him with similar news, but it wouldn't be helpful to tell her that. He looked at the girl, so different from her brothers and sisters in both looks and build, and saw the sorrow in her eyes. He knew, as many did, how close the two younger O'Leary children were, for there was a largish gap between them and the others. Now the girl must be twenty or so. He remembered the time before her birth when Norah had come to see him and asked him to speak to her husband, who she'd said had forced himself upon her. She was pregnant again because of it and she didn't want the child: Francis her youngest had been six and she'd thought four children enough for anyone.

Of course he could no nothing for the woman, but tell her firmly that she had to be grateful for any children that God sent her. He also said that it was not a woman's place to refuse the husband to whom she had promised obedience in the marriage ceremony. Dermot, he'd said, had rights. And he must have insisted upon them –

for Anthony had been born just two years after Jenny. Altogether the priest thought Norah O'Leary had had little to moan about in those days with a fine handsome family and Dermot able and willing to work all the hours God sent to provide for them and not spend it all in the pub. Not all women were as lucky. Of course, her disability would have been hard to bear, he could understand that, and then to lose Dermot had been a big blow. Her children would have been a fine consolation for her, if the damned war hadn't taken the young men of the family away. Thank God, he thought, she still had the girls – and Geraldine, now married, was still near at hand.

Father O'Malley had liked young Anthony. He'd been a fine boy, like his brothers before him. As mischievous as the next, though – not averse to taking the odd sip of Communion wine when he was serving on the altar, or filling his water pistol with holy water, as he recalled. But that was boys for you. The priest sighed. He'd have to go up and see Norah and try to offer the poor woman some comfort.

On the way home, Jenny decided to go to her Gran O'Leary's, for she knew no one else would bother to tell the old lady about Anthony. Norah herself hated her mother-in-law. Not that she was a great one for liking people generally, but she really seemed to loathe Maureen O'Leary. She called her fat and common, and said she'd only put up with her on sufferance while her husband was alive, and now that Dermot was dead, she refused to have anything more to do with her.

14

Jenny didn't care if her Gran O'Leary was common, but the woman her mother described scathingly as 'fat' Jenny herself would have called 'cuddly'. Her lap was just the right size for a child to snuggle into, in order to lean against her soft and very ample breasts, while her plump arms were the most comfortable and comforting pillow Jenny had ever known. Maureen O'Leary always had an apron tied around her waist and her feet were encased in men's socks, especially during the winter, with downtrodden slippers or old boots on top. Jenny didn't care either that her gran cursed and swore a bit and hadn't had the benefit of a decent education, Gran O'Leary was the only woman who'd ever shown her any love in her young life. She could never remember her own mother giving her a cuddle, or tucking her up in bed at night.

But then, as her Gran said, you couldn't make people what they were not and she had to accept that. Jenny knew her Gran had loved Anthony, and it was right that she should be informed about his death; the four eldest O'Leary children had little or nothing to do with old Mrs O'Leary, because Norah had wanted it that way. Jenny thought it a shame, especially as she'd had so much to do with them all when they'd been small, but Maureen had never complained – at least not to Jenny. She'd once told her that Dermot had had very little influence over his elder children because he'd been away so much. First the Great War had claimed him, and then, once they'd come to England, he'd had to find work and money enough to support his mother's

15

family as well as his own.

Dermot had become a driver in the armament factory his uncle worked in, and had taken on any number of contracts to earn the money he needed. Maureen told Jenny that once he'd left the house, he might not come back into it for a week. That was how it came about that Norah and her mother, Eileen Gillespie, had the rearing and ruination of Jenny's older brothers and sister.

However, it was all water under the bridge, now. Her brothers and sister were grown up and could make their own decisions – yet they never went to see their gran though she lived but two streets away, in Westmead Crescent.

That afternoon, Maureen O'Leary took one look at the anguished eyes of her granddaughter and drew her into her arms. She wept as Jenny gave her the news. She cursed Hitler and the whole German army and the German nation, and Jenny lay against her and wondered why she still couldn't cry.

Even her gran's lodger Peggy McAllister was upset when she heard of Anthony's death. The McAllisters were friends of her gran who lived in Ward End and when the family had been bombed out in August, Maureen offered their eldest girl Peggy a temporary home with her. Since then Peggy had become friendly with Jenny, and she had even met Anthony when he'd visited his gran on his short leave in late September.

'It could have been our Mick,' she said to Jenny. 'He's desperate to join the RAF and he's eighteen just after Christmas. It'll break Mammy's heart if anything happens to him.'

'It isn't only the servicemen though, is it?' Maureen said, dabbing her eyes. 'I mean, your whole family could have been killed in the raid that blew up your house. Those poor Londoners are getting it every night, and hundreds killed there.'

'It's happening all over the country,' Jenny said. 'And the Coventry raid five days ago killed over fifteen hundred people and injured many more will at least put paid to the stupid people who think being two hundred miles from the coast is some sort of deterrent. I think, and so do many more, that we will be next. All our defences have been stepped up. I'm on duty tonight, as it happens.'

'Och, girl, they'll understand if you go down and explain,' Maureen said tearfully. 'They'd not expect you in tonight if you tell them about Anthony.'

Jenny shook her head. 'I'd rather not just sit and think,' she said. 'God knows, there'll be time enough for that – and Anthony wouldn't want me to stay away, especially if there should be a heavy raid tonight.'

Maureen didn't press her granddaughter further, but Jenny knew it wouldn't be so easy for her to convince the ones at home. 'I'll have to be going anyway,' she said, getting to her feet. 'They'll all be sitting there waiting for me to make their tea.'

'I must be away too,' Peggy said, 'or they'll be handing me my cards.'

Peggy worked the night shift at BSA –

Birmingham Small Arms – in Armoury Road, making Browning guns for Spitfires, and it was one hell of a trek from Pype Hayes out there every evening. Maureen secretly thought the reason she stayed on with them and didn't look for something nearer, was because she was sweet on her son Gerry, and Gerry certainly more than liked her. In fact, Maureen thought, Peggy would be hard to dislike as she was lovely to look at with her thick hair so dark it was nearly black, and eyes to match, and her full mouth in her heart-shaped face. But best of all was her kindly nature and sense of humour. Maureen would welcome the girl as a daughter-in-law, for Gerry was thirty-three and a fine age to marry, but he was too shy to speak his mind to the girl. Maureen thought him a fool and hoped he wouldn't dally too long, or someone else would snap the girl up.

Jenny knew what was in her gran's mind, but her own was still full of her brother, and as she made her way back to the house, she wondered why she didn't look in the least bit like him. Like his three brothers and Geraldine too, Anthony had had deep brown eyes and hair, a nice-shaped nose and mouth, and flawless skin. The boys were all acknowledged as handsome and Geraldine known as a stunner.

Jenny's face was longer than theirs and went to a point at her chin, and though her eyes were brown, they were much lighter than the other O'Learys'. Her nose had no shape to it at all and was powdered with hideous freckles, and her mouth was too big and her lips too thick. But worst of all was the mop of auburn curls that refused to lie flat, or be tamed in any way. She was plain if not downright ugly – and if she'd had any doubts about it, Norah O'Leary would have dispelled them, for all the years of her growing up, she'd told her how ugly she was.

Not, in fact, that she'd grown up very much, for while the boys all touched on six foot and Geraldine was a willowy five foot six like her mother and other grandmother, Jenny was just five foot. She'd grown till she was about twelve, then stopped, and she had few womanly curves and little bust. In fact, she looked more like a young boy than a young woman, especially when she wore the trousers that women were finding so comfortable and practical these days.

Even her sister had said she'd be left on the shelf if she didn't make the most of the few attributes she had – and indeed, there had never been anyone killed in the rush to take Jenny O'Leary out.

Now though, Norah was pleased that Jenny had turned out plain. As the only unmarried daughter, she'd spend her lifetime looking after her; it wasn't as if she'd ever have a better offer. Norah considered she'd had a miserable life since she consented to marry that oaf Dermot O'Leary, but she'd made him pay for it. Now it was Jenny's turn. She'd always championed him anyway, and even looked like him and all his common relations. Norah knew she would never feel the same about Jenny as she did about her beautiful daughter Geraldine, who'd never argued with her in the whole of her life. There had been just one distressing incident in her teens when she'd been

19

all for marrying someone unsuitable. But Norah had soon put a stop to that. Jenny was a different kettle of fish altogether.

When Jenny returned from her gran's, it was to hear the priest had already paid the two women a visit. Norah immediately demanded to know where Jenny had been for such a long time; she was furious when she found out. Didn't Jenny have any thought for her feelings? Surely she knew that Maureen O'Leary was the last person on God's earth she'd have wanted her to see. 'Why,' she asked plaintively, 'do you take such pleasure in upsetting me and today of all days when I'm trying to come to terms with the death of my son?'

Jenny couldn't understand her mother. Did she honestly think Gran O'Leary should have been kept in the dark? Anthony was her grandson too, and she had loved him dearly. Surely she had a right to know!

But in this sort of mood, there was no reasoning with Norah, as Jenny knew from bitter experience. She gave a sigh and, deciding she might as well be hung for a sheep as a lamb, told her mother she was on warden duty that night and had no intention of asking to be excused. At first Jenny thought her mother was going to have a fit; naturally, everyone blamed Jenny for the upset. 'You are unnatural,' Norah declared, and Jenny could see that the others agreed with her. No one could understand her attitude. Geraldine was still at the house but she couldn't stay late for she had the children to get to bed. She said she assumed that Jenny would be there that evening to offer their mother some measure of comfort. Jenny gave a grim smile, knowing her mother would never take comfort from *her*. She was just used as the whipping boy.

It had been Anthony's idea that she work as an ARP warden or at least that she do something for the war effort. He'd told her about the women working on the shopfloor of factories doing jobs that had once been traditionally male, and of those driving buses and trucks and ambulances, and how proud he was of them all setting to and running the country in the absence of the men. His words had inspired Jenny and, having some knowledge of First Aid, she offered herself as an ARP warden and now reported for duty two evenings a week at the warden post in Tyburn Road.

Norah had then said that if Jenny was going to leave her alone in the evenings, as well as the day, she wanted her mother to move in with them, at least till the end of the war. Jenny disliked her Grandmother Gillespie, for Eileen resembled her daughter Norah in looks and temperament, but there was no point in complaining, Norah would only point out that it was her name on the rent book. Eileen had moved in, and before many weeks had passed, Jenny thought that if she hadn't had the warden post to escape to, she'd have strangled the pair of them!

She particularly needed to get out that night. Before, she'd always given in to the family and done what they wanted, but not this time. 'Mother, Anthony would want me to go,' Jenny said steadily.

21

'Oh, you know that, do you, miss?' Norah sneered.

And suddenly Jenny could almost see Anthony in front of her eyes and hear his voice in her ear. 'Go on Jen. Stand up to Mother for God's sake, or she'll destroy you.'

'Yes – yes, I do!' Jenny shouted back at her mother. 'He gave his life doing what he thought was right, but the war hasn't finished because Anthony has died. He wouldn't want us to give up. If there is a raid tonight, more people might be injured and killed. I *have* to go.' And then, as her mother made no reply, she lifted her chin defiantly and went on: 'And I *am* going, just as soon as I've made us all something to eat.'

Norah stared at Jenny. Always before she'd given in under pressure; this was a new tack entirely. 'Then go,' she said, 'though what earthly good *you'll* be I don't know, for you're as small as a child and about as much use.'

Jenny stared back at her mother for a minute, then turned from her without a word, though she trembled inside as she went into the kitchen to start on the tea. She heard Geraldine call goodbye to her mother and grandmother, completely ignoring her. Jenny told herself she didn't care; she'd made a stand now and had to stick to it – and the sooner she got the tea over and was on her way, the better she'd feel.

Chapter Two

As Jenny was struggling with the news of her brother's death, just a couple of streets away on Paget Road, Linda Lennox was looking at her mother Patty Prosser with concern, a frown creasing her brow. 'Are you sure you're well enough to get up, Mom?'

Patty looked at her daughter and smiled. She was a good kid, she thought, 'I can't stay in bed all my bloody life, now can I?' she said. 'The sooner I'm back to work and you back to school the better.'

'Yeah, but you ain't gotta rush it. You know what the doc said.'

'Yeah, I know what he said, and between the two of you I'd be wrapped in cotton wool. Don't worry, Linda – I'll have to see how I am when I'm up, won't I? If it's too much I promise I'll go back to bed, but I'm bored bloody solid, and it's too much trouble and cost to have a fire in the living room and the bedroom.'

'It ain't no trouble, Mom, honest,' Linda protested. 'The bedroom would be like an ice box without a fire. Dr Sanders said you had to keep warm.'

'I know, but today I'll get up and sit by the fire downstairs for a bit, all right?'

'OK,' Linda conceded. 'I'll make us both a cuppa, eh?'

Patty's face still looked pasty white, Linda thought, but at least she wasn't coughing quite so much any more. She knew what had given her the chest infection; it was that trip to the Bull Ring the previous Saturday to buy her some new shoes. Her mom had already been full of cold. Their good neighbour and friend Beattie Latimer had told her to leave it a while, for the day had been wild, squally and cold, not a day to be going anywhere, but Patty said Linda could wait no longer for shoes. And she couldn't really. Her summer sandals hurt her toes, they were so small and her pumps didn't keep her feet warm or dry, despite the cardboard Linda put inside them.

Still, they didn't have to go as far as town to buy shoes and Linda guessed her mom wanted a gander at the Bull Ring after the bombing raids on it in late August. She did herself, and when Patty had told Beattie not to fuss, it was just a cold, she'd believed her.

They'd had a great day, for much as she loved her two little brothers, George and Harry, Linda enjoyed having her mother to herself at times. And Beattie, despite her disapproval, agreed to mind the two little ones so that they could go together.

They'd both been shocked by the devastation. They'd read about it, of course, and seen pictures in the *Evening Mail* and the *Despatch*, but seeing pictures and hearing about it was one thing; being there was quite another. Much of the rubble from inside the shops on the bottom end of High Street down towards the Bull Ring had been cleared over the past weeks and the empty shells of the

24

shops leaned drunkenly one against the other.

At first, the Bull Ring itself had seemed much the same as ever. The bag lady was still there chanting, ''Andy Carriers,' as she had for as long as Linda could remember, and opposite to her was the man selling Alcazar razor blades. There didn't seem quite so many barrows though, and the fish stalls were severely depleted. 'I heard tell they were going to start selling whale meat,' Patty said. 'But I can't see any sign of it.'

'Ugh,' Linda had said in disgust. 'Don't you go buying any of that.'

'Now, now. You ain't never tasted it, so how can you say that,' Patty had admonished. 'Any road, you might be glad of it before we're finished, with all this rationing.'

Linda had doubted she'd ever be that desperate, but wisely didn't argue further.

She'd always loved the buzz and clamour of the Bull Ring, the mingled smells of the goods on offer, and the chatter and hubbub of the crowds, mixed with the cries of the vendors shouting their wares. Hawkers had been spread about Nelson's Column, their wares laid out in suitcases with lookout boys on the corners in case any rozzers came that way. Linda knew you had to watch what you bought from hawkers. She'd heard of a woman who'd bought a watch from them for five bob. When she couldn't get it to go, she took it to a watch repairers, who took the back off and found there was nothing inside. 'Daft 'aporth she must have been,' Beattie snorted when she'd told the tale. 'I'm sure I'd make certain the bloody thing worked before I'd

25

hand over five bob.'

Linda was sure she would too, but she had felt sorry for Thelma Grimshaw, the mother of her best friend Carole, who had once bought a pair of silk stockings at a bargain price from a hawker, only to find there was no foot in one of them! But still, that day the hawkers had been doing a brisk trade. It was mainly black-market stuff and there'd been clusters of people around them, seeing what they had to sell.

The fruit and veg stalls no longer had the array of stuff they'd had before the war. There were no bananas or oranges, just a few piles of mangy-looking apples, some rock-hard pears and small bunches of grapes. There were plenty of potatoes and onions, carrots and swedes and some tired-looking lettuces and small tomatoes, but little else.

However the sight of the Market Hall had taken Linda's breath away for a moment or two. Open to the sky, it was still a fine old building, and the old lags were still there on the steps with their trays of bootlaces and matches and hair grips. Linda and Patty went up the steps to gaze at it and saw that the people had begun returning. They'd been sheltered from the elements by canvas awnings, the Market Hall had been cleaned up and was now back in business.

Linda remembered Beattie telling them all about it just after the bombs had landed. 'Bleeding animals running all over the place,' she had said. 'God it must have been a sight.'

Linda had felt sorry for the frightened creatures. A visit to Pimm's Pet Shop was always one of the highlights of any trip to the Bull Ring when she'd been younger. The shop had a wide variety of animals – hamsters, guinea pigs and rabbits, together with adorable kittens or boisterous puppies that nipped playfully with their sharp little teeth. Then there were the birds; she used to spend ages standing in front of the budgies trying to get them to talk. The canaries she recalled, always sang so beautifully, and occasionally there'd even be a parrot or a mynah bird.

There were no pets now, and the clock the children and many adults had been fascinated by was also gone. There were fewer flower-sellers than before the war, Linda noticed. This came as no surprise. Everyone was digging up their lawns and gardens now to grow vegetables. They had been urged to 'Dig for Victory'.

She herself couldn't ever remember having flowers in the house, or growing in the garden. Patty had told her that her father had tended the garden nicely before he got too sick, they'd had vegetables in the back and flowers in the front, and he'd often cut a bunch and bring them into the house for his wife. But eventually he'd grown too ill to see to the garden and Bert Latimer came to mow the lawns. The vegetables and flowers went to seed and died; Ted Prosser, her second husband, never had any interest in it. Linda remembered Patty's sad face as she'd said that, and she thought if ever she had any spare money, she'd buy a bunch of flowers to cheer her up.

As she followed behind Patty, she saw Jimmy Jesus taking his place by St Martin's Church. 'Look, Mom!'

27

'He's early today,' Patty remarked. 'Must have plenty to say.'

They'd stood a minute to listen to the old down-and-out with the long white hair and beard that had given him his name. 'Though your souls be as black as pitch, if you repent of your sinful ways, your soul can be washed cleaner than the whitest snow by the blood of the lamb,' Jimmy began.

A few hecklers shouted at him from the crowd, but Jimmy Jesus took no notice and opened up his Bible. 'Oh, Gawd blimey, come on, chuck,' Patty had urged. 'I ain't in the mood for a bloody sermon today.'

Linda followed her mother as she made her way towards the Rag Market, but sneaked a look back at Jimmy Jesus as she went. He'd always fascinated her; though she couldn't understand all he said, she liked the sound of his voice which was surprisingly gentle and without an accent of any kind.

The Rag Market was used as a fish market through the week and the reek of fish was still there; Linda wrinkled her nose at the smell, but she knew as well as anyone that this was where the bargains were to be found. Sure enough, after a little bit of haggling, Patty had got a pair of stout shoes for Linda costing three bob, as well as plenty of cheap vegetables, a few apples and some fresh fish at a very reasonable price. Patty was pleased with herself and it wasn't until they were on their way home on the rickety, smoky tram that she'd begun to cough; the next morning, Sunday, Linda phoned for the doctor

28

from the phone box on the corner.

She didn't mind sending for Dr Sanders now. He'd become a good friend to them all. She remembered the first time she'd gone to see him early in August. Patty had collapsed five days earlier.

Linda told the doctor it was the telegram that had brought it on, but she knew it wasn't, not really. Linda guessed that her mother was secretly glad when she got the telegram to tell her that her second husband, Edward Prosser, would not be coming home from Dunkirk. He'd been a bully and Linda knew he used to hit her mom. She'd hated Ted Prosser for what he did to Patty and because he was horrible to the boys. There was another reason for hating him too, but she had never breathed a word to her mom about it – wouldn't ever have to now, 'cos that pig was dead and gone and couldn't hurt them any more.

However, when Patty had read the letter that came later, she had dropped like a stone to the floor in a dead faint. Dr Sanders had put her condition down to delayed shock and depression, and he prescribed tablets. He hadn't informed the Welfare Authorities about the family though he knew he should have done. Instead, he'd arranged for a District Nurse to call daily until Patty was on her feet. He'd said it was too much for any twelve-year-old, coping with a sick mother as well as the housework and cooking and looking after her two little brothers aged three years and just twelve months, even with the quite considerable help she got from the next-door neighbour.

When Patty recovered, he'd got her a job in Armstrong's on the Lichfield Road making cartridge cases; he also used his influence to get a place for George and little Henry at the day nursery across the road.

It was great now, Linda thought. Money wasn't quite so tight; they no longer had to hide from the rent man and could begin to pay the doctor's bill, though he'd told them there was no rush. It grew better still when Beattie talked her Bert round into letting her take a job too. She'd said she was bored solid at home with the lads fighting and her daughter married and living in Leeds, and anyway, she wanted to be doing her bit. But it meant that she'd pop in in the morning, help to get the boys ready and help Patty bring them back in the evening. Linda knew they had a lot to thank Beattie for. Even now, with Patty ill again, she'd taken the boys and left them at the nursery on the Monday and that day, Tuesday too, knowing that Linda would have her hands full as it was.

Patty watched her daughter bustling about, getting a meal for the two of them. 'We'll put the wireless on later, bab,' she said. 'Have a bit of music to cheer us all up.'

They hadn't had the wireless very long and it was still a novelty. Patty had wanted one at home because they always had 'Worker's Playtime' on at the factory and she loved to sing along to the songs. When any of the girls said how terrific her voice was, she always replied that they should hear her daughter Linda, as hers was even better, and she tried hard to remember the words of the songs to teach Linda in the evening. Then she heard of the 'never never' or 'hire purchase' scheme where you could make a down payment on a wireless, then pay so much back a week. But oh, the excitement in the house the Saturday it was delivered!

Linda had looked as if Patty had given her the Crown Jewels. 'Can we afford it, Mom?'

'Let me worry about that,' Patty had said. 'Any road, we need to hear the news, don't we, or this flipping lot will be invading us and we'll know nowt about it till the church bells start to ring.'

'Oh, Mom!'

'I'm only joking,' Patty said. 'But we do need to know what's happening. If it gets too miserable we can always turn the dial to summat else, eh? They have good plays on, the girls at work were telling me.'

The thing they enjoyed the most was singing together, and they'd join in the old favourites belting out from the wireless. Beattie loved to hear them. Patty and Linda had been singing together ever since Linda was just a nipper, but it had all come to a stop when Patty married Ted Prosser. Didn't like to hear it, Patty had said. Didn't like much, if Beattie's opinion had been asked. Didn't seem to take to Linda either and resented any closeness between her and her mother. But then he didn't go great guns for his own babbies either. Funny man altogether and Patty was better off without him, not that she went around telling her like, but she was.

Patty knew what Beattie thought, for even if she said nothing, her face spoke volumes. They'd been neighbours since she'd come on to the Estate in 1930. Patty Lennox she'd been then, of course, and she thought she was in heaven getting one of the new houses on the Pype Hayes Estate, after living in one room in a rat-infested house in Aston since her marriage three years previously. She was so proud and kept the place like a new pin. She enjoyed looking after her husband and little girl, and hoped there would be more children to fill the house with their chatter.

However, when she lost her dear husband Billy to TB in 1932, Patty was glad she only had Linda to see to. It was Beattie who'd been her support then and helped her to pull herself together for the sake of her child. Later it was Beattie, too, who minded Linda when Patty did cleaning at the Norton pub. Patty also worked behind the bar a time or two to make ends meet, and that was where she met Ted Prosser. She often rued the day, for the man had hard fists, a vicious temper and a short fuse which grew shorter according to the amount he'd drunk. Added to that, he kept Patty short of money and when he did give her any, often borrowed it back to supplement his beer money.

Patty knew her daughter disliked him and there was something else, a wariness that had always come into Linda's eyes when they spoke of him; and she never wanted to be left alone with him in the house. Patty had her suspicions, but didn't know how to raise them with the child. What if she was wrong and put all sorts of ideas in her head? She'd thought Linda would come to her if there had been anything, but she hadn't. That apart, Patty soon knew she'd made a grave mistake marrying Ted Prosser, one she'd pay for, for the rest of her life because she couldn't see him agreeing to divorce. When she received word of his death, she felt little grief; her overriding concern was how she'd feed and clothe three children.

But the letter from the Corporal told her of a husband she didn't recognise. He'd given up his place in a boat leaving Dunkirk for the Corporal because he'd been injured and lost his life because of it. The Corporal said Ted had been a brave fine man and her loss must be a grievous one and he said also he would be recommending him for a bravery award. His description of Ted Prosser bore no resemblance to the bully he'd become to his wife and Patty knew if she'd glimpsed that brave and selfless soldier the Corporal appeared to know, she'd have considered herself proud to be married to him. The fault must have been hers, she told herself. She'd failed to recognise Ted's good points and had annoyed and frustrated him in some way, so he'd been forced to lash out at her and go to the pub to escape. It had been those feelings that had overwhelmed her. She'd thought she was no good as a wife or a mother and everyone, including the children, would be better off without her. Now she knew that wasn't true. It was just possible that Ted Prosser would have returned from the war a changed man, but privately she doubted it. What she didn't doubt was the love she had for her children, and that encouraged her to get better, helped by medication from the doctor.

33

Linda was relieved that Sunday when the doctor said her mother would soon be up and about again. He said chest infections were rife in the winter and it was nothing to worry about, and she'd soon be back at work. Linda was glad she'd be leaving school herself in a couple of years, for then the money problems would be easier and her Mom might not have to work so hard. One thing she did know was that they didn't need a man to look after them.

Just once her mother had said, 'Well, I've had two husbands and that's one too many, but without Ted there would be no George or Harry, and I wouldn't want to be without them, would you?'

Linda would not. To be without her brothers was unthinkable, but she remembered the times Ted had come home drunk from the pub and the sounds of slaps and punches and the screams of her mother. The next day Patty would host a black eye, split lip, or bruises on her cheek and Linda thought it was a bloody high price to pay.

If her mother stayed up that evening, maybe she could get her to tell her about her real father again, she thought. They'd take the photographs out of the shoe-box in the glass-fronted cupboard in the alcove and Linda would study her mother in her wedding dress and the father she could scarcely remember, stiff but smart in a suit anyone could see he was unaccustomed to wearing. There were others – one of him cuddling her in his arms as a baby, and one of him holding her hand in the wilderness of a garden he had eventually tamed, according to her Mom.

There were more of them both in the tended garden, pushing her on the swing he'd built for her and another helping to blow out the three candles on the day of her third birthday party. After that she knew he became sick, but when her mother spoke about how much he'd loved Linda and how happy they were together, it often brought a lump to the young girl's throat. Patty had told Linda how much she missed Billy when he died, and Linda supposed that was why she'd married Ted Prosser. She didn't ask her, though; she never mentioned the man's name if she could help it.

She glanced out of the window. Although it wasn't yet half past two, the dark autumn day had turned dusky and Linda knew she would soon have to attend to the blackout. She loved the cosiness of their house in the winter's evenings. Once the supper things had been washed and put away and the little ones were in bed, the thick red curtains would be drawn across the bay window cutting off the hated blackout curtains. Then Linda and Patty would sit in front of the fire; Patty could now afford plenty of coal. They'd talk, or listen to the wireless, or play cards, or knit socks and balaclavas for the troops. Tonight, Beattie would be with them as her Bert was on nights at the Dunlop, but Linda didn't mind that; she liked Beattie.

Suddenly there was a pounding on the door, and Linda opened it to see Beattie herself outside, standing with Harry in the pushchair and George holding on to the handle. 'Beattie,' she said in surprise.

'Let me in, girl, this cold goes through you like a bleeding knife.'

Linda stood aside and Beattie marched into the living room, surprised to see Patty sitting by the fire. 'What are you doing up?' she asked.

Patty's mouth had dropped agape. 'Never mind me,' she said. What are *you* doing home at this time of day?'

Beattie began unstrapping Harry as she explained. 'Got a call about my sister Vera from the hospital. Silly bugger's fell down the stairs and broke her leg bad. They're keeping her in so it mustn't be straightforward. She's in the General. She wants me to go and see to their Vicky and her husband Lennie.'

'Doesn't she live in Sutton Coldfield?'

'Yeah,' Beattie said and added, 'I hate the bloody place – all kippers, curtains and no drawers. Too bleeding posh for any air raids. And Vicky's well able to look after herself and see to her dad – she's a year older than Linda who could do it with her eyes shut. Any road, the doctor said she was getting upset and agitated, so I said to tell her I'll go. I might then get to see our Vera herself at visiting time this evening.'

'What a shame,' Patty said sympathetically.

'Ah well. My old man will have to look after himself and all,' Beattie said. 'I'll go round and see him in a bit, before he goes down for the night shift.'

'D'you want a cup of tea, Mrs Latimer?' Linda asked as she unzipped a squirming Harry from his siren suit and put him down on the floor.

'Thought you'd never ask, girl,' Beattie said,

folding up the pushchair and putting it in the hall. 'Me tongue's hanging out. And what's your Ma doing up out of bed?'

'You'd better ask her,' Linda said, making for the kitchen with George behind her, his teddy bear Tolly, trailing after him. He'd had Tolly since he was a baby and though he knew he couldn't take the toy to the nursery, it went everywhere else and it was the first thing he made for when he came home in the evening.

Inside the living room, Beattie looked across at Patty and thought her rather pale. 'You're not overdoing it, I hope?'

'With our Linda in charge?' Patty said. 'You must be joking.'

'You gave her a right bloody turn, I'll tell you,' Beattie said. 'Bloody great fool you were to go out with that cold on you.'

Patty shrugged. 'Least it gives you a chance to say, "I told you so",' she said with a smile, and went on, 'Don't fuss, Beat, I can't bear fuss and I was bored stupid upstairs. I'll go to bed early tonight and be as right as rain in the morning.'

'Don't think of coming into work this week,' Beattie lectured. 'And don't forget, I won't be able to take the babbies to nursery tomorrow, being as I'll be living it up in Sutton-bloody Coldfield. My Bert will have to see to himself tomorrow morning.'

'He can come here for his breakfast if he wants,' Linda said, coming in with the cups of tea on a tray.

Beattie accepted a cup from Linda and said, 'No ducks, you got enough on your plate as it is looking after the nippers and all. For Gawd's sake, Bert can make himself a few slices of toast and a cup of tea. Won't kill him, will it? Might even make him appreciate me a bit more, eh?'

'Aye, and pigs might fly,' Patty chuckled and to Linda she said, 'Pull the curtains, bab. We need a light on in here – it's as black as pitch.'

Linda did as she was bid, glad to shut out the cold night. The rain hammered on the panes like hailstones and she shivered. 'Hate to be out in this,' she said.

'Yeah, pity them Londoners trekking down the Underground night after night,' Beattie said. 'God, it doesn't bear thinking about.'

'Yeah, and the papers going on as if it's some great party, as if they choose to do it,' Patty said. 'Bleeding fools. I'm glad my sister Lily's out of it any road. She was right down by the London docks, you know? How she was supposed to look after all those kids down the Underground, or somewhere just as bad, I don't know. Any road, she was all for going back home when no bombs fell. It was only her hubby Sid who made her stay; he'd got himself a good job and the kids were settled into schools. I told her to stick it out. I bet she's bloody glad now.'

'Basingstoke she was sent to, weren't she?' Beattie said. 'Where's that then?'

'Down south somewhere,' Patty said vaguely. 'Don't rightly know for sure, just know it ain't in London.'

'Point is,' Beattie said, 'my Bert said it shows you now, after the raid on Coventry, that being so very far from the coast is nothing – and you got to admit, Birmingham makes a lot of stuff – armaments, tyres, planes and lots of military vehicles. If Jerry gets wind of it, he'll come for us, I reckon.'

Both Linda and Patty shivered and Patty scooped the toddling Harry into her arms and hugged him as she cried, 'For Gawd's sake, Beat, put a sock in it! Proper Job's comforter you are. If Hitler's got something up his sleeve for us, I hope he waits for the warmer weather, that's all.'

Beattie drained her cup of tea and getting to her feet she remarked with a laugh, 'Well, now I've cheered you up right and proper, I'll go and do the same to me old man. Bye, all.'

Linda saw Beattie out, and as she came back in Patty remarked, 'Right little ray of sunshine, ain't she, our Beat?' Linda laughed and took the tray of cups back into the kitchen and hoped in her heart of hearts that Beattie was wrong. The August raids had been quite frightening enough, when she and Patty had to sing to the children to calm them down, but as they'd eventually lain across the bunk asleep, her nerves had gathered into knots and her throat became so dry it was hard to swallow.

She gave herself a mental shake. What was she doing, worrying about something before it even happened? She saw George looking at her frowning face and wondered how much he had understood of Beattie's words. No need for him to be worried anyway and she smiled at him and said, 'D'you want a drink of milk, George?'

The lad nodded his head. 'Can I have summat to eat and all?'

'In a bit,' Linda told him. She knew both boys had a cooked meal at the nursery. 'Tell you what, I'll do you some toast on the fire later and I'm sure we've got a bit of jam left in the jar.'

'I'm hungry now though,' he complained.

Linda poured some milk into a cup and handed him one of the apples they'd got from the market on Saturday. 'Have this for now,' she said. 'I'll get your tea later.'

Mollified, George sat up at the table cuddling Tolly in his arms and swinging his legs as he watched Linda bustling around, preparing a nourishing meal for her mother. 'D'you think we'll be bombed, Linda?' he asked. 'Beattie does.'

'She's Mrs Latimer to you,' Linda said sharply. 'And I don't know if we'll be bombed, George. But we'll be all right – we've got the shelter, haven't we?'

Her brother wrinkled his nose. 'I don't like that shelter, it's smelly and cold and dark,' he whined.

'It ain't dark, George,' Linda said. 'I've put a hurricane lamp in there and that will soon light the place up. We can take blankets to wrap ourselves in if we have to go down there. 'Fraid I can't do much about the smell.'

She ruffled his dark hair and said, 'But why are you worrying, eh? It might never happen. Hitler's probably finished with us now. Maybe it's someone else's turn.'

She didn't believe it, but George did. In a way Linda wished she was still small and could be reassured so easily. But at least she'd taken the worry away from her little brother's eyes and she bent and planted a kiss on the top of his head.

40

Chapter Three

Jenny realised almost as soon as the door clicked behind her that night, that she'd forgotten her torch. No wonder – she'd been in such a state of agitation after the row, when she'd insisted on reporting for duty that night. The point was, it was a disaster not to have any light at all on those blacked-out nights, for you couldn't see a hand in front of your face. Instead of going back indoors and facing her family again, she began to pick her way cautiously over the ground. So many people had been killed on the roads during the first months of the war because of the blackout, that Stan Walker, who worked with her at the warden post, said he reckoned it was Hitler's secret weapon. 'He ain't gonna fight us at all,' he said with his wheezy laugh. 'He's just going to let us kill ourselves in the bleeding 'orse road.'

White lines were painted along the kerbs and on the running boards of cars and, though they were now allowed shielded headlights, it had made little difference. There were few cars on the Pype Hayes Estate anyway and the white lines were barely visible on a dark moonless night.

Everyone hated the blackout. Norah never stopped going on about it and made no effort to comply with regulations. She would have sat by uncurtained windows, the light shining like a beacon outside and eaten the entire butter ration

41

in one meal if Jenny hadn't watched her. Ignoring the blackout carried a fine of £200 and Jenny couldn't afford to indulge her mother.

As usual though, pangs of guilt began to stab at her as she made her way to the ARP post and she wondered whether she should have stayed at home that night with her mother. She hoped that Norah and Eileen would be all right but she doubted, even if there was a raid that night, that they'd use the Anderson shelter in the garden which her brothers had erected before they went away to war. Being sunk into the earth, it was inclined to flood; her next-door neighbour Mr Patterson had helped Jenny to pump it out just the previous week. He'd floor-boarded it for her too, as he'd done his own at the beginning of the war, and put a seat one side and two bunks at the other. He'd even loaned her his old oil-heater to warm the place up, and Jenny had bought a kerosene lamp to put in there for a light. She'd used the shelter herself in the August raids, and while it wasn't the most comfy place in the world, it hadn't been so bad.

Her mother was adamant, however, that she would not go grubbing in some underground tin shack like an animal, and that was that! Eileen felt the same. The two women had taken shelter under the stairs in the pantry that opened off the living room when the bombs came a little close. People said you were just as safe there – and maybe you were. Jenny was powerless to do anything about it, anyway. She could hardly force them to take shelter if they didn't want to.

She hadn't quite reached the post when the

siren wailed out a warning. Before it had faded away she saw the planes approaching, though in the dark it was the drone of them that alerted her first. They were nearly overhead before she saw the shapes of them in the sky. The first planes dropped incendiaries, making the blackout irrelevant as the night was suddenly lit up like daylight; now she saw the second column of planes flying in formation behind them. She actually *saw* the bomb doors open and the bombs topple out fins first and then nose down towards their targets. She heard the first crashes and crumps, and remembering where she was supposed to be making for, she increased her pace.

Jenny knew with a dread certainty that there would be more grieving families before the night was over. She also knew that the news of Anthony's death had to wait. This was not the time for the luxury of tears.

Linda was toasting bread for her brothers' tea with a long-handled toasting fork over the glowing embers in the grate when the siren went off. She jumped so suddenly, the toast fell off the fork and dropped into the fire. 'Oh, bloody hell.'

'What's up?' Patty called from the kitchen, where she was boiling a kettle.

'I've dropped the perishing toast.'

'They wouldn't have had time to eat it anyway,' Patty said struggling into her coat. 'Go and get the hot-water bottles out of the boys' beds, will you, love? That shelter will be perishing. I'll fill the flask up with hot tea.'

Linda looked at her mother with concern. She was right, the shelter would be freezing – the very last place Patty should be spending the night. She scuttled hurriedly upstairs and hoped the raid wouldn't go on very long and they'd be able to come back inside soon.

The bottles would keep them a bit warmer anyway, she thought, and she tugged the blankets off the beds for good measure. Downstairs, her mom was pouring the contents of the teapot into the flask. She smiled at Linda and said, 'Nothing's so bad if you can have a cuppa, eh?'

'Not half.'

Yes, it would be nice to have hot tea, Linda thought. The vacuum flask was a wonderful invention and very expensive, but Patty had come home with one a few weeks before, bought from someone at work with contacts.

'Take all that lot down the shelter, Linda,' Patty said, handing her the flask as well. 'Then come back and give me a hand with the babbies.'

'You'd better turn the gas off under the stew, too,' Linda said, and hoped the raid wouldn't last long because her stomach was growling with hunger. It was as she was returning to the house that she saw a fleet of bombers heading their way. 'Hurry, Mom,' she said as she ran in.

'I'm coming,' Patty said. 'I've got Harry's bottle ready and a packet of biscuits I put by in case this might happen. Get your coat on. I'll do Harry, you see to George.'

She went into the pantry and could hear the drones of the planes louder and she looked at Linda in sudden fear. There sounded like

44

hundreds over their heads. Both boys picked up the tension of their mother and sister, and Harry started to grizzle as Patty struggled to fasten him into his suit. But she took no notice and then she picked him up and handed him to Linda. 'Take him down,' she said. George trailed after his mother, dragging his beloved teddy bear Tolly behind him, his coat flapping open because he hadn't let Linda stop to fasten it.

A resounding crash, terrifyingly close, startled Patty. Her hand closed around the biscuits on the top shelf of the pantry. The sooner they were under cover the better, she thought, and she turned with such suddenness, she almost tripped over George who was clinging to her skirt. The intensity of the raid had unnerved her totally and she screamed, 'Let go, George, let go! Come on, let's get to the shelter quick.'

George was too scared to loose his mother's skirt and, as another bomb landed too close for comfort, he gave a yelp of terror. Patty bent to pick him up with a suddenness that took him by surprise and Tolly fell from his arms on to the pantry floor.

'Tolly,' he cried, but Patty was stopping for no threadbare teddy. She dashed after Linda out of the back door and into the comfortless shelter in the back garden.

Warmed by the hot-water bottles and wrapped in the blankets, they sat huddled on the bench. It was bitterly cold. Patty doled out biscuits by the light of the hurricane lamp she'd hung from a protruding screw on the shelter wall. 'We can't eat them all now,' she told George as he

45

clamoured for more. 'We might be here some time.'

'Can we have a cup of tea? I'm gagging,' Linda asked.

'Not yet,' Patty said. 'This could go on for hours and it would be daft to have drunk it all then.'

Linda said nothing, but her stomach continued to rumble; the biscuits had done little to fill her up and a cup of hot tea would have been comforting. The crashes and explosions all around them were frightening the boys and Linda began to rock Harry to and fro as she and her mom started to sing to the boys as they'd done before to calm them down. They started on all the nursery rhymes they'd ever known to encourage George to join in, and then all the rousing war songs to counteract the explosions and the tremors they felt even through the shelter. In time the lateness of the hour, Linda's rocking motion and the sucking of the warm milk caused little Harry's sobs to ease and his eyelids to droop. But George suddenly sat up straight, all sleepiness forgotten as he said, 'I want Tolly.'

Linda raised her eyes questioningly to her mother, who said, 'He dropped it on the pantry floor when I picked him up to run in here.'

Linda knew of George's devotion to Tolly. 'He'll be all right, George,' she told him. 'He's looking after the house.'

George lifted a tear-streaked face and said, 'No he ain't. 'itler will bomb him.'

'No, he won't, George.'

'Yes, he will. Else why we in 'ere?'

46

Linda couldn't answer that and as George began to cry again, she said, 'Don't worry, he'll be all right.'

Patty unscrewed the flask and poured out a half-cup for George. 'Here,' she said to Linda, 'see if this will shut him up.'

Patty took Harry from Linda and tucked him in the bunk with a hot-water bottle and a blanket, and left him sucking the last of his warm milk while Linda was blowing the hot tea until it was cool enough to give George.

'Beattie's well out of this tonight,' Patty remarked.

'Oh yes, didn't she say Sutton Coldfield's too posh to bomb?'

'Got no industry, that's why,' Patty said.

'She'd better stay there then,' Linda said, 'than put up with this. This isn't a place I'd like to spend much time in.'

Patty's chest was hurting her again but she tried to control her coughing so as not to worry Linda. 'I agree with you,' she said at last. 'These shelters are not the healthiest places in the world, but we must be safer in here than out there. Our Beattie won't stay longer than she can help at her Vera's. She always says she can't stand her, nor the place where she lives. Apparently they never got on, even as kids. But there you are, blood's thicker than water when all's said and done.'

'Well, she's lucky to be there tonight at any rate, ain't she?' Linda said. 'If she was here, she'd be sharing our shelter and probably our biscuits too.'

Patty opened her mouth, but before she could

say anything George handed Linda back the empty cup, wiped his mouth with his sleeve and said, 'Can we go and get Tolly now?'

'God, child, I'll brain you in a minute,' Patty cried.

'It's stopped,' George said flatly.

The raid hadn't stopped exactly, but the explosions were further away, certainly. 'I'll run back to the house and fetch Tolly for you,' Linda said.

'You'll do no such thing.'

'It's eased a bit. Listen.'

'Any minute they could be back.'

'I'll only be a tick,' Linda said. 'You know our George won't settle without that flipping bear.'

George began to whimper and cry again. 'I want Tolly, I do. Get me Tolly, Linda.'

'Honest, Mom, it won't take me a minute,' Linda said. 'Pour me a cup of tea and I'll be back to drink it.'

She was out of the shelter before Patty could stop her, glad for a moment of the blast of cold air after the stale damp mugginess of the shelter. The air smelt smoky and the night sky was lit up by searchlights; there was an orange glow everywhere. Her ears were filled with the loud tattoo of anti-aircraft guns, the drone of aeroplanes and the sirens of the emergency services.

She'd almost reached the house when she saw the formation of planes that seemed to have come from nowhere and were heading straight towards her like menacing black beetles. She bolted in the back door; the sooner she got George's bear and was back inside the shelter the better, she thought.

She'd reached the living room and turned on the light when a whooshing sound seemed to knock her off her feet and take all the breath from her body. She lay where she'd been thrown for a moment or so. The house had been plunged into darkness and debris continued to fall all around her. Linda knew a bomb had fallen terrifyingly close and her house had been caught in the blast. She was frightened to death, trembling in every limb, fearing at any moment the house would fall on top of her.

She could see nothing. The darkness was so thick she felt she could almost touch it. Yet she told herself to keep calm, and to try and remember where she'd been in the room when the blast had knocked her over.

Cautiously she got on to her hands and knees and began to crawl frantically over the rubble, whimpering with fear and knowing there was just one place where she might be moderately safe and that was the pantry. However, in the pitch black, she had no idea if she was even going in the right direction.

She found the remains of the pantry door first, and crawled over it into what remained of the small room. She was only just in time. As she lay, panting with fear, the house began to give ominous creaks; there was a sliding, splintering sound and Linda curled in a ball with her hands over her head as with a roar the house collapsed. There was a crash of falling masonry, the smell of brick and plaster, and the stink of charred wood.

Never in all her life had Linda felt such intense

terror and she broke out in a cold sweat. The dust swirling in the air was gritty in her eyes, stopped up her nose and filled her mouth, threatening to choke her. Any minute she expected to be buried alive.

Eventually, things stopped moving and there was no sound at all – only a deep silence. She moaned in relief, almost surprised that she was still alive. She tasted blood in her mouth and realised she'd bitten her bottom lip and hadn't been aware of it. She was so tense, every bone in her body ached.

She was mighty glad her mom knew where she was. She even knew where it was Tolly had dropped out of George's fingers, so she could pinpoint exactly where Linda would be right away. Until then she knew she just had to stay calm and eventually they'd dig her out.

It was hard though to remain calm, all alone in the dark, and soon she began to shiver with cold and shock. Had she been injured anywhere? She felt all over her face and extended her arms, very gingerly one at a time, not sure how much space she had. She did the same to her legs and gave a sigh of relief when she found there was room to stretch them out fully. It was a fairly large space, she reasoned so there'd be plenty of air if it was a long time till she was rescued. Suddenly, there was a loud crack above her head and she opened her mouth in a scream. But before she was able to utter a sound and before she could pull her legs out of harm's way, the bottom of the stairs collapsed on top of them. The stairs had held the weight of the house and of the houses adjoining, and the pain that ran through Linda's body was agonising. She was also stuck fast. At first she couldn't believe it and began wriggling and struggling, but it achieved nothing but more pain.

She forgot about being brave and staying calm. She wanted her mom and she began to shout for her, but her mouth filled with dust and she started to cough. She thought she was going to die, die here all alone in the blackness, and tears poured down her cheeks as she continued to yell for help.

Eventually though, she was too tired and her throat too sore to shout any more and she lay quiet, shaking all over. She tried to calm herself; she wouldn't be there long. People were probably looking for her right now. She listened intently, but couldn't hear anything. Maybe the raid was still going on. She had to be patient; they'd come as soon as they could.

When her fumbling hands came into contact with fur, she realised she'd found Tolly and was absurdly pleased. She'd thought he would have been buried under the rubble that had once been their home. George would be pleased at least, she thought, by the return of his beloved bear, but her mom would be cut up by the loss of the house she loved. Linda wondered where they'd all live. Something would have to be found for them; they could hardly camp out in the street. Mom would sort it all out, Linda thought sleepily.

She wished she could see her, or hear her voice. She cuddled Tolly, surprised how comforting it was. The bear smelt of her brother George and she leaned her head against the toy and closed her eyes. She wanted to sleep, to pass the time away till she was rescued, and she thought of all the tales her mother had told her about her real father. She pictured his face before her as he had been in his wedding photograph. 'Oh, Dad,' Linda whispered into the darkness. 'I wish I could remember what you really look like. I wish you were here now.' That was the last thing Linda could remember. It was as if a deep peace came over her and eventually she slept.

Chapter Four

Phil Rogers, the chief ARP warden, surveyed what was left of what had once been six houses, virtually opposite Paget Road Senior School. He and several wardens like himself had worked through the teeth of the continuing raid to pull people from the rubble and now as the planes still droned above in the black sky and with the crashes and thumps and explosions all around them, he said, 'We'll have to leave the rest; I can't risk any more lives. There's an unexploded bomb in the school playground and everyone has to be evacuated out of the area.'

Jenny was feeling very sick. She'd helped pull apart the buckled corrugated iron and burst sandbags of the Anderson shelter in the garden of the end house to get at the woman with the two little boys. She'd fought the nausea that rose in her throat as she pulled out the little crushed bodies, one little boy was just a baby, the other only slightly older. 'Poor sod lost her man at Dunkirk,' one of the neighbours said as she was being carried to one of the three ambulances standing by.

Oh God, Jenny thought, a whole family killed through this stupid, stupid war. She felt anger and hatred towards the German nation and in particular, the bombers, bringing such misery into people's lives.

The first three houses were reduced to a mountain of rubble; the fourth had no upper part, but part of one of the downstairs walls still stood; the fifth had been sliced clean in two.

'Bleeding good job Beattie was out of the way tonight,' the woman said as she passed Jenny.

'Beattie?'

'Beattie Latimer, her what lived next door to Patty Prosser.'

'What, the woman who was killed?'

'That's the one,' the woman said. 'Reckon she'd have been a goner an all, I do, but she's been at her sister's all afternoon. She told me herself when I met her coming in from work this afternoon and her old man's on nights down the Dunlop.' She shook her head sadly and gathered her own two children closer to her. 'Bloody shame it is. Proper shook me up, to see a family wiped out like that. I mean, it's bad enough losing your house, ain't it? You spending your life building it up like, and then it's smashed to bits, but then you look at the likes of Patty Prosser and you thank God for what you've got left.'

'Come on missis,' Phil shouted. 'Let's get you and the babbies out of it. Hitler ain't finished with us yet.'

And he hadn't. Bombs still whistled from the sky, as they marshalled the women and children and a few men down Paget Road. The incendiaries that had fallen had set up pockets of flames that lit up the black sky, but did nothing to take the damp chilling coldness from it and all the families shivered as they hurried along.

Jenny, watching them, shivered herself, and

54

Gladys, a fellow warden, asked, 'Are you all right, Jenny?'

'Oh Gladys, how could anyone be all right after what we've just witnessed?'

'God, don't I know it.' Gladys said. 'But you've been quiet all night.'

'*So would you if you'd just learnt your brother had been shot down*,' Jenny could have said, but she didn't. Too many people had been killed that night and she felt particularly sorry for the two little children who'd been crushed to death in the one place the government had promoted as a safe place to shelter. But she couldn't say this either, or she would bawl her eyes out and she was glad the light was too dim for Gladys to see her face.

Gladys was one of the women Anthony had talked about. She drove the double decker buses around the streets of Birmingham and he'd been proud of her for doing a traditionally male job. Jenny didn't know how she managed it because Gladys was no bigger than she was, though a lot stouter. But she'd said it was much easier to be out driving a bus than sitting at home worrying about her lads, who were both away fighting. Jenny guessed that work was as much a life saver for Gladys as it was for her, and so she gave a sigh and said, 'I'm all right Gladys, just tired like everyone else.'

As the news came through to the post that night, it was obvious that the Luftwaffe was out to try and paralyse many of the factories making things for the war effort. One of the prime targets was the BSA, Birmingham Small Arms, where Peggy

McAllister was working the night shift. She'd always told Maureen and Jenny that in the event of a raid, she'd be all right, for there was a large reinforced basement to shelter in.

However, that day, smoke vapour had been dropped over the factory by a German plane, forming a ring over it and when Peggy went into work, all those leaving the day shift were on about it. Then as the raid began, the incendiaries dropped first were able to pinpoint the factory accurately. This led the way for the lone bomber who followed to drop three high-explosive bombs, with such precision that the badly damaged, blazing, four-storeyed building began to collapse into the basement.

Even the firemen, having exhausted the hydrants and drained the canal, could not contain the fire. They concentrated their efforts instead on getting people out. Many were trapped, some were buried by machinery, badly injured or burned. Peggy was one of the fortunate ones, although she had a number of cracked ribs and a deep gash on her head that needed stitching, and a mass of cuts and bruises. Later she lay in the General Hospital and remembered her friends and colleagues that had been badly injured and killed that night and knew she was lucky to have got off so lightly.

Jenny went home at seven o'clock on the morning of the twentieth of November to wash and change her clothes. She met the accusing red-rimmed eyes of her mother as soon as she went in the door. 'Here she is, the heartless bitch.'

Jenny was in no fit state for this after the traumatic night she'd had and she fought to control herself. 'Mother, I know Anthony's death is a shock and I'm heart sore about it myself. But last night was the heaviest raid I've ever seen. I was needed.'

'There you go, you see,' Norah said bitterly. 'Other people are always more important than your own.'

'What good would I have done, stopping here?' Jenny asked. Her voice broke as she went on, 'If I could do anything to bring Anthony back I would, but he's gone. We ... we must accept it.'

'Accept it? I've sat up all night with bombs pounding around me and cried for my son.' Norah glared at her daughter and burst out, 'Oh, you're a wicked selfish girl.'

Later, getting ready for work, Jenny wondered if her mother was right, for as yet, she'd shed no tears for Anthony. She really didn't know how she would cope without him. But she was so shocked and stunned by the events of the previous night, she knew she wasn't really thinking straight.

At work the supervisor looked at the white pallor of her skin and her black-ringed eyes and sent her home again. But Jenny didn't want to go home, she needed to rest, to try and sleep for hours and hours, but she'd get no peace in the house with her mother and grandmother.

Instead, she found herself drawn to the wreckage facing the school. The unexploded bomb had been defused at two that morning, but the wreckage had been untouched.

There was another woman staring like she was. She was quite tubby and had a nondescript brown coat and a headscarf covering her frizzy grey hair. She looked completely flabbergasted. She turned to Jenny with anguished eyes, tears streaming down her face, as she said, 'Bleeding mess, eh?'

Jenny nodded.

The woman pointed and said, 'Used to be my house, that did.'

'Then you're Beattie, the one they told us was away?' Jenny said.

'That's right. Was you here last night then?'

'Yes,' Jenny said. 'When I have my other hat on I'm an ARP warden. I'm terribly sorry about your house.'

'So am I duck,' Beattie said. 'Me and my Bert will have to lodge with our Vera, and the snobby cow can't turn us away. But what I can't get over is Patty and the nippers all gone like that and yet they were in a bleeding Anderson shelter. Lived right next door for years and never a cross word between us. God it's hard,' she wiped tears from her eyes and said, 'And young Linda an' all.'

'Linda?'

'Her daughter, Patty's daughter. She was only twelve.'

'There was no girl with them.'

Beattie stared at her. 'There must have been.'

'There wasn't,' Jenny insisted. 'I was here at the scene.'

'Could she have been blown out of the shelter?' Beattie asked.

Jenny shook her head. 'No. It collapsed inwards. We had to move sandbags and corrugated iron to get them out.'

'Didn't they have a list?' Beattie demanded. 'Who was in charge?'

'Phil Rogers.'

'Oh him,' Beattie threw up her hands in despair. 'He's no bleeding good. His mother's the same, I was at school with her. As for him, he couldn't organise a piss-up in a brewery.'

Jenny had the desire to laugh at the expression on the outraged woman's face. What, she wondered, was the matter with her? Was she mad to want to laugh when a child was missing, possibly dead. The laughter bubbled within her, high and hysterical. Beattie, far from being offended, put her arms around Jenny's shoulders and said, 'There duck, there.'

The laughter turned to racking sobs. Jenny spluttered through her tears in an attempt to explain. 'I'm so sorry. You see, my brother was shot down yesterday as well.'

'Oh, you poor sod,' Beattie said, and the sympathy from a perfect stranger opened the floodgates at last. Beattie led her to the kerb where they both sat down and she held Jenny in her arms while the tears streamed from her eyes. When the paroxysm of grief was spent, Jenny lay, worn out, against Beattie who then said, 'I've got to look into this business of Linda being missing, but I don't want to leave you by yourself. Is there anyone I can take you to?'

'My gran's,' Jenny said not wanting to go home. 'She lives in Westmead Crescent.'

Maureen O'Leary was half demented herself

when they arrived with the news that the BSA where Peggy had worked on the night shift had been attacked the previous night. Gerry had been like a mad man until Peggy was able at least to send news that she was safe and in the General Hospital, nothing then would do, but he had to go up there. 'I've put in enough hours overtime,' he'd said to Maureen. 'They can do without me for once.'

'But son, she says she's not badly injured, and thank God for it.'

'I have to see for myself Mammy,' Gerry said looking at his mother bleakly. 'My life's nothing without her. I thought you knew that.'

'I guessed, lad,' Maureen said. 'And I should tell the girl if I were you and put her out of her misery. I'd have done the same for my own man. Go on and satisfy yourself.'

And then, not half an hour after he left, she opened the door to her granddaughter who was being helped by a woman she'd never seen before.

'What in God's name is the matter with you?' Maureen cried, putting her arm around Jenny and drawing her inside, where the girl sat on the settee sobbing with her head in her hands. 'What is it?' Maureen asked Beattie, but Beattie didn't answer. It wasn't her tale to tell.

'I have to be off,' she said.

'Will you not stop a while?' Maureen said.

'No, ta all the same,' Beattie said. 'I have things to do, and you two need to be alone.'

When Beattie had gone, Maureen went into the kitchen and came back with a cup of tea that she pressed into Jenny's hands. 'Drink that,' she said, 'and then for God's sake, tell me what it is.' And then she sat very still and said, 'It's no one else is it child? You haven't had another telegram?'

Jenny shook her head. 'None of the family,' she said. 'It isn't that. It's just that last night was a terrible raid and I saw some awful sights.' She looked at her gran and said, 'Beattie, the woman who brought me here, had her house destroyed and her neighbour, a young woman with three children, was killed and her two young sons with her. The daughter is still missing; she's only twelve years old.' Jenny's hands shook so much she was in danger of spilling the tea.

'I know pet. It's this awful war.' Maureen said, and put her arm around Jenny's shoulder.

'Yesterday, I told myself that Anthony had a sort of choice,' Jenny said. 'I mean, he chose to be a pilot, but he'd never choose to die, he loved life too much for that. This morning, I suddenly realised I'd never see my brother again. I'll never see him smile or hear his laugh or have a joke and argue with him. Oh Gran, I don't think I can bear it.'

'You'll bear it cutie,' Maureen said sadly. 'You'll never forget Anthony like you've never forgotten your daddy, but you'll learn to live without him.'

Jenny knew her grandmother was right, she'd have to learn to live without Anthony, however hard it was.

'I'll tell you what,' Maureen said, 'you need a good feed and a sleep. Then you'll feel better able to cope.'

'Oh no, Gran.'

'Oh yes Gran,' Maureen said. 'Sit you down and drink that tea before it goes cold. I'll just be a minute.'

After a bowl of stew and another cup of tea Jenny did feel better, but she was still very tired and her gran lifted her legs onto the settee and covered her with a blanket.

She slept deeply and didn't wake, not even when Gerry came back and said he was away to see the priest because when Peggy came out of that place they were to be married as soon as was humanly possible, and no one was going to stop him.

Then Beattie came to see how Jenny was. 'Tell her we're searching the bomb site,' she said. 'It'll be for a body, I dare say, for if the child's under it she doesn't stand much chance.'

'There's always a chance,' Maureen said.

Beattie thought she could only say that because she hadn't seen the mountain of rubble, but she didn't disagree with the older woman.

Linda had given up the chance of being rescued. She seemed to have been inside her black tomb for ever and was in so much pain. She'd screamed in agony when she'd woken up and had shouted and yelled, but no one had heard. There was no one there. It was like everyone in the whole world had disappeared. She didn't know how long she'd lain there, but it seemed a long time. When she'd first woken up and opened her eyes she'd shut them quickly, because such intense dark frightened her. She would have said she wasn't afraid of the dark, like George was, but this dark was different.

She shivered with cold and fear, her legs were throbbing and she cried out with pain. God, she'd never felt pain like this and she wasn't sure she could stand it. She was soaked because she'd had to wet her knickers, she couldn't ever remember doing that before. She lay on her back and let the tears trickle out of her eyes and run unchecked down her cheeks.

Phil Rogers looked mournfully at the mountain of debris and said, 'You sure there's someone in there?'

'Course I ain't sure,' Beattie said. 'But if she ain't in there, where the hell else is she? All I know is, if you'd checked the bloody list last night, you'd have known she was missing, at least.'

Phil looked at Beattie and remembered the previous evening. Pockets of incendiary fires had lit up the sky and bombs had been raining down as they tried to evacuate people from the area of an unexploded bomb in Paget Road School playground just yards from houses. He knew it would have been easy to miss one young girl in that nightmare. They daren't use heavy lifting gear whilst there was even the remotest chance of someone being alive inside it. He knew how impossible a feat it was going to be to clear the area by hand, but Beattie had begun to shift the bricks already. 'Come on you daft 'aporth and put your bleeding back into it,' she cried.

When Jenny woke, she was determined to go and help after hearing Beattie's news. She impatiently swallowed the sandwich and drank the scalding hot tea that Maureen insisted on before she'd let her leave the house. She gave little mind to her mother and grandmother. They can look after themselves for once, she thought, and maybe it will do the pair of them good.

She hadn't quite reached the bombed site, when she saw Beattie detach herself from a group moving debris, and run down the road to Jenny. 'You'll never believe it,' she said, 'but we've heard her. Or at least, we heard a scream from somewhere, so she's still alive, but we don't know exactly where she is.'

Jenny wondered how the child had survived so long. The bomb that had killed her mother and brothers and landed on the house fell at about seven o'clock. She'd been incarcerated for nearly twenty-four hours.

Doctor Sanders was there on standby. He was very worried, because since the one petrified scream an hour or so ago there had been nothing, though they'd knocked and called repeatedly.

Suddenly one of the rescuers said, 'I reckon there's only one place she can be.'

'Where's that then?'

'In the pantry,' the man said. 'It's well known. You're safe there as in a shelter, built under the stairs as it is. That's where she'd have made for if she'd got any sense, I'd say.'

Nearly everyone agreed with that and the rescuers began to concentrate on the debris at the very edge of the stack where the side of the house and stairs would be. They worked feverishly for hours in the black bitter cold night using the inadequate light from shielded torches. Jenny's coat was now filthy dirty and her fingers blistered, her nails were all broken and her back felt as if it was ready to snap in two, but she made no word of complaint. But when Maureen O'Leary appeared with a tray of tea and buttered soda bread for them all later, she could have kissed her. 'Any news?' she asked Jenny.

'None for hours,' Jenny said. 'When I first got here Beattie said they'd heard her scream. Since then there's been nothing. Let's pray she is taken out alive Gran.' Maureen could only nod her agreement.

Through the evening, many workers had dropped out and others had taken their place. Even Beattie had been to a neighbour's house where her Bert had slept before putting in a few hours helping the rescue attempt before he went back to work that evening, and Jenny's Uncle Gerry had come to help after a day at work. He'd also been to visit Peggy at the hospital, but he said none of that to Jenny: in his opinion she had enough on her plate already.

Gerry had been there about an hour when there was a sudden shout. Wearily and hopefully Jenny lifted her head. 'I've found the front of the house,' someone shouted and indeed he had, for though there was no front door or bay window left, the bottom of the stairs that once led from the tiny hall had eventually been uncovered.

However, it was soon apparent that the stairs could not be moved at all, the weight of the house was resting on top of them and if the child

65

was in the pantry, the stairs could be protecting her.

Before long they'd uncovered a couple of roof beams that had fallen against the staircase, leaving a tiny triangular-shaped hole, filled with broken bricks and tiles, and Jenny knelt down and began pulling them out with her hands.

'Steady girl you'll have the lot down.' Beattie cautioned. 'Take it easy.'

But Jenny was impatient to get to the child and the others felt the same way, helping all they could. Soon, though, they'd pulled the debris out as far as anyone could reach and stood looking at the small hole. 'It might be like that all the way to the pantry, filled with rubble,' Jenny said. 'The stairs are probably taking the strain, stopping the big stuff falling down. Someone could get in there and perhaps find out.'

'Oh aye,' one man said. 'Nowt but a midget could get in there.'

'I could,' Jenny said.

Everyone turned and stared at her and eventually Gerry said, 'You couldn't do that. It's too risky, you could bring the lot down.'

'What's the alternative?' Jenny snapped.

There was no answer to that. Gerry felt he ought to forbid Jenny to go – he was after all her uncle – but he knew Jenny, she'd probably take no notice of him anyway. He felt bad that he couldn't offer to go himself, but he was far too big. God, but it was a dangerous operation for a young girl. Far too dangerous.

Jenny had already removed her scarf and coat, begrimed with dust and dirt, and handed them to Beattie as she asked for the loan of a torch. 'Won't you be scared to death?' Beattie said.

Jenny looked at the black, uninviting hole and suppressed a shudder. Scared to death was an understatement. She was absolutely petrified. Since she'd been a small child she'd been terrified of closed-in spaces, worried to death she wouldn't be able to breathe. Somehow she had to conquer her fear, or commit the child to never being found alive.

So she looked Beattie straight in the face and said, 'No, not really. I'll be fine.'

'You know what you have to do?' Phil Rogers asked Jenny, handing her his flashlight, as she crouched at the tunnel mouth.

'Course I do.'

Phil Rogers nodded and stepped back. Jenny looked around at all the faces before taking a deep breath and going in head first. 'Oh God, I hope she'll be all right,' Beattie said and everyone echoed the same sentiment as Jenny's legs slowly disappeared into the tunnel.

Chapter Five

Jenny O'Leary's heart was pounding against her ribs, the breath rasping in her throat as she tried to contain her panic. Every nerve in her body urged her to get out of the bombed house *now*, while she had a chance. Progress was pitifully slow; there wasn't room either side of her for her elbows, so she had to pull herself along by her hands. Her whole body rested on broken bricks and tiles and shards of glass. Her arms were grazed, her hands and her legs torn and bleeding, but she bit her lip and pulled herself on across the rubble, inch by painful inch.

The space was so small she had to keep her head down and her mouth and eyes filled with dust and grit. Suddenly she stopped too frightened to move any further. She couldn't breathe and knew she'd die in this futile attempt to rescue Linda Lennox. The girl must surely already be dead! The tears came then and she sobbed and prayed more intensely than she'd ever done before. 'Oh God, help me.'

Strangely, she did feel eased, though the roof of her mouth was still dry and her hands clammy. She forced herself to count to ten slowly and take deep breaths to prove that she could. Afterwards she felt a little better; she focused on the entombed child and inched herself a little further.

She wondered after a while how long she'd been in the tunnel. It seemed for ever. Surely the pantry wasn't as far as this? Perhaps the tunnel led somewhere else entirely, or nowhere at all. Panic threatened to overwhelm her again; she moaned in great distress, dropped the torch and it went out.

'Oh God! Oh God!' In the pitch black she scrabbled frantically. To be stuck here in the pitch dark was the most frightening moment of her life. She'd not stand it! She'd go mad!

Then suddenly, her grasping hands found the torch again and despite the shield, as she turned it on, the little tunnel seemed flooded with light and she sobbed with relief.

A little further on, she realised the roof seemed further away than it had been. She found she could raise her head and did so, glad to be able to get away from the plaster and brick dust if only for a moment or two.

The space got bigger still. Soon Jenny was able to lift herself on to her knees and progress was slightly quicker. Then she came to an area where she could crouch and when she swung the torch this time, she saw why. The beams holding up the first floor had fallen against the stairs, but as the stairs rose so the space beneath them became larger. She sat for a moment, glad of the respite, and considered things.

The pantry must be near, because it was fitted under the stairs and anytime now she could be coming to it. It could well be blocked and yet she mustn't miss it. She must search every few inches.

Even then she nearly went past it. It was the groan that alerted her. The girl was still alive, but she was obviously in a lot of pain. Frantically, she swung her torch, all fear for herself forgotten. She swung around onto her knees, searching every nook and cranny wishing and hoping the child would groan again or cry out, anything to help her find out where she was.

'Linda,' she cried as loud as she could. 'Linda, where are you?'

Silence, total silence. 'Linda?' Jenny shouted again after a few minutes. 'Linda, please! Oh Linda, for God's sake!'

And then it came, a long low groan to the left of where Jenny sat. She swung around and examined the wall which seemed totally blocked with a solid lump of wood except for a narrow space at the top.

She pulled herself up and peered over, playing the torch around. The missing girl lay so white and still she might have been a corpse, her legs held fast by the staircase that had semi-collapsed on top of her.

Jenny gasped. She knew she had to get through that gap to rescue Linda, and it would be a squeeze, even for her. Discarding her tattered blouse, suit, stockings and shoes without a thought, she crouched shivering in her slip.

The widest part of the human body is the head and Jenny was soon aware of this as hers took a great deal of manoeuvring to get through the small aperture. But at last she was on the other side, and kneeling by the unconscious child.

Linda was covered in grey dust. Her face was

thick with it, but with cleaner trails as if she'd cried for some time. Her brownish hair was matted beneath her and she lay on a bed of fragmented bricks, an old teddy bear in her right hand. Compassion flooded through Jenny. 'Linda,' she said softly and then much louder, but there was no response.

Sudden fear gripped Jenny. Was that shuddering groan she'd heard the final whisper of life? She tried to feel for a pulse in the wrist and throat, but her lacerated hands could feel nothing, so very gently she laid her ear across the child's chest and could have cried with relief when she distinctly heard the heart beating – faintly it was true, but definitely there.

But how could she, rouse the girl? She couldn't bring herself to smack her face. In fact, to touch her in any way could hurt her, seeing the way her legs were pinned. Eventually, Jenny ripped the bottom of her slip into strips and spat liberally on the first one and wiped it across the child's face.

Linda had been drifting in and out of consciousness for some hours. She hated waking from the blissful oblivion for she woke to fear and loneliness and intense pain, stronger than she'd ever felt before, so strong it drained her of energy. Every bone and pore in her body seemed on fire and she burned with a fever that Jenny was aware of as soon as she touched her. In her lucid moments, Linda had heard people calling her, but it had seemed so far away and nothing to do with her at all.

But this was different, a stroking of her face and

71

her cheeks, reminiscent of her mother who used to do that when she was small. She came to reluctantly, almost afraid to open her glazed eyes.

But when she did, she was gazing into deep brown ones, very like her mother's. Someone was patting her face gently and it felt so soft, like a pillow. So soft, she closed her eyes again, but then the same someone called, 'Linda.'

'Mom.' She knew her mother would come for her. Linda's eyes opened again, but the face looking down on her was not her mother's. 'Who are you?' she asked in a voice slurred with weariness and the agony of constant and unremitting pain.

The person didn't answer, but tears rained down her face. Eventually, she controlled herself and said, 'Oh Linda, I'm so glad I've found you.'

Linda was confused. She wasn't lost; she knew where she was. She was in the pantry. Suddenly, it all came back; she'd nipped in to the house to find Tolly, George's teddy bear. She still had him in her hand. 'I'm in the pantry,' she said. 'There was a bomb.'

'I know, my dear.'

'I came back for Tolly, he's George's bear.'

'George?'

'My little brother. He'll be glad he's safe.'

Jenny remembered the small dead bodies carried past her the previous evening and a shiver went through her. She had to keep off the subject of the girl's family at all costs. 'Are you in much pain?' she asked.

Linda gave a brief nod and even that small movement caused such a severe spasm throughout her body that she nearly passed out again. 'It used to be just my legs,' Linda said wearily, when she recovered her breath. 'Now it's everywhere.'

'Oh, God.' Jenny thought, and tears stood out in her eyes.

'It's all right, it's not so bad now you're here.' Linda said. 'Are you going to get me out?'

Jenny held one of Linda's hands and stroked it gently as she said, 'There are people outside waiting to help, but we couldn't do much till we found out where you were. I ... I need to go back and tell them and then they can really start moving to get you free.'

'Oh, please don't go!' Linda cried, her eyes wide with alarm and terror. 'Oh, please! Oh please!' Tears coursed down her cheeks and Jenny could hardly speak. She knew it would take all the young girl's reserve of courage to stay by herself in the dark again while she alerted those waiting outside.

'I must,' she said, 'don't you see? They can't start moving anything about, until they know where you are.'

'I can't bear it if you go.'

'Please, Linda, try and understand,' Jenny said. 'I promise I'll come back and stay with you till you're rescued.'

'Do you promise, God's honour, on your mother's life?' Linda asked, and shivered as she imagined the fear of being left alone again.

'Yes,' said Jenny firmly. 'Yes, I do, and I'll get something for the pain you're in too. Dr Sanders is out there.'

Vague memories stirred in Linda's befuddled

brain and she said, 'Yes, he came to see my mom. He's nice. Is Mom all right?'

Oh God, Jenny thought. Instead of answering she said again, 'I must get back and tell everyone you're safe as quickly as possible.' She got to her feet gingerly, wary of jarring the child. 'Don't expect me back too soon,' she warned. 'The tunnel is very narrow and in places I have to lie flat and drag myself through, but I promise you I'll be back.'

'Be as quick as you can,' Linda said and shut her eyes tight so she wouldn't see when the stranger disappeared and she was in darkness and alone once more.

When Jenny emerged from the tunnel, a cheer rose up. She was covered head to foot in a film of yellow-grey dust and clad only in a torn and filthy slip that hung on her like a tattered rag. As she shivered from reaction and cold, a woman stepped forward with a blanket to wrap around her.

Maureen ran towards her granddaughter, tears coursing down her face, for she thought she'd never see her again. She was shocked at the sight of her; even in the dim light of the torches she could see the mass of raw gravel grazes on Jenny's face. Her nose had not escaped and there was a green/blue bruise swelling under her left eye. The deep gashes on her arms oozing droplets of blood were hidden by the blanket, but the legs sticking out from it had jagged slash-marks along the length of them and blood was dripping from them on to her bare, blistered feet.

'She's there in the pantry like we thought,' she said wearily. 'The stairs have collapsed on her, trapping her legs, but apart from that she's all right.'

'Oh my darling girl.' Maureen cried, wrapping her arms around Jenny's shoulders. She saw her wince and stood back. 'Come away home now,' she said firmly. 'You've done enough for one night.'

'Go home. Gran?' Jenny echoed incredulously. 'Don't be silly, I have to go back.'

'Oh no, my girl,' Dr Sanders put in. 'Doctor's orders. You must go and rest now.'

'How can I?' Jenny cried. 'You're not my doctor, but you are that young girl's. Would you have me abandon her and renege on my promise?'

'Can we argue about this at home?' Gerry interrupted. He turned to the doctor and said, 'Whatever is decided, Jenny needs treatment I'd say, and if she stays here much longer, she'll die from the cold.'

So saying he lifted her as if she weighed nothing at all and stilled her protests. 'Be quiet, Jenny, you have to get your injuries treated, some food inside you and some clothes to cover you, before any decision is reached.'

'I'm going back,' Jenny said mutinously.

'We'll see.'

'I *am!*'

'All right,' Gerry snapped back. 'But let's take one thing at a time.'

He was striding down the road as he spoke and Jenny relaxed when she realised she wasn't being

75

taken all the way home, only to her gran's house. Maureen and the doctor were following behind. Once inside, Dr Sanders quickly washed the dust and grit from her and bandaged her arms, hands and legs and put salve on her face, and the smarting pain of it all subsided a little.

Then, dressed in thick trousers, shirt, pullover and boots, she was given a bowl of Irish stew, a cup of tea so strong the spoon could have stood up in it on its own, and was sat before the fire. The latter was nearly her undoing. The crawl through the tunnel and back had taken it out of her mentally and physically, and with a full stomach and the heat of the fire, Jenny felt incredibly drowsy. Her eyelids were so very heavy; surely she could shut them for a wee minute or two...

Suddenly she jerked herself back to wakefulness. How long had she slept – an hour, half an hour, a few minutes? She had no way of knowing. The clock now showed just after two o'clock in the morning.

She looked around at her gran and the doctor accusingly, knowing they would have let her sleep till morning and not tried to wake her. 'I can't believe you let me drop off like that,' she said.

'Cutie child, you've done enough,' Maureen said.

Jenny made an impatient movement with her hand. 'Linda Lennox is just twelve years old and has lost all belonging to her. She's lain for hours, cold, frightened and alone in total darkness, injured and in constant pain. I promised her I would go back and I will. I've never broken a

76

promise in my life and I think this is the most important one I've ever made.' She looked at the doctor and said, 'I wouldn't answer for Linda's mental condition if she's left much longer in that place alone. I said I'd try and get her something for the pain too.'

'But now we know where she is, it won't be long till she's out.' the doctor said. 'They were ordering heavy lifting gear when we left.'

'Don't treat me like an idiot,' Jenny said desperately. 'You know as well as I do, it will be hours yet. The stairs pinning Linda to the pantry floor are holding up the whole of the upper floor and part of the other house is leaning against it too. It will be some time before she's reached, let alone rescued.'

'But at least she will be rescued now,' he said. 'You did well detecting her.'

'I did well?' repeated Jenny. 'That girl is almost delirious with pain, and when they eventually lift the stairs off her legs ... well, I don't think she'll stand it. She needs something to kill the pain, and as soon as possible, I'd say.'

Dr Sanders regarded Jenny shrewdly. 'I can't get in there to give her an injection – you know that,' he said. 'Surely you're not proposing you administer it?'

'Have you a better idea?'

'It would be incredibly dangerous.'

'It's all incredibly dangerous,' Jenny said dismissively. 'She's not lying in a feather bed at this minute either.'

Maureen was open-mouthed at the way Jenny was attacking the doctor. She'd never heard her

77

speak that way to anyone before. She hoped the man would put it down to shock and not be offended. Jenny didn't seem to care if he was or not, because she cried out, 'She needs help *now!* Why can't you realise that?'

'Hush, mavourneen,' Maureen said, dropping down on her knees before the settee and gathering her weeping granddaughter into her arms. 'Everyone knows about the wee wean and sure it's terrible news, so it is. But why does it have to be you that goes back in?'

Jenny wiped the tears away and said, 'Because I'm small, Gran, the only one that has any chance. There were even places I was nearly stuck too.' She gave a shuddering sigh and went on, 'I'm the only one who can keep her company.'

'But the whole place could collapse on top of you both,' Dr Sanders said gently.

Jenny swallowed the terror she had of going back into the dreadful tunnel and retorted, 'I know all that. What I want to know is, are you going to help me, or sit up all night talking about it?'

Dr Sanders remembered suddenly the first time he'd seen Linda Lennox. She'd come into his surgery with half a crown in her cardigan pocket which he could guess was all the money she had in the world, and asked him if it were enough for him to visit her mother who'd collapsed. He'd seen the family many times since, and been impressed by the courage of both the mother and daughter. Linda was the same slight build as Patty, with a little elfin face, deep blue-grey eyes, a dainty nose and a fine mouth; her rich brown hair was wavy and fell to her shoulders, but her chin was well defined and Dr Sanders knew her to be a determined little thing.

But he also knew she'd been devoted to her younger brothers and she'd had a special bond with her mother. He couldn't begin to comprehend the depth of her loss, or how she'd cope with it. He also knew she'd be very frightened, and if anyone needed a friend at this moment, it was Linda Lennox. Surely if the O'Leary girl was brave enough to go back in that tunnel, he was brave enough to trust her to administer morphine to alleviate the child's pain. Really there was no other option anyway.

So in the end Jenny had her way, although most were astonished that she was going back to stay with the child because of a promise she had made. At last one of the official rescue workers who'd appeared with lifting gear, saw her determination and knew she wasn't to be dissuaded. 'At least go better equipped this time,' he said. 'You know it might take hours before we reach you.'

'I know.'

She was given a flashlight which she could push in front of her into the tunnel and a water bottle which was strapped to her back. High energy biscuits used by the Forces were tucked into one of the breast pockets of her shirt, and a blanket was tied to her belt so that she could drag it behind her.

In the other breast pocket, she carried the precious morphine injection. The doctor was still apprehensive as he measured out the dose. 'I'm worried about giving her too much,' he said. 'She's quite slight as well as small for her age.'

'She's in terrible pain,' Jenny reminded him.

'Even so ... just try and keep her alert. Don't let her sleep if you can help it. Keep talking to her.'

'Yes, all right,' Jenny said. She was impatient to be on her way before further objections could be raised.

She gave her gran a hug then knelt before the tunnel; the old lady's eyes were wet with tears and her lips moved constantly in prayer to the Virgin, who'd tasted sorrow in her own life and would understand the gnawing worry she had for Jenny.

Jenny had been in the tunnel about half an hour when Gerry decided to call it a day. It was after three o'clock in the morning and he knew he'd be needed in at work in the morning. The city was in a perilous position, with half the gas pipes in the centre ruptured, leaking or unusable, and it would be some time before Jenny reached the trapped child and even longer till the search-party located them. Meanwhile he was asleep on his feet and if he wanted to be any good at all in the morning, he knew he had to rest. His mother, too, looked dead beat, and he went over and put his arm around her. 'Come on, Ma,' he said. 'Let's away home for a wee while.'

'Away home when my dear grandchild is in that hell-hole?' Maureen cried, but though her voice was strident, Gerry knew she was at the end of her tether.

'Ma, she'll be in there hours yet,' he said.

80

'Honest to God we can do nothing more and when she is eventually rescued, then she'll need you.' Maureen knew Gerry was right; she was too tired to think straight or be any bloody use to anyone. She doubted she'd sleep, but even to rest in the warm would be nice. Gerry put his arm around her and led her away.

Willing hands took the places of those who dropped out as the night wore on. The tale of the child who lay buried under tons of rubble and the girl not much older who'd crawled in to give her comfort, had spread like wildfire across the estate, and people came from all over to lend a hand. It was heartening Maureen thought, as she made her way home, in a world where values and common decency seemed to have been turned on their heads.

In the tunnel the going was tough. Conscious of the needle in her breast pocket, Jenny tried to keep her upper body raised as much as possible, but that meant the water bottle dragged on the roof. Occasionally, it got stuck altogether and she would have to hunker down and wriggle free, hurting her face again. But though she felt the water bottle to be an encumbrance, she knew it was vital; she dreaded puncturing it and seeing the precious water trickle away.

The blanket hampered her progress considerably, it kept getting stuck on things and had to be shaken loose – not an easy task in such a small space. Jenny wished many times she could leave it behind, but knew she couldn't; she knew they'd need it, Linda was probably near frozen stiff already.

When she eventually reached the slit in the top of the piece of wood blocking off the pantry, she knew she couldn't struggle through it this time. Not only was she wearing more and thicker clothes, there was also the morphine syringe that she couldn't risk breaking; nor did she want the biscuits to be reduced to useless crumbs.

She called out reassuringly to Linda as she unstrapped the water bottle and the blanket and pushed them through the small gap. There was no answer. Jenny hoped she hadn't dropped into unconsciousness.

Impatiently, she set to examine the wood. Surely there was some way of enlarging the gap? She swung the flashlight around. The wood was balanced on one side on a heap of bricks: if she could kick them away, the wood could drop another twelve inches or so. It would be enough for her to get into the pantry where Linda lay. But had she the courage to do so, because to move anything was extremely dicey?

But then, she thought, what choice did she have? She might as well have stayed in front of her gran's fire all night otherwise. Gently she scraped away at the powdery gravel around the bricks, and then began to push at them one by one. They seemed wedged fast: Jenny had to exert more and more pressure. Eventually, she braced herself against the wall and pushed hard with her feet. At first they moved slowly and then suddenly they came out in a rush. There was a terrific roaring above Jenny's head as a beam fell, glancing off her shoulder and causing her to cry out, and a pile of masonry, broken pieces of plaster and charred timbers fell and filled the tunnel behind her, effectively sealing it off, so if she'd wanted to get out she'd be unable to. Jenny wasn't aware of it at once: she was aware of nothing but the dust swirling around her as thick and acrid as smoke. It stung her eyes and caused them to stream with tears, and filled her nostrils, and she felt she would choke with it as she coughed and coughed till her stomach ached.

Outside, the rescuers heard the roaring boom too, as loud as thunder. Those on the pavement saw the rubble drop several inches and the whole mountain of bricks began to tilt and sway. For some time after the dust had settled around Jenny in her tunnel, it dislodged bricks, plaster pieces and glass shards outside and they continued to slither on top of the pile, and so it was a while before the rescuers could begin again. 'I think the little lady's had it this time, don't you?' one man said.

'Don't you believe it!' Stan Walker, Jenny's fellow warden and one of the rescue team, stated forcibly. 'I've worked with Jenny at the warden's post for some time now, and I'll tell you she's one of the best.'

'No one's saying she isn't, man,' another protested. 'It's just ... well, everyone knows what that noise means.'

'Bloody good job her gran's gone home. I reckon she'd have collapsed if she'd heard and seen that.'

There was a murmur of agreement and then someone said, 'Let's hope she hasn't upset the lot and brought it all down on the child she was trying to save.'

This was a sobering thought and Stan burst in eventually with, 'That's defeatist talk and what Hitler would expect of you all. Whether they're alive or dead, let's get them out of that hell-hole, even if it's just to give them a Christian burial.'

At Stan's words there was a small cheer. 'That's telling them, mate,' a man said from the back. 'Come on, you lot – where's your Brummie grit? Let's get to it,' and without another word the men turned to their task and redoubled their efforts.

Down in the tunnel, despite the dust still swirling around her Jenny saw she had achieved her objective; the wood had dropped sufficiently to let her climb inside to where Linda lay. Light-headed with relief, for she really thought she'd had it that time, she got to her feet shakily and clambered over the wood partition to the injured child.

Linda was unconscious and delirious, she was mumbling on about her mother and little brothers in a way that brought tears to Jenny's eyes. She hoped that she had some nice kindly gran or aunt to take care of her after all this, for the thin undersized child certainly looked as if she needed someone to see to her and help her over the terrible tragedy of losing her mother.

'Linda,' Jenny said gently, 'remember me?' She saw the slight frown on Linda's face and knew she not only had no idea who she was, she probably couldn't even hear her. 'I said I'd come back and stay with you, do you remember?' Linda's eyes flickered shut again and Jenny went on doggedly, 'I've spoken to the doctor. He's given me an injection for you to take away the pain, is that all right?'

There was no response and Jenny realised she'd have to administer the injection anyway. She eased Linda out of one sleeve of her coat and rolled her cardigan up. As she moved the flashlight nearer, she was more nervous than she'd ever been in her whole life. It took all her reserves of courage to stick the needle into the flesh of the bunched up arm, as Dr Sanders had shown her, and press the plunger, especially as Linda flinched as she did it.

The child was shivering with cold Jenny realised as she gently pulled down her sleeve and eased her into her coat again and buttoned it up. She brought over the blanket and put it around the two of them, then lay down beside Linda and put her arms around her, trying to warm her with her own body.

She must have dozed off, for when she woke, Jenny didn't realise where she was for a moment or two. Then she saw a pair of solemn, blue-grey eyes staring into hers in the flickering beam of the flashlight. The child's voice was slightly slurred – with the morphine Jenny supposed – but her mind seemed lucid enough as she said, as if she couldn't believe it, 'You came back.'

'I said I would.'

'I know.'

'You didn't believe me?'

'I tried to, I waited a long time.'

'It took a long time,' Jenny said. 'I told you that.

I'd also cut my hands and legs getting to you and I had to have them dressed. Not that it did my hands much good,' she added, because though her legs and feet had been protected by heavy-duty trousers and boots, the bandages around her hands were filthy dirty and were virtually ripped to shreds.

'Would you like a drink of water?' she asked.

'You've got water?' Linda said, amazed. 'I've dreamed about having a drink. My throat is so dry.'

'You can't take too much,' Jenny warned. 'It might have to last some time. I have special energy biscuits too. Are you hungry?'

'I was,' Linda admitted. 'Terribly hungry. It went off, but I'd love a drink.'

She lifted the water bottle to her mouth and had the urge to drink and drink until it was all gone, but when the water had just taken the dust from the back of her throat and done nothing to slake her thirst, Jenny put her hand on the bottle. 'I'm sorry,' she said, 'but you can't have any more just now.'

'No?' Linda said with a sigh.

'How's the pain?' Jenny asked.

'Better, much better,' Linda said.

Jenny sighed with relief. 'That's the injection your doctor gave me to give you,' she said.

'You gave me an injection?' Linda's voice was high with surprise.

'I did,' Jenny said with a smile. 'I was scared stiff, I've never done such a thing before. I'm glad it's worked.'

'Who are you?'

'My name's Jenny O'Leary,' Jenny told the child, 'and I live in Pype Hayes Road. I know you are Linda Lennox because your neighbours told us all about you.'

'Have you seen Mom?' Linda said. 'She'll want to know I'm all right – has anyone told her?'

'I don't know, love,' Jenny said gently.

'And my brothers,' Linda went on. 'I bet they was dead scared in that raid.'

'I expect so, love,' Jenny said miserably, unable to keep the depression out of her voice.

'Were they hurt or summat?' Linda demanded and Jenny realised she could probably read the distress on her face. 'They should have been all right,' she went on, 'they was in the shelter.'

'Linda, I'll have to turn the lamp off,' Jenny told her. 'We may need it later and we're just wasting the battery now. Will you mind?'

'Not now you're here,' the young girl confided. 'It was horrible on my own.'

'Well, I'm going nowhere, so don't you worry,' Jenny said. She clicked off the lamp, glad of the velvet dark around them concealing the deep sorrow she felt for the child beside her.

Chapter Six

Linda was talking about her father. She'd been talking about him for some time and Jenny encouraged her; it was better for her to talk about him than ask searching questions about her mother or little brothers. She knew that when this was all over, Linda would have to live with someone, so she listened, hoping to hear of a nice gran somewhere, or a kindly aunt to help Linda over the tragedy of it all.

She felt it such a shame that her father hadn't survived to see his daughter grow up. But she'd had a stepfather for four years; maybe he had relations she could live with.

She waited until there was a lull in the conversation, and then probed gently, 'What about your stepfather Linda? Did you get on with him?'

She heard the sharp intake of breath and then Linda hissed, 'I hated him. I wanted him to die. I was glad when he went off to war and every day I wished he'd never come home again. I was glad when we got the telegram.'

Jenny was so shocked by the venom in the child's voice, she said not a word and Linda went on, 'I bet you think that's dead wicked don't you?'

The Catholic church would, Jenny knew, but she didn't say that. Instead, she said gently, 'Why did you want him to die?'

''Cos he used to knock me mom about,' Linda said. 'He was big, like an all-in wrestler, he was. Mom used to say he was as broad as he was long – he was near enough – and he used to hit her, 'specially when he came from the pub. I used to think he'd kill her; I reckon he could have too. She used to have black eyes and bruises on her cheeks, me mom did. She always said she fell. But I knew she never, 'cos I used to hear him.'

She stopped and there was a pause and Jenny was loath to break it, feeling sure Linda hadn't finished. After a minute or two, she began again, but her voice was so low, Jenny had to strain to hear. 'I'll tell you something now I've never told a living soul, not even Mom. Not 'cos I didn't think she'd believe me, but 'cos I didn't want her to be upset. I mean, what could she do about it anyway?'

There was another pause and part of Jenny wanted the child to go on with her tale, but the other half of her recoiled from it. In a way she was semi-prepared for what came next. 'He used to touch me, you know, my ... my privates, like. He told me I'd get to enjoy it, and when I was bigger he'd do more exciting things that I'd get to enjoy more. But I never did, I hated it, and I hated him, I did, and I was glad he died, so there.'

Jenny imagined Linda's little face contorted with hate as she almost spat the last words out. She felt for her hand and held it tight, although her own was still semi-bandaged, and said, 'That was awful for you Linda, but not all men are like that, you know.'

She felt she had to get that point across, but Linda said firmly, 'I know that. My own dad wasn't and there's lots more who don't do that sort of thing.' Then suddenly she changed her tack and asked, 'Was your dad nice?'

'Very,' Jenny said firmly. 'But he was born to a totally different life from yours and mine, because he was brought up in a cottage in Northern Ireland in a village called Cullinova.'

'Is that why you speak funny?' Linda said. She knew all about Irish people. Most of them went to the St Peter and Paul's Catholic church on Kingsbury Road on Sunday morning, and her mom always said they were odd. They couldn't eat meat on Fridays but could get tanked up on a weekend and beat up their women then go and tell it all to the priest who would say it was all right. Then, her mother said, they often went and did the same thing the next week. But Jenny didn't talk like the Irish people she knew, and yet she didn't speak Brummie either. 'You don't speak like Irish people,' she said. 'Not ones I know, any road.'

'Well, I was born here,' Jenny said. Her mother had worked hard on them to eradicate all traces of an Irish accent and had insisted the children call her and Dermot mother and father, instead of mammy and daddy. But Jenny had always called her father Daddy in her head, and used the name whenever they'd been alone.

'Maybe that's it,' Linda said, and added, 'tell me about your dad. I've told you all about mine.'

Jenny only hesitated briefly. Somehow they had to fill the hours until they were rescued, and she

didn't want Linda to start to fret over her family
again and so she told her of the young boy who'd
worked on the estate of his English master,
Fotherington. First he worked on the land and
then as a ghillie or a boat boy and later was a
groom in the stables.

Linda was fascinated, as this was all new and
different to her life.

'When did he marry your mom?' Linda asked.

'Not long after he got a cottage of his own,'
Jenny told her. 'But my mother had a totally
different upbringing, in a large house with
servants and so on. But my mother's father died
when she was in her late teens, and they found
they weren't rich any more. Her father had run
up huge debts and everything, including the
house which had to be sold.'

Linda thought that was sad and Jenny supposed it was. Her mother must have felt
desperate, especially when her own mother,
Eileen Gillespie, had a nervous breakdown
through it all and was taken into a hospital in
Derry, leaving her all alone.

'Good job your dad was there then,' Linda said.

'Yes,' Jenny said, remembering how her father
had adored Norah Gillespie for years, though
he'd never expected anything to come of it.
Suddenly there she was, educated to the hilt, but
fit for nothing, and destitute into the bargain.

'So they got married?' Linda said.

'Yes; in time her mother, Eileen, recovered and
moved in with them. My three brothers and
sister were born and things were very difficult for
my mother, for she'd not been raised to cook and

clean, you see.'

'Who did it then?'

'My father's mother, Gran O'Leary,' Jenny said. 'She taught my mother basic housework and cookery and showed her how to cope with the babies when they came, and Daddy did his fair share too.'

Linda screwed her eyes up, glad Jenny couldn't see her, for she thought Jenny's mother sounded like a silly cow. Everyone knew that housework and babbies were women's work. 'Why did they come to live in Birmingham?' she asked as the silence between them lengthened, but Jenny's reply was stopped for suddenly, there was a shout above them. 'Are you all right down there?'

Jenny gave a sigh of relief. 'We're fine.'

Cor blimey, thought the man who'd broken through close enough to communicate with the girls. They're alive!

That cheered him, for as the icy night had drawn its freezing cloak about everyone, hope had died among the rescuers. It was hard to keep working in the dark and intense cold, when all you expected to recover from your efforts were two corpses. God, when he took the news back, it would make everything seem worthwhile.

But none of his thoughts did he portray in his voice. He forced himself to speak calmly, in order that neither of them was alarmed as he shouted down, 'We'll start moving the heavy stuff now. Don't be alarmed at the noise. We might disturb some dust and that. Wanted you to be prepared. Take some time, I'd say, because we might have to shore it up as we go.'

92

'That's all right,' Jenny said. She knew they'd need to take extreme care, but however nerve-racking it would be, it was the first step to their release. She felt lightheaded as she thought that in a few hours they might be free and out in fresh air again. The air around them had got extremely muggy and she wondered how much air there was left but she definitely didn't want Linda worrying about it, so she said brightly, 'This calls for a celebration! What about another biscuit and a drink of water?'

Linda laughed. 'You're a proper daft bugger, you are,' she said. 'But you're dead nice with it.'

For a while all that could be heard was the sound of crunching. Linda finished her biscuit and said, 'I feel as if I've known you all my life. I reckon our mom will be really grateful to you, coming back like you said you would. She'll want to thank you, I know she will. You'll like my mom; she's nice.' There was a pause and Linda said, 'You ain't that keen on your mom, are you?'

Jenny hesitated a moment or two and then decided to tell the truth. 'I don't like her that much,' she said. 'I don't think she's that keen on me either.'

'Why not?'

'I don't know,' Jenny said wearily. 'I don't really think she wanted any more children for one thing. She already had four. Then I don't look like the others either. I take after my dad's side of the family. I look just like my Gran O'Leary did when she was young, and I'm glad because I think the world of her.'

'Well, I think you've got a lovely face,' Linda

said firmly. 'I can't see much of it, but you look really friendly. Tell you the truth, I ain't been so pleased to see anyone in my life as I was to see you. I thought I was going to die all by myself.'

'Oh but that's different,' Jenny said. 'I mean in your position I'd have been pleased to see Dracula.'

'Hmm, I suppose so,' Linda agreed and then with a spark of humour added. 'You're nicer looking than Dracula though, not much mind, but a bit.'

Jenny marvelled at the young girl's spirit.

They lay in silence for some time, then Linda said, 'Talk to me some more, Jenny.'

'What about?'

'Tell me about your gran and what she did when she first came to Birmingham.'

'Well, she went to work in the Jewellery Quarter,' Jenny said.

'Oh I'd love it there,' Linda cried. 'I've only been once in my life. What did she do?'

'She made watch chains, bracelets and necklaces,' Jenny said. 'At first she operated a press to cut out the rough for the men to work on, but then she learnt how to do it herself. She knew how to enamel brooches and badges too.'

'I'd love to do that,' Linda said again.

'Well you can if you'd want to, I'd say.'

'If the war ain't over, I'll probably have to work in munitions,' Linda said glumly. 'Mom likes it, but I don't think I will.'

'Sometimes we have to do things we don't like.' Jenny said. 'But the war won't last for ever, will it? Eventually all the workshops and factories will make other things just like they did before the war. We're lucky in Birmingham.'

'Why?'

'Because it's the workshop of the world. Don't you know that?'

'I never heard that before.'

Jenny gave a little laugh. 'I didn't understand it when Daddy told me either,' she said. 'It means Birmingham makes so many things, small things like safety pins and nuts and bolts, up to bicycles, motor bikes and cars, while related firms like Dunlop make rubber for the tyres. We also have our own jewellery quarter and thriving brass industry. It means, not only are there lots of jobs, but there's also a variety of them, see? You can do more or less any job you want, if you set your heart on it.'

She was glad they'd both been warned about the noise the rescuers might make because it was unnerving. The sides of their space beneath the stairs kept groaning and shaking, and plaster and brick dust began to trickle down on them. Jenny found herself holding her breath, expecting any minute for the lot to crash in on them, burying them both. She wondered how Linda was bearing up against the new danger that seemed to be around them, and when she felt a small hand tighten around hers, she knew the level of panic within her. 'Don't worry,' she said. 'They know what they're doing.'

'I know,' Linda's voice was a mere whisper. 'My legs are beginning to pain me again.'

Jenny wasn't surprised. They had been trapped a long time; small wonder the morphine had

95

begun to wear off. 'If my mom was here, we'd be singing together,' Linda said with a stifled sob. Jenny felt she had to take the child's mind off the pain in her legs if she could, so though she hated any reference to Linda's mother, in case it should lead to awkward questions, she said, 'Did you used to sing a lot?'

'Sometimes,' Linda said. 'Once we sang all the time but that was before Mom married that Ted Prosser, and then we stopped 'cos he didn't like it. Mom's got a lovely voice and we had a good old sing-song in the shelter, for the babbies you know. They was scared to death – so were we really – but in a way it was worse for them, 'cos they don't understand nothing do they?'

'No,' Jenny said, and before Linda could say anything else about the little boys that Jenny had seen crushed to death, she went on, 'why don't you sing here for me, now?'

'On me own?' Linda said.

'Why not?'

'I'm no good without Mom,' Linda said. 'And I'd feel proper daft.'

'Why?' Jenny said. 'It isn't as if I can even see you.'

Linda considered Jenny's words. It was true, no one could see her and no one but Jenny would hear her, either, and she could often forget things when she sang. Perhaps the pain in her bloody legs wouldn't be so bad either. 'I'll sing for you,' she said. 'It's me mom's favourite. It ain't mine. I like something a bit jollier, but she sings along with this whenever it's on the wireless.'

'What is it?'

'A Nightingale Sang in Berkeley Square,' Linda said, and without another word she opened her mouth and began, '"When true lovers meet in Mayfair, So the legends tell..."'

Jenny was stunned by the beauty and clarity of the voice. It was so sweet and clear and perfectly in tune, it moved Jenny to tears. For a child to lie flat on her back for so many hours in total darkness and in dreadful pain, all alone until Jenny had eventually reached her, and still to be able to sing like she did, she thought was truly wonderful. Jenny realised, as Patty had, that Linda had a great gift.

Outside, the raw winter's day was beginning again. The pearly grey dawn eventually gave some light to the rescuers, some of whom had toiled through the night. Then the rain began, pounding the pavements and stinging their faces in icy spears, the wet making the rubble pile slippery and slimy and more unstable than ever. It was hard to continue to move the rubbish away with wet hands, their fingers aching and made clumsy with the bitter cold.

And yet, no one wanted to give up now the girls had been located and it had been established both of them were alive and well. Those who had work that day had gone back home to prepare for it. But there were others to take their place.

And then into that grey, depressing, rain-sodden morning, came the sound of singing and what singing! 'It's one of the girls down there,' one man remarked.

'She sounds like a nightingale herself,' another commented. A third rubbed his hands over his eyes and said, 'I call that real courage. Let's put our backs into this and get those two girls out quick.'

Dr Sanders, who'd been home for a brief rest before morning surgery, returned after it to see what progress had been made. By then Linda was singing, 'I'm going to hang out the washing on the Seigfried Line', after a rendering of 'The Quarter Masters Stores', and 'We'll Meet Again'.

Dr Sanders knew who it was. Beattie had told him of Linda's love of singing and the quality of her voice, but he was amazed she was still able to sing after being incarcerated for so long. 'How much longer?' he asked impatiently. 'That pain-killer I gave the girl to take in will be wearing off soon.'

'Another half hour should do it, Doc,' one of the men said. 'You don't want us to lift the stairs up off her yet, do you?'

'Not till I examine her,' Dr Sanders said. He wasn't sure of the extent of the damage. Linda's legs could be smashed to pulp and once the stairs were lifted, she could bleed to death. It might even be that one, or both, of the young girl's legs would have to be amputated. God, he hoped that wasn't the case. But then, only the previous week, he'd dined with a friend and colleague from London, who'd just done such an operation on a young boy. The boy had been caught in an air raid and pinned down as the building fell on him. Dr Sanders' friend had amputated both legs below the knee on the dust-laden pavement, with only the light from a couple of shielded hurricane lamps, and with bombs dropping all around them. It made Dr Sanders' blood run cold to think of it. 'I'm off to do a few visits,' he said. 'I'll be back in a little while to see how you're doing. Send for me if you need me before; my receptionist will know where I am.'

'OK, Doc.' The man who'd spoken watched the doctor walk away and sighed. He wouldn't want his job in this war for all the tea in China.

Linda eventually stopped. 'I can't sing any more,' she said. Jenny heard her breath coming in short gasps and knew the pain had taken over again. She could do nothing but hold her close and pray. Slowly the conversation above became distinguishable from the low rumble heard previously. Now she could hear actual words and she knew any minute they would break through. The darkness was not so dense now she noticed. It was grey rather than deep dense black. Then suddenly it was over and light flooded in. A cheery face looked down at her. He looked exhausted and had red-rimmed eyes, but his face near split in two when he saw the girls cuddled up together. 'By God!' he exclaimed. 'Have you out in a jiffy ducks. Who was it giving the concert then?'

'Linda,' Jenny said getting to her feet. 'But she's in terrible pain again now.'

'Doc's here,' the man said. 'You hurt at all?'

'No, not really,' Jenny said, shaking herself free of the blanket and struggling to her feet. But her head swam as she stood up and she staggered like a drunk as she made her way over to the hole the man had made.

'Catch hold of me, ducks,' the man said. 'We'll get you out in two shakes of a lamb's whisker.' Jenny lifted up her hands and the man whistled when he saw them. 'Thought you said you wasn't injured?' he said. 'You won't be able to hold anything much with these hands. I'll catch hold of your arms. Don't worry, I'll soon have you up.'

And he did. Another man came to help and they hauled her upwards. For a moment she was suspended in mid-air, and then she lay on the top of the rubble panting. She gulped at the fresh air thankfully and didn't mind the numbing cold, nor the icy rain that was still pelting down.

'How's the child?' the doctor asked Jenny, as she tried to stand unsteadily, supported by the two rescue workers.

'She's been OK till a little while ago,' Jenny said. 'The morphine's wearing off now.'

'I guessed as much.' Dr Sanders said grimly. 'I'm going down immediately,' he told the men and they nodded briefly. Then to Jenny he said, 'There's an ambulance waiting. You use it.'

'There's nothing wrong with me.'

'There's plenty,' he said, 'and I'm afraid I must insist. There's another one on the way for Linda and she won't be out for a while yet. I'll have to examine her before they can even begin to start moving the staircase. You get yourself away.'

Jenny was surprised how weak she felt and she knew if it hadn't have been for the two men either side of her she'd have stumbled on her face more than once. She was surprised at the knot of people gathered who gave a cheer as she appeared. Her gran was there, brought from the house when Jenny's release was imminent. She was in her old brown coat and didn't seem to notice the rain pouring down that had plastered her hair to her head.

Geraldine was there beside her. Jenny was touched that she'd come to stand, like her gran, in the rain.

'Mother's been beside herself with worry over you,' Geraldine said, a hint of censure in her voice. 'What a foolhardy thing to do.'

Jenny was too tired and worn down to make any sort of answer, but her gran wasn't having Jenny spoken to like that. She said impatiently, 'This isn't the time or place to discuss things. Do you want to ride in the ambulance with your sister or not?'

'No,' Geraldine said. 'I must go back to grandmother and mother; they're minding the children for me. We'll probably be up later to see you.'

Jenny waved her hand wearily, and Maureen just waited until they had Jenny settled before climbing in beside her.

'Well, she's not going away without one of her own beside her,' she said and she gave a defiant wag of her head from which droplets of glistening rain fell. Jenny smiled and closed her eyes.

When she woke in the General Hospital the following morning, Jenny felt refreshed and more in charge of herself. Even though her hands and legs were heavily bandaged, she wondered why she was using up a valuable bed that could be used for someone else. All day she fretted about it, but when she attempted to go to the bathroom

101

before lunch, her legs felt so wobbly she was afraid they'd give way, and a scolding nurse brought a wheelchair and assisted her into it. 'There's nothing wrong with me,' she protested. 'Not really.'

'You are totally exhausted,' the nurse said. 'And suffering from exposure and shock, and you've inhaled a lot of dust. As well as that, you had a lot of nasty lacerations on your body, and some of them have become infected, including those on your hands. Is that list enough to be going on with?'

Jenny was surprised, but it certainly explained the weakness she felt. 'Don't rush to get better,' the nurse said with a smile, as she helped her into the toilet. 'You'll only put yourself back if you do. We'll tell you when we want you to sling your hook. All right?'

'All right,' Jenny said.

'D'you want to get tidied up after lunch?' the nurse went on. 'A reporter from the *Evening Mail* wants to interview you and take a photograph. If you feel up to it, that is.'

'Interview me?' Jenny said in surprise. 'Why?'

The nurse laughed. 'You're quite a celebrity my dear,' she said.

'Linda should be the celebrity.'

'Linda is far too ill to be interviewed. Too ill for visitors really.'

Jenny felt her heart sink. She settled herself into the wheelchair again and asked anxiously, 'She will be all right though, won't she?'

'Let's hope so,' the nurse said, pushing Jenny back to her bed. 'And at least they managed to save her legs.'

Jenny was glad about that, for she'd been worried about it. 'Does she know about her family?' she asked.

'No,' the nurse answered. 'She's not strong enough for news like that yet. Mind you, they won't be able to hold out much longer. She's asking all the time, so I'm told.'

And Jenny knew she would be.

But if Linda wasn't well enough for visitors, Jenny had plenty. Even her mother had made the journey once and came in a taxi with her grandmother and Geraldine – and her sister-in-law, Jan, had also been. One day she was surprised by a visit from Babs and Lily from the office at Dunlops. They brought her a little basket of fruit donated by the greengrocer on the Tyburn Road, and a sack of papers that had her picture and story of the rescue plastered all over them. Her mother and grandmother had talked about her in glowing terms and spoke of her considerate and conscientious attitude.

'*In spite of personal grief,*' her mother was reported as having said, '*for Jenny had just learnt of the death of her beloved brother, she reported for duty that night as usual She is truly a remarkable girl.*' Underneath the reporter had written: *Anthony O'Leary was shot down over France. He was one of our brave Battle of Britain pilots to whom we all owe so much.*

The evening papers carried the interview with Jenny herself, and she was described as 'a dainty, pint-sized girl with a lovely freckled face and a gorgeous shock of auburn curls, who, despite her size, had the heart of a lion.'

The whole thing embarrassed Jenny, yet she could see how proud Babs and Lily were of her. They said everyone at work felt the same way and had all signed the card they'd brought in. She knew her mother and grandmother would revel in the attention.

The next day Jenny had the bandages removed from her hands and Linda endured the first of her many operations. The nurses said she would be ready for visitors in a day or two. Jenny was anxious to see her, but she was also concerned about where Linda would go when she recovered. She'd passed on all that she'd learnt about Linda's relations to the authorities, but had heard nothing of the outcome of any investigations they'd done.

In the end, it was Beattie who told her. Jenny had never seen Beattie looking so sad as she did one afternoon when she came in to see her. Beattie laid a packet of sweets on the bed, gave a sigh and said, 'How are you ducks?'

'I'm all right,' Jenny said. 'In better shape than you, I think. What on earth is the matter?'

'Oh, it's young Linda,' Beattie said. 'I popped up to see her first. Poor little bugger. She's been told about her mom and brothers today.' Beattie paused. 'Apparently she went wild, yelling and screaming and lashing out at them all, throwing things.' There were tears in Beattie's eyes. 'Had to be sedated again, the nurses were telling me.' She looked at Jenny and tears ran down her face as she said, 'How the bleeding hell will she stand it? Answer me that.'

Jenny couldn't, and could only guess at the extent of the child's grief. She'd suffered agonies over Anthony's death, and even now if she thought about him for too long, the tears could flow. But to lose everyone in the world must be soul-destroying. 'Let's hope that who ever she goes to stay with has an understanding nature, and will help her cope,' she said.

'That's another thing,' Beattie said. 'Not one of them can or will take her, 'cept the feller in Australia. You ever heard of a kiddie being sent to the other side of the world to a man or family she's never seen. 'Specially with all them bleeding U-boats around. She wouldn't stand a chance. Remember that ship with all those kiddies on board, sunk on its way to America? Anyway the welfare people won't wear it.'

But what about the aunt that lives in Basingstoke?'

'She'd have her and willing, but hasn't the room,' Beattie said. 'She came down to see her, a nice woman but she was telling me she has eight boys already and they're all living in a little two-bedroom place. All they could give her I expect when she was evacuated, and she really has no room for the child at all.'

'That's it then?' Jenny said. 'Where will she go?'

Beattie shrugged. 'Orphanage I suppose,' she said. 'I'd take her like a shot if I hadn't had my house blown up, 'cos she's a great kid. But I can't land her on my sister as well.'

'No, I see that,' Jenny said. 'But, oh God Beattie, an orphanage!'

'I know. Bloody awful.'

'Tragic,' said Jenny. She knew Linda, that brave free spirit, would never fit into the rigours of an orphanage. She knew they'd crush her. Who there would care that her world had been torn apart? She'd just be one of many.

Jenny felt very depressed when Beattie had left. She tossed and turned in bed all night.

And in the hour before dawn, as she lay tired, but too emotionally charged for sleep, she wondered for the first time if it wouldn't have been better for Linda to have died with her mother and brothers. And she turned her face to the wall and sobbed.

Chapter Seven

'How is she?' Jenny asked the nurse at the door to the children's ward.

The young Irish nurse shook her head sadly. 'Desperate,' she said. 'It breaks your heart, so it does, to see her.'

'Is she sedated still?'

'No,' the young nurse said. 'But sure, she might as well be. She lies as still as a statue, withdrawn into herself you know, and never speaks more than yes or no – that's if you get her to talk at all.'

'Can I see her?'

'I'll have to ask Matron,' the nurse said. 'But I'd say it can do no harm. You are the young lady who was rescued with her, aren't you? I've seen your picture in the paper.'

Jenny nodded, blushing, unused to such fame, and she blushed still further when the nurse continued, 'We all think you're ever so brave – the whole hospital was talking about it.' But then she noticed Jenny's blushes and touching her on the arm, said, 'I'll just go and have a wee word with Matron.'

Matron agreed with the nurse that Jenny's visit couldn't harm Linda. 'In fact, my dear,' she said, her stern features relaxing for a second in the ghost of a smile, 'you might be the one to make her take an interest in life again.'

Jenny doubted it as she looked at the child, as

107

pale as the pillow she lay against. Her face was expressionless, her arms still by her sides. She seemed unaware of anything – the hospital side-room where she lay alone, the drip feeding into her arm, a cage protecting her legs at the bottom of the bed.

'Linda,' Jenny said gently.

The child turned her head and Jenny was shocked by the hopeless look in them. There was not a flicker of recognition; she was like the living dead. For a moment Jenny regretted rescuing the girl. Hadn't she thought it might have been better if she'd died, along with her mother and brothers?

Yes, but she *hadn't* died. She had her whole life before her, and it could be a good and fulfilling life. She took one little thin hand in hers and said, 'How are you feeling?'

What a stupid, inane remark! She thought instantly, but Linda appeared not to have heard her. Jenny's eyes flitted around the room and came to light on a worn-looking teddy bear propped on the bedside cabinet. She'd seen it once before, by the light of a torch, and knew it was Tolly, the bear Linda had come back to the house to fetch. It had been that bear that had saved her life. She remembered Linda saying that George would be so pleased she'd found him, and a lump rose in Jenny's throat.

This would never do, she told herself fiercely. She put out her hand and gently stroked the bear with one finger and Linda's head moved to watch.

'Talk to me, pet,' Jenny said softly.

Linda's eyes met Jenny's and she snapped out

108

in hurt anger, 'What about? The weather?' Her voice was little more than a whisper and she closed her eyes with a sigh, as if the mere effort of speaking had exhausted her. Then Jenny saw tears seep from the corners of her closed lids, slide down her cheeks and soak the pillow. She wondered if these were the first tears Linda had shed. They said she went mad, screaming and shouting and had to be sedated, but had she cried at all, like Jenny had that terrible morning when she'd sobbed in Beattie's arms at the loss of Anthony and the terrible things she'd witnessed the previous night?

Risking rejection, she held Linda's hand tight and looking into the child's eyes she said, 'I'm so sorry about your mother and little brothers.'

Linda's eyes opened wider. No one in the hospital had spoken of the tragedy since she'd come out of her drugged sleep. She'd lain in bed and the doctor's words had vibrated in her head, but the nurses tried to jolly her along and talk to her as if she was two years old. And no one said anything about her family; in fact they carefully avoided the subject, as if it was better to pretend they'd never existed at all.

It mattered much more to her than her crushed legs, but that was all anyone would talk about. They told her of the operations on them and that she'd be as right as rain in time, not that she believed them and the nurses said she was a lucky girl. Linda thought wryly she'd hate to meet an unlucky one, and many many times she regretted returning to the house that evening.

Her Uncle Sid had sent a letter to her from

Australia. He said how sorry he was, and how he regretted being so far away, and said once the war was over she could come and live with him and his family and be welcome. Linda supposed it was nice of him, but 'when the war's over', was like saying 'when the world ends', or 'when the clouds fall out of the sky'. Any road she didn't want to go and live in Australia. She didn't even want to live in Basingstoke with her Aunt Lily, though she liked the plump motherly woman who'd bought her a small basket of fruit.

She felt completely alone in the world, and that was the hardest thing of all to cope with. If only she had a photo of her mother, of the boys and her father, but all the family snaps had been in the shoe-box in the house, and were destroyed along with everything else. Beattie had searched the ruins for her, but there was nothing left. Her sense of desolation was total. 'I expect I'll forget what they look like eventually,' Linda said to Jenny.

'You won't. You'll carry them in your heart always.'

'Huh,' Linda said. 'I ain't got nothing to remember them by, not one thing 'cept our George's teddy bear. Dr Sanders said he'll take me to see their graves when I'm better and out of here for good. I'd like that. I'll take some flowers and that and make it nice.'

Her voice ended on a slight sob and Jenny squeezed her hand tightly and said, 'I'll go with you if you want.'

Linda shrugged. 'I don't care. Do what you like.' She brushed the trailing tears away from her

110

eyes impatiently and said, 'You knew they was dead all the time, din't yer?'

Jenny hesitated for a brief second. 'Yes,' she said, her voice so low, it was almost a whisper.

'Why din't you tell me? All the time we was together and you never said a word,' Linda demanded angrily.

'What could I say?' Jenny cried. 'You'd lain for hours alone, cold, in pitch dark and in pain. How could I add to that?'

'You mean, I might just have given up,' Linda said, reading her mind. 'And you'd have been bloody right, too. In fact, I wish you hadn't bothered to get me out at all.'

'Don't say that!'

'Why shouldn't I?' the younger girl said harshly. 'You told me you wanted me to talk – well, this is what I want to talk about.'

Watching Linda, Jenny saw her face full of self-pity and though her heart ached in sympathy, she knew that Linda feeling sorry for herself would destroy her. Her own mother had done just that for years – and because of it, she'd taken no interest in anyone else besides herself. It had soured her life. And she wasn't going to let it sour Linda's. So she said quite sharply, 'OK, let's talk about it. Let's talk about the people who laboured for hours to release you. Let's talk about the men, and some women, who worked all through the bitterly cold night with the rain lashing down, and then went straight on to work the next day.'

'Well,' said Linda mutinously. 'They needn't have bothered.'

'They bothered because they thought you were brave and plucky,' Jenny retorted. 'They might not have been so keen to get you out if they'd thought you were just going to give up.'

'What d'you know about it, any road?' Linda cried. 'What have I got to look forward to, now, anyway?'

'Oh Linda, I know how you feel,' Jenny said. 'At the moment it hurts like hell and you can't really believe it, but it does get better with time. My gran says you never forget your loved ones, a piece of your heart goes with them, but you have to learn to live without them.'

'How the hell do you bloody know?'

'I know, because it happened to me too,' Jenny said sharply. 'The day of that massive raid we had a telegram saying the youngest and favourite of all my brothers had been shot down. He'd just turned eighteen in June.'

There was a short silence while Linda thought about what Jenny had said. She knew she was being unfair taking it out on her. Eventually, she said in a very quiet voice, 'I'm sorry, Jenny, I know I'm being an ungrateful sod, but I'm as scared as hell. Where am I going to live when I get out?'

Jenny forced herself to speak brightly, 'You'll be looked after, don't you worry.'

'Where? In a home?'

Jenny couldn't deny that and didn't try. Instead she said, 'The children's homes are lovely today, and there will be plenty of others for company.'

'I want to stay here,' Linda said obstinately. 'I want to stay with my friends and at my old school.'

112

'Maybe they'll find you a city orphanage,' Jenny said. 'Tell them how you feel when the time comes,' but even as she spoke, she wasn't at all sure that children's feelings were considered that much.

Linda was obviously of the same mind. 'I'll tell them,' she said, 'but d'you think they'll listen, or care?'

And Jenny couldn't face her and say that they would. Instead she said, 'It will only be for a couple of years. You'll be at work then and have more choice in what you do and where you live.'

'Yeah, I know,' Linda said. Again there was a small silence between them and then Linda said, 'I thought shelters were bloody safe?' and Jenny saw the tears beginning to trickle down the girl's face.

'Not for a direct hit,' Jenny said gently. 'Nothing could stand up to that.'

'But they didn't suffer?'

'Not for a moment,' Jenny assured her. 'They wouldn't have known a thing about it.'

'I feel... I feel so bloody awful,' Linda said with a sob. 'It's not fair that I survived and they didn't.'

The tears came then – a wild torrent that spurted from her nose and eyes and threatened to choke her. Nurses came running, but when they saw the child gathered into Jenny's arms as far as the drip and the leg cage would allow, and saw that she too was sobbing, they withdrew.

'About time,' the Matron said to the doctor, recognising the tears as a good sign. 'I honestly thought that lass was heading for some sort of breakdown.'

113

The doctor nodded in agreement. 'Perhaps now she'll begin to make some improvement,' he said.

'We can only hope so,' the Matron said grimly.

As the taxi pulled up outside Pype Hayes Road, the neighbours ran forward to welcome Jenny home. Others stood in the doorways and waved and cheered and Jenny, though embarrassed, was touched by their concern. A man from the end ran up with a jar of honey. 'From my own bees Jenny,' he said. 'Enjoy it.'

Mrs Patterson, their next door neighbour, had baked a cake and everyone said they were glad to see her back safe and sound. Jenny was touched to see that Geraldine and Jan and their children had come down to the house to see her, and had been absolutely staggered when her grandmother arrived at the hospital in a taxi to bring her home.

The table was laid as for a party, full of things not seen since pre-war days. There were plates of chicken and ham sandwiches and a dish of tomatoes that Jenny found were from Mr Patterson's greenhouse. But the bowl of hard-boiled eggs astonished her: her mother said they were from a man who kept hens. The cold sausages were a present from the butcher. 'Sit up and eat up now,' she told her, 'before it's all spoiled.'

It was all wonderful, and Jenny was only sorry her appetite was not able to do it justice, especially the jelly and blancmange the children demanded she try, and the cake baked by their next-door neighbour, that Geraldine pressed on her. 'Go on,' she said. 'Being thin is one thing, but you're just plain skinny, Jenny.'

'You could do with more meat on your bones certainly,' Jan, Seamus's wife said. She herself was comfortably plump, and would have liked everyone else to be the same size, but she was a nice person and Jenny liked her. She wished Gran O'Leary had been invited because she could have done with her support that evening. She was going to make an announcement which she knew would spoil some of the joy of her home-coming for her family. But she knew she had to do it today: it had been growing in her ever since the previous day when Linda had cried in her arms.

Knowing it was best to get it over with, Jenny began as they sat drinking their second cup of tea. 'I went to see Linda yesterday,' she said.

'Oh, how is she?' Norah asked. Jenny knew she hadn't the slightest interest.

'Very down,' Jenny said. 'She knows the full extent of the tragedy now.'

'Has she any family to see to her?' Jan asked.

Jenny shook her head, 'No one.'

'Ah, poor soul.'

Jenny blessed Jan for her sympathetic nature. 'Yes it's a shame isn't it? She has got an aunt and an uncle, but he's in Australia, and the aunt hasn't got the room with a big family of her own.'

'Be an orphanage for her then,' Norah said.

'Not necessarily,' Jenny said. Everyone stopped and looked at her. Jenny paused for a moment or two, and then said, 'She could come here.'

'Don't be ridiculous!'

'I'm not,' Jenny protested. 'She could sleep in my room in my bed; neither of us is very big.'

'Jenny, my dear,' Eileen said, in her most patronising voice. 'It would not be at all suitable. We don't know anything about the child's background.'

'Sod her background,' Jenny said, so intensely angry she didn't care what she said.

'Jenny!' the exclamation came simultaneously from Eileen and Norah.

'Don't "Jenny" me, and treat me like an idiot,' she said, rage boiling inside her. 'The child I spent hours with is virtually alone in the world. She has no one. They were wiped out in the raid that left *you* unscathed!'

'I understand you are upset over the child and a little overwrought yourself perhaps,' said Eileen. Jenny had the desire to swipe the smug expression off her face. 'So, despite the way you've spoken to us, and the language used, we shall make allowances. You'll find she'll soon settle down, dear. The orphanages today are marvellous places, I believe.'

'How d'you know? You've never been inside one.'

'Jenny, don't be so rude and argumentative,' Norah said, siding as usual with Eileen. 'Mother's only expressing an opinion. Now, we have no objection to your being friends with the girl and visiting her if you feel you must, but that's as far as it is to go.'

The only way she could maybe change their minds was to appeal to their puffed up pride.

They'd enjoyed having their pictures in the paper and their account of Jenny, who they described as a 'wonderful daughter and granddaughter', had raised their esteem within the neighbourhood. So Jenny said, 'If you were to agree to take Linda on, it would look good for you.'

'How, pray, do you work that one out?'

'Well think of the headlines,' Jenny said. 'Selfless widow offers home to orphan. The newspaper would be interested. In these days of bad war news, human interest stories are sought after.'

She saw the two women were thinking about what she said, and so she went on, 'I don't care how it's done. You two can take all the credit, as long as Linda is allowed to come here to live.' She paused and then went on, bravely determined. 'But if you don't agree to this, I will go to the papers myself and tell them Linda's story. I will tell them I wanted to offer her a home here with me, but you would not hear of it.'

'Don't you dare threaten me, miss,' Norah snapped.

'I'm not threatening you Mother. I'm just telling you what I intend to do,' Jenny said, marvelling at how calm she felt. She knew she'd won the fight; she saw it on their faces as they glanced at each other. But before they were able to make a reply, the sirens sent up their unearthly wail. The adults looked at each other almost in disbelief. 'Oh God,' Geraldine breathed. 'It's starting again. Oh God!'

'It may go over,' Jenny said, seeing her sister's terror mirrored in the faces of her children.

But it didn't go over. It was far too dangerous for Jan to walk home, and Jenny insisted Jan and Geraldine and their children use the shelter, as she knew neither her mother, nor grandmother would go into it. It would be cramped with them all inside, and probably damp and cold too, and she was glad she had taken the loan of Mr Patterson's oil heater, even though it smelt to high heaven.

Seeing how frightened the children were of the planes droning over their head, and the crashes of explosions, and remembering what Linda had done to calm her brothers, Jenny began to sing every song she could think of, in an effort to still their panic.

Jan realised what she was doing immediately and began a rendering of the silly songs Eddie and Rosemarie would know from school. Geraldine didn't join in, but she did stop shivering quite so much and the children grew enthusiastic, especially when none of the bombs fell terribly close.

Eventually, the heavy air and late hour got to Jamie and Declan and they were put down in the bunks to sleep. Even Rosemarie and Eddie were drowsy and lying back on their mothers' knees, Eddie with his thumb in his mouth for comfort.

Too tired to sing any more, the women fell to talking in low voices so as not to disturb the children. At first they didn't discuss the subject Jenny had broached at tea, but skated around it. Eventually, Jan said, 'Were you serious about having that wee girl to live with you?'

'Yes,' Jenny said. 'Never more so.'

118

'Do you dislike Mother so much?' Geraldine asked.

'I dislike her attitude,' Jenny said. 'What is so wrong with her and grandmother that they can't extend the hand of human friendship to another person in need?'

'Well,' said Geraldine, 'they do know nothing about her.'

'She's young and orphaned,' Jenny snapped. 'What else is there to know?'

She glanced at the children and saw they had their eyes closed. She lowered her voice to a whisper as she said, 'Linda's little brother George was about the same age as young Declan and Harry was a baby, younger even than Jamie. Think on that.'

Geraldine and Jan did think of it and instinctively shuddered: Jenny, seeing she had their sympathy, went on, 'Linda was like a little mother to them, the next-door neighbour, Beattie, told me. There was just her and her mother, you see – her own father died when she was small, and then her stepfather was one of those left behind on the beaches of Dunkirk.'

No need for them to know what sort of man Ted Prosser really was: Jenny wanted them both to feel sympathetic towards the young orphaned girl.

'Oh, the poor wee thing,' the kind-hearted Jan said. 'And then to suffer like she did, being buried like that.'

'I can see how you feel somewhat responsible, Jenny,' Geraldine said. 'And if she has no one else...'

'She hasn't,' Jenny said. 'The only one that would have taken her has eight boys of her own already and lives in a two-bedroom terrace house in Basingstoke. Beattie would have her like a shot, but she's been bombed out herself and is lodging with her sister.'

'So, you think it's up to you?' Jan said.

'Yes. Do you understand why?'

'Oh, indeed. I think the poor wee thing has already been dealt a bad enough hand in life.'

Oh bless you Jan, Jenny thought, and turning to her sister she said, 'What about you Geraldine?'

Geraldine had been moulded by their mother. But this had touched on her protective feelings as a mother and she knew that were she to have been blown to kingdom come by a bomb, she'd not have liked either Eddie or Rosemarie to end up in an orphanage. 'I can see how you feel sort of responsible for her and maybe it would be the charitable thing to look after her, at least for the time being. I'd hate one of mine to ever end up in an orphanage.'

Jenny's mouth dropped open in astonishment and she grasped Geraldine's hand in hers. She knew Geraldine's resolve would crumble before any opposition, particularly if it came from their mother. But to say she understood what Jenny was doing, and why, was a form of breakthrough. 'I won't forget how you supported me tonight,' she said and both of the older women were moved by the passion in Jenny's voice and they smiled at each other as the 'All Clear' blasted out its reassuring sound.

Chapter Eight

'What else can you do, cutie dear?' Grandma O'Leary said to Jenny the following day. 'The child hasn't a one belonging to her. What are you to do, but offer her a place to lay her head?'

'That's right, Jenny. You can't let her go into a home, not when you have the room,' Peggy put in.

The approval of her gran and Peggy washed over Jenny, healing her spirit that was bruised from the blistering argument she'd had that very morning when she'd reopened the topic with her mother and grandmother.

'I'd have the wee thing here myself,' Maureen went on, 'if it wasn't for my Gerry and this one here, tying the knot next spring. The small room will be empty, but I've a feeling it won't be long before that's in use as a nursery.'

'Gran,' Jenny said, as Peggy blushed.

Maureen gave a gentle push to her future daughter-in-law. 'You have to get used to things like that, my darlin'. You can't be blushing every time I open my mouth.'

'She's awful, Gran is,' Jenny said to Peggy. 'And she'll never change.' In a way, she was a little jealous of Peggy and the closeness between her and her gran, but she told herself she was being stupid.

She smiled across at Peggy as she spoke. The

121

other girl was still recovering from the raid on the BSA. Gerry had been all for an early marriage, but both Peggy and Gran had been against it.

'Mad galoots to want to marry in the middle of the winter,' Maureen had said.

'Anyway,' Peggy added, 'I'm not hobbling down the aisle with my ribs bound up and my hair in a state. Besides, Mammy and Daddy want a bit of a splash, wartime or not. I'm the first to be married in our family and Mammy says we'll do it in style. If we're too hasty, she says people will think there's a reason for it.'

So that had been that. Gerry had been overruled and the wedding was fixed for the very end of March 1941. According to Jenny's gran, he'd been amazed at the fuss a wedding entailed. 'What did you think, lad?' she cried. 'Did you think Peggy should put on a costume and yourself a suit, and the two of you could pop along to the priest, without a body belonging to you being there, as if you were going to the pictures?'

'No, of course not,' Gerry lied. 'But does she really need a fancy dress and bridesmaids? Don't you think it's a bit unpatriotic?'

'No, I don't,' his mother had snapped. 'In this mad world, where the innocent are dying daily, what is unpatriotic about wanting to give the girl a good send-off on her wedding day? Would it help the country any if it was hidden away as if it were something to be ashamed of?'

Gerry had no answer for his mother, but really it didn't matter. Unpatriotic or not, Peggy was having a wedding dress she could be proud of, and at least three bridesmaids.

'Have you decided on who you're going to have?' Jenny asked Peggy. She knew two were Peggy's sisters and presumed another would be a cousin, or friend of the family.

'You,' Peggy said to Jenny with a brilliant smile. 'Will you do it?'

'I'd be honoured to,' Jenny said, touched that Peggy should even consider her. 'What about fittings and measurements and things?'

'Leave it a wee while,' Peggy said. 'There's no rush.'

'No, except I've got time on my hands now. The hospital doctor said I wasn't to think of going back to work yet. It's mad, I feel great and I'll end up murdering my mother and grandmother if I'm home much longer with them.'

'Look on the bright side cutie,' Maureen said. 'At least it gives you time to visit the wee girl in hospital.'

Jenny sighed and said, 'I suppose it does. I'm on my way there now. She doesn't get many visitors, you know – it's too far for her friends to go. Her teacher has been up once, and Beattie pops in, but that's it really.'

'I'll take a wee dander up to the hospital myself,' Maureen said. 'The days must hang heavy on her.'

'I'll go along with you,' Peggy said.

'You'll not,' Maureen said. 'What will his lordship say if I let you go gallivanting?'

Peggy laughed. 'Visiting a sick child is hardly gallivanting,' she said.

Jenny left them arguing amicably over it and made for the tram.

Linda was feeling very low when she saw Jenny enter the room, but she tried to smile, because she was grateful to the older girl for making the effort to visit her. Jenny came almost every day. Linda hadn't really believed she would, but she hadn't let her down, even though it was a trek to Steel House Lane from Pype Hayes.

'Hi. How are you today?' Jenny asked.

Linda shrugged. 'All right.'

'I got you some comics,' Jenny said.

'Thanks,' Linda said flatly.

Jenny took Linda's hand. 'I suppose you get bored?' she said sympathetically.

'What d'you think?' Linda snapped, snatching her hand away. Almost immediately, she was ashamed of herself. It would serve her right, Linda thought, if Jenny didn't come again. The thought of long days stuck in this place without the other girl's visits to look forward to made her eyes fill with tears.

Jenny knew Linda was depressed; Matron had warned her about it. She decided to get straight to the point.

'Linda,' she said. 'When you're well enough to leave hospital, would you like to move into my house?'

Linda's eyes opened very wide. 'Your house!' she repeated. 'Live with you, you mean?'

'That's right,' Jenny said.

The other girl's eyes shone. 'You mean it, really and truly?'

'I do.'

'That would be great.'

'It won't be for some time, you know,' Jenny said.

'I know, I don't care. I was worrying about where I was going to live,' Linda said. She studied Jenny for a minute or two and then said, 'What about your mom?'

'What about her?'

'Won't she mind me coming to live with you?'

'No, of course not.'

Linda was lying back on the pillows watching Jenny, and she suddenly said, 'She will though, won't she? Your mom ain't happy about it, I can tell.'

Jenny opened her mouth to voice another denial, when Linda suddenly said, 'I know when you're lying. Your eyes dart about all over the place.'

Jenny laughed and said, 'All right then. My mother isn't all that keen, to tell the truth. But she'll come round.'

'I don't care if she doesn't,' Linda said. 'If I had to choose anyone to live with, it would be you, and as long as you're happy about it, that's all I'm bothered about.'

And Jenny put her arms around Linda and gave her a hug. She knew all the rows with Norah were worth it, to give Linda something to smile about at last.

The news of where the orphaned Linda Lennox would live when she was finally released from hospital, soon filtered through the Estate. Many thought that Norah O'Leary might be a stuck-up cow and her mother too, but their hearts were

125

obviously in the right place to open up their home for a child. Jenny never told the true story, but let people believe the decision was one her mother had made.

To Dr Sanders, who knew the type of women Jenny's mother and grandmother were, it seemed out of character for them to offer an orphan a home, especially a tough cookie like Linda Lennox. He was worried about the whole situation and knowing they'd have no privacy in Jenny's house to talk, he waited for her in the car park one evening as she left the hospital. He made the excuse he'd been visiting a patient and Jenny was certainly glad to see him. The winter's day was raw and cold and inclined to be foggy. Her feet throbbed and she had no wish to stand at a freezing tram stop for hours on end.

She slipped gratefully into the car and with an impish grin said, 'We'll have to stop meeting like this.'

'If you say so,' Dr Sanders said in the same vein. 'I could always let you out now, if you're worried about your reputation.'

'Don't you dare,' Jenny cried. 'It's lovely to be chauffeured home like this.'

'Then sit back, enjoy it and shut up.'

'Yes, sir!'

The doctor drove in silence down the darkened city streets for a moment or two. He'd noticed the exhausted pallor of Jenny's skin as she sat beside him, and guessed it was the trek to the hospital wearing her out. But he knew Jenny well enough now to know it would do no good to mention it. Instead he said, 'Are you looking forward to Linda coming to live with you?'

'How do you know about it?' Jenny asked. 'I've never mentioned it and it's only just been decided.'

'Jenny, I work on the Estate,' he reminded her. 'The story is on everyone's lips.'

'Well,' said Jenny, recognising the truth of his words, 'the answer to your question is yes and no. Yes, I'm looking forward to having Linda's future settled, and she's happier than she's been for a long time.'

'But?' prompted the doctor.

'It's my mother and grandmother,' Jenny burst out. 'They're so anti towards the child.' She chewed her thumbnail anxiously and then went on, 'Between them, they've given me hell for years. I'd hate them to do the same to Linda. I mean, I won't always be there to protect her.'

'Then, is it wise of you to offer her a home at all?' Dr Sanders asked.

'Maybe not. But what's the alternative?' Jenny asked. 'A children's home? Indifferent foster-parents? At least I do care for her and she cares for me. And she'll have all the rest of the family.'

'But your mother...?'

'Mother and Grandmother refuse to discuss it,' Jenny said.

'What if they refuse to have her at all?' Dr Sanders suggested gently.

'Oh God. That would really break Linda's heart,' Jenny said, and added after a second or two, 'but Mother won't do that.'

'How can you be so sure?'

'Because if she did that, I'd leave home and

she knows it.'

'Where would you go?'

'I'd join the WAAFs,' Jenny shrugged. 'I wanted to right at the start of the war, but all the family said it was my duty to stay and look after Mother. If she said Linda definitely couldn't come, I'd be off.'

'Aren't you under-age?'

'I'm twenty,' Jenny said. 'And Anthony joined up at eighteen, but if Mother and Grandmother do kick up, I'd just wait. I'll be twenty-one in April. It's not long, and I can do what I like then.' She looked out at the drab, blacked-out city centre. 'Linda on the other hand, is still only a kid; she needs to be with people who will take good care of her. How else will she ever cope with the tragedy of losing her family?'

Dr Sanders didn't know. The same question had been nagging at him. Linda's physical injuries would heal, of that he was certain, though it would take time. But the mental scars would take sensitive handling. The best cure he knew for what ailed Linda was love, the kind that Jenny had for her. He said, 'Jenny, would you like *me* to talk to your mother?'

Her reaction surprised him. 'Oh, God no. That would make her worse.'

'Why?' he asked, genuinely puzzled.

'She hates doctors,' Jenny said.

'Good Lord! Why?'

'I suspect, and so does Gran O'Leary, that it's because our family doctor knows what a fraud she is and has probably told her so. Listen,' she went on, 'Mother is supposed to suffer from

128

severe arthritis. Now I know she's not half as bad as she makes out, as I've seen her myself, walking around the house quite normally when I've spied on her through the window. Yet when I've gone into the house minutes later, she's groaning, with a blanket placed over her legs.'

It wouldn't have been the first time a patient had exaggerated their ailments, or even invented them altogether, Dr Sanders thought. It had always flabbergasted him that some people would do that. His predecessor, Dr McKenzie, said that such people usually had psychological problems which were just as real and important as their imaginary physical ailments. However, Dr Sanders had neither the time nor the training to delve into people's minds and he knew Jenny O'Leary well enough to know she was not lying. 'We must try and break down this animosity to the medical profession in your mother,' he said. 'What if she ever needs a doctor one day?'

Jenny shrugged. 'She hasn't yet,' she said. 'But I suppose she might. After all, she's getting older and Grandmother is older still.'

'Let me come and see them and talk to them about Linda.'

Reluctantly, Jenny agreed, but in the event she needn't have worried. Dr Sanders was respectful and charming to the two older ladies, complimenting them on their youthful looks and figures, before mentioning Linda's name. Then he told them how he admired their selfless decision to offer her a home with them. Eileen and Norah were flustered. Flattered beyond measure at the young doctor's praise of them, they hesitated to lose his good opinion by telling him they didn't want the girl near them, let alone living with them.

Instead, they found themselves saying, 'It was the least we could do.'

Then Dr Sanders spent time commiserating with Norah's disability and discussing the modern treatment and tablets now used to alleviate the symptoms of arthritis. Norah was pleased he'd taken an interest but said she didn't think there was much could be done for her. 'I've been a martyr to pain all my life, Doctor, and that's the truth,' she said and Dr Sanders was sympathetic.

'For a doctor, he appears to be quite a pleasant young man,' Norah conceded after he left. 'At least he cares, not like that old charlatan we had before.'

Eileen agreed with her daughter, but Jenny said nothing. It was amazing, really, that they liked him; they liked so few people. The kindly smiles and greetings Eileen had received, once word got round about where Linda would live, had been firmly rebuffed.

'But why?' Jenny had cried when she'd been told.

'Why?' Norah snapped. 'We don't want people to become familiar, that's why.'

Linda was waiting impatiently for Jenny to come. She had something special to tell her: the doctor had said she could go and spend a few days at Jenny's for Christmas.

Further operations were planned in the New

Year. The New Year was aeons away, but Christmas wasn't and Linda knew she wanted to spend it with Jenny more than anything in the world. She was much happier about going, now she'd had visits from Gran O'Leary, and Peggy who spoke with a much stronger Irish accent than Jenny's. Peggy had told her she'd been injured herself when the BSA was hit, the same night her lot had copped it. They both said when she lived with Jenny, she could visit them anytime, for sure they were only two streets away.

Even Jan and Geraldine had been up to the hospital on separate occasions to make the acquaintance of the child Jenny had spoken so passionately about. Jan thought Linda a lovely and brave wee girl; she had sat beside her for an hour and talked to her easily about her mother and brothers and the better place they'd all gone to.

She told Jenny her heart had been sore for the child who hadn't even a vestige of faith to hang on to. 'She needs you, Jenny,' she'd said. 'She'll give you love and gratitude for the rest of her life.'

'I don't want gratitude,' Jenny had said. Years later she was to remember those words, but at the time they were said, she meant them. But she did want love. She craved it as much as Linda did, and she knew there was a special bond between them.

Geraldine thought Linda was too quiet – sullen, she called her – and not quite their sort. 'But I thought I might as well see her, seeing as you're quite determined to bring her here to live,' she said. 'But I'll tell you now it won't work,' and

131

Jenny realised her sister had been got at. Her brave words in the Anderson shelter the day she'd come home from hospital had been torn apart by their mother.

Linda could have told Jenny how Geraldine had sat uneasily on the seat by the bed and made it apparent she'd rather be anywhere than in a hospital with a child she'd never set eyes on before. She spoke empty words of welcome in a clipped voice and a smile that didn't reach her eyes and Linda was glad she left after about fifteen strained minutes. Jenny knew that Linda hadn't taken to her either, but whatever the problems Jenny was still determined to have Linda home for the Christmas break, even if just for a day or two because the girl wanted it so much, even though she herself was as nervous as hell.

There were practical considerations to make too. Linda would still have a plaster cast on her leg and would be in a wheelchair, so ramps would have to be made to go in the kitchen door and the outside toilet beside it. Then there was the problem of carrying her up and downstairs night and morning. Jenny wondered if she could borrow a commode from the hospital, because she'd never be able to use a chamber pot under the bed if she was taken short in the night. But those were problems she'd solve on her own. She told Linda that she was delighted at the doctor's decision and couldn't wait to have her at the house. Inside, she quailed at the prospect of breaking the news to her mother, that Linda was coming home for a few days, a lot earlier than they'd imagined.

Two evenings later, Jenny was startled by a knock at the door – they didn't get many visitors. She was even more surprised to see the figure of Dr Sanders standing on the step.

'Can I come in, my dear?'

'Of course,' Jenny said, and wondered why she'd said that. 'Of course' wasn't in the vocabulary of her mother and grandmother, and she wondered would they mind her asking him in.

She needn't have worried, for after his first visit, the good doctor had her mother and grandmother almost eating out of his hands. He hadn't been in the house two minutes when he mentioned the fact of Linda coming home for Christmas. Jenny was surprised he knew, but he seemed to know everything.

'I must say, I'm surprised,' Norah confided. 'Jenny tells me the child's legs will still be in plaster and she'll be in a wheelchair. Really, I'm not sure she's fit to be let out, even for just a couple of days.'

'You're probably right,' Dr Sanders agreed gravely. 'But you see, it's Linda's *mental* state the hospital doctors are worried about.'

'Mental state!' Norah said. She had a horror of mental illness.

'Ah, yes,' Dr Sanders said. 'The poor girl faces more painful operations in the New Year and her spirits have been so very low. After all, she knows she won't be able to leave hospital for some months and that seems a lifetime away. This was to give her a little boost. I must say, I was glad to

133

hear the news myself.'

The two older ladies had no option but to look suitably pleased. 'It will buck her up tremendously,' he said, and both women nodded their heads sagely. 'The point is,' the doctor went on, 'the hospital is doing a sort of concert on Christmas Eve. Any patients who are fit enough can do a turn, and the doctors and nurses will supply the rest of the entertainment.'

'Yes?'

'Well, it appears Linda is singing some carols on her own. She has a wonderful voice, you know – a natural talent!' Then he glanced at Jenny and said, 'Of course, you'd know that yourself. She sang when you were both trapped, didn't she?'

Jenny saw her mother and grandmother's eyebrows raised in surprised enquiry; she'd told them virtually nothing of what it had been like trapped hour upon hour and they'd never asked. 'Yes,' she said, answering the doctor. 'I thought it might keep her spirits up. Her legs had begun hurting her again. I thought it might take her mind off it all.'

'You did well,' the doctor said warmly.

'Stop it!' Jenny blushed, not used to praise of any kind. 'I'm really not any sort of special person. Anyway, surely you haven't called just to embarrass the life out of me.'

'No,' said the doctor with a smile, and Jenny thought he should smile more. It made him look younger and far more human. 'I really came to ask you all if you'd like to go to the concert? It would make Linda's evening if you could. Most of the patients have relatives booked to come and watch, but Linda...'

'Is a bit short on relatives,' Jenny put in. 'Don't worry, Doctor, I'll be there.'

'I'll pick you up at four-thirty,' the doctor told Jenny.

'Fine. I'll be ready,' she said.

Jenny saw him to the door and they talked for a few minutes about Linda and the coming festive season, and then he inclined his head and said with a smile, 'Till Christmas Eve then, Miss O'Leary,' and Jenny answered in the same vein: 'Till Christmas Eve, Dr Sanders.'

When Jenny went back into the living room, she expected her mother and grandmother to be full of questions about Jenny's experience in the tunnel, though they'd never shown any interest before. In a way, she hoped they wouldn't be; they would only be disparaging and scornful about the whole episode, she knew. But they said nothing at all. She wasn't to know that, as she saw the doctor to the door, Norah had turned to her mother and said, 'Well.' The way it was said spoke volumes.

Jenny knew her mother and grandmother were irritated by the doctor's words to her and it didn't take much to guess at the reason why. But then, she decided, there was nothing she could do about it and she rubbed her hands together and said, 'It's real parky. Shall we have a cup of tea?'

'I should think so, after all this time,' Norah snapped.

Jenny made no reply. Instead she smiled pleasantly and went through to the kitchen.

The day after this, Jenny bumped into Beattie at the hospital. It was Saturday and Beattie's day off, and she said she'd thought to take a look at the little lass.

'Gawd girl, I'm glad to see you,' Beattie declared. 'I've got a parcel of clothes at home for Linda. It's from our Vera's daughter Vicky. Thirteen she is, but not a bit like Linda. She's developed, you know – *bosoms* an' all.' She gave Jenny a nudge and went on, 'Bit of a madam, an' all, by all accounts. I told our Vera she'll have to watch her. The bleeding town's teeming with soldiers from the barracks.' She sighed and said, 'Any road, that ain't my problem and I did get her to part with her stuff, but you'll have to alter it, if it's not to make Linda look like a bleeding scarecrow.'

Clothes! Jenny hadn't given them a thought. She knew the hospital would probably find Linda something to come out in, but what sort of something was another matter. And she wanted her to look nice for Christmas. She thanked Beattie, who said she'd drop the stuff around the next day.

And when Jenny saw the quality of the clothes, she sighed with relief and knew Linda would at least be adequately dressed. She found, too, that Peggy and her gran had already anticipated Linda's needs. Peggy had knitted her a beautiful Fair Isle jumper in russet red and green, interspersed with yellow and Wedgwood blue. It would go a treat over the plain navy kilt from Beattie's bundle, that just needed the buttons

136

moving and the hem turning up to fit Linda like a glove. Maureen had knitted the girl a navy cardigan. Jenny was overcome with their kindness. Her mother and grandmother had contributed precisely nothing. They would never change, Jenny knew, and she thanked God from the bottom of her heart that she had Gran O'Leary and *her* family at her back.

Chapter Nine

Jenny was excited about the prospect of Linda's first Christmas in her home. She made paper chains and hung them around the living room, and displayed the few Christmas cards they'd received on the mantelpiece. She brought the wooden Christmas tree down from the loft for the first time since her father's death, and she washed its spiky leaves and stuck it in a bucket to steady it. Many of the things for the tree were home-made, by Jenny and her sister and brothers, and they brought back so many happy memories as she hung them around the branches. Interspersed with them were silver balls and novelties her father had bought over the years.

Neither her mother nor her grandmother had much time for Christmas. 'Just an excuse for over-indulgence and drunkenness,' her mother was fond of saying. 'We're celebrating Christ's birth. It's a time for reflection and prayer, not giving each other expensive and often quite unsuitable presents, and eating and drinking too much.'

As a child, Jenny had always been disappointed by her mother's reaction. No one else's mother seemed to feel the same way about it. Even the priest was not above accepting presents from parishioners, she noticed, especially bottles of whisky, for which he seemed to have a great liking. Dermot O'Leary had said the world would be a dull old place if time wasn't made for a bit of jollification now and again.

He also said, at a person's birthday you buy a present and have a wee party to celebrate it. Surely, he'd said, on Christ's birthday, the celebration and present giving should be the greater?

Norah had answered her husband with a disapproving sniff. Without Dermot's enthusiasm, Christmas for the O'Learys would have been a bleak affair indeed. Christmas 1939 had been just that, Jenny remembered. The room had not been decorated, nor any Christmas cards displayed and there had been no tree. Norah had said it wasn't seemly with the family in mourning. Jenny had managed to buy a small present each for her mother and grandmother, who'd come to stay for the holiday, but there was little to spare for fancy food, though she had bought a chicken for the actual day itself. 'It's not seemly to make a fuss in wartime,' her mother had decided, 'even if your father hadn't died only just months ago.' Geraldine had come to tea and for the children's sake they'd done their best despite Norah.

This time it would be different, she decided. Most people on the Estate seemed to feel sorry for Linda, Jenny found, and a collection had been taken at the Dunlops. Almost five pounds was collected and delivered to Jenny the weekend before Christmas.

Armed with this staggering sum and her own

139

savings, she went to the Bull Ring the following Saturday. Beattie's niece, Vicky, had given her old coat for Linda, but it would have swamped the girl. Jenny could have cut it down, but she was loath to do so; it still wouldn't have fitted her across the shoulders or on the sleeves, and she would have spoilt the cut of it. Linda was bound to grow, and Vicky's coat would come in handy later.

Thanks to the generosity of her workmates, Linda could have a new coat for that winter. Jenny found just the right one – a warm woollen coat in dark maroon, with a velvet collar just a shade darker, and a matching hat. She got it in C & A Modes for £2 19s 11d. A bargain!

Then off she went to the Bull Ring. Vicky's underwear drowned Linda and her shoes were about three sizes too big, so she set about replacing these items. Then she went on to buy some pretty bangles, necklaces, hair bands and slides from Woolworth's, and a few sweets for Linda's stocking. Jenny's own personal present for her were two books, favourites of her own as a child, *Robinson Crusoe* and *Alice in Wonderland*. She smiled as she anticipated Linda's pleasure.

She also bought gifts for Jan and Seamus' small sons, and for Geraldine's children, too. She found a shawl for her mother and gloves for her grandmother. She'd bought the inevitable socks and cigarettes for her brothers Martin and Francis and was about to send them off when she received word that they all had a spot of unexpected leave and would be home on Christmas Eve. Jenny was glad of it, and hoped that would make it a better Christmas for Linda.

Linda looked so beautiful that Jenny felt a lump in her throat. She sat in the wheelchair, looking as composed as if she'd done sing-songs at concerts every day of her life, and only Jenny, who knew all of her moods by now, was aware of how nervous she really was.

Linda had discarded the hospital gown and put on the nicest dress she and Jenny had ever seen. It had been in the bundle Beattie had given, but Beattie had explained: 'Our Vera didn't buy that. It came in a parcel from her old man's uncle in America. Modelled on a dress worn by Shirley Temple, or some such.'

Jenny could well believe it. The dress was pure white silk with a lace overskirt. At the neck and edge of the long sleeves was a trim of peach. The petticoats made the skirt stick out so much it surrounded Linda like a beautiful fan, and the ends of the underskirts which showed beneath the dress, were trimmed with the same peach colour. Over it all was a little bolero, knitted in the softest peach angora, and across the front, a white silk rose was embroidered.

Linda had been speechless when Jenny had produced it earlier that afternoon when she'd arrived at the hospital with Dr Sanders. It even fitted better than any of the others, because Vicky had so hated to part with it, she kept it long after she'd outgrown it. Linda looked a treat. Jenny had brushed her hair till it shone and tied it back with one of the ribbons she'd bought in the Bull Ring.

141

Jenny was proud of Linda's hair which she'd washed the previous day; it hung halfway down her back now, and auburn highlights glinted in it. Dr Sanders remembered the lank greasy locks of the child in the surgery the first time he'd seen her, and was amazed at the transformation. 'You've done marvels for that girl, Jenny O'Leary,' he'd said. 'And for that reason alone, you can shout at me as much as you like.'

Linda felt like a fairy princess. She could hardly believe she owned this lovely dress, or the coat and hat and other things that Jenny had bought her for Christmas – presents from the people she worked with. 'Santa delivered it all a day early,' she teased Linda. 'He didn't want you to freeze to death on the ride home.'

Linda smiled back. She knew Santa Claus didn't exist, she'd tumbled to it a couple of years before. She'd gone along with it, of course, for the babbies, but if Jenny wanted her to believe in some bloke in a red suit, then she would. To be honest, if Jenny had asked her to leap into the fire, she'd seriously consider it.

During these past few weeks in hospital, as she'd been wrestling with her intense grief at having her family wiped out, Linda had also acknowledged the debt of gratitude that she owed certain people like Beattie and the doctor and all those rescue workers who had toiled to release her. But to Jenny she owed an over-whelming debt. She loved the older girl with all her heart, and vowed she'd never, ever hurt her in the whole of her life, and if Jenny should ever ask

142

her to do anything for her, if it was in her power at all, Linda would do it. And when she sang later, she sang for Jenny alone as a sort of thank you.

Peter Sanders was stunned by the quality of Linda's voice.

'She's phenomenal,' he whispered to Jenny. 'I never imagined she would be this good! Oh Jenny, her talent should be fostered, developed.'

'There will be no money for that, Doctor,' Jenny said sharply. 'When Linda comes to live with us, she'll have to understand that. If she had the choice, I'm sure she'd rather have love than singing lessons.'

'I'm sorry,' Peter said. 'That was crass and thoughtless of me. You're right, of course. The girl herself won't have thought of developing her voice further either, I shouldn't think.'

And she hadn't, of course. But she lapped up the lavish praise they heaped on her head and going back to Jenny's in the car, as she leaned back on the seat and said contentedly, 'I'm so happy, I could bloody well burst.'

Linda had loved the Midnight Mass she'd attended with Jenny. Jenny said she didn't have to go, but Linda knew she'd want to go herself, but wouldn't if it meant leaving her behind in a strange house with just her mother and grandmother for company.

Also her brothers had left word that they'd see her after the Mass. Linda hadn't met them yet, for they'd arrived while she and Jenny were at the hospital concert. They'd gone out for a cele-

143

bratory drink and would go straight on to church from the pub.

Linda was a little nervous of meeting Martin and Francis; she hadn't much experience with men. 'Do they know about me?' she'd asked as Linda pushed her down the dark streets towards the church.

'Yes, I wrote and told them.'

'Do they mind?'

'Why should they?'

'Well, your mom did.'

'Oh Linda.' Jenny said, 'I told you how it is with her. It's her way and it's not a nice way, but there it is. We have to put up with it.'

'I know,' Linda said wearily, and decided to say no more on the subject.

The church was packed and Jenny knew they'd have little chance of seeing anyone till the service was over. She was ushered to a seat at the side where there was ample space for Linda's wheelchair beside her. Linda was enthralled by it all, the decorated church and the altar bedecked with cloths of white and gold, with a golden box in the centre and golden candlesticks on either side of it. There were big vases of flowers to either side of the altar and the scent of them rose in the air. A Christmas tree stood at one side, with little coloured glass balls tied on to it, and a nativity scene to the other showed the stable where Jesus had been born.

Linda wasn't used to going to church and she looked around in fascination.

The confessional box was to one side of the altar, and remembering what Jenny had told her, she imagined herself going in there and telling a strange man all her secrets and the bad things she'd done. What if you told him something really awful and he was annoyed with you, or told someone? Jenny said that couldn't happen, but you never knew with some people.

There were lots of statues too. One, Jenny had whispered, was the Virgin Mary, and others down the side of the church were called 'Stations of the Cross'. 'What's that?' Linda had whispered back.

But the Mass had begun and Jenny said, 'Ssh, I'll tell you later.'

The priest was dressed in white robes embroidered in gold like the altar cloths, and behind him were two small altar boys dressed in black shirts with white apron things on top. The service began. Linda loved the beautiful singing that rose and fell as the congregation sang the Latin responses, even though she could understand none of it. She was glad she knew her carols well because they sang them and she tried to join in for the others she didn't know so well.

One thing she was not keen on, was the man on the Cross with the bleeding hands and feet, and even dribbles of blood on His face from the thorns pressed into His head. She knew he was Jesus, she'd learnt that much at school, and that He'd died on the Cross, but she didn't know whether she'd want to be looking at Him every Sunday.

She'd listened to the priest telling them the story they all knew about, Joseph and Mary stranded in Bethlehem without a place to stay.

'Nowhere for the Son of Man to lay His head,

but a manger in a draughty stable,' the priest said.

Privately, Linda thought that no big deal. No one had been bothered where she'd lay her head either, till Jenny had said she could move in with her. And she knew she was only one among thousands. Birmingham had had a number of raids since the one that had flattened her home, London was still pounded every night, as were many other industrial cities, and she imagined that many people were homeless. She guessed there were plenty of people laying their heads in most peculiar places just at the moment. They would be glad of a stable they could have all of their very own, and if Jesus was supposed to live on earth like everyone else, it was probably right that He didn't have a real place to live either. The priest was going on as if He should have been born in a palace, and Linda thought that plain daft. She glanced at Jenny, but couldn't read the expression on her face and filed her questions away to ask later.

All in all though, the service was quite good, then in the porch Linda met Martin and Francis for the first time. Everyone was wishing one another a 'Merry Christmas'. It was too cold to hang about. Wispy vapour trailed from people's mouths into the crisp and frosty night air as they spoke, and Jenny tucked a blanket around Linda's legs. Francis offered to push her home.

Linda was glad to see when she got into the house, that Jenny's mom and gran had gone to bed. Martin pushed her into the living room, for the kitchen was like an ice box. She had known that Jenny's mother wasn't wild about the idea of her going to live with them and she told herself it didn't matter. She'd probably just be a bit off with her – sharp perhaps – but Linda could cope with that. What she hadn't bargained for was the way Norah had looked at her earlier with cold eyes and a curled lip; apart from that, she'd not acknowledged her presence at all. She'd not even said hello.

The grandmother Jenny hadn't mentioned much and Linda had assumed that this Mrs Gillespie would be all right about it eventually. Linda had never had a grandmother, but lots of her friends had. Grans were usually kind and nice and often cooked scrummy things to eat. They would slip you the odd copper or two for a comic and queued for hours if they heard there was chocolate on sale, and might bring you a bag of sweets when they came to tea. Gran O'Leary was like that and she'd told Linda to call her Gran too, like Jenny did. Somehow, Linda didn't think she'd ever call Jenny's other grandmother anything but Mrs Gillespie – that's if she ever addressed her at all.

'Are you going to sleep on us, Linda?' Martin asked, giving her a playful poke.

'No, I ain't,' Linda said spiritedly, but she was drowsy. It had been an eventful and emotional day, and she could easily have dropped off. The fire had nearly gone out when they'd arrived but Francis had poked some life into it and put some small pieces of coal on to heat the room a little.

'Here, eat this and then it's bed for you, or you'll be good for nothing tomorrow,' Jenny said, handing her a mug of cocoa and a plate of bread and dripping.

Linda took it from her. She knew she'd have to stay in Jenny's house once she came out of hospital, and live here until she was grown up. She wasn't absolutely happy about it, but she'd rather that than an orphanage. As for the two horrible old women, and she could hardly believe they were related to Jenny – well, if they didn't like it, they'd have to lump it!

'Come on lazybones,' Martin said. 'I've got to carry you upstairs tonight.'

'Not before she cleans her teeth and goes out to the toilet,' Jenny put in.

'Well, hurry up. I need my beauty sleep.'

Linda looked at him from head to foot and remarked drily, 'You don't half.'

The boys laughed so loud, Jenny put a cautionary finger to her lips. 'Ssh, you'll have them both down,' she said, indicating the front bedroom with her thumb.

That sobered everyone a little, though Martin still had a smile on his face as he carried Linda up the stairs some minutes later. She was a cheeky monkey all right, he thought, a grand plucky little girl altogether. Jenny followed behind to help her get undressed and tuck her in with a hot-water bottle at her feet and Linda smiled happily and snuggled down.

And it was wonderful when Linda woke up on Christmas morning and saw the stocking hanging on the end of her bed. She tipped it upside down and out fell coloured pencils, a proper fountain pen, pretty hair-slides and

148

bangles, and lengths of ribbon in a little wooden box. Underneath was a small bar of chocolate, a silver sixpence and an orange. Linda knew Jenny must have queued for hours for that orange, and a lump came into her throat as she imagined Jenny searching the shops for things to please her.

She hadn't had a stocking herself for years, though she'd helped fill George's the last two years and told him the story of Father Christmas coming down the chimney. She thanked God for Jenny; she knew in the whole of her life she'd never be able to repay her for what she'd done.

Watching from the bed next to hers, Jenny was pleased that Linda liked everything she'd taken such pains to choose.

'Come on, Linda,' she said. 'Put them away now and I'll cook us some breakfast. I'm famished and freezing cold, and I bet you are, too.' Linda scooped everything back into the stocking while Jenny went to see if one of her brothers was awake and would carry Linda down the stairs.

Jenny surveyed the dining table with pride. It had been lifted out of the bay into the centre of the room, and the two leaves pulled out of the middle to extend it to its full length. Kitchen stools and bedroom chairs had been brought in as well as dining chairs to accommodate everyone as Geraldine, Dan and the children were joining them for the meal.

Martin, as the eldest man, carved the two crispy golden chickens that Jenny had acquired

149

from Stan Walker, her fellow ARP warden who kept chickens in his back garden. They sat sizzling on the roasting plate, and ready on the sideboard, on the thick ironing blanket used to protect the surface, were the dishes containing succulent roast potatoes, sprouts, mashed swede, carrots and slices of stuffing, and gravy in a jug. And it was all as delicious as it had looked and smelt. Jenny tried not to think of the one member of the family who would never come back and share in Christmas dinner again, but just be grateful for those who had returned.

Martin and Francis were better company than she remembered. Freed from their mother and grandmother's dominance they'd blossomed, and what gladdened her heart most was they'd gone out of their way to make Linda welcome and include her in things. They'd delighted the women of the house with their presents; a pair of fully-fashioned silk stockings from Francis and a bottle of Californian Poppy perfume from Martin.

'Now don't ask any questions about where we got those from,' Martin warned.

'Whatever do you mean, Martin?' Norah asked, holding her son's gifts as if they were highly explosive. 'I hope you haven't obtained these things dishonestly?'

'Not dishonestly, Mother,' Martin said with a laugh. 'By that I mean, we didn't steal them, but we did get them illegally.'

'Martin, you know how I feel about the black market!' Norah exclaimed. 'We can't accept them.'

The old Martin would have mumbled an apology and been embarrassed at his mistake and Francis would have been worse, but the new Martin just shrugged. 'If you don't want them, I'm sure Jenny and Geraldine would be glad of extra,' he said.

And Francis added, 'Really Mother, it is about time you moved into the world ordinary people live in.'

'What on earth has that to do with receiving black-market goods?'

'Everything,' Francis said. He gave a sigh and went on, 'Go all pious on us and refuse if you want, but don't expect Jenny and Geraldine to feel the same. They looked pretty damned pleased to me.'

'We are,' Jenny said firmly. 'And I for one have no intention of refusing. Thank you very much, both of you. I'm afraid the socks and cigarettes I have for you both seem pretty ordinary in comparison.'

'We'll be grateful for them though,' Francis said. 'They march us for bloody miles, our socks don't last five minutes and fags are always handy.'

The other presents were received with pleasure, though Jenny barely got a thank you for the soft shawl she gave her mother, or her grandmother's gloves, but then she didn't expect it so she wasn't disappointed.

It was Linda's reaction to the books Jenny gave her that was so unusual. She held them in her hands and stroked them almost reverently, but made no attempt to open them as she said, 'Oh, thank you, thank you! I've never, ever had a book

151

of my very own. I don't read much, see.'

'You mean you can't read?' Geraldine said, and her voice was scornful.

Linda was no fool; she'd heard Geraldine's tone and she said sharply, 'No, I din't say that. I can read. I ain't bloody stupid. Just that I've never had the bleeding time.'

There was shocked silence. In the pre-war days, no swearwords or blasphemous language were allowed in the house. Today, Francis had sworn twice, but Norah had excused him; he was, after all, in the Army now and mixing with all types – and added to that, he was a man. For a child to use such language, and on the Good Lord's birthday too, it was – well, it was indecent.

Linda didn't know what she'd done, but she was aware of the charged atmosphere, and being Linda she asked, 'What's up?'

Before Jenny could offer any sort of explanation Eileen cut in, 'What's up?'

'If you were my daughter, miss,' Norah said icily, 'I'd wash your mouth out with soap and water this very minute.'

Then Eileen rounded on her. 'Yes, don't you bring your gutter language here, my girl.'

'Come on Mother, Grandmother, lighten up,' Martin said feeling sorry for Linda and the way the two old ladies had leapt on her. 'The kid didn't say anything that bad.'

Linda stared at him. Now she understood. She supposed she should apologise, but her mother never got into a fit if she swore a bit.

Francis saw Linda was upset and he didn't think it was fair on her first visit to the house. He remembered how astounded he'd been in church when he'd heard her sing for the first time. She didn't know all the carols, but with those she did know, her voice rose above everyone else, crystal clear and pure. Many heads had turned to look at the young girl in the wheelchair singing her heart out.

He thought only to deflect the anger of his mother and grandmother as he said, 'How about giving us a bit of a sing-song Linda, with it being Christmas and all.'

Linda's face was pink with embarrassment and anger. She didn't want to sing, certainly not for the two po-faced harpies who sat in judgement on her. They looked at her as if she'd crawled from under a stone and all because she'd said a few swearwords.

But then she caught sight of Jenny's face, and though she said not a word, Linda knew she wanted her to sing for her family. If Jenny wanted it, how could she refuse? Linda shrugged off her bad humour and said, 'What do you want me to sing?'

Norah and her mother were annoyed that Linda should have the limelight, and Norah especially was cross that this hussy's presence in the house had caused her sons to answer her back. They'd never done *that* before. She didn't blame her boys, however, but the disruptive influence her daughter had introduced into the house. And she'd never encouraged her own children to show off like this.

'Sing "Silent Night", Linda,' Jenny suggested. Linda cleared her throat and began. A silence

153

developed in the room as her voice rose; even Rosemarie and Jamie stopped their play to listen and stare, and Dan forgot he'd been filling his pipe for an after-dinner smoke; it slipped from his fingers, scattering tobacco over his good clothes. He seemed not to notice, but sat almost mesmerised by Linda's voice.

When the carol eventually drew to a close, there was a hush before Martin and Francis began to clap and the others joined in. Somehow it seemed the appropriate response. 'Give us another,' Francis said, when the clapping eased eventually.

'I only know three carols right through,' Linda said, 'but I know lots of other sorts of stuff. I used to sing with me mom. Join in if you like. I don't like doing it all on my own.'

'Not with the carols,' Martin put in. 'We'd never hear your voice, but we'll join in with the other songs if we know them.'

And of course, they did. Everyone knew 'Hey Little Hen', 'Run Rabbit Run', and 'Follow the Yellow Brick Road', followed by some of the famous wartime songs. Only Norah and Eileen sat prim and unyielding with a pained expression on their faces, and obviously had no intention of taking part.

The winter's day was drawing in. It was time to pull the blackout curtains, put up the shutters in the other rooms and turn on the lights. The boys went around the house doing that, while Jenny made a cup of tea for them all and laid the trays for her mother and grandmother with chicken sandwiches and a couple of sausage rolls she'd found the recipe for in the *Evening Mail*, with little meat and lots of mashed vegetables instead, and a mince pie each.

After a cup of tea, the family was dispersing: Geraldine, Dan and the children to their own home to spend some time together; Martin and Francis off to visit friends; and Jenny had arranged to take Linda to Maureen's for the evening. Norah and Eileen were not happy about everyone leaving, but Jenny didn't really care.

Two streets away, a party atmosphere prevailed at Gran O'Leary's. Her two daughters, Celia and Betsy, had arrived with their husbands and children. Irish music played on the wind-up gramophone, and food and drink were arrayed in the kitchen for all to help themselves, which they did. Linda thought she'd never had such a good time. It wasn't the food alone either, it was the friendliness of everyone there, and their acceptance of Linda as part of the family.

Hours later, the gramophone had ground to a halt. A large hole had been made in the food and drink in the kitchen, and Celia and Betsy had eventually sat down, breathless from dancing the reels and jigs all evening.

'I think I'll make us all a drop of tea,' Maureen said, looking around her family. 'Beer and whisky is all well and good, but you can't beat a drop of tea.' Jenny knew it was her grandmother's way of winding up the night and though it was late, she knew Linda hated returning to the house where Norah and Eileen cast their evil eyes over everything, poisoning it for others.

Just before midnight, as the cups were being

155

drained, there was a furious knocking on the door. When Jenny went to open it she saw her brothers, Francis and Martin outside, both quite merry, but for all that she was glad to see them. She knew they weren't in the habit of coming to wish their gran a Merry Christmas, and she saw tears glisten in the old lady's eyes as she held her grandsons close. To Jenny, it was another indication that they'd broken away from their mother's influence, and she couldn't be sorry about that.

'We thought we'd better come and see the old besom,' Martin said, with a lopsided grin.

'About time you did,' Gerry said sharply, and the two boys shifted uncomfortably. Maureen rounded on her son.

'Well, they're here now, aren't they? Don't be moaning at them. Christ alive, isn't it Christmas Day, one day of peace in the crazy world?'

Gerry held out his hand to his two nephews and said, 'The old woman's right for once. Merry Christmas to the both of you.'

'I'll "old woman" you in a minute, my lad,' Maureen cried, as the men shook hands. But her heart wasn't in the rebuke, and Jenny, watching her, realised how much her brothers just appearing like that had meant to her.

She knew her grandmother would be embarrassed if she thought anyone had seen how moved she was, so in order to give her time to compose herself she said, 'Well, I'm glad to see you at any rate. You can help me push Linda up the hill.'

Pointing to Linda, Gerry said, 'Jenny will

definitely be needing a hand. That wee girl has done nothing but eat since she came in. She'll be a couple of stone heavier going home, I'd say.'

'I will not.' Linda retorted, but there was a smile on her face. She liked Gerry, for all he was a tease. She didn't want the night to end, but she was tired and she leaned back in the wheelchair and said, 'I've had a bloody marvellous day.'

Jenny was glad her mother wasn't there, but her gran didn't swoon, or shout, or even look shocked. Instead she said, 'I'm pleased you have, girl, and so would your mammy be, because she'd never want you to be sad, now would she?'

Linda considered her answer carefully and then she said, 'No, no she wouldn't. She laughs a lot, me mom. At least, I mean ... I mean she used to.'

'Then I'd say she still does,' Maureen said decisively. 'If I know anything, she's up in Heaven this minute, laughing fit to bust because her fine daughter's had a bloody good day. What d'you say, Linda?'

Linda, her eyes shining, said, 'Yeah, I think you're right.'

'Then don't you ever feel bad or guilty about enjoying yourself, d'you hear?' Maureen said.

Linda promised she wouldn't, and Jenny pondered on the wisdom of her gran, who often had the ability to say the right things at the right time, as she walked home arm-in-arm with Francis, while Martin pushed Linda's chair.

Chapter Ten

It was the quiet week between Christmas and New Year, the men had returned to their unit and Linda had been transferred to the orthopaedic hospital on Bristol Road to prepare her for the second round of operations, due at the beginning of January. Jenny yawned. She'd returned to work the day after Boxing Day and had found it more tiring than she had expected. She was very glad it was Thursday and there was just one more day before the weekend.

Her mother had dozed off in her chair, she noticed, and she crept quietly into the kitchen thinking it would be great to drink a cup of tea in peace just for a change, for even her grandmother was out visiting her old next-door neighbour in Erdington.

She put the blackout shutters up at the kitchen windows so that she could turn the light on and made a swift cup of tea, then sat at the table savouring the peace and quiet.

A knock on the door, sudden and loud, made her jump and she almost spilt the tea into her lap. She went to the door, wondering who it could be, for they had few visitors.

Peering through the gloom of the winter's evening, Jenny saw a young man dressed in Air Force blue, and, for a split second she thought it was Anthony. She staggered in shock and the young man's arms shot out to prevent her falling. 'Are you all right?'

'Yes, it's just... I'm sorry,' Jenny said. 'For a moment, I thought... My brother was in the RAF.'

'Was your brother Anthony O'Leary?' the man asked.

Jenny gave a brief nod and the young man continued, 'My name is Bob Masters and I was your brother's Squadron Leader.'

It was what Jenny had longed for – someone to talk to about her brother, to tell her something of his life as a RAF pilot, and whether it was as marvellous as he always maintained. She opened the door wider and said, 'Please come in.'

She supposed she should wake her mother, but she didn't want to, not yet. She wanted to talk to Anthony's Squadron Leader alone first. She put her finger to her lips and understanding immediately the need for silence, he crept behind Jenny into the kitchen, where she immediately filled the kettle again and put it on to the gas.

'I'm delighted to meet you at last,' Bob said. 'I feel as if I know you. Your brother spoke of you often.'

'Did he?' Jenny said. There were tears in her eyes. 'We were very close, Anthony and I. I have three other brothers, but he was my favourite.'

Oh God, she thought, she was going to cry and in front of this young man whom she'd never met in her life before. God, he'd be so embarrassed. She got up and swilled the teapot out under the sink, though it probably would have taken more water, to try and keep a check on her emotions.

Bob guessed she was trying to control herself and for a minute or so, there was silence in the room which was broken by the kettle coming to the boil.

Jenny poured boiling water on to the leaves in the pot and said, 'Was he a good pilot, my brother? It matters, you see, because it was all he wanted to do. If he died doing ... doing something he was good at, then maybe ... maybe it isn't so bad.'

Her voice was husky and Bob guessed that tears lurked behind Jenny's eyes. Gently he took the two cups from her that she'd brought out of the cupboard, and pressed her down on to one of the kitchen chairs. He poured out the tea and passed a cup to Jenny and sat down with his own opposite her. Jenny sat clutching her cup as if she was mesmerised.

Now Bob leaned forward and said, 'Let me tell you about your brother.' And Jenny heard that her brother had been a first-rate pilot, brave and seemingly without fear, and his death had been a tragic loss to the entire squadron. Bob told her of the young man he'd come to love and admire as a brother. 'For his sake I'm here today,' he said.

Jenny looked into Bob's dark brown eyes with the long black lashes, and read the sympathy there. 'It's so hard, you see,' she said painfully. 'We had the telegram, of course, and then his effects were sent over ... and it was almost as though he'd never existed. It's not having a grave, I suppose. It would help if we'd had a proper funeral service and a grave to tend, but there was just nothing but a commemorative Mass.'

'Believe me, I know,' Bob said, and he did, for this wasn't the first visit he'd made in this way, but the one which had affected him the most. He took Jenny's tiny hand between his own, and though she was embarrassed, she didn't pull it away for she found it strangely comforting...

For the first time she realised how dark-skinned Bob Masters was. It was as if he had a deep tan. His mouth was wide and generous and his chin firm; his hair was so black and silky, it shone with a blue tinge. She noticed how powerful his hands were; she gazed at the black hairs on the back of them and his long fingers and square nails.

'I'm holding you up,' Bob said suddenly, dropping Jenny's hands and getting to his feet.

'No, not at all,' Jenny said, although she hadn't even started on the tea. Facing him she asked, 'Do you think my brother died happy?'

'I think he died doing something he loved,' Bob said, 'and when you think of it, few can say that.' He put his hand in his inside pocket and said, 'He gave me something for you. He left a letter with me in case anything should happen to him.'

'For my mother?'

'No, for you,' Bob said. 'He was quite specific.' He withdrew an envelope from his pocket and placed it in Jenny's hands. She looked at the dear familiar writing and felt tears well in her eyes. Bob saw the raw emotion in Jenny's face and he said gently, 'I'll leave you now. You'll need to read your letter in peace.'

And though Jenny did want to read her letter in privacy, she didn't want Bob to leave. He was the last link with her brother. 'No, please,' she said.

'Please don't think you're intruding.'

Bob stood up straight and asked, 'May I call again? I have a spot of leave and nowhere particular to go at the moment.'

'Oh, please do come,' Jenny said. 'During the day my mother will be here and my grandmother. I'm sure they'd be delighted to meet you. I will be at work, I'm afraid.'

'Fort Dunlop – that's right, isn't it?' he asked.

'How do you know that?'

'I told you – your brother spoke of you often,' Bob said and added, 'Could I pick you up from work tomorrow? Perhaps we could go somewhere and talk.'

And Jenny knew she would meet the good-looking man who had been her late brother's Squadron Leader, whatever it took. 'Yes,' she said. 'You could pick me up outside the factory at half-past five?'

''Til then, Miss O'Leary,' Bob said with exaggerated formality and with a slight bow he was gone. She didn't see him to the door, but stayed in the kitchen with the letter crushed in her hand, and the second the front door closed behind Bob Masters, she ripped the letter open.

Dear Sis

In some ways I hope you'll never receive this letter, because that will mean I'm dead and there is so much yet I'd like to accomplish in my life. But I know that my death will not have been in vain and almost expected, for after every sortie, there are men missing. When the call goes to 'scramble' I feel my legs turn to water with fear. We are all scared, and anyone who

162

tells you different is a fool, or a liar – and neither is to be trusted. But when you are up there in the sky, fear leaves you and yet you know that if you make one slight mistake, you will not get down alive. You face your own mortality daily, and the fact that you are reading this letter, means that I have come to the end of mine.

I believe I have played my part in attempting to halt the monster creeping over Europe like a vengeful dragon, burning and destroying all in its path. I believe if Hitler had succeeded in destroying the Air Force, he would by now be occupying our islands – our Navy would have been bombed out of the water. So accept my death as the sacrifice to be paid, remember me with pride, but please, Jenny, get on with your life.

I know you face as much danger as I do. I went out with a young Cockney girl once who told me how the ARP wardens beaver on throughout a raid to reach the trapped and injured. I won't urge you not to take risks, for this war will not be won that way, and win it we must.

I will instead ask you to do the best you can and do not allow yourself to be a martyr to Mother. You're not martyr material and remember, she is not half as helpless as she makes out. Remember also this is our one crack at life, and despite my death, I don't consider I threw mine away. I'll hate you to do that with yours.

OK, lecture over – time to go.

Till we meet again,

Love, Anthony xxxx

It was if Anthony was in the room talking to her, and Jenny felt profoundly comforted. She heard

163

the front door open and knew her grandmother was back. And here she was, sitting in the kitchen with tea not even started and the blackout curtains not pulled across the living room windows. She pushed the letter into the pocket of her skirt and went into the room, knowing she'd have to tell them about Bob's visit and knowing also she'd get it in the neck for not waking her mother up.

However, when Jenny did go in, her mother was already awake and she attacked her immediately. 'Left me in the pitch dark, and the fire nearly out as well.'

'I'm sorry, Mother, but you were asleep.' Jenny said, pulling the blackout curtains together so they could turn the light on.

'I was not. I was just dozing,' Norah said indignantly. 'And what's more, I haven't had a bite since lunchtime. You've not made so much as a cup of tea since you came in.'

Jenny poked up the fire and put on some small nuggets of coal before she said, 'I'm sorry. I would have started the tea, but we had a visitor.'

When she said who it had been, her mother was further incensed that she hadn't woken her up, and Jenny was tempted to say that if she'd just been dozing as she'd maintained earlier, she would have woken up herself.

'Didn't you think I had a right to see him too?' demanded Norah, and Jenny knew she did and felt guilty. 'You take too much upon yourself, young lady.'

'I can't believe you spoke to Anthony's Squadron Leader on your own without informing your mother,' Eileen put in. 'Your selfishness leaves me almost speechless.'

'He's meeting me after work tomorrow,' Jenny said. 'You'll see him then.'

'And why, pray, is he meeting you?'

'I don't know.' And Jenny really didn't know. She couldn't understand it; it must be something Anthony had asked him to do.

Despite that, she dressed with care the next morning, discarding her navy costume as dowdy and picking the dark red one with the soft pink blouse that she normally wore for Mass. She pulled on the pair of silk stockings she'd got as a Christmas present from Francis, and polished her best black shoes with a Cuban heel.

She didn't normally wear much makeup, but that morning she creamed her face well and dusted it over with powder in an attempt to hide the freckles. She rouged her cheeks and put the merest touch of lipstick on her lips, but her eyes she left alone; they were big enough and the lashes long enough to need nothing else.

She gazed with despair at her unruly mop of auburn curls, pulling her comb through them ruthlessly; they went their own way as usual. But still, she told herself, Bob knew she looked like some sort of freak and he'd still said he'd meet her. Her hair would have to do. She dabbed the Californian Poppy scent Martin had given her behind her ears and on her wrists, and was ready for work.

A couple of hours before the hooter heralding the end of the working day, Jenny began to get anxious. She wondered what Bob meant about 'talking to her'. Hadn't he said all there was to say? She didn't know how to talk to boys *or* men – she'd had no practice. She'd enjoyed her brothers' visit home over Christmas, but she hadn't talked to them properly; she'd only discussed current issues like how the war was going. And of course they were never interested in her views, only their own. They'd always managed to imply she was just a woman and wouldn't understand.

Still, she had to meet Bob Masters now, she'd said so and that was that. And there was no point making a big deal of it either – so why did she feel the need to touch up her make-up and reapply her scent just before half five?

As soon as they left the office building, the icy blast of wind hit the huddle of people making for the gate. 'Isn't it perishing?' one shouted.

'Aye, it's for snow I'd say.'

Jenny, tucking in her scarf and lowering her head against the onslaught, thought they could be right. You could smell the cold, and when you took a breath in, it hurt your teeth and caught at the back of your throat.

'Too bloody cold for snow, mate,' someone called.

'Too bloody cold, you daft bugger? Have you seen the North Pole?'

There was laughter at this, but Jenny was too unnerved to laugh. She hoped Bob was waiting for her. If she had to hang around, she'd stick to the ground in cold like this. The grey-green mist from the canal just in front of the main gate began to swirl around them, only now it was mixed with the oily black smoke from the Smokey Joe's that were lit every evening to cover everything with dense smoke to confuse the enemy.

Jenny hated the Smokey Joe's. Everyone did. The acrid smell of burning oil was bad enough, but worse were the black smut particles that settled on clothes and was the very devil to get off. Jenny hoped anxiously her coat wouldn't be spoilt. It was a saxe-blue colour with a wide full belt, and cut in military tradition. It was pure new wool and the smartest coat Jenny had ever owned. She'd bought it from a draper's shop on the Kingsbury Road for £8 10s, and she'd had to pay in for it over eight weeks. She didn't normally wear it for work, but kept it for Mass, like they jaunty tam o'shanter her gran had knitted for her in blue with stripes of cream and pink to match the scarf. But there, she'd worn it now and if it was ruined she had only herself to blame.

And then suddenly it didn't seem to matter, for there at the tram stop Bob stood waiting for her, his hand stuffed into his greatcoat and his collar turned up against the cold. Jenny smiled; she wasn't aware how it transformed her face or how Bob suddenly felt – as if his heart had stopped beating. He went towards her and took her arm companionably, saying as he did so, 'I thought we'd take the tram into Birmingham. We can eat there and then go to the cinema or something. Unless there's something you'd rather do?'

'I can't,' Jenny gasped. 'I must go home, my mother–'

'It's all right – I've seen them,' Bob said. 'I

called in this afternoon. I also visited your other grandmother, Mrs O'Leary. Anthony asked me especially to go there if anything happened to him, you know. Anyway, I explained to your mother that I was taking you out tonight and they're all right about it – they said they'd manage.'

Surely though, this was beyond what could be expected, Jenny thought. Whatever Anthony had asked him to do, surely it hadn't included taking his sister out for the evening? But she allowed Bob to help her into the tram and it wasn't until they were sitting down together that she said, 'You don't have to do this, you know.'

'Do what?'

'Take me out like this.'

Bob looked at the girl he'd only just met but had heard lots about from Anthony O'Leary. He'd said his sister was a smasher and so she was. She was so dainty and small, she looked like a child, especially with the sprinkling of freckles across her face. But there was nothing childlike about her full sensual lips that he was very tempted to kiss, nor the large beautiful brown eyes. The auburn head of curls framing her face, despite the tam o'shanter, was her crowning glory. At that moment, Jenny's eyes looked troubled and Bob said, 'I know I don't have to. I *want* to.'

'But why?'

'Why?' he repeated in a surprised voice. 'To get to know you better, to give you a good time. Why any man takes out a pretty girl, I should imagine.'

But she liked to get things straight. 'I'm not

pretty,' she said. 'And I'm not fishing for compliments, or being shy, so don't think it.'

'No, you're right,' Bob said. 'You are more than pretty, you are beautiful.' Jenny went to interrupt and he put up his hand. 'Now, now, Miss O'Leary,' he said with mock formality. 'You must let me have my say, and I say you're beautiful, and my opinion must be considered.'

Jenny smiled, 'You are a fool,' she said, and Bob felt his heart hammering against his ribs as he saw how the smile lit up her face.

Steady! He told himself. You hardly know the girl. But he was aware that he wanted to get to know her better, and Jenny felt the warmth of his praise wash over her. She didn't feel such a freak now but she certainly wasn't pretty or beautiful. The man was mad, she decided, but very kind. 'And another thing,' she said. 'I'd say you need your eyes testing.'

Bob burst out laughing and squeezed Jenny's hand tight. 'Your brother said you were a smasher and he was right, you are,' he said. Jenny blushed crimson and knew there was nowhere else she'd rather be at that moment than beside Bob Masters in a tram going towards the town and so she sat quiet with her hand in his and just enjoyed the experience.

Linda watched Jenny come into the ward with a young man following behind and she hoped she had a boyfriend at last. She'd asked her once about boys and Jenny had said she had no one special and wasn't particularly bothered about it. 'I'm not so popular with men,' Jenny had said.

169

Linda thought that was plain daft, especially as Jenny was so pretty. Linda wished she had curly hair like hers, especially when it shone like gold in the light. And her face was so friendly-looking, too; even her freckles seemed friendly. Anyway, she thought, she seems popular enough with the bloke she came in with because he keeps smiling at her.

Bob would rather have been holding Jenny close in some dim-lit cinema, than visiting a child in a hospital bed, but he hid his reluctance well. Jenny had told him about Linda as they'd eaten their tea in Lyon's Corner House in the city centre, and gently, but firmly, she'd explained that much as she would like to, she couldn't go to the cinema that evening. She told him all about Linda and though she played down her part in the rescue attempt, she did tell him of Linda's incarceration and the fact that her family had been wiped out.

After that, no one could be churlish enough to make a fuss about seeing the girl, though Bob did say he was surprised Jenny was allowed to visit so often. 'Haven't the hospital got rules and things?' he enquired. 'When I was in having my tonsils out, my mother was only allowed to visit on Sunday afternoons. They said it upset the patients too much, but I missed her a great deal. There were complications and I was in for three weeks in the end.'

'For Linda the rules have been relaxed somewhat,' Jenny told him. 'In the beginning they encouraged visitors because she'd sunk into a deep depression. Now though, there's just me and the family doctor, and her old next-door neighbour, who can only really visit at weekends, who come regularly.'

Bob did wonder why Jenny was such a frequent visitor, for she'd only told him she was one of the ARP wardens who had worked to locate Linda's position in the rubble. Knowing Jenny's reluctance to tell anyone of her part in the rescue, Linda regaled Bob with the tale of her bravery and he was amazed. Jenny looked so slight and small, as if she needed looking after, and yet she'd put her life at risk for an unknown child. He was also surprised that Jenny took her responsibilities so seriously, that she was prepared to offer Linda a home with her when she eventually left hospital.

Anthony hadn't told him of that side of Jenny's character. He'd been very fond of his sister, but annoyed by the fact that she'd allowed herself to be browbeaten by his brothers and Geraldine, and dominated by their mother. 'She lets them upset her, and they know she gets upset,' he'd said. 'I wish she'd develop a thicker skin. It gives my mother and grandmother some sort of malicious pleasure to reduce Jenny to tears.'

Maybe the war and the atrocities she must have seen as a warden had helped to harden Jenny O'Leary, Bob thought. Undoubtedly, her frail appearance was deceptive. He wondered if Anthony had ever noticed his sister's decisive lift of her chin, the way she had of speaking that would brook no argument and the glint in her beautiful eyes. Oh yes, Jenny could be stubborn enough all right and fully ready to dig her heels

171

in about something she felt passionate about.

And she felt both passionate about and sorry for the little orphan Linda Lennox, that much was obvious. Bob had to admit the child herself had something. He had a feeling that soon she would develop into a beauty and yet it wasn't that alone; she had a charm all of her own and a delightful sense of humour.

It was plain Linda liked Bob. Jenny had wondered if she would be jealous of her bringing someone else, but she wasn't. She was very interested in him and he found himself telling her all about his family, his Italian mother Francesca, his father Malcolm and his sister Juliana. He told her how he'd known as soon as war broke out which of the services he would apply to join, and went on to describe the men in his squadron and what a bomber pilot's off-duty life was like.

Linda listened fascinated and so did Jenny. Anthony had been sure of what he was going to do in the war as well. No one had put obstacles in *his* way. She wondered if Bob's mother had objected at all, especially as Italy was now our enemy, or just waved him off with a brave smile and worried about him constantly, dreading the sight of the telegraph boy stopping at her door. Jenny remembered the night the unthinkable and dreadful had happened to her. She wished for a moment she hadn't met Bob. What if he was the next one she heard of, shot down? She gave a sudden shiver and he turned and said, 'You all right?'

'Fine.'

'You don't look it. You look deep in thought.'

'Maybe I am.'

'Do you want to share them?'

'They're not worth sharing,' Jenny said more sharply than she'd intended. 'I think we should be making our way home soon. They'll be settling the children for the night any time now.'

Bob opened his mouth, but before he could reply to this, the door opened and Beattie came in. She brought in the cold of the night, and Jenny noticed her woolly hat was pulled tight down on her frizzy hair and her cheeks were glowing red. But she smiled at the group around the bed and the girl in it and said, 'What's all this then?'

She really meant, 'Who is this then?' as Jenny well knew. She introduced Bob and Beattie said she was pleased to meet him. She gave Jenny a knowing look. Jenny ignored it and said, 'I thought you don't visit in the week?'

'I don't much,' Beattie said, she then nodded to Linda and said, 'Ain't that right, ducks?'

'No, you don't,' Linda said. 'But I'm glad you're here today.'

'Well,' Beattie said, 'I thought if I hadn't have got out tonight, I'd have given our Vera a clout in the gob.' She glanced at Bob and said with a grin, 'Vera's me sister, dead refined and all she is, like Jenny here. I never had the corners bashed off me, I am as I am. D'you know,' she demanded of Jenny, 'what that mean-minded bugger called me today? Common. Common, huh! At least I ain't ashamed of where I came from, like she is. She calls herself respectable. Well, if that's respectable, you can stick it! She wants to look to her

173

daughter and I told her so and all. Always gawping at the bleeding soldiers up Sutton Park she is. Man mad, the girl is. Mind, if she was ever to fall pregnant, our Vera would die of shame. Wouldn't be so respectable then, would she?'

'If you're sure about that, I mean, if Vicky really is doing something wrong, maybe you should have a word with your sister,' Jenny said.

'Well, I ain't sure, am I?' Beattie said. 'Not absolutely certain, like. It's more a feeling, and she has that sort of look – you know? But when I tried to tell my sister, she said I had a mind like a bloody sewer, thinking mucky thoughts about her precious Vicky.'

Jenny suppressed another smile. Tact wasn't Beattie's strong point and she wasn't really surprised that Vera had been annoyed when Beattie attempted to put her wise about her daughter. Heaven knows what Bob Masters thought about it all. But it wasn't really her business, and they ought to be getting back home before the hospital threw them out.

She got to her feet and bent to give Linda a kiss, saying as she did so, 'See you tomorrow.'

'You don't have to come, if you don't want,' Linda said.

'Why wouldn't I want to?'

'Well, you might want to go out with him,' Linda said, giving a nod in Bob's direction.

'If you want to go out with your young man, you go,' Beattie said before Jenny was able to utter a word. 'You're only young once, I say. Don't you worry about Linda here – I'll come and visit her. I usually come Saturday anyway; I'll

174

just come over earlier, that's all, Tell you what,' she said conspiratorially to Linda, 'I'll bring some Christmas cake and mince pies, eh, and we'll have a feast.'

'Yeah, fine,' Linda said. She looked from one to the other and went on, 'The doctor came round today. He's thinking of operating on Wednesday.'

'Bloody hell, New Year's Day,' Beattie said. 'Let's hope they're up to it, if they've been partying all night.'

Jenny saw the look on Linda's face and could have cheerfully strangled Beattie. 'Is it definite?' she said.

'I don't think so,' Linda said. 'I don't know really.'

'I'll see if I can have a word with someone when I come in on Monday, all right?' Jenny said. 'There probably won't be anyone here on Sunday with the authority to tell me anything.'

'OK,' Linda said.

'Now you have a day off tomorrow and don't worry about a thing,' Beattie said, nodding meaningfully at Bob and Jenny.

Bob turned and gave Jenny a smile of triumph and she felt her heart turn over and hoped she wasn't blushing. She got to her feet quickly and said, 'We'd better make a move.'

Outside they slithered and slipped on patches of black ice. The blackout made it even more difficult to see and the icy blasts of air took their breath away. It was too cold to chatter, but Jenny didn't want to talk anyway. She wanted to walk with Bob. Cuddled up together for warmth, the pair made their way to the tram stop. 'Now where

175

to?' Bob said, as they sat down on the swaying city-bound tram.

'What d'you mean?'

'Well, what do you usually do after visiting Linda?'

'Oh, I lead a very exciting life,' Jenny said with a grin. 'I go straight home and have a cup of cocoa and go to bed. Course, I used to visit the warden post two nights a week once, another den of iniquity, but the doctor's forbidden even that until the spring.'

'And quite right too,' Bob said. 'I should think you need a break after all you've been through.'

'That's nonsense. I'm perfectly all right now,' Jenny cried.

'OK, let's say I'm glad you don't have to be there, tonight at least,' Bob said. 'Let's be a couple of devils and do something wild, like go for a drink in a city centre pub.'

'You're on,' Jenny said with a smile. 'But I'm afraid I can't recommend one. I've never been in any of them.'

'Oh, I'm sure we'll find one to suit,' Bob said airily.

And they did, of course. The Taverners at the top of New Street by the Town Hall.

Bob knew that a large part of Birmingham city centre had been flattened by bombs, but they decided against going down for a look that night. 'We'd see nothing in the blackout anyway,' Bob said, 'and there's always tomorrow.'

Jenny wondered what plans Bob had for the following day and decided it wasn't her business. She had no claim on the man and she told herself to be satisfied with the evening they'd spent together.

'What will you have to drink, Jenny?' Bob asked as they went in through the door of the pub. She didn't know. She'd only ever tasted sherry and hadn't really liked it. 'There's no point being too fussy, anyway,' he said. 'It all depends on what the pub has in. I'll fetch you a drink most ladies like. That's if I can get it, all right?'

Jenny found she did like the port and lemon that he placed in front of her. Having taken a cautious sip, she smiled at him and said, 'That's nice.'

'Don't you start getting a taste for it,' Bob warned. 'I don't want your mother and grand-mother after my blood for encouraging you to drink.'

'Don't be silly, I'm twenty years old.'

'I don't care how old you are,' Bob said. 'That pair you live with would string me up, I'm sure.'

'I don't think they'd care that much what happened to me,' Jenny said. 'But that's enough about me and my family. What about yours?'

'Mine?' Bob said. 'What d'you want to know?'

'Well, you have a slight Midlands accent,' Jenny said. 'Do you live far away?'

'Jenny,' Bob said, 'I was brought up on Grange Road, and my parents live there still – or at least they do when there isn't a war on.'

'Oh,' said Jenny. Grange Road was not far from the Pype Hayes Estate. In fact, it was almost on the edge of it, but it might as well have been a million miles away. All the houses in Grange Road were big, and many had maids and even cooks in them. But when Bob had arrived at her house the previous evening, he'd said he had nowhere special to go. Now it appeared he had parents to visit and a comfy house to live in.

However, he went on to explain: 'No one's in the place now, unless you count Paddy and his wife Dora, who are sort of caretakers while my mother is away. They used to work for us but agreed to come and oversee the place when Dad insisted on packing my mother off to Devon, to live with his sister, at the beginning of the war. Not that she'll stay long, I don't think. She's bored stupid and wants to be back home now the raids have eased.'

'What about your sister? Didn't she go with her?' Jenny asked.

'You don't know Jules to ask a question like that,' Bob said. 'She wouldn't bury herself in the country, doing good works, when there was a war to be won. She's in the Wrens and based in Portsmouth at the moment.'

'And your father?'

'He's in Intelligence and we're not at all sure of where he's based, though of course we can write to him, care of the military.'

'Haven't you been near the house at all?'

'Oh yes. I went last night. Dora fussed all over me, fed me as if I'd been on a starvation diet. They knew I was coming – I'd sent them word. My room was all ready for me when I got home last night. A fire lit in the grate, and hot-water bottles in the bed. Sheer luxury.'

'If you ask me, you're spoilt,' Jenny said. 'We've never had a fire in a bedroom in the house, ever.

Not,' she added, 'that my room has even got a fireplace, but my parents' room had and the one my brothers shared.'

Bob raised his hands in a gesture of surrender. 'I am, I admit it,' he said. 'But you see, it wasn't all my fault. We can't help what we're born into.'

Jenny realised he was right. No one could help it, and Bob went on: 'After this war, the class system will disintegrate. It will have to.'

'No, it won't,' Jenny said. 'It didn't after the last one, did it? And millions lost their lives. My father told me it was supposed to be the war to end wars, and how they'd come back expecting a land fit for heroes. In the end, many of them came back to the dole queue and hunger and deprivation. It will be the same after this one; the heroes will be forgotten.'

'No, they won't,' Bob insisted. 'They can't be. You're right about the last war, the whole thing after was a damned scandal. Those in power conveniently forgot about the slums many lived in and the unemployment many were coming back to. And this time the government didn't even make adequate provision for them in the event of air-raid attacks.'

Jenny knew what Bob said was true. Londoners bedding down nightly in the Underground was a well-known fact now, and eventually emergency measures had been set up for them, reluctantly, by the authorities.

'We had a young trainee arrive from London a few weeks ago,' Bob said. 'His whole family had been bombed out since October, and since then his mother and three youngsters hide out at night in an underground warehouse. Apparently there are thousands of people there. They put up barricades for some privacy, and he said the chemical toilets they have now are a great improvement on the buckets they used to have to share. My God,' Bob groaned, 'the ironic thing is, these warehouses used to house dray-horses, and they were shipped out of that part of London to somewhere safer. Do you hear that?' he said to Jenny. 'Somewhere safer for horses. So, they knew this area by the docks would be heavily bombed, and they ignored all the signs and did sod all to protect the people.'

He stopped then, and looking at Jenny said, 'I'm sorry, I shouldn't be yelling at you about it. It's just ... this young Cockney lad says his mother, and younger brothers and sisters, are more in danger than he is. It worries him.'

'I bet it does,' Jenny said grimly. 'And it *is* awful, and now everyone agrees it is. But afterwards, these people will be forgotten, like last time.'

'No, no, I don't think so,' Bob said, 'and that's partly because of evacuation.'

'Evacuation!'

'This time, the poverty and deprivation have been brought into other people's homes. Those in the country have been shocked by the city children's appearance. Some have never slept in a bed or sat up to a meal, never handled a knife and fork and have lived on a diet of chips and bread and jam or dripping. Some have been sewn into their clothes, or have brown paper underneath their thin clothes in an attempt to offer more protection to the children. Many wear hob-nailed boots – well patched and cobbled, people say. But worse, there are those who wear canvas plimsolls with cardboard in, to keep their feet dry.'

Jenny knew this was true. She'd seen children going to Paget Road School with inadequate footwear and no topcoat in the depths of winter. The *Evening Mail* gave away free boots to the poor and they wouldn't do that if there was no need for it. She was just glad it *had* all been brought to other people's notice.

'You mark my words, this will push the Beveridge recommendations along quicker after the war,' Bob said.

Jenny was glad she knew what the Beveridge Report was; her father had talked to her about it. It sounded too good to be true – a free Health Service, family allowances to help the poorer families, and old-age pensions for the elderly. But here was Bob agreeing with it all, and saying it would all come true.

She hoped he was right. It would mean people like her brother Anthony and Linda's family had not died totally in vain, if a better Britain was built at the end of such an awful war, whenever it was. 'D'you want another?' Bob said.

Jenny realised she'd finished her port and lemon. She wanted to talk some more to the man who so interested her, so she smiled and said, 'Oh, yes. Yes, please.'

It was late when Jenny got home, much later than she usually arrived and she was glad that both her mother and grandmother were in bed.

She was in no mood to be quizzed and have her evening spoilt by poisonous spiteful remarks. She wanted to lie in bed and go over the whole evening she had spent with Bob, when for a short time, she'd been found desirable and attractive by a man, for very possibly the first time in her life. And there was another day tomorrow. If, after that, the relationship went no further, and really there was no reason for it to, then at least she'd have this time to remember. With that thought in her head, she turned over and went into a deep sleep.

Chapter Eleven

Hand in hand, they strolled around St Philip's churchyard in the centre of town. It was too cold for strolling really, it was a day for marching along, arms swinging, to get the circulation going. Instead, they meandered slowly and in the end Bob took Jenny's gloved hand into his own pocket – making the cold day an excuse to cuddle closer.

The air was so icy it hurt one's throat to try to talk, but it didn't matter, the silence between them was an easy and companionable one. Jenny had been up at the crack of dawn in order to be ready for Bob who was coming to collect her at one o'clock. She'd got the rations in, given the house a lick and a promise, left the beds to change for another week and washed only the essentials, leaving the ironing to Sunday, whatever her grandmother would say on the subject.

But she said none of this to Bob. She didn't want to talk about her relations, and certainly not spoil the day with complaints. She wanted instead to imagine that this smart and handsome man was walking around town with her because he truly wanted to. She wished Bob had nothing to do with Anthony and didn't feel he had to be kind to his sister.

And if she were to chatter nonsensically about nothing at all, as she was wont to do if she was nervous, Bob might regret he'd asked to see her again, and she wouldn't be able to bear that. She might only have this one day with him, so for this one day, she would pretend.

She didn't have to pretend the thudding of her heart against her ribs however, and pressed against him like she was, she was surprised he was unable to feel it. Maybe he did, maybe he knew how his nearness affected her. She went hot with embarrassment at the thought and Bob turned to look at her. 'All right?' he said.

Jenny nodded, she couldn't trust herself to speak. The look in Bob's deep brown eyes had made her legs feel suddenly weak. 'We've been out in this long enough,' he said. 'Let's find ourselves somewhere to have a nice hot drink, shall we?'

'All right,' Jenny said, her voice little more than a whisper. Anything he wanted she would have agreed with, and they quickened their pace towards the town centre, the people and the cafés.

Bob had not been into the centre of the city since the raids. He'd heard about them of course, but seeing it was something else. Where Marshall & Snelgrove had stood was now just a heap of rubble. 'There's talk they're going to level this, and build a big marquee over it for dances and concerts and things,' Jenny told him.

'Fairly nippy on a night like this, wouldn't you say?'

'For a concert maybe,' Jenny said with a laugh, 'or anything else where you had to sit still for long. A dance would probably be all right. You'd have to prance round all evening, mind, or you'd

184

stick to the floor with the cold. Still,' she shrugged, 'it might come to nothing, and it will be spring or summer before anything's done.'

'And it might be better than leaving a gaping hole that's neither use nor ornament,' Bob said.

But nothing could disguise the mess the bombers had made of the bottom end of High Street, and Bob was struck speechless by the devastation in the Bull Ring. Every time he took his plane up, certainly in the early Battle of Britain days, he knew he risked being killed or maimed, like the other young airmen in his Squadron, but he, like they, accepted those risks. What he *couldn't* come to terms with was what the ordinary person in the street had had to put up with – even children like Linda who'd had her whole family wiped out.

'We've got to win this damned war,' he said grimly, and his hand tightened around Jenny's and she saw his eyes were troubled.

Then he seemed to give himself a mental shake and went on, 'But for today, let's try and forget it for a little while. We'll go for a cup of something to warm ourselves up, walk around the shops a bit and then maybe go to the pictures. What d'you say to that, Miss O'Leary?'

Matching his bantering tone, Jenny said, 'That would be most acceptable, Mr Masters.'

It was a shame the city centre looked so drab, Jenny thought afterwards, fortified by a steaming bowl of soup and feeling much warmer. The shops were a disappointment, now that the afternoon had turned into a dusky evening. None of the sparsely decorated windows were lit up as

185

they used to be. No Christmas lights twinkled outside the shops or in strands across the street. And once inside the shops, there was little to buy. Jenny remembered that the shops used to be very busy getting ready for the January sales at this time of year. People would queue for hours and hours to get in first, and whenever Jenny had gone as a child she'd been buffeted from side to side by the heaving crowds.

Now the scurrying shoppers scarcely looked about them and seemed anxious just to do what they had to do and head for home. Jenny felt it was rather depressing and hoped Bob didn't feel bored by the whole thing.

He didn't appear bored. He seemed not to find her company too tedious at all, and she couldn't really understand it. She was surprised at the offer to go to the cinema. She really thought he'd thank her for the pleasant afternoon and be off to spend his last evening with someone more exciting than herself.

She was very worried about going to the cinema with him anyway. She'd listened to enough of the other girls' tales around the office to know what went on. 'Groping,' her friend Babs called it, 'like a bleeding octopus.'

Jenny had been appalled. 'Do you ... do you let them?' she'd asked.

Babs had smiled. 'There ain't no one law about it, Jen. Some you do, some you don't. It all depends.'

'Depends on what?' Jenny had been desperate to know.

'How much you like them. How much of a

186

good time they give you.' Babs had leaned towards Jenny, and went on in a lower voice, 'Thing to remember Jenny is, if you let them go too far in the flicks, they'll think you're ready to go further once they get you outside, see?'

No, she didn't see. It was like a minefield and people just seemed to know the rules. How did they? Why did she worry so much over it? And how far was too far? If she let Bob put his arm around her, would he take that as an indication that she might sleep with him later? Surely not. The whole thing was ludicrous! But what if his hand should snake down her neck and cup her breast like her first date had done, so long ago? She couldn't allow that, he'd think her fast – and what if he wanted a kiss? She went hot at the very thought. She wouldn't mind a kiss, in fact she'd love him to kiss her, but you couldn't go round kissing strange men, a little voice of reason said in her head. Was he a stranger? He'd been Anthony's friend, but so probably had half the airfield, the annoying little voice said again. Would you kiss them all because they could claim an acquaintance with Anthony?

Oh shut up. For a horrified moment, Jenny thought she'd spoken aloud. She hadn't, but Bob had seen the definite shake of her head. 'Are you all right?' He asked again.

'Yes, fine – never better.' Jenny's voice was high and brittle-sounding and her face tense.

Bob wondered what she had been thinking about so intently to upset her, but he didn't know her well enough to ask. Instead he said, 'Have you seen *Gone with the Wind?*'

187

'No,' Jenny said. 'I must be the only person in the world who hasn't.'

'I haven't either,' Bob said, 'so that'll make two of us.'

'I know a lot about the film,' Jenny said. 'The girls at work have told me virtually everything about it.'

'Don't you just hate friends like that?'

'Well, I don't suppose they ever thought I'd see it,' Jenny said. 'I don't get out much, you see.'

Bob squeezed Jenny's hand again and said, 'Well, you can tell them all about it on Monday. Let's hope you're not disappointed.'

Jenny knew she wouldn't be, not with him by her side anyway.

Night had fallen in earnest as they'd toured the shops and Bob said, 'If we go into the next showing of the film, we could eat when we come out and I'll still have plenty of time to see you on to the last bus before my train. Would that be all right, or would you prefer to eat before we go in?'

'Oh, afterwards definitely,' Jenny said. 'Heavens, it's no time since we had the soup.'

They made their way to the queue forming outside the Odeon in New Street. The people, now well used to queuing, were friendly and carefree, out for a night's entertainment. Jenny realised there were a fair few girls of her age, some in groups, some with young men, most in uniform of some sort. This was the life other young women lived, she realised, not the one of duty and drudgery that she had for herself.

'Blistering cold, ain't it?' a voice shouted from the crowd.

'Too cold for Jerry, I'd say.'

'They won't be over tonight, too much cloud.'

'Better be thankful for small mercies, eh?'

Bob took Jenny's hand in his again. 'That's one blessing,' he said. 'They're right. There'll probably be no raid tonight, the cloud's too thick. I should have thought of it though. Last night and tonight, we were risking it really.'

'Well, it's OK,' Jenny said. 'Anyway, I wanted to come. Don't worry, there hasn't been a raid for ages.'

It hadn't been ages, not really, but the last thing Jenny wanted was for Bob to start worrying enough to take her home.

But then, she told herself, why should he worry at all? They'd only met the day before. To Bob this must be just a diversion, a way to spend a few hours' leave when he had nowhere else to go. She should face facts and not be reading stupid romance into everything he said.

Suddenly a man went past whistling 'A Nightingale Sang in Berkeley Square', and memories tugged at Jenny. 'That's what Linda sang,' she said, 'when we were trapped together, you know?'

'What?'

'That song, "A Nightingale Sang in Berkeley Square",' Jenny said. 'She sang to pass the time at the end. She said she and her mother used to sing to her brothers sometimes to stop them being so scared in the shelter. She has a marvellous voice, you know.'

Bob smiled, glad that Jenny couldn't see it. She was dotty over Linda, he knew, and felt a

189

measure of responsibility for her, for as well as sitting beside her for hours in the bomb-damaged house, she had helped dig her mother and brothers out of the wreckage first. He doubted she had such a great voice at all. His mother had taught music before the war, but then most of her pupils had vanished, evacuated privately or with their schools, and his father insisted on Francesca herself going to a place of safety.

Bob remembered the mothers who would come with children they claimed could sing like angels or were gifted on the piano. Seldom had their claims been justified. He recalled the early cater-wauling sounds that would come from the music room, that his mother could turn into a passable singing voice. Or the clumsy child thumping on the piano, whom she could turn into a satisfactory pianist, but none of them were gifted.

'I would love to have the money to have her properly trained,' Jenny went on. 'I'm sure she could make something of herself.'

Bob said nothing, but maybe if his mother came back to live in Birmingham as she kept threatening, she could listen to Linda and see what she thought. The girl was probably as bad as all the others, but it would please Jenny and he'd like to please Jenny, but he'd say nothing for now.

Jenny thought his lack of response was because he didn't like her talking about Linda. She'd not thought of her all day, and now she felt guilty standing in a cinema queue and not visiting the child in hospital. She vowed to store up all she

190

saw to tell Linda the following day.

The visit to the cinema was not at all the traumatic event that Jenny had anticipated. Once seated, Bob pulled a package from his pocket and gave it to Jenny. 'I didn't dare give you this in daylight, in case you were set upon,' he joked.

Inside was a box of chocolates, a small box, but all the same! Her eyes widened with surprise. Everyone knew sweets were hard to get, and chocolate – well, that was virtually unobtainable. 'Where on earth did you get them?' she whispered.

'I have shares in the local sweetshop,' Bob said, and in the dim light Jenny saw the sparkle in his eyes and the quirk of his mouth. 'No really, I did get them from the local shop. I worked there from when I was twelve, you see, first delivering papers and then behind the counter when I was fourteen, after school and Saturdays and holidays and things. They have a soft spot for me and I always call and see them when I'm home. If they have anything under the counter, they usually slip me the odd thing. I called in this morning, and they gave me the chocolates to give to my young lady.' He smiled again and set Jenny's heart dancing as he said, 'So they're yours.'

Steady, steady, Jenny told herself. He doesn't really mean I'm his young lady. It's his way, part of his charm. No need to get excited.

With that established, the evening was marvellous. The film was as wonderful as the girls at work had said it was, and all that Bob did was hold her hand. She should have been relieved she didn't have to fight him off, and rebuff any liberties he tried to take. However, human nature being what it is, Jenny was surprised to find herself rather disappointed.

Later, they ate in a little pub that was also a restaurant, just off New Street. Jenny ordered steak and was given a piece of tender, juicy meat the like of which she had not seen since the pre-war days. She was not used to alcohol and the wine Bob ordered went to her head rather. 'Where do they get it all from?' she asked. 'This beautiful food, wine and everything?'

'Better not ask too many questions, sweetheart,' Bob advised. 'Eat and enjoy.'

'For tomorrow we die,' Jenny continued, and then clapped her hand over her mouth, horrified at what she'd said. 'Oh God, Bob, I'm sorry.'

'It's all right,' he said easily. 'Don't worry so much.'

Don't worry so much, Jenny thought. I *need* to worry. I need my bloody tongue cut out! How could I have been so crass and insensitive. In a short time, I will say goodbye to this man who has been so very kind to me. He will return to all sorts of dangers, and I'm sitting here ill-wishing him. It was like an evil omen that sent a shiver right down her spine.

Bob saw her anxious face and said, 'Look, sweetheart, it doesn't matter.'

It did matter though. Anthony had told her how superstitious many pilots were, and about the good luck charms many carried with them, even into the cockpit. It put a blight, a restraint over the rest of the evening, and Bob felt it too, Jenny was sure.

He was as courteous as ever, though, as they walked to the tram stop. Jenny wished she could go to the station with him to see him off, but she knew she'd never get home if she did. As it was, Bob felt bad that he wouldn't be able to see her right home. 'It's all right,' she assured him. 'Really it is.'

'If you're sure,' he said.

'I'm sure.'

Bob seemed ill-at-ease, Jenny thought, and she wondered at it, as he usually appeared so confident. She was totally unprepared for his next question.

'Jenny, will you ... will you write to me?'

'Write to you?' Jenny couldn't believe what Bob had asked. She would have thought he'd never want to think of her again, but here he was asking her to write to him.

'I've copied my address out,' Bob said, pressing a piece of paper into her hand. 'Will you write?'

'Of course, if you want me to.'

'Thank you,' he said. The tram came clattering towards them and he bent and kissed Jenny – a soft, almost tentative, kiss on her lips. 'God bless, Jenny. See you soon,' he said. Jenny, her eyes blurred with sudden, unexpected tears, stumbled up the stairs of the tram.

'Careful ducks,' the conductor said with a wide grin, holding out a hand to steady her. 'Should take more water with it.' He rang the bell and the tram gave a lurch and rattled away. When Jenny was able to look out of the window next, Bob was nowhere to be seen.

Almost a week after her meeting with Bob, Jenny spotted a letter on the mat addressed to her as she descended the stairs. Unfortunately the living-room door opened just then and Eileen scooped up all the post. Jenny knew the letter was from Bob. She'd written to him on the Sunday afternoon, thanking him for the pleasant evening and day that they'd spent together, and said how much she enjoyed it. This must be his answer. She went into the living room and saw that Eileen had handed the letter to Norah, who seemed to be studying it intently.

Jenny felt anger bubbling inside her. 'I think that's mine,' she said.

'In my day, young ladies' letters were always read by their mother,' Eileen said.

Jenny snatched the letter from her mother's hand and retorted, 'Good job it's *not* your day then, isn't it, Grandmother? Or that I'm a young lady either, I suppose. Isn't it grand that I'm an ill-mannered, inconsiderate bitch?'

'Jenny, what an expression!' Norah complained peevishly.

'It's only what you say about me.' Jenny said. 'It might be couched in different terms, but it means the same.'

'I don't know what's got into you, really I don't,' Norah said. 'All this fuss about one letter. I bet it's from that airman. And we know nothing about him.'

'You liked him. He called to see you on Friday, and you made him tea. He told me you got on fine,' Jenny cried. 'He was Anthony's Squadron Leader, for goodness sake! Anyway,' she went on, 'half the girls in Dunlop write to servicemen.'

'Well, you know what I think of those hoydens you mix with down there.'

'Do you know what?' Jenny said angrily. 'I'm sick of your "I'm better than everyone else" attitude and I'm sick of your bad-mindedness. Now if you don't mind, I will go upstairs and read my letter!'

Jenny stormed out. When she reached her bedroom she was shaking with reaction. She was so tired of fighting over every blessed thing. Surely she should be afforded a little privacy at her age?

In the end, the letter was a bit of an anti-climax. Bob wrote that he'd been delighted to have had her company, and maybe they could do it again the next time he had leave. He signed it *All the best, Bob*.

Jenny crumpled the letter up in disappointment and tossed it into the bin. Then she took it out again, and smoothed it out, not willing to give her mother or grandmother the chance to read the almost cursory note. What did she expect, she asked herself. That Bob would swear undying love for her and say he could no longer live without her? Really, Jenny thought, I need my bloody head examined.

On 22 January 1941, British and Australian troops captured 25,000 Italians in a battle to regain Tobruk, as Jenny told Linda when she went into the hospital later. 'Where are they going to put them all?' the girl asked.

'According to Beattie, Sutton Park,' Jenny said.

'Don't be daft!'

'I'm not, I don't say *those* prisoners, but certainly some,' Jenny said. 'She told me not long ago that the Displaced Persons' camp in the park was being strengthened to house prisoners-of-war. There will be camps all over the country, I expect. I mean, you can't just give them a smack on the hand and release them.'

'No, I know that,' Linda said, 'but it means we have to feed them and look after them, and that?'

'Well, what would you do – starve them to death?'

'No, I suppose not,' Linda had to agree, reluctantly. 'But I wonder if they get the same rations as us. I bet they get more. There's probably laws and that, saying they've got to have stuff we can't get because they're soldiers.'

'I don't know, Linda,' Jenny said with a smile, and added, 'but, I suppose I could enquire when they're in residence.'

'Oh you,' Linda said with a laugh as she gave Jenny a push.

Jenny was glad to see Linda was recovering the good spirits that had brought her through so much. One day a nurse brought in a pile of wool for her to knit balaclavas for the troops, and another brought old issues of comics she'd collected from the local newsagent.

But really she lived for visitors, and Jenny did her best to go as often as possible. Beattie still went, of course, and Gran O'Leary was always willing to pop along and help cheer the child up.

But Peggy no longer had much spare time, for the doctor pronounced her fit for work at the end of January. With the BSA burnt down and the workers dispersed to other factories, Peggy applied to change her job and Jenny got her set on in one of the offices in the Dunlop. Peggy was glad to be back at work and earning, and began to put something away each week for her bottom drawer. Jenny was pleased to have the girl's company there and back as they travelled to work on the tram.

Peggy's hair had grown again now and looked quite respectable, but much shorter than before, as she'd had the rest bobbed to match the regrowth. Both Linda and Jenny thought the short bob suited Peggy, but she wasn't sure herself and said she hoped it would be long enough to have it shampooed and set before the wedding day. Linda listened avidly as they talked about the bride's dress and those of the bridesmaids, and the head-dresses and the flowers and the guest list. She just about remembered her mother marrying Ted Prosser, not that there was much to remember really, just a man mumbling things in a little room full of chairs. Only Beattie and Bert were there, and afterwards there was a sort of party in the Norton pub. Linda had hated it all, like she'd hated Ted's mates and their slack lips and beer breath and their big sweaty hands pawing at her.

But Peggy's wedding sounded like the fairy-tale wedding she'd dreamed of for herself, and she was determined to do whatever it took to help her be there for the big day.

Even Bob appeared to be caught up in the excitement of it all, and he wrote and told Jenny

197

that he might have leave the weekend of the wedding. He didn't know how much, or even if it were definite yet, but he'd let her know. Jenny hugged herself with delight at the prospect of seeing him again.

Then the doctors told Jenny that Linda would definitely be well enough to attend the wedding. 'Her right leg will have a calliper fitted, because that leg is much weaker than the left,' he said. 'It sustained a nasty injury. But as long as she's able to return to hospital for treatment, there's no reason any more for her to occupy a bed.'

'So she can go home?'

'After the wedding, certainly.'

Jenny couldn't wait to tell Linda the good news. She was over the moon, though she did complain sometimes about the physiotherapy she'd begun as soon as the plaster casts had been removed. She told Jenny how much her legs ached afterwards but Jenny knew, despite that, she'd think it all worthwhile now that she was definitely going home at last.

Linda was singing 'Ave Maria' at the wedding. She wasn't at all sure how they'd all managed to talk her into it. It had all been connected with her excitement in knowing that by the end of March, she would be living with Jenny for good. Then Peggy came to see her and told her it would make her day if she'd sing and Linda could see that Jenny wanted her to as well. They both sang the piece to her so that she had an idea of the tune, and copied out the words, and suddenly she found herself saying she would do it.

Later, she wished she hadn't agreed, because there were deep ugly scars running down both her legs. The right was worse than the left, but the calliper hid most of that. And that was another thing, her calliper. It was heavy and ungainly, and very difficult to walk with. In the beginning, she had listed to one side to compensate for the weight of it, and she still wasn't certain that she walked completely straight.

She was sure she'd make a complete fool of herself, but she'd have to do it now. If she complained, it would sound as though she was thinking just of herself, but she'd give anything to be hidden in a church pew along with everyone else. If only she had a long dress to wear! But then she could hardly ask Jenny to provide one, not after all of those clothes of Vicky's that she'd been given.

Jenny had noticed Linda's slight restraint when she visited, and also the way she'd seemed to lose interest in the wedding preparations, but her gran had said maybe she felt a little out of it not being involved. Jenny supposed that was right. She didn't ask her. She knew Linda wouldn't like to think she'd offended her in any way and if she spoke about it, Linda might think she'd upset her. So she said nothing and Linda worried about it and wished the day was over and done with.

There were just five days to go to the wedding when Peggy's youngest sister, Maria, fell down some cellar steps and broke her leg quite badly.

Peggy was understandably upset and so was the girl, who had been due to be one of the brides-maids. Jenny felt very sorry for her and called to see how she was going on the following evening. Peggy had just got in after visiting her in the Children's Hospital where she'd been taken and told Jenny she was very depressed about the whole thing. The doctor had said she'd definitely not be well enough to attend the wedding, let alone be a bridesmaid. 'It's not to be wondered at,' Jenny said. 'It must be a great disappointment with the bridesmaids' dresses made and every-thing.'

'There's no help for it,' Peggy told Jenny, and went on with a sigh, 'Maria was upset, but as I said, she has another sister and three brothers to go yet. She'll have her turn as bridesmaid again, before she's much older I'd say. Our Leonie is courting strong, so Mammy told me last time I was over.'

Jenny still felt sorry for the little girl who was probably bitterly disappointed, but she didn't bother saying anything at home. She'd told them about Peggy, and how she was to be a bridesmaid at her wedding, but they went on as if she hadn't spoken, so she said no more about it. But still, she thought, as she let herself in later, I'll have to tell them that the wedding takes place this Saturday, and that Linda's coming to live here permanently from the night before. Whatever they say, it will not make the slightest difference.

'It was your gran's idea,' Peggy said next day on the tram. 'After all, the dress is made and it's a shame to waste it, and Linda is singing so she is part of the service anyway.'

'It won't fit her, will it? Your Maria is only ten.'

'Aye, but a bit bigger than Linda I'd say,' Peggy said. 'We can measure it up against the clothes you altered for her at Christmas. That's not a problem, the point is, would she like to be a bridesmaid?'

'She'd like the dress – what young girl wouldn't?' Jenny said. But would she like hobbling down the aisle with everyone watching her? She didn't know the answer to that. 'I'll ask her tonight.'

But Linda was delighted. It solved the problem of her scarred legs and the calliper; both would be hidden under the layers of petticoats and pale apricot satin which would fall to the floor. She could picture the dress for she knew it was exactly the same as Jenny's, and Jenny had described it in detail.

'We wondered whether you might feel awkward walking down the aisle?' Jenny said.

'Not really,' Linda said. 'I'm getting better every day. I just have a slight limp now and I've got two more days to practise, because you're not fetching me until after work on Friday, are you?'

'No. Dr Sanders has offered his services again,' Jenny said.

'I reckon he's sweet on you,' Linda said. 'Bob had better watch out.'

'Linda!' Jenny cried. 'What a thing to say! The doctor is just being friendly, that's all, and Bob is just a friend.'

'Oh yeah, course he is,' Linda said sarcastically.

201

'You need your bottom skelped, young woman.' Jenny said, but with a laugh.

Afterwards, she told herself Linda was being ridiculous. She was just a child still and everyone knew they had funny notions. It was just coincidence that she'd bumped into Dr Sanders sometimes in the hospital as she was visiting Linda, and the brief visit he'd made to the house at the weekend was merely to offer his services to bring Linda home on Friday evening. Jenny had been grateful to him for the offer, and he'd never said anything awkward or even mildly suggestive to her.

Not that he was an unattractive man. He wasn't old either, she was sure, for though the beard and moustache made him look older than his years, his eyes were young and, she'd noticed last time, deepset and so dark they looked almost black. But she knew Peter Sanders was definitely not interested in *her*. She wasn't even sure if Bob was, not in the way Linda meant. But then Linda was still of an age to believe in fairy stories, such as that of the prince marrying the beggar girl and living happily ever after. Jenny was only too well aware however, that life seldom worked out like that.

Yet, when she got into the doctor's car after work on Friday evening, Linda's words reverberated in Jenny's ears and she smiled at the doctor a little self-consciously. 'All right?' he said, as she slid into the seat beside him.

Jenny nodded.

'A bit nervous, I suppose?'

'Not really,' Jenny said, a little puzzled and added, 'nervous of the wedding, you mean?'

202

'No, not that. I meant nervous of having Linda home for good?'

'Not particularly,' she said, but she didn't speak the truth.

Dr Sanders wondered if Jenny knew how bad she was at hiding her feelings. He heard enough Estate gossip to know how much Jenny's mother and grandmother were disliked, and the decision to have Linda to live there had little to do with them, but much to do with the young girl beside him, no matter what they told him the first time he called. 'Linda's terribly excited,' he said. 'I popped in yesterday.'

'I didn't see you.'

'You'd long gone by then,' Peter Sanders said. 'I had to have a patient admitted last night, and I went in the ambulance with her because she lived alone. While I was there, I nipped along to see Linda. She should have been asleep, but she was too excited.'

'She'd better sleep tonight or she'll be like a wet rag tomorrow,' Jenny said grimly.

'And isn't she performing too?'

'Well, I suppose you could call it that. She's singing "Ave Maria".'

Dr Sanders nodded 'She told me,' he said. 'I might just come and listen. Linda has asked me to. Eleven o'clock, she said?'

'That's right,' Jenny said. 'At St Saviour's Church in Ward End, which was Peggy's church before she went to live with Gran and where the rest of the family go. She moved over there yesterday, to stay with a neighbour till after the wedding.'

203

'Well, the bride and groom could hardly leave from the same house.'

Jenny smiled and said, 'It wouldn't be very traditional, would it?'

'And terribly bad luck for the groom to see the wedding dress too soon.'

'So they say.'

Dr Sanders cast a quizzical eye at Jenny and said with a smile, 'Can I take it you scorn these old customs, madam?'

'Let's just say I think a happy and successful marriage has more to do with love and compatibility, than catching a glimpse of a wedding dress.'

'Ah, there speaks the voice of experience.'

Jenny laughed out loud. 'OK,' she conceded. 'I know little about it, I suppose. But that's my opinion.'

'And have you anyone you love and feel compatible with?'

Jenny was surprised by the direct question, then quite annoyed. The doctor had no right to ask such things. It wasn't any of his business. Despite herself, she felt her face flush and was glad the inside of the car was so dim. Into the silence that had fallen between them, Peter Sanders said, 'Sorry Jenny, out of order. I had no right to ask. Forgive me?'

'There's nothing to forgive,' Jenny said. She thought of Bob and wondered did she love him? She was happy to see him certainly, and her heart seemed to beat faster when she was near him, but she didn't know if that was love. And she had no idea how he felt about her; and as for compatible,

204

how much did either of them know of one another after such a short acquaintance? She only knew that at this moment, he was probably on a train travelling to the Midlands from the South, in order to spend his leave attending the wedding of her friend because she'd asked him to.

'It was just that if you have no one special, I'd like to take you out one evening,' Peter said. 'I'm sure I could get tickets for the theatre, if you'd like that?'

Jenny sat in stunned silence. Linda was right, she thought, he *has* got designs on me. She looked across the car at the doctor and wondered how old he really was. Only about thirty, she decided, certainly no more and quite a handsome man, distinguished-looking. She wondered how and why he'd become attracted to her. Surely he couldn't just be being kind, like Bob? She wondered briefly if Bob would mind her accepting a date with the doctor, but then why should he? It wasn't as if he was her real actual boyfriend, as if they were going steady or anything, and he probably dated other girls when he was at the camp. She'd just never asked him, thinking it wasn't her business.

'I ... I think I would like that, Dr Sanders,' Jenny said.

She heard the doctor sigh and realised he'd been nervous and felt rather sorry for him. 'Shall we say next Friday then, about seven?' Peter said. 'I'm not free till then anyway. I could pick you up from your house.'

'That would be lovely, thank you.'

'There's just one more thing.'

'Yes?'

'Do you think you could manage to call me Peter? I don't think I could last a whole evening with someone who calls me Dr Sanders.'

Jenny burst out laughing. 'No, I suppose not,' she agreed. 'But really I didn't know your name before, and anyway I wouldn't have felt right to address you as anything other and Dr Sanders when I was consulting you professionally.'

'Well, this Friday I won't be wearing my doctor's hat,' Peter Sanders said. 'So my name will be Peter, all right?'

'All right,' Jenny agreed, with a smile.

They had little time to say much else on the matter for the doctor had swung the car into the hospital car park. But when Peter Sanders stopped the car, he leaned over, squeezed Jenny's hand and said, 'Go for it, Jenny, and don't let anyone get you down,' she was glad of his support. She waited for him to lock the car and they then walked into the hospital side by side.

Chapter Twelve

All eyes were on Peggy the next day as she walked down the aisle on her father's arm. She looked truly beautiful. Her hair had grown long enough for a shampoo and set, and it fell in lovely waves around her heart-shaped face. Jenny felt a lump in her throat as she saw her arrive.

But though everyone turned to watch Peggy's progress, people were also intrigued by the smallest bridesmaid, who by concentrating very hard, walked slowly behind the bride with a barely perceptible limp. Some knew who she was, some had no idea, but most were aware that she'd stepped in when Peggy's little sister had injured herself.

Linda took her duties very seriously. She knew she had to walk behind Peggy slowly, her steps matching the bride's and on no account was she to tread on the train which would be spread out behind her. Her hands, which were clamped around the dainty posy, were damp. Beads of perspiration stood out on her forehead, and her heart was thumping so loud she could hear it even over the strains of the organ playing the 'Wedding March'. She wondered if Jenny was as nervous as she was, and worried that she wouldn't be able to sing properly, though she'd practised for hours in hospital.

Glad to reach the relative safety of the pew

facing the altar, she sank thankfully on to the seat. Jenny leaned across and pressed her hand and whispered, 'Well done,' and turned and flashed a smile at Bob sitting two rows behind them.

Bob wished Jenny could have sat by him. The service seemed interminable. He'd forgotten how long Nuptial Mass took. But still, he was glad he was there, it was important to Jenny, and Jenny, he was beginning to realise, was becoming more and more important to *him*. He wasn't sure if he loved her; he'd seen many of his mates go down that road, some even getting married – often to people they barely knew. The excuse was always that there was a war on, and who knew whether you would still be alive the next day, week or month? But what if you *did* survive? Bob thought. Fancy finding yourself married to someone you couldn't get along with, or even hated! No, he decided. When he married, and he didn't intend it to be for years yet, it would be to someone he loved, war or no war.

Jenny wished she'd had time alone with Bob before the service. He'd come down to Gran O'Leary's house, from where they were all leaving, to travel with them in the car. But Jenny had been busy and preoccupied, and she imagined there would be little time to talk together all day. And he'd have to leave the following evening. She wondered if it was wise to have invited him this weekend; it wasn't as if he knew many people. Maybe it would have been better to have asked him to try and make it one ordinary weekend. Yet she'd wanted him there, to sort of show him off to the family. She wasn't really being fair she knew, because everyone would assume he was her steady boyfriend.

However, it was too late to worry about any of that now. The bride looked a picture and her Uncle Gerry was as smart as she'd ever seen him. Now they'd been pronounced man and wife and the Mass was nearly over. It was almost time for Linda to sing.

Linda saw the sign Jenny made and, struggling to her feet, she made her way to the space in front of the altar, thinking she'd been mad to agree to perform and convinced she'd make an utter hash of it. Her damaged legs knocked together and her mouth felt dry as she faced the sea of unfamiliar faces. She was scared out of her wits.

But then as the organist struck up the opening notes, all nervousness suddenly left her and her voice rose sweet and clear. There was absolute silence as if the congregation had been stunned, and indeed many were. Among them was Bob. Jenny had not exaggerated the child's talent, he realised. He knew she was the sort of pupil his mother had waited half a lifetime for, and when he wrote and told her, she'd come galloping back from Devon, and he knew she would train Linda as Jenny had dreamed – and not for money either. Her pleasure would be to see this young star reach her potential. But for now he would say nothing to either Linda or Jenny. He would write to his mother tonight and take it from there.

Bob was surprised to find how much he'd

enjoyed the day. He was very glad to see that Jenny had ordinary, friendly relations to make up for the mother and grandmother he'd already met and hadn't liked, however pleasant they'd been to him on the surface. He also enjoyed being able to hold Jenny legitimately close, as they danced to the band at the pub where the reception was being held. 'What will we do tomorrow, sweetheart?' he said as they danced almost cheek to cheek.

Jenny's heart plummeted. 'I can't see you tomorrow, Bob,' she said anxiously. 'At least not alone. I must bring Linda.' She saw his face darken and wished, once more, she'd been able to meet him before the service to explain.

'You can't give your whole life up for that kid, you know,' he said, and though his voice was low, his face was grim.

'I do know,' Jenny said. 'But my mother and grandmother were wicked to her last night. Not in what they said, but how they said it, you know. I didn't expect a welcoming committee, but I did expect them to be civil to the child.'

'Linda's tough. She'll survive bad manners.'

'I know that, but it's her first day.'

'And tomorrow's my last for some time.'

'I know that too.' Jenny could have cried. Both of them had stopped dancing; neither was in the mood. Bob took Jenny's arm stiffly and led her to one of the tables. 'I'll get us both a drink,' he said coldly, but he didn't even bother asking what she wanted. I've done it again, Jenny thought, as she watched him walk away. He'll not want to see me again now.

From across the room, Linda watched Jenny chewing on her lip nervously. She'd seen the strained conversation between Jenny and Bob on the dance-floor, and the abrupt way Bob had left Jenny sitting at a table alone, and she knew they'd had a quarrel. She could even guess what it was about. Linda herself had been neither surprised nor upset by the behaviour of Norah O'Leary and her mother, Eileen. It was only what she'd expected after the way they'd gone on at Christmas, and she'd steeled herself not to feel bad about it, but Jenny had been made miserable.

Linda was glad though that she hadn't to stay in with them all day on Sunday. She wouldn't have done anyway. She'd have made her way down to Maureen's. But she was really pleased that she had arrangements made already, and was going out with Dr Sanders. Jenny hadn't seen Peter Sanders outside the church door, she'd been fussing with Peggy's dress in the porch, but Linda had gone to speak to him. Linda hadn't been sure he was going to come and was delighted, but she hadn't had time all day to say a word to Jenny about it.

She walked across and sat down at the table beside Jenny and smiled. 'It's been a great day, hasn't it?' she said, though she was tired and her legs ached but she wouldn't admit it and had stubbornly refused to use the wheelchair the hospital had given her.

'Yes, yes it has,' Jenny said, but her eyes still looked troubled as they scanned the bar.

'I ... I haven't had a chance to talk to you till

211

now,' Linda said, 'but I think you ought to know Dr Sanders has asked me to go out with him tomorrow.'

'Out with him?' Jenny repeated.

'To see my mother's grave,' Linda said. 'I told you he promised he'd take me when I was well.'

'Yes,' Jenny said. 'I remember, but I thought we were going to go together.' She felt strangely hurt.

'Well, we will another time,' Linda said cheerfully. 'Dr Sanders did ask about you, but I said you'd probably be going out with Bob. You are, aren't you?'

Was she? How the hell did she know! Maybe not. After all, he didn't want to go out with an idiotic girl who'd thought Linda would be dependent on her for company. God, she felt stupid. 'I suppose so,' she said. 'I'm not sure.'

'Well, here he is on his way back,' Linda said. 'You can ask him. Dr Sanders is picking me up outside the church after nine o'clock Mass.'

'You're going to Mass?'

'I'm going with you. You did say you usually go to the nine o'clock one, didn't you?'

'Yes, I did. I do,' Jenny said. 'But there's no need for you to go.'

'I know that. I want to.'

'I don't want you to feel under any pressure.'

'I don't,' Linda said. 'I never went to any church before, but it's not a bad way to start Sunday, and anyway I want to give it a try. After all, it must mean something to all your family.'

'We were born into it, and brought up in it,' Jenny admitted. 'I never really thought about it, to be truthful.'

Linda didn't say anything else because Bob was beside them, a pint in one hand and in the other a smaller glass. Jenny thought, from the colour of it, it was probably a port and lemon like she'd had before. Bob smiled a tight smile at them both and said to Linda, 'Mrs O'Leary is looking forward to your company tomorrow. She's expecting you to call.'

Jenny stared at Bob. Though he was addressing Linda, Jenny knew he meant her to hear what he had to say. He'd obviously gone to her gran and said Jenny hadn't wanted to go out and leave Linda in the house on her own, and her gran had said the girl was welcome at her place. Why hadn't she thought of that herself, or let Linda make her own plans? 'Oh, I can't tomorrow,' Linda said. She gave a little smile and went on. 'I've already got a date. I'll go and see Gran and explain.'

Jenny watched her limp away and turned to Bob and said, 'I'm sorry.'

Bob smiled. He sat down and took her hand. 'It's all right. I do know how responsible you feel for Linda.'

'It's just that ... if you knew how it is at home...'

'I do know. Anthony often talked of it,' Bob said. 'But I wanted you to myself tomorrow.'

'Well, we'll have the rest of the day,' Jenny said softly. 'After Mass, that is.'

'Ah, Jenny you shame me,' Bob said. 'I should by rights be going to church alongside you. My mother would be pleased, but I'm afraid I'm out of the habit now.'

'You're a Catholic?'

'I was brought up that way,' Bob said. 'As all children of a mixed marriage must be. My father was christened Church of England and never bothered much with any of it. I think he became a confirmed agnostic as the war began taking its toll of lives.'

'What about you?'

'I never thought deeply about any of it,' Bob admitted. 'My mother let Julie and me choose when we got to sixteen. I felt there were far better ways to spend a Sunday morning, but Julie carried on going for some time, till she went to Portsmouth, in fact.'

'And your mother?'

'Oh, she is a Catholic born and bred,' Bob said. 'She says it's not something you choose to be, it's what you are born into. Catholicism will never let go of my mother and she will never let go of it. It's ingrained in her.'

Jenny understood that only too well. She'd never have missed Mass on a Sunday, unless she was near dying and would have felt incredibly guilty if she had, even to go out with Bob. He saw her puzzled look and kissed her nose lightly. 'Don't worry, sweetheart. I won't ask you to risk your immortal soul. I'll pick you up after nine o'clock Mass with a picnic packed ready, and you pray for good weather.'

'Where are we going?'

'You'll know soon enough.'

Jenny didn't care where they went as long as it was together. She wondered if Bob guessed how much she thought of him, and how often.

Possibly, it would scare him if he'd guessed. She was sure he wanted their relationship light and free and she knew her greatest battle to have Sunday off was still to be faced. Never ever for as far back as she could remember, had she had a free Sunday. After Mass she would make the dinner and then wash up the dishes while the two older women dozed and chatted before the fire. Jenny then, in an agony of boredom, would take herself to her gran's or even Geraldine's.

She'd always steered clear of the parks, however nice the day, for no young man had ever asked her for a walk on a Sunday, and the sight of couples strolling arm-in-arm always produced a pang of envy. But now she had a young man to walk with, she thought, and her mother and grandmother could go to blazes if they didn't like it. She was spending the day with Bob whatever they said.

Linda and Jenny sat together in the church, for Linda had no desire to sit at the front with the children. They all went to the Abbey School in Erdington as it was the nearest Catholic school, not Paget Road like her. She knew none of them and stuck like glue to Jenny. She saw them all go to the rails for Communion as well, like most of the guests had done the day before at the Nuptial or Wedding Mass. Jenny had explained all about Communion and what it meant in the Catholic Church, and that to be able to take part, you had first to be received into the Church and then fast from midnight the night before.

'Why?' Linda had asked.

Jenny didn't think it was the time or place for a theological discussion. 'It's just something you have to do,' she said. 'It's a sort of miracle.'

Linda knew all about miracles. They said Jesus could make the blind see and the lame walk and raise people from the dead. Now that, she decided, was a miracle worth having, but she didn't feel there to be anything miraculous about Mass. She didn't worry about it, though. It was, she decided, just one more confusing thing.

There were many other things that confused Linda about the Catholic Church and one of them was not eating meat on a Friday. Jenny had told her that it was because Jesus Christ had died on Friday. But there was nothing Linda and her mom had liked better than a piece of fish if they had the money to spare. Egg and chips was another of her favourite meals. She didn't reckon it was any hardship to do without meat on Friday, or any other day either.

The church was different from her last visit, which had been to Midnight Mass on Christmas Eve. She looked around. There were few flowers in the church itself and Linda was surprised because it had had flowers before, and that had been in December. Jenny whispered that it was because it was Lent. Linda didn't understand what difference that made. The priest at least looked quite magnificent in his shiny embroidered purple robes and the stole of the same material around his neck.

She felt her eyes stray, as she knew they would, to the statue of Jesus hanging on the Cross. His eyes were open and His face creased with pain.

Linda remembered that after her first visit, Jenny had told her that as well as bearing the suffocating pain of the crucifixion itself, He carried the sins of the world on His shoulders so that when people died they could go to Heaven, as no one who'd sinned could be let in.

'Why not?' she'd asked.

'It's the way it is. The Devil himself was a fallen angel who sinned and was cast into Hell. So, to protect the sinners of the world, Jesus died to save us all.'

It had seemed monstrously unfair when Jenny had first explained it, and it still did. 'I thought you said God could do anything,' Linda objected.

'He can. He does,' Jenny said, and added, 'if you pray enough that is, and have faith.'

'If I was God, I wouldn't have let my son get crucified. I'd have let anyone I liked into my Heaven. I'd have told the Devil to go to Hell.'

'He was there already, Linda,' Jenny had said with a laugh.

'Well, he could have stayed there for my money.'

'People wouldn't have been able to go to Heaven then.'

'Course they would. I'd have let them in if I was God. You said God can do anything, that He is all-powerful. Jesus could raise the dead and all that. I'd have said that was a lot harder to do than letting the odd sinner into Heaven, wouldn't you?'

And Jenny couldn't really find words to argue. Many of Linda's questions had caused her to

217

examine her faith more closely. She'd been brought up to pray, worship and believe, but Linda had no such constraint. Norah and Eileen would have been scandalised if they'd heard some of the questions Linda asked, or the comments she made, but Jenny welcomed them because they made her think.

That morning, however, the Mass seemed to take for ever. She hoped both that Bob would be waiting for her, and that the picnic he'd promised was substantial. She'd had no breakfast as she'd been at Communion and her stomach felt yawningly empty.

But eventually, the Mass drew to a close and they filed out of the church into the spring sunshine. Many people spoke to them, but neither Jenny and Linda had any desire to linger; their eyes were focused on the road at the end of the drive where Jenny could see Bob waiting for her, a haversack strapped to his back.

Dr Sanders was out of his car leaning on the bonnet talking to Bob and he smiled when he saw the two girls. They pushed the wheelchair in front of them, for though Linda needed it on the long haul to church, she refused to get into it for the short walk to Peter Sanders's car. 'I thought you were never coming,' he said. 'Did you pray for us all in there?'

'Do you need prayers, Doctor?' Jenny asked lightly, and Peter answered: 'Show me a man who doesn't.'

'Are we going straight to the graveyard?' Linda said, cutting straight across their banter.

'No, we're not, young lady,' the doctor said.

'We're going first to my home, where if you're lucky my mother will make you a mug of cocoa and offer you a biscuit perhaps, while I cut some daffodils from the garden. Then we'll go.'

'Oh great,' Linda said. 'Jenny should come to your house, too. She's not even had breakfast.'

'Hasn't she? She's very welcome.'

'No, no, it's all right,' Jenny said. 'Really.'

'I forgot you'd probably have taken Communion,' Bob said. 'But it's fine, Doc. I have enough food to feed an army here. We'll stop and have a late breakfast.'

'Where are you heading?'

'Sutton Park.'

'Well, you have a grand day for it,' the doctor said, opening the car door for Linda to clamber laboriously inside. 'I'll take this little minx out to lunch afterwards, and then we might take in a film somewhere.'

Linda gave a squeal of excitement for she hadn't expected further treats, but the doctor leaned forward and said quietly, 'I don't want to bring her back home too soon. My mother's expecting her for tea.'

'You're very kind,' Jenny said. 'Thank you. I'm sure Linda appreciates it.'

'Oh, I was at a loose end anyway,' the doctor answered easily, folding up Linda's wheelchair to put it in the boot of his car.

Jenny saw some of her fellow parishioners streaming out from the church path looking askance at the young girl the O'Learys had taken in sitting in the doctor's car, and himself putting the child's wheelchair in the boot. Then there was

219

young Jenny O'Leary herself, deep in conversation with a young man. That will keep them guessing over their Sunday dinner, Jenny thought, and to give them further food for discussion, she linked her arm through Bob's and gave him a dazzling smile.

'He's a nice bloke, that doctor,' Bob said, as they began to walk towards the bus stop. 'Did you know he went to Linda's family funeral?'

'Yes, he told me,' Jenny said. 'He seems to think a lot of Linda. Sort of feels responsible for her.'

'He's not the only one,' Bob said with feeling. 'If you ask me, Linda Lennox is a lucky kid.'

'How can you say that?'

'Oh come on, Jen, I know she's had a bad time, but everyone's bending over backwards to help her now,' Bob said.

Jenny was silent. In a way she could see what Bob way saying, but he hadn't listened to Linda talking about her mother and little brothers like she had, and sensed the feeling between them. She knew she'd never be able to replace her family, however hard she'd tried. She was sure Linda would never totally get over her loss either, though she seemed to have come to terms with it now. If she, her family and Peter Sanders could help her, then she was glad to be able to do it.

'What's up?' Bob said. 'I haven't upset you, have I?'

'No, of course not, I was just thinking.'

'Oh dear, that sounds ominous.'

'Not really. It wasn't anything important. I was just mulling things over in my head.'

They'd reached the bus stop and stood waiting

for the Midland Red bus to take them to Sutton Coldfield so that they could walk to the park. 'Are you very hungry?' Bob said. 'The bus is due at half ten. What I mean is, can you wait to eat until we get to the park?'

Jenny's stomach growled with emptiness, but she said with a smile, 'Of course. Anyway, I can hardly stand in the street with a sandwich in my fist. If that got back to my mother she'd die of shame.'

'People don't die of shame,' Bob said dismissively. 'But still, I should have thought about it. I could have called for you after the service at your home, and then you'd have had a chance to eat some breakfast.'

'It's not important, really it isn't,' Jenny said. 'Peter Sanders didn't know what to make of it though,' she grinned. 'He probably doesn't know you have to fast in order to take Communion.'

'Peter – is that the doctor's name?'

'Yes. He told me to call him that, and I suppose it is silly to call him "Doctor" all the time. It's like him calling me Miss O'Leary.'

'I didn't think you knew him that well,' Bob said sharply.

Jenny could see the bus in the distance and she totally missed the odd note in Bob's voice. 'It's coming,' she said.

'Do you know the fellow well?' Bob asked again impatiently, ignoring Jenny's reference to the bus.

'Not well, I suppose,' Jenny said easily. 'I used to meet him at the hospital now and again, and he's been to the house a couple of times. He's been very helpful with transport, taking me to hospital for the concert on Christmas Eve and ferrying Linda back and forth and things like that.'

'Do you like him?' Bob asked.

Jenny looked at Bob. 'What a daft question. Of course I like him.'

The bus arrived with a squeal of brakes and Jenny leapt on to the platform before Bob could assist her and made for the stairs. 'I love riding on the top deck,' she said. 'Do you mind?'

Bob shook his head and nothing more was said until they were sitting together on the upper deck, when he began, 'You were telling me how much you like Peter Sanders.'

'Was I?' Jenny said. 'Well, I do like him and I don't understand why you're being so funny about it. He's taking me to the theatre on Friday, as a matter of fact.'

'He's *what?*' Bob was staggered by the stab of jealousy he felt at Jenny's words, and at an unreasonable hatred against the man he'd previously thought of as an 'all right bloke'. He wondered what was the matter with him, and why it hurt suddenly that she should even consider going out with another person.

At his exclamation heads had turned and Jenny said, 'Ssh.'

'I won't ssh,' Bob said. 'What d'you mean, you're going out with him?'

Anger blazed in Bob's eyes and Jenny was annoyed. He had no right to dictate to her. 'Hang on a minute,' she cried. 'Why the hell shouldn't I go out with him?'

Bob knew Jenny was right. There was no reason at all why she shouldn't go out with other people. He'd made no move to tell her she was special to him, and hadn't really been aware she was until now. The thought of her seeing someone else chewed him up inside. He'd been afraid of commitment, he realised. Even the previous day during the wedding, he'd been unsure whether he loved Jenny O'Leary or not. What a bloody fool he'd been, when just to look at her made his whole body tingle, and when she touched him, or they danced together, he felt like he was on fire. Oh yes, now he knew he loved Jenny and the sooner he told her the better. He took her hand in his. It felt stiff and unyielding because she was still so cross with him. His heart thumped in sudden fear. Maybe she wasn't ready for a declaration of love, maybe she didn't feel the same way and he would frighten her off, but he couldn't go on the way they were and pretend not to care, not if she wanted to see someone else.

'Because,' he said roughly, 'you're my girl, and I don't want you dating other men.'

Jenny could only stare at him. What was he talking about? She couldn't ask him either because the conductor was there jingling his leather bag and shouting, 'Tickets please.'

Jenny waited until the conductor had gone back down the stairs before she hissed, 'What do you mean, I'm your girl?'

'Well, you are – aren't you?' Bob said. 'I mean, I'd like you to be.'

'But you hardly know me.'

223

'Of course I know you. You and your Grand-mother O'Leary were all Anthony talked about, and when I saw your photograph I was very interested in learning all he had to say. Jenny, I've been in love with you for months, bloody fool that I am. I hardly knew myself, until now.'

'You can't have been,' Jenny said. She was floored by Bob's declaration, flattered certainly and a little suspicious.

'Why can't I?'

Jenny stared at him wondering if she should say that he couldn't care for her or he'd have tried something on in the cinema, or given her a more passionate kiss. Even the previous day at the wedding, although he'd held her close, his kisses had been not the least disturbing. But what would he think of her then, she wondered. No, she couldn't say any of it. So instead she said, 'You don't really know me. You just know *of* me. How can you say I'm your girl after such a short acquaintance?'

'I don't know,' Bob said. 'How does anyone know how these things happen? I just knew I was interested in the picture of Anthony O'Leary's sister, from the moment I saw it tucked inside Anthony's wallet. And, when I saw you standing in the doorway, the day I came to tell you about Anthony's death and gave you his letter I ... I knew I'd found someone special.' And, he thought, I refused to recognise it. He'd treated her like many of his previous dates, and now he had to know how Jenny felt. 'How do you feel about me, Jenny?' he asked.

How did she feel? Pleased to see him certainly,

or far more than just pleased? Her stomach went into knots when she thought of him and her heart thudded almost painfully against her ribs. 'I like you,' she admitted at last.

'Like me?'

'I like you a lot,' Jenny said.

'You don't love me just a little?'

'I don't know,' Jenny said. 'How do you know when you love someone?'

'I can't explain it,' Bob said. 'But I'm sure I love you.'

'Oh Bob.' Tears blurred Jenny's eyes. Those were words she never thought she'd hear a man say to her. Surely such a handsome man couldn't love her? Surely he was just playing with her feelings?

'What is it?' Bob said, seeing her woebegone expression.

'Oh, Bob, please don't just joke about this, or try to be kind. I can't bear it,' Jenny said.

'Who's being kind?'

'You can't mean you love me, not really?'

'Why on earth not?'

'Oh, look at me, for God's sake!' Jenny cried. 'We've had this discussion before and I told you then to get your eyes tested. I'm not attractive to men! My mother and sister Geraldine told me so many times that, not only am I plain, I also put men off by my attitude. I've never had a boyfriend, Bob.'

Bob laughed, and Jenny, almost in tears, was outraged. 'Don't laugh. It's bad enough to look like I do, without being laughed at.'

'Oh God Jenny, I'm not laughing at you,' Bob

said, trying to control his mirth. 'I just can't believe you see yourself like this.'

'But I don't look anything like Anthony, or the others,' Jenny wailed.

'Well, not everyone likes the same type of person, and a good job too,' Bob said. 'You appeal to me, Jenny. I think you're beautiful and I told you that once before too. I want to be someone special in your life.'

'Oh Bob, I wish I could believe that.'

'If we were off this damned bus I'd prove it to you,' Bob said, and Jenny leaned against him with a sigh. He cuddled her up close and Jenny would have been happy to stay like that all day.

Chapter Thirteen

Jenny hovered outside the house that evening, waiting for Peter Sanders to return with Linda, for she needed to tell him their date for Friday was off. After the time she'd spent in Sutton Park with Bob, she knew the feelings she had for him meant it wasn't right for her to go out with another man.

Peter wasn't surprised at Jenny's news that there was someone special in her life. Not only had he seen the depth of feeling in Bob's eyes that very morning, but Linda was quite keen to go on about it too. 'Jenny doesn't know,' she said. 'She's flipping barmy at times, she is. Thinks she's ugly, just 'cos she doesn't look like the others.'

That had been news to Peter and he wondered at it. Jenny wasn't stupid: why couldn't she see how striking she looked? He thought. True, she didn't resemble her mother, but she had a beauty of her own, and her courage and determination belied her slight frame and made Peter want to look after her.

He wasn't sure when he'd fallen in love with Jenny, but now the feeling was getting between him and his sleep. It was hopeless, he recognised that. Jenny was not the sort of girl to give her heart lightly and it had been obvious that Bob Masters loved her and she certainly felt something for him. Peter knew she'd never viewed him as anything other than a friend.

His mother would say that there were plenty more fish in the sea, but when you have the prize in your sights, no man likes to settle for second best. However Peter was not one to sulk over things he couldn't have, though he drove home deep in thought.

He was glad that at least Linda had had a nice day. She'd got on remarkably well with his mother Mabel, who'd told the child snippets of gossip about the neighbours, that Peter wasn't sure had any basis in fact. However, after seeing Linda smile and hearing her laugh, he said nothing. He knew the visit to the grave might be upsetting and traumatic, and if she could have a bit of enjoyment first, he wasn't going to stop her.

And the visit to the grave *was* upsetting, although Linda explained how she knew the important part of her mother and brothers wasn't buried under the mound of earth. Often, she'd said, it was a whiff of a certain scent or a snatch of a song that could still make her cry, yet seeing the grave brought the horror of it all to her mind again. She arranged the flowers Peter had cut for her in the pot his mother had found. The tears ran from her eyes as she said goodbye to her mother and George and little Harry all over again.

Peter had watched from a respectful distance while a lump formed in his throat. He was mightily glad he was taking her out to town for a slap-up meal afterwards and then on to see *The*

Thief of Baghdad at the Odeon cinema in New Street. And so for her, the day had ended splendidly after all. He'd been surprised he'd enjoyed it so much. He'd done it because he'd promised Linda as a sort of duty and he hadn't expected to get much pleasure out of it, but he had.

Mabel Sanders came upon her son that evening, sitting in the living room and staring into space, with quite a large whisky in a glass beside him, and a look on his face she could only describe as bereft. She didn't need a crystal ball to know who'd put it there and it wasn't the child with whom he'd spent the day.

He'd never stopped talking about a certain Jenny O'Leary, ever since the rescue of Linda. She was sure he wasn't aware how often he brought her name into the conversation, or how his eyes softened as he did.

Mabel would have given her life for her son, but she knew she couldn't help him through this. It was obvious even from the little that Linda had said to her, that Jenny loved another, and from the look on Peter's face she must have told him how things were. She sighed heavily, but didn't go into the room. Instead she crossed to the stairs and slowly made her way to bed.

Peter heard her. He was surprised she hadn't come in to wish him good night, but very glad. He felt he couldn't have taken her chatter that night without snapping the head off her, and she didn't deserve that.

He sipped his whisky and remembered his mother saying that Norah O'Leary's bad humour was something to do with some dreadful tragedy that had happened in Ireland. 'Years ago, you understand – when The Troubles were at their height and terrible things were happening all the time,' she'd said. 'She blamed her husband for it, apparently. Of course, I don't know all the details.'

'Really, Mother?' Peter had said. 'You amaze me. You must be slipping.'

'Don't be so provoking,' his mother had reproved. 'I'm interested in people, that's all.'

'Nosy would be a better word.'

'Perhaps. Call me what you like. Anyway, that's why she took to her bed, people say.'

'Who took to her bed?'

'Why, Norah O'Leary, of course! People say she was always snooty anyway, but when she became disabled, it was done as a form of penance for her husband. She had him running after her for years.'

'So, you've examined the woman and with your extensive medical knowledge, you know that she is suffering from nothing more than resentment and revenge?' Peter had suggested sarcastically at the time. He hadn't met Jenny then.

His mother had flapped a dismissive hand in front of her face and said, 'Scoff, go on, I don't mind. But that's what people say.'

'Mother, people used to say the world was flat.' But for all he'd scorned the gossip his mother had collected, he did remember what she'd said about the marriage between the amenable Irishman for whom everyone had a good word, and the aloof woman he'd married, who seemed

230

to have ideas above her station. He also remembered that when the father had died, some of his own patients had shaken their heads; they reckoned that the young lass would be landed with the job of looking after her mother. There wasn't one that hadn't thought it wasn't a daughter's duty to do just that, but they'd still pitied her.

The antagonism aroused by Linda's presence in the house did not abate as the days passed. Eileen and Norah ignored her as much as possible. They seldom or never spoke to her by name, but leapt on Jenny for any small misdemeanour, real or imagined. Jenny soldiered on and Linda often thought the two older women needed a smack in the gob to teach them some manners, but she kept these thoughts to herself.

Twice a week Jenny was at the warden post. She'd discussed this with Linda and offered to give it up for a while, but Linda wouldn't hear of it. She knew it was only through Jenny being a warden that she'd been rescued at all, and she wouldn't ask her to stay and keep her company when she could be doing some good elsewhere.

Jenny felt the same, but although the raids had increased through April, few bombs, landmines or incendiaries fell anywhere near Pype Hayes. She often felt useless as she made tea and chatted to Stan while she did a bit of knitting. She was restless, and often worried about Linda back at home and missed Gladys who'd asked for a transfer to a city centre post. Gladys's youngest son had been killed just after New Year. A month later, her elder son was posted as Missing – and that had seemed to suck the very life out of Gladys. Then she'd seemed to pull herself together again. 'Those buggers took my lads,' she said. 'And, I'm not going to let their deaths be in vain. I've got to be where I can be of some use.'

Jenny sympathised with her determination, but she now had a responsibility to care for Linda and, she thought, the child had suffered enough losses in her short life. 'Anyway,' Stan said, 'maybe Hitler's finished with us at last.'

Maybe, Jenny agreed, and thought to herself that it would be lovely if she could believe that.

Just before Easter, one Wednesday night, the sirens blared out at ten o'clock in the evening. Linda had gone to bed and Jenny was in the kitchen preparing supper for her mother, grandmother and herself before she joined her. The sirens had caused her to jump and drop some of their precious tea ration on to the floor as she was spooning it out of the caddy at the time.

Eileen and Norah looked at each other across the fireplace with no sign of panic. Jenny knew that they would only take shelter under the stairs if the planes were heard heading their way. Really it was Linda she was worried about. The youngster was terrified of air raids – in fact, any loud noises – and after her experience, it was not to be wondered at.

Jenny got another cup down and poured out four cups of tea. Leaving two for her mother and grandmother, she took the other two up to the bedroom. There was little sleep for the girls that night, and though none of the planes came close enough to cause them to take shelter, the raid was severe. They sat at the window most of the night and watched as the city centre burned and the night sky glowed a reddy orange colour, and they held each other tight and wept.

That same evening, Francesca Masters, Bob's mother, had decided to come home. She'd mouldered long enough in Devon, she decided. Anyway, she was intrigued about the young girl Bob had written to her about and who, he claimed, sang like an angel. Francesca would have imagined a romantic attachment, had it not been for the fact that the girl was only twelve years old. But something had caused him to wax lyrical about the young girl's talents and abilities, because neither he nor his sister, Juliana, had the slightest interest in music, to her great disappointment.

Long before they reached New Street Station they were stopped. In the black night they could see bombers pounding the heart out of the city and Francesca felt cross that she'd been sent away like some fragile hot-house plant, while others had stayed and lived and worked with danger at their shoulder all the time.

Eventually, the train was shunted into a siding to await instructions before continuing. There was no food or water and only basic amenities, but none of the passengers grumbled. They'd all seen what was happening just a few miles away and it seemed very unpatriotic to make a fuss. Most, including Francesca, settled down for a long, uncomfortable night and she reflected long and hard on what she had actually been protected from, and why.

It was Easter Saturday before Jenny heard that Gladys was one of the casualties of that bombing raid. 'Fellow came round to tell me,' Stan Walker said. 'Decent of him really. He said he knew she'd once worked here along with me, and he found my address in her diary in her bag.'

'What happened?'

'She was rescuing folk when the building caved in,' Stan said. 'Never stood a chance.'

The news of Gladys's death really upset Jenny. She couldn't seem to lift the depression. She tried, for Linda's sake, but the girl wasn't fooled. What was really affecting Jenny was the fact that she had nearly put in for a transfer like Gladys had. Every time she thought of Anthony, she'd wanted to, but then when she remembered Linda, she'd felt she couldn't put herself at so much risk. And Gladys had died. If Jenny had been there, she might have died too. Many did, including the sick and doctors and nurses at the General Hospital when it was hit so badly that Lewis's department store had to open their basement to the wounded.

She knew the city centre would never be the same. High Street and New Street were burnt out. Gone also was the Odeon cinema Peter had taken Linda to on New Street, and the Prince of Wales Theatre in Broad Street that he would have taken her to, if their date had ever come off. The fires had been so fierce, it had been eight o'clock the next morning before they'd been brought under control. Jenny was affected with a deep and severe depression and Linda, remembering her mother's similar complaint, wondered if there was any way she could lift her out of it. But in the end it was Maureen who thought of something to help Jenny.

Jenny's twenty-first birthday was on 27 April, and Maureen had been considering having a party for her the day before, which was a Saturday. She was determined on this when she saw how low and dispirited her granddaughter was after the raid which had killed her friend Gladys. 'It's honestly not to be wondered at though, is it?' Peggy said, one evening when Maureen expressed concern. 'But sure, Gladys wasn't the only one killed that night. I think a party would be the right thing.'

And so the preparations for it went on. Peggy asked their workmates and Maureen the neighbours, and Linda wrote to Bob after copying his address from the book in Jenny's handbag.

'He won't be able to come, you know,' Maureen warned. 'He'd never get leave.'

'Aye, I believe he near had to stand on his head to get the weekend off for my wedding, Jenny told me afterwards,' Peggy put in. 'But still, you're right to tell him, for knowing Jenny, she'll not have said a word.'

Linda was very excited about it.

'What a pity you won't be able to dance at it though,' Linda's friend Carole said sadly one day at school, looking at the heavy calliper still encasing one of Linda's legs. Carole was fanatical about dancing and the Duke Ellington sound, and the jitter-bugging craze coming over from America.

'I'd rather be able to walk than dance,' Linda said. 'Anyway, I don't mind. This is Jenny's twenty-first. Don't you worry – I'll be able to dance fine at my own.'

And then, just two days before the great day, Bob was invalided home to recover from shrapnel wounds in his leg. He'd given Jenny no indication that he'd even been in the military hospital, and it was a total shock to see him arrive at the door on Thursday evening. 'Don't fuss,' he said, when Jenny had recovered a little and realised he was hurt. 'They've got all the muck out now and I've been sent home for a week or so, until I heal properly.'

But Jenny wanted to fuss. Bob sat in the living room with her mother, grandmother and Linda, telling them about the dogfight that he'd survived and not only survived, but got the plane down in one piece though shot to blazes. Jenny listened at the door, only too well aware that he could have been just another statistic of the war, another young pilot shot down like her brother. Would she cope if that happened to Bob? It didn't bear thinking about, but in facing up to it, she realised two things. The first was how much Bob was beginning to mean to her, and the second was that however sad she was about Gladys's death and however guilty she felt, life had to go on.

Later, as Bob and Jenny walked in the warm spring evening she said, 'Is this harmful for your leg? Should you be walking like this?'

236

'It's good for me,' Bob told her. 'It's what the doc told me to do – go for walks to stop it stiffening up, you know. He even said I'd find it more enjoyable if I found a pretty girl to walk with. I pity any other poor chaps given the same advice, because I've captured the prettiest girl in the British Isles.'

'Bob, you are a fool,' Jenny said, but she couldn't resist laughing at him.

'Ah, but you love me for it don't you?' Bob said, and was pleasantly surprised when Jenny said, 'D'you know, I think you may be right.'

Bob brought her to an abrupt stop and turning to face her he said, 'Did you mean that?'

'W ... what?' Jenny startled, but knowing full well what he was asking.

'About loving me?'

'Yes.

'Say it,' he commanded.

'I ... I can't.'

'You can,' Bob said. 'It's easy, and gets easier the more often you say it. Listen; "I love you, love you, love you",' he said, planting a kiss on her two eyes and her nose.

'Don't,' Jenny said, trying to pull away. 'We're in the street, anyone could see us,' and she looked around fearfully.

'Don't dodge the issue, Jenny O'Leary,' Bob said, and in a wheedling tone continued, 'Come on, put a chap out of his misery.'

Jenny looked into Bob's deep brown eyes and her legs felt as if they were made of jelly. Sweat broke out under her armpits and also on the palms of her hands that Bob was holding, and she said softly, 'I love you, Bob.'

After all that, how could the party be other than a success, especially after Bob presented her with a mizpah. Jenny had never heard of one, so Bob had to explain that one person wore one of the pendants, and you gave the other to someone you loved. The message could only be read when the two split halves were put together. The message on Bob and Jenny's mizpah said; *The Lord watch between me and thee while we are absent from one another.*

Jenny was delighted with it, and vowed she would wear it always. In a way, she thought of it as a sort of talisman. While she wore the mizpah she was calling on the Lord to keep them both safe, and surely she thought, He would honour such a wish. That and the party, when friends and relatives came to share in Jenny's coming of age, was like a bright light in a dark world when the war seemed to be escalating and ordinary people, as well as servicemen, were being killed in droves.

But Jenny was determined to forget about war for this one night, her birthday, knowing that there wasn't one person there who didn't wish her the very best. Linda was so glad to see that Jenny seemed to have recovered her good spirits; she didn't care whether it was the party, or Bob that had worked the magic, she was just glad to see her happy and like her old self again. And Jenny was so happy, little frissons of it kept leaping up inside her when she looked at Bob, or held his hand, or danced with him. It lent a sparkle to her eyes and a glow to her face, and most of the people in the room knew that something had happened between Jenny O'Leary and the young man with the limp, who was dressed in Air Force blue.

Much later, after most of the guests had gone, Bob and Jenny went out into the garden. Jenny was glad of the blackout, which ensured that no one could see them as Bob took her in his arms; his kiss seemed to melt her very bones. Bob didn't want it to end there either, but he told himself to have patience. One day this woman would be his wife, of that he was determined. Until then, he would show her proper respect and not frighten her to death.

To help him keep this resolve he broke off a little, though he still held Jenny close as he said, 'Would you like to come and meet my mother tomorrow?'

'I thought your mother was in Devon?'

'Not any more,' Bob said. 'I told you she wouldn't stay. Mind you, her timing is priceless. She decided to come home the night of that big raid in Birmingham. She said her train was held up for hours in sidings outside New Street Station. But anyway, she'd back now.'

'Does she want to see me?'

'Of course she does! Any mother would be curious to meet the girl who's captured her son's heart.'

'Oh Bob, do be quiet,' Jenny said, glad he couldn't see her face which she knew would be flushed crimson.

'It's true!' he protested.

'I hope you didn't say that. I'd be too embarrassed to meet her,' Jenny said.

Bob kissed her gently on the lips and admitted, 'No, sweet Jenny, I didn't. She does want to meet you though, and is more than curious about our Linda.'

'Why?'

'Because, my dear, my mother is a music-teacher,' Bob said. 'Much to her disgust, Jules and I have no musical talent of any sort, though she made us both learn piano and even that...'

'Bob,' Jenny interrupted. 'What are you talking about?'

'Linda's singing,' Bob said. 'I told her about it, and she said she would like to hear what she can do. You did say you wanted Linda to have the chance to be professionally trained.'

'Why did you never say your mother was a music-teacher?' Jenny demanded.

'You never asked.'

'Oh Bob, you are so aggravating,' Jenny sighed. 'And though I'm sure your mother is very good, you must know I can't afford to pay anyone?'

'My dear Jenny, she doesn't want paying.'

'But, if she's a teacher ... I mean, it's a business for her.'

'Believe me, when she hears Linda sing, she will teach her for the joy of it,' Bob said. 'Anyway, I've already said you'd go.'

'Oh, have you?' Jenny said, still annoyed. 'Next time, I'd like to be given the choice before you start arranging things. What time does your mother want us there?'

'I suggested that I came to collect you both after dinner, which will give us some time to

240

ourselves in the afternoon, while Mother talks to Linda. Later we'll all have tea together.' He cocked his head on one side and said, 'Are those arrangements to your satisfaction, madam?'

Jenny was forced to smile. 'Yes, I suppose so,' she said. 'Though I don't know what Linda will make of it.'

'Well, don't ask her now,' Bob warned. 'Come on and show me how much you love me.'

And Jenny went into Bob's embrace and returned his kisses with a passion that surprised them both. Bob held her tighter still and thanked God he'd found such a girl, and Jenny said a silent prayer to keep Bob safe and sound until the end of the war.

In truth, Linda wasn't all that pleased to be asked to go and sing in front of a strange lady, however good she was at music, and not pleased either that it had all been arranged without asking her. But Jenny wanted her to go, Linda knew, so she said nothing about it.

Both girls were awed by the house which was approached by a curved driveway, hidden from the road behind high privet hedges. The house was quite square and solid-looking, built of red brick. In front of it were well tended lawns, and there were flowerbeds in a riot of colour beneath the bay windows which lay on either side of the oak studded front door. 'Mother is expecting us,' Bob said, and opened the door and ushered them inside.

Linda left her wheelchair in the porch and they both stepped into an oak-panelled hall, which seemed bathed in sunshine from the big landing windows. The parquet floor beneath their feet gleamed, Jenny guessed, from years of polishing and a large carpeted staircase went up from the centre.

As Bob took their coats, a lady came out of one of the rooms on the ground floor with her hands outstretched, and Jenny noticed the long slender fingers bedecked with rings.

Francesca was darker-skinned than Bob, and her hair, tied up with decorated combs, was just as black and shiny. Her eyes were oval-shaped and deep brown, her classic nose was perfect like you might see on a sculpture, and her lips were full. Even her neck, the one thing that betrayed a woman's age, was unlined and graceful, and from her ears dangled hoop earrings.

But for all her loveliness, her eyes were kind and her smile of welcome genuine. She grasped Jenny with one hand and Linda with the other. 'I am so glad you could come,' she said. 'Roberto has told me so much about you. I longed to meet you both.'

Roberto! Jenny thought. Of course, that would be his full name. He'd just been Bob to her. She caught the light of mischief in Linda's eyes and knew she was amused by the name Francesca Masters called her son, and hoped she wouldn't laugh. She needn't have worried. Although she might tease Bob about it later, Linda had more sense than to laugh at his mother.

Francesca drew them towards the room she'd come from, but slowly because the calliper on Linda's leg was hampering her. Their feet sank into a thick carpet which was beige and deep red, and Jenny looked around the room. A three-piece suite of beige velvet, with plump dark red cushions, was pulled up in front of the ornate fireplace. A curly red rug lay before the gleaming hearth with its shiny brass fender and cosy crackling fire.

'Do please sit down,' Francesca said, and Jenny sat on the settee with Linda beside her. She had an urge to touch the wallpaper, above the panelled wood. It was a Regency stripe in beige and red to match the carpet, and Jenny knew it would have a velvety feel to it. She'd also have liked to stroke the dark red brocade drapes at the windows, but she did none of these things of course and kept her hands firmly in her lap.

She felt slightly uncomfortable, for although she knew that Bob came from a far richer home than herself – she'd known that from the beginning – she still felt slightly intimidated in these surroundings.

Bob had told her that Francesca would now be taking over the role of gardener, keeping the weeds under control and 'digging for victory'. But Jenny still found it hard to imagine the graceful, impeccably dressed Francesca in overalls, grubbing around in the dirty soil for a few vegetables. Linda had glimpsed the back garden through the conservatory windows and she said it was so big it was like a small park, and what's more, one that was beautifully looked after – in fact not a weed in sight, she'd told Jenny.

Bob came limping in with a tray of tea then and

243

smiled at her, guessing she was nervous. He sat down beside her and gave her a hand to squeeze.

The movement brought Francesca's eyes round to her again, and she said, 'My Roberto tells me you are a very brave lady. I believe this, too.'

Jenny smiled at the woman, and said, 'He probably makes it sound worse than it was.'

'Well,' Linda argued, 'It couldn't have been much worse.'

Jenny's face flamed in embarrassment and Francesca, seeing her discomfort, attempted to change the subject. 'Is your full name Jenny, my dear?' she asked.

'No, it's Jennifer,' Jenny said. 'But I've always been called Jenny.'

'Ah, this is the way of the British people,' Francesca said. 'Their lives are too busy. They rush, rush, rush so much they haven't time even to give a person their full name. So, I am Francesca and yet I'm called Fran. My Roberto becomes Bob while Juliana is Jules, and my husband Malcolm is known as Mal.'

'That's just the way things are, Mother,' Bob said. 'I think Jenny is friendlier than Jennifer.'

'Maybe so, but it is strange that no one uses their rightful given name,' Francesca said. 'But, Linda at least is just Linda. And, I believe you sing, my dear?'

'I sing a bit,' Linda admitted, accepting a cup of tea from Francesca. 'I don't know if I'm any good.'

'In a little while we shall find out,' Francesca said. 'Is that what you wish?'

Linda didn't know what she wished, but she

knew it was what Jenny wanted. She glanced across at her and said, 'Yes, please.'

'We will see what you are made of shortly,' Francesca said. 'For now, drink your tea and we will talk.'

And how they talked! At first Linda felt rather resentful of this woman, who seemed to want to know everything about her and her family; it had nothing at all to do with singing. But then she realised it was true interest and that Mrs Masters really seemed to care and sympathise sincerely, when Linda explained about her mother and brothers being killed. Francesca went on to ask Linda about any experience she'd had in singing, which of course had been nil – unless you counted the singing she'd done for fun.

'That is amateur singing,' Francesca said, 'and no bad thing. For I can teach no one to sing well, unless they have a burning desire to use their voice. You appear to have that. We will see, and if it is there, I will develop it. You want this too – yes?'

Linda really wasn't sure, but felt she could do nothing but agree.

Francesca smiled, and said, 'Come my dear, we'll go into the sitting room, and find out what you can do.'

The sitting room faced the back of the house and the door to it led off the large square hall. Francesca led the way and Linda felt her mouth to be so dry, she wondered if she'd be able to sing a note. When Francesca opened the door and she stepped over the threshold she was almost sure she wouldn't.

There was a thick, green, patterned carpet on the floor and a large, very expensive-looking piano opposite her, with a stool made of the same wood with a tapestry seat on it. Black armchairs were arranged before the fireplace, which was black and gold with brass ornaments on the mantelpiece. A firescreen in Chinese designs, again in black and gold, hid part of the empty hearth from view, and a gilt-edged mirror hung above it on the wall.

There were shelves fitted in the two chimney alcoves, and all along one wall from the floor to the ceiling; they were filled with more books than Linda had ever seen in her life. She stopped and stared.

Seeing Linda's amazement, Francesca was slightly amused, but knowing there was probably little enough money in Jenny's house for books, she said to the girl, 'Those are mainly my husband's, for he uses this room as a sort of office. They are all catalogued and we'd be sure to find something to suit you if you'd like to borrow some books now and again. Malcolm had the children's classics removed from the nursery and stored them down here as Roberto and Juliana grew up. I'm sure you'd enjoy *The Railway Children* by E. Nesbit, if you haven't read it already. It was one of my Juliana's favourites.'

The first books Linda had ever owned had been given to her by Jenny at Christmas and she looked at the beautifully bound books and said, 'You mean it?'

'Of course I do,' Francesca said briskly. 'I wouldn't have said it if I didn't. But let's leave the subject of books for now, my dear. Come over to the piano and I'll see what you're made of.'

What Linda was made of, impressed Francesca very much. She was excited, like any teacher would be, at finding a gifted pupil and she knew Linda had exceptional talent.

The afternoon sped past as Francesca tutored Linda on scales and pitch and snatches of songs which she had her repeat over and over. Eventually she closed the piano, and said, 'Enough, my dear. Your throat must be raw. I'm a hard taskmaster, I'm afraid.'

'No,' Linda said. 'I'm all right.'

'And will you come and see me every Saturday morning?'

'Yes,' said Linda, and added honestly, 'I'll be glad to.'

Linda was tired on the way home and her legs hurt; she was mightily glad of the wheelchair. Jenny could see how exhausted she was and felt sorry for her. It was a month from Linda's thirteenth birthday, the first one her mother wouldn't be there for and Jenny was determined to do something special for her.

'What would you like most of all for your birthday next month?' she said.

Linda could have said, 'to have everything back the way it was,' but she was no longer a child and had to accept that her mother and brothers were dead and gone; no wishing in the world would bring them back. There was no sense either in mentioning anything about it and upsetting Jenny, who was trying to be kind. 'Well now,' she said, her head on one side as if she was attempting to think, 'I'll tell you what I'd like. I'd like to get this bloody calliper off my leg and to never need this stinking wheelchair ever again.'

'Is that all?' Jenny said sarcastically. 'That's all right then. For a minute or two, I thought you were going to ask for the impossible. I'll go straight into the hospital on my way home from work tomorrow, and tell them it must be done, because you say so.'

Linda grinned and said, 'Maybe I could settle for going to the pictures, or you could take me for a meal if you're feeling flush, or to the theatre, or all three if you like.'

'And maybe I could just tip you out of this wheelchair if you're not careful,' Jenny said. 'It had better be me that thinks up a treat for you before you bankrupt me altogether.' And she knew whatever it took and whatever it cost, she was determined to give Linda a birthday to remember.

Chapter Fourteen

May, 1944

By 1944 Linda had been living with the O'Learys for three years. Gone now was the rather puny, undersized child; and in her place was a young lady. She still had a small frame and would never be tall, but she was a very pretty girl with a good figure, her best feature being her large eyes.

Martin and Francis had a few days' unexpected leave in late May of that year, arriving home just a few days before Linda's sixteenth birthday. Both boys had always liked her and showed it, and had teased her as if she'd been a younger sister, but this leave Martin realised the child Linda had gone. He watched her as she bustled around the kitchen that Saturday afternoon preparing the evening meal for them all as Jenny and Peggy had taken a trip to the Bull Ring, a rare treat now for them both to get out together.

'Nearly sixteen, Linda,' Martin commented. 'How's it feel then to be getting on, nearly an old lady now?'

'No doubt I'll be able to cope with it,' Linda answered drily.

'Sweet sixteen and never been kissed, eh, Linda?' he teased.

She glanced up at him and smiled. 'That would be telling.'

'Oh, hoity toity miss,' Francis said. 'Does Jenny know your little secret?'

'No one knows my secrets, otherwise they wouldn't be secrets, would they?'

'She has you there,' Martin said, and gave a bellow of laughter.

'Ssh,' Linda cautioned and pointed her thumb at the door.

The two men knew what she meant. Their mother hated them chaffing and teasing Linda. In fact, she hated them going anywhere near her at all. Neither of them could understand her attitude. Linda had been living with the O'Learys for some time, after all. Martin thought she should have got over any antagonism and he would tease Linda if he wanted to. 'Don't be scared of her,' he said. 'We're doing no harm.'

'I'm not scared of her,' Linda said scornfully.

'Martin! Francis!' came a sudden authoritative voice from the living room.

Linda gripped the edge of the sink, so tightly that her knuckles showed white, and then she jerked her head and said, 'You'd better go. She wants you.'

'I'll go when I'm good and ready,' Martin said.

Heedless of her wet hands, Linda gave him a push. 'Go on,' she said. 'The two of you go and see what she wants and leave me to get on.'

'I'll go when I'm ready,' Martin said again. 'After all, what can she do?'

'To you, nothing,' Linda said grimly. 'I know full well if she gets into a temper who will bear the brunt of it.'

'Come on, Martin,' Francis said, his smile

gone. 'Linda's right. Anyway, we've only got a forty-eight-hour pass. Let's not upset the old girl more than we have to.'

'Oh no, we mustn't upset her,' Martin said bitterly. 'By God, when this war's over there'll have to be some changes here.'

But then, he knew there would be. If his plans went the way he wanted, he'd be married as soon as this whole thing was over. He'd marry his girlfriend Dora tomorrow if she'd go for it, but she didn't seem to want to rush things. She'd drive him mad if he didn't get answers soon, because he'd dated her for six months and knew her to be good and kind, with a body a man would sell his soul for. The point was, it was *his* soul she was worried about. But he couldn't give a toss that all her people were in the Sally Army and that she'd been heavily involved herself until she'd enlisted. Martin could just imagine his mother's face if he joined her church and marched up the Pype Hayes Estate banging his tambourine. The vision and her probable reaction had made him smile.

But when he told Dora, she hadn't seen the funny side of it at all. 'Talk to her, Martin. Let her know we worship the same God.'

Talk to her? It would be like talking to a man-eating shark and would make no difference either. Dora didn't know his mother. But whatever Norah said, with or without her permission or blessing, he was going to marry Dora and the sooner Dora realised that, the better he would feel.

But Francis was right. There was no point in

251

upsetting his mother now. Martin gave his brother a push and Linda a shrug of his shoulders before going into the living room. Linda watched the men leave with relief and went back to the sink for she had plenty to do, and she wanted the evening meal to be ready before Jenny got home from town.

But as she peeled and chopped the vegetables, her mind wandered back over the last three years she'd spent in the O'Leary household. It had been difficult for her in the beginning, and not just because of the attitude of the two older women. Geraldine had been antagonistic too then, and though her boys had been friendly enough, she hadn't seen that much of them. Only with Jenny, Seamus's wife Jan, and particularly Maureen and her family, did she feel completely at peace.

In many ways they'd been her lifesavers because in the early days she'd found it very hard to live with people who seemed to so actively dislike her and were resentful of her presence. Another person who'd always given Linda's battered ego a boost was Francesca Masters.

Over the years, a friendship had developed between the woman and child so keen to learn everything she had to teach her and not just in music and singing either. Going through her enormous collection of books had opened up new horizons for Linda. It had even spilled over into other school subjects such as maths, which Linda had found so difficult in the past. Francesca had always been willing to help her in such subjects, and Linda found she enjoyed

252

school more when she wasn't constantly behind.

The teachers had been pleased and surprised at her progress and presumed Jenny was helping her at home, and Linda didn't tell them any different. No one knew of her singing lessons and that's how Linda wanted it. People would think she was peculiar as it was, wanting to learn to sing properly, so she told no one of her visits to Francesca Masters. Eventually as the months passed, despite the strained atmosphere of the house, Linda felt more able to cope.

She'd been a bit anxious though about Christmas 1941, but she wasn't alone, for no one had been really looking forward to Christmas that year. The war was dragging on: as Maureen O'Leary remarked, it seemed like they were all taking one step forward and two back all the time.

In November 1941, they were told of the massive losses in shipping – 750,000 tons scattered over various ocean beds between July and October. 'How can they manage with losses like that?' Jenny had asked her gran one day in dismay.

'It's desperate all right,' Maureen said. 'And how many men did we lose on those ships? That's another loss.'

'Aye, that's another tale altogether,' Peggy had said. 'All we can be glad of, is that the only one sailor lost his life, when the *Ark Royal* finally sank.'

Linda supposed they should be glad, but to lose an aircraft carrier of such a size, which was torpedoed on 14 November, was a major blow.

So she could understand the adults' despondency a little. This deepened when the Japanese, who already occupied parts of China and Indo-China, much to America's disquiet, bombed Pearl Harbor on 7 December.

America was thrust into the war, whether they wanted to be or not, and many thought it was about time. No one however, was prepared for the scale of the massive Japanese onslaught. The world had looked on in horrified amazement as the following day, the Philippines, Thailand and Singapore were bombed and further Japanese troops landed in Malaya. By December they occupied Bangkok and were granted free passage through Thailand by the frightened government.

And so it went on, battle after battle. Christmas had been a fairly muted affair, although the O'Leary household, or certainly Jenny, Geraldine and Linda herself, had tried to make it a more festive occasion for the children's sake. But it had been difficult.

The Japanese marched on as 1942 dawned and Allied Forces withdrew to Singapore. It was said to be impregnable despite the heavy bombing raids inflicted on it since the beginning of the war. However, it fell to the Japanese on 15 February, and 64,000 British, Indian and Australian defenders were forced to surrender after 9,000 had been killed in combat. Winston Churchill, speaking to the nation on the wireless later, described the Fall of Singapore as the 'worst disaster and largest capitulation in British history'.

American GIs began arriving in Britain and

Linda had her first sight of them when she was taken into the Orthopaedic Hospital to have her calliper removed for good, just before her fourteenth birthday. It had been a great day for both her and Jenny, who had gone with her and treated her to lunch afterwards to celebrate her freedom from the heavy iron that had imprisoned her leg for so long. For the first time since the accident, Linda felt she was just like other girls.

The next day she told Maureen of the Yanks she'd glimpsed from the windows of the taxi as they'd travelled through the town. Maureen knew many girls' heads had been turned by the GIs, as they were smarter in dress than the average British Tommy. Besides all that, they also seemed to have an unlimited supply of money, chocolate, chewing gum and even nylons for the chosen few.

In fact, tales of their exploits were told far and wide. Beattie, who'd become a great friend of Maureen's over the years, had told them what it was like living amongst them as she'd dropped into Maureen's one evening in June, just a month or so after Linda's fourteenth birthday. 'Taken over a shed they have, the Yanks, by the railway station in Sutton Coldfield,' Beattie had said. 'A big shed, mind. Have to be bleeding big 'cos that's where they're dealing with all the US mail. Imagine that? But I tell you, Linda; you can't walk down the bleeding street without being accosted. Our Victoria's in her oiltot,' she went on. 'Wearing make-up now – lipstick, rouge, the lot. And the clothes she wears! I said to her the other day, is there any point putting that on? There was so little of it, you know. Course, she wasn't best pleased and her mother said I should leave her alone.'

'Oh, come on, Beattie,' Maureen grinned. 'Don't be on about her all the time. The girl's only young.'

'You don't know her,' Beattie said darkly. 'And she's not only young, Maureen, she's a bloody fool.'

Maureen had pushed a cup of tea and plate of scones across the kitchen table. Beattie stopped to draw breath, and taking up a scone she split it and buttered it lightly, before she said, 'I don't know how you get the stuff to make things like this.'

'Well, it's just flour, a bit of fat and a bit of milk.' Maureen was glad to get off the subject of Beattie's niece. 'It fills a hole, anyway.'

'It certainly does,' Beattie agreed. 'Have you tried the horsemeat yet? That fills a bleeding hole as well.'

'Aye, Peggy got some down the Bull Ring,' Maureen said. 'Jenny got some too, didn't she, Linda?'

'Yeah,' Linda answered. but added. 'She didn't dare tell her mom and the other one though. They think it was beef. You wouldn't know the difference, 'cept it takes more cooking. It's better than the whalemeat they sell, any road. I never thought I'd eat that stuff.'

'Aye, but that's not so bad made into fish pie, and at least it's something else to eat on a Friday,' Maureen said.

'And better than dried egg that doesn't taste like egg at all,' Beattie put in.

'Still and all, it makes a meal,' Maureen said. 'And God knows we can't afford to be choosy. Stop moaning now and let Linda tell you her bit of news.'

'What's this?'

'It's about what I'll do after July. You know, when I leave school,' Linda told her.

'What's that then?'

A smile played around Linda's mouth as she remembered back to that day, nearly two years before and how excited she'd been, but she'd said as nonchalantly as possible, 'I've got a job in the jewellery quarter in Hockley. Only they don't make jewellery now – they make radar parts.'

'God, how did you get that then?'

'I went to see the Headmistress, Mrs Daniels,' Linda said. 'Jenny told me to, 'cos she knows I've always wanted to work there. Mrs Daniels recommended me.'

'Good on yer kid,' Beattie said sincerely. 'You go for it, if it's what you want.'

And it was what Linda had wanted. Most of her friends, including her best friend Carole, were going into dirty noisy munitions factories where people said the smell of cordite would near choke you to death. Jenny had said that Linda might have to fight for what she wanted. And so, armed with an astonishingly good report and a personal recommendation from her Headmistress, she'd set out with her knees knocking together for an interview at Wall's Jewellers in Pitford Street just three days after the calliper had been removed.

Linda knew she'd looked good that day. She'd worn a blue suit that had been one of Vicky's.

257

Jenny had put it away hoping Linda would grow to fill it, and she had. She wore a crisp white blouse under it and Jenny had loaned her a pair of her blue shoes. She'd offered her a loan of her precious silk stockings as well, but Linda refused them. Her legs were now as straight as anyone else's, but they were thin, almost shapeless and still badly scarred, and though the doctors and nurses said the scarring would fade, Linda was very self-conscious about them and was happier with them covered up with thick lisle.

Her hair had grown long down her back and she'd worn it in plaits to school. After washing it the night before the interview, Jenny had brushed it until it gleamed the following morning and then plaited it into one long braid, which she rolled into a bun shape at the back of Linda's head and fastened with grips. Dressed in her good clothes and with her hair up, Linda was surprised how old she looked suddenly. It was as if she'd shed her childhood.

She'd felt the familiar butterflies in her tummy when she alighted from the tram in the city centre and made her way through the little cobbled streets by St Paul's. The Wall's building, like most of the places, had once been a dwelling house, but had been converted to a workshop.

She'd been interviewed by a Mrs Jenkins and Linda hadn't been in her office five minutes when she knew she was a snobby cow. She had a long nose, ice-cold blue eyes that glittered spitefully, and a thin tight mouth, and she held the report and headmistress's letter as if both were infected with anthrax.

Still Linda remained polite and answered her questions respectfully, and to her delight, got the job. She was better pleased when she was shown the fascinating workshop and her boss Mr Tollit, whom she liked on sight. To her great relief, he told her there was little communication between the workshop and the office staff. 'If you're ever summoned there, lass, it's usually to deal with some complaint,' Mr Tollit had said.

Linda had thought it plain daft that the workshop and office staff didn't mix, but then she wasn't there to change the system, but work within it. She remembered so well the first day she started work. She finished school on Friday 17 July and had arranged to begin work the following Monday. 'Take a wee holiday first,' Jenny had urged. But Linda wanted no holiday. She wanted to get out and earn some money, she had a big debt to repay.

The workshop was made of wood; it was low and dark, and reminded Linda of a very large garden shed. Very little light came from the small grimy windows that looked out onto the narrow cobbled street. The bare floorboards had such deep cracks between them that Linda thought if anything fell down them, it would be the devil's own job to get it out again. She was to find out this was very true.

Mr Tollit was a fairly old man who'd been working in the same place for thirty-five years. 'Of course, before the war we made jewellery, and blooming good jewellery too,' he'd said. 'But now we all make radar parts, and in time, you'll learn to make them too.'

Linda didn't doubt that she would, because she wanted to succeed at this job. She was seated like all the others, mostly women all older than her and another man besides Mr Tollit, on a bare three-legged stool. It took her bottom days to get used to the hardness of that stool, she remembered. Their benches were circular with semi-circular recesses cut out where the stool was placed, and a gas-light hung above each bench sending a pool of light over it all.

There was very little noise and people didn't talk much as they worked. Linda soon realised the job of assembling the radar parts needed precision and concentration, and she talked as little as the rest. Often though, they had *Workers' Playtime* on the wireless and that eased the boredom a little. Mr Tollit was pleased with Linda. By the end of the first week, he'd told her she had jeweller's fingers and she was ridiculously pleased to find something she was good at.

Linda had been at work just over a week when the sirens went off as the O'Learys were sitting down to tea. No one could quite believe it, for it had been a full year since any air raid at all. 'Maybe it's a false alarm,' Eileen said.

'And maybe it isn't,' Jenny replied, getting to her feet because she was on duty. 'I'd best be off as soon as possible, just in case,' she said. Then she looked at Linda and said, 'Go down the shelter if it turns out to be the real thing, OK?' She knew it was no good asking her mother and grandmother.

Linda's eyes were alarmed. She didn't want to go and sit in some shelter on her own. Jenny saw her fear and said, 'Go next door, if you like. The

Pattersons won't mind you sharing.'

'Can't I go to Gran's?'

'Not if there's a raid on over here, you can't,' Jenny answered briefly.

Eileen had got to her feet. 'That's it,' she sneered. 'Look after the girl. You haven't a thought in your head for your mother and myself.'

'You won't go to any shelter,' Jenny said wearily. 'You never have.'

'I didn't say anything about a shelter. I'm talking about you expressing concern for us.'

'Oh Grandmother, please. I must go,' Jenny said. 'If this is a raid, everybody could be needed.'

'Then go!' Eileen said. 'All your life you have put other people before your dear mother.'

Knowing it was no good arguing, Jenny said not a word, but just glared at her grandmother before she left the kitchen and went upstairs for her coat. Linda, left in the kitchen, felt the old lady's eyes bore into her back as she collected up the plates. She said nothing and tried not to look at her, but carried the dirty things to the sink as they heard the barrage of ack-ack guns barking into the night and the distant drone of the planes.

'See what you've done, girl!' Eileen spat out at last, as Linda filled the kettle for hot water.

'Me! What have I done?' Linda cried. Normally she didn't retaliate, but she felt the accusation was unfair.

'Destroyed the family, that's what,' the old lady said. 'You've set the children against their mother.'

261

'I ain't! I never did! That ain't fair!' Linda had burst out.

And it wasn't fair, yet she knew what the old lady meant.

If sides had to be taken in this family conflict, Linda knew what sides the family would take. They couldn't understand, and in no way condoned, the way their mother and grand-mother treated Linda. Martin and Francis weren't averse to saying so, and Jenny of course consistently championed Linda.

But it wasn't Linda's fault. If Jenny's mother and grandmother had been the slightest bit welcoming, instead of treating her as if she was invisible half the time and the rest turning on her viciously, she'd have been friendly with them, if only in gratitude for allowing her to share their home. Many times in that first few months, Linda remembered how she'd wanted to walk out, and it was only the thought of Jenny's face that made her stay put. Then there was also, of course, the little matter of where she was to go; she'd never been over-burdened with choice. However, from the day she got a job, she knew she'd stay because her wages would ease the financial burden considerably. For that reason alone, she would have to learn to put up with the old dragons.

She'd heard Jenny call goodbye and the slam of the front door, and she had looked at the old lady, drawn herself to her full height and said coldly, 'Do you know, I think you're mad, quite mad?'

Then she'd walked past her startled, hate-filled

face, glad the old lady would be unaware of her own trembling limbs, opened the back door and stepped into the garden. Although the raid was still in progress, the thumps and crashes were far away, by the city centre. Jenny told her she wasn't to go to Maureen's in an air raid if it were overhead, but it wasn't. Anyway, Linda reasoned, if she'd stayed in any longer with that vindictive old woman, she'd have done her a mischief, and so she set off.

Many times over the years, Maureen O'Leary's home had been Linda's bolthole, as it had been Jenny's before her. She was there again two days later when the sirens wailed out for the second time.

Jenny had told them the first raid killed and injured many people, mainly in the city centre, who, believing it to be a false alarm, hadn't taken to the shelters. 'And the Americans, of course, had never seen the effects of a raid,' she'd said. 'People say the city centre was full of them. They were more scared than the average Brummie who'd been through it so many times before, but at least now, perhaps they have some idea of what our country has suffered.'

And was still suffering, Linda thought as she brought her mind back to the present and checked that the pie in the oven was browning nicely. Anyway, she had to get on. Jenny would be in soon and fair clemmed with hunger. Jenny and Peggy seldom had a day out in the Bull Ring now, since the birth of Peggy and Gerry's small son Dermot, eighteen months before. Although Peggy had returned to work when Dermot was

263

four months old, leaving him in Maureen's capable hands, she disliked asking her to look after him at weekends, feeling it was putting upon her. However, there were bargains to be had in the Bull Ring, and both women had been anxious to go. Though Jenny could say nothing about it to Linda, she was hoping to find her a nice wrist-watch for her sixteenth birthday. Linda was unaware of that, but did think Jenny deserved an odd afternoon off at times and here she was, having a trip down Memory Lane instead of getting a meal ready when she came in. She set out into the living room with her hands full of cutlery to lay the table.

They had to have the dinner over and done fairly soon that evening too, she thought, for she was appearing at Whittington Barracks, just outside Sutton Coldfield, as part of a concert party put together to entertain the troops. She'd seen the advertisement in the *Evening Despatch*. 'Entertaining the troops it said, straight up,' Linda told the girls at work. 'There's auditions next week.'

'I could entertain the troops,' one of the women said with a laugh. 'One at a time, like.'

The other women laughed, and then Linda went on, 'Why don't you try though?' and as the laughter mounted again she cried, 'Not that way. Seriously – singing or summat.'

'Cos, me ducks, I ain't got a scrap of talent in anything like that,' the girl replied. 'Singing and dancing ain't in my line, like,' she went on impishly. 'I'd be better off at other things now and I'd have said the soldiers would be bloody

264

pleased. Proper entertained, they'd be.'

The raucous laughter rose again and someone else shouted, 'We could form a troupe of strippers.'

'Somehow, I don't think that's the sort of show they had in mind,' Mr Tollit said mildly, and added, 'Now, get back to your work before her in the office comes down to see the cause of our hilarity.'

The women grumbled, but quietly, for they knew what Mr Tollit said was true, and they returned to the job in hand. 'Pity that Mrs Jenkins don't go in for a bit of stripping and entertaining herself, eh ducks?' one of the women whispered to Linda. 'That's what the matter is with her. Silly old cow is as frustrated as hell.'

Linda wanted to laugh but she didn't, because she spotted Mr Tollit's eyes on her and didn't wish to get anyone into trouble. She bent over the bench, but the idea of the concert party kept going around in her head and she mentioned it at home to Jenny.

'Why not try it, love,' Jenny said. 'I'd say you'd be doing them a favour and didn't Francesca Masters tell you, you had to keep singing?'

Francesca had wanted Linda to apply for the College of Music, when she told her she could teach her no more, but she'd refused. 'There are scholarships,' Francesca had said. 'Jenny would not have to pay a penny.'

Linda had looked at Francesca pityingly and said, 'Come on, Francesca, you know that isn't the end of it. What about the books I'd need, and you said they like you to be able to play at least one instrument. How would Jenny afford that? Then there's the cost of keeping me at school for years.'

Francesca didn't answer. She knew Linda felt guilty about the expense she'd already cost Jenny. She couldn't altogether blame her for she knew, certainly at the beginning, that Jenny had often had a job to manage. She could have helped Linda, helped them all, and taken joy in doing so, especially someone with such a talent in music, but she knew neither Jenny nor Linda would accept that; a fierce pride would prevent it. 'Francesca,' Linda had said, 'don't think I'm not grateful – please, *please* don't think that. But I owe Jenny so much. And, it's not just money either. You know that.'

'She wouldn't want you to feel this way,' Francesca had once said.

'How do you know what she'd have wanted?' Linda had asked her angrily. 'I'll tell you how it is at home, Francesca. Jenny has been trying to squeeze a quart into a pint pot. All she had to manage on until now is the pittance of a widow's pension that her mother gets and what she brings home each Friday. Soon I'm going to add to that and make life easier for her. Nothing you can do would convince me that my duty lies in any other direction, and even if I was the best singer in the whole world, I would still choose to find a job some other place that pays a wage.'

Francesca gave in. She knew Linda had her mind made up. 'All right,' she'd said, 'but you have a rare talent, Linda. Don't let it dwindle away to nothing. Keep singing. Sing at every

266

opportunity. Who knows, you might use it yet?'

Linda had never recounted this conversation to Jenny, though she did say that Francesca had said she'd taught her all she knew and had advised her to keep singing. Jenny was no fool, but she knew it was no good raising Linda's hopes. There was no money for her to continue any sort of education in music and that was that. Francesca had taught her so much already and with that, Jenny thought, she'd have to be content.

So, when Linda came home from work with news of the concert party, she was enthusiastic. 'They're holding auditions,' Linda told her. 'I don't suppose it will hurt to go along. And if I don't get in, I've lost nothing.'

But Jenny knew if she sang from the heart, as Francesca urged her to do, she would be taken into the concert party without a second's thought. Linda's shining eyes, when she came home from work the day of the auditions, told their own tale.

They were a motley crew who called themselves, 'The Brummagem Beauties'. There was a compère/comedian called Bill Fletcher who also owned a van with windows in the sides and seats at the back. He said he would ferry the group round, provided he got an extra petrol allowance. Then there was a pianist/singer called Flora McMillan, a man who played an accordion while three Brummie girls of Irish extraction did Irish step-dancing to the music, and a conjuror by the name of Sam Phelps, who, being a farmer, was able to claim exemption from the call up, and a small group specialising in funny acts and sketches based loosely on Army life. Linda was by far and away the youngest. They dubbed her their 'little nightingale'.

At first, despite her initial encouragement, Jenny was worried about Linda touring the West Midlands with people she didn't know terribly well, and of necessity, meeting servicemen in large numbers. Her mother termed it 'common', when she got to hear of it. Her grandmother said she was 'reverting to type' and even Gran O'Leary asked Jenny if she didn't think she was a mite young for such things.

Jenny hated to forbid Linda to do something she looked forward to so much. But, with her full-time job, work at the warden post and the household to run, she hadn't the time or energy to accompany Linda. However, Linda, knowing of Jenny's concern, asked Bill Fletcher and the conjuror Sam Phelps, the two she got on best with, to meet her and reassure her she'd be safe. Bill Fletcher was a solid man in his fifties who had two daughters of his own, both grown, one married with a husband away fighting. Knowing Linda's tender years, he'd already decided to look out for her. Linda, lacking a father's influence, had found Bill's paternal attitude very comforting. Sam Phelps was a younger man in his early thirties. He too was a married man with two children. Linda saw Sam like another Martin, Francis or Gerry in her life. Both men were genuinely fond of Linda and were prepared to guard her well from any unwelcome advances. After meeting them, Jenny knew any fears she had about Linda were groundless and she gladly gave her permission for Linda to go ahead.

Linda found she loved singing to people, though she'd been very nervous at first. Because she was still self-conscious about her legs, Jenny fashioned a floor-length dress that didn't look like it belonged at a wedding, from the bridesmaid's dress she'd worn at Peggy's wedding (for Linda had long since outgrown her own). With her legs covered, Linda felt much more confident. She didn't realise what an enchanting figure she made, dressed in apricot satin with her long hair decorated with a ribbon of similar hue used like an Alice band, so that her long hair cascaded over her shoulders. She looked like a beautiful, slightly-built child.

But when she opened her mouth to sing, it was a different story, and before she was very far into her first song, any shuffling, fidgeting and murmuring from the crowds would stop. By the end, a pin could be heard drop in the halls and mess rooms they performed in, and there was always a pause before the stupendous applause.

'Always guaranteed to quieten an audience, our little nightingale,' Flora, the older singer-pianist had sneered cattily one day, as she left the stage to the shouts of 'More... More!' her voice was nowhere as good as Linda's and she knew it, and so did the audience.

'Good job someone can, ducks,' one of the Irish dancers had put in. 'Go on, Flora, see if you can do any better.'

And as Flora, face aflame, had strode on to the stage, the Irish dancer pressed Linda's arm and said, 'Don't mind her. She's just bloody jealous.'

'It doesn't matter,' Linda had said, and it was true, she didn't really care, for she knew the audiences truly liked her voice and she was experiencing the heady excitement of success, albeit in a small way. During the year, she'd also seen more of Birmingham and the West Midlands than she'd ever seen before. They'd been a lot to Castle Bromwich aerodrome, where the young trainee pilots and their instructors were based with 605 Squadron, and some of the American units were also sharing the base.

There were plenty of other service bases in or around the confines of Birmingham, where the group had always been made more than welcome – like the Aston Barracks that housed the Paras, and the Royal Engineers who were based at Smethwick, Cannock and Tunstall in Staffordshire. St George's Barracks in Sutton Coldfield was the home of the Royal Warwickshire Fusiliers, and Whittington Barracks was the base for the Royal Staffordshire Regiment.

Whittington Barracks was used as a training barracks for newly arrived American servicemen. Many of the young GIs were homesick, and the concert party was in great demand to entertain them.

That particular night, Linda was more nervous than ever, because Jenny was coming to see her for a change, and Martin and Francis had demanded they be allowed to go too. 'There'd be no room in the van,' Linda had protested when Jenny had suggested it that morning. 'We'll squeeze one in at a pinch, but never another two as well.'

'You needn't worry your head,' Jenny said. 'Peter Sanders has offered to take us all.'

'Peter Sanders! God, is he coming too?'

Jenny smiled. 'It would seem so, my girl. Your fame has gone before you.'

'Oh, shut up, Jen.'

'Linda, what are you worried about?' Jenny put her arm around the other girl's shoulders. 'Look pet, I wrote and told the boys what you were doing and obviously they're curious and anxious to see you perform. As for Peter Sanders, you know what an interest he's always taken in you, and it won't be the first time he's heard you sing. Remember that Christmas Eve in the hospital?'

'This will be totally different.'

'Ah, yes. Then you were just an untrained child,' Jenny said. 'Cheer up, love. I can't get to many of these things, and I'm really looking forward to it.'

So there it was, and now in a couple of hours' time, Linda would be standing up before rows and rows of servicemen, knowing that some of her new family would be watching her, along with her good friend the doctor. Her stomach tied itself in knots at the thought.

But then she was plunged back to the present again, for Jenny was at the kitchen door, telling Linda of her trip to the Bull Ring and emptying her bag on the table, displaying the goodies as she did so, and Linda felt a rush of love for her. She wished she could put her arms around her and say so, but she'd be embarrassed and Jenny might think her proper daft. But then Jenny turned to look at her and said, 'You're a grand

271

girl to have the meal ready for us all, Linda. I don't know what I'd do without you, and I often bless the day you came to live with us.'

The words brought a lump to Linda's throat. For Jenny, Linda would gladly have stood on a bed of nails. After that, singing a few songs to please her was nothing at all. She busied herself at the stove to hide the emotion Jenny had stirred up within her. When she had full control of herself again, she said with mock severity, 'And if this meal isn't to be spoilt, we should eat it quick,' and she lifted the pie from the oven as she spoke.

Jenny opened the door for her to put it on the living room table. 'You're a right bossy-boots when you want to be, aren't you?'

Linda answered pertly, 'It takes one to know one, they say,' and she passed into the living room with a flourish as Jenny followed behind her laughing.

Chapter Fifteen

Bill Fletcher looked across at Linda, and quietly, so the others in the van shouldn't hear, he said, 'OK, ducks? You seem all at sixes and sevens tonight.'

'I'm fine,' Linda said. What else could she say? How could she explain to Bill about the full-scale tantrum Norah O'Leary had thrown that evening, when she'd found out that her two sons home for the weekend only, were spending Saturday evening watching 'that wretched girl making a disgusting exhibition of herself'.

She'd sat at the table that night in honour of her sons being home, instead of having her tea on a tray by the fire. She'd risen to her feet as she'd yelled at Linda, and stood surprisingly steady for one claiming to be crippled with arthritis.

Her lips had been drawn back as if she was in contact with something distasteful as she'd screamed at her: 'You're nothing but filthy scum, gutter trash, and you've succeeded in breaking this family apart! I'll never forgive you. Do you hear?'

The shocked 'Mother!' was said by the three young people in unison, but ignoring the censure, Norah had spat at Jenny, 'And you've encouraged her.'

'Mother, that's enough!' Martin was on his feet and so was his brother. 'That was unforgivable.'

Jenny groaned silently. If her mother wanted further proof that Linda had taken the boys away from her, then Martin had just given it to her.

'Unforgivable, you say,' Norah had screamed at her sons. Both of them were staring at her with shocked faces. 'She wheedled her way in here with the help of that one there,' and at this she jabbed a finger at Jenny, 'another conniving ungrateful little slut. There's a pair of them I have to put up with.'

'Stop it, Mother! What's got into you?' Francis cried, while Martin came round the table and put one hand on his mother's arm and the other arm around her shoulders. 'Sit down, Mother,' he said, though he was as confused as his younger brother by Norah's actions. 'You'll be ill if you go on like this.'

Norah shook off his restraining hands. '*Ill*, you say? *They've* made me ill – the pair of them – your sister and the fawning sly creature she brought in here.'

Linda's head shot up. She'd lowered it only so Norah wouldn't see the tears that threatened to brim over her eyelids, but Norah's last words made her angry, too angry to cry. She stared at Jenny's mother scornfully. Eileen saw the defiance in the young girl's look and snapped, 'Have you no shame, girl? Don't you see what you have done?'

'No,' Linda snapped back. 'No, I bloody well don't. I've done nothing to either of you.'

'Don't you dare bring your gutter language here, girl,' Eileen said disgustedly, and Linda saw red.

'I will if I want, because what you two say is worse. You just use posh words, but they're just as horrible.'

Eileen's chest heaved. Norah leaned across the table and jabbed Linda in the chest with each word. 'You broke up a happy home.'

Jenny was staring at her mother as if she was crazy. Leaning her hands on the table she pulled herself to her feet and cried, 'Don't make me laugh. Happy? When was *I* ever happy?'

'This is what I say, she's an ungrateful slut,' Norah said, appealing to her sons. 'This is what I must put up with every day.'

'Can't we all sit down and talk about this reasonably?' Francis put in.

'No, we can't!' Linda had had enough and she was too angry to be cautious. 'I'm fed up being reasonable and biting my tongue when I'm called names and accused of things.' She looked at Norah with hate-filled eyes and saw a woman out of control, her hair awry, her eyes wild, her whole face contorted with loathing and anger, and spittle forming at the corners of her mouth. 'D'you know what I think?' she said coolly. 'You don't really care what I think, but I'll tell you anyway. I think both of you are clean barmy.'

With a shriek and a roar, Norah lunged across the table and actually had her hands around Linda's throat, before Martin, Jenny and Francis were able to pull her off. 'Go upstairs,' Jenny said to the shaking girl. 'Go and get changed.'

'Will you be all right?'

'We'll be better without you,' Jenny assured. 'Go on.'

Linda went, leaving Norah, seated at last, sobbing long tearing sobs and being comforted by her sons and her mother. Jenny went into the kitchen to make tea. She'd have put a drop of brandy in her mother's, if she had any, hers too, for she was shaking like a leaf. For this to happen on her brothers' short leave saddened her. She'd been on the receiving end of these tantrums before, but her brothers had never seen them. However, it was the thought that Martin and Francis preferred to go and see Linda's performance than sit with her, that had brought things to a head with Norah because her unreasonable hatred of Linda went deep.

Upstairs, Linda sat on the bed she shared with Jenny and shook with delayed reaction. The tears came at last. It wasn't fair, the things that old bugger downstairs had called her, nor had she done anything. They just loathed her she knew and showed it plainly. Well, she loathed them too, so that was all right and she wouldn't say she was sorry, even if Jenny asked her to.

She couldn't tell any of this to Bill, nor how Jenny came in and chivvied her to get ready. She hadn't felt like it at all. In fact, she was so worn out by everything, she had the urge to crawl into bed and sleep. But she thought of letting down all the young servicemen and allowed Jenny to help her dress and brush her hair.

She thought she'd stopped her shivering and was in control of herself when she climbed into the van, and yet Bill had noticed she was agitated about something. She wondered if Francis and Martin would turn up to the concert now and thought probably not. Jenny might not even come. Such was human nature that although before she thought she'd be too nervous to perform well if they came, now, when she thought they might not, she knew she'd be disappointed.

She would have been surprised if she'd heard the conversation going on between the two brothers a little time after she'd left the house. Jenny was washing the dishes, a job Linda usually helped her with, and they'd gone upstairs to change. 'I suppose we'd better knock this business of going to see Linda perform tonight on the head?' Francis said.

'Why?'

'Come on, Martin. You know why.'

'Because our mother would blow a fuse?'

'Well, yes.'

'You can do what you like, little brother,' Martin said, 'but I'm damned if I'll be held to ransom in this way. Can't you see what she's doing? She wants us tied to her apron strings, but I'm afraid she'll never have me like that.'

Francis sucked in his lower lip and thought about what Martin had said. He knew he was right, and yet he'd never been as brave as his brother and hated unpleasantness and rows. He was a bit like Seamus, who'd always given in for a quiet life. But this was a bit different. A stand had to be made, both for his own self-respect and for the sake of the young girl taken into their household, and for his sister Jenny. He'd seen his mother in rages before, though seldom directed at him or his brothers, or even Geraldine.

Guiltily, he remembered it had always been Jenny who received the tongue lashing, as well as his father before he'd died. He'd never questioned it then nor thought it odd. He'd grown up that way and that's how his family was. It had been moving away that had changed him and opened his eyes to the fact that other families didn't behave like his.

'Our dear mother is a conniving and domineering bitch of a woman,' Martin told his younger brother. 'She gave Father hell for years. You remember how she'd talk to him at times, and for no reason at all?'

Francis nodded. 'She talks to Jenny and Linda like that now,' he said. 'I've noticed that.'

'She's always used Jenny as the whipping boy. It was so much part of our lives and Jenny so much younger, we probably weren't aware of it. At least I wasn't.'

'I was aware of it,' Francis admitted. 'I was a lot younger than you, remember? I just thought it was normal behaviour. Mother was always telling us how naughty Jenny was.'

'Hmm,' Martin said. 'Makes you wonder now, doesn't it? Well, I'm not going to let Linda down. Mother will have won then. You do what you want, Francis, but I'm going out tonight with Jenny in this doctor fellow's car.'

Francis thought for a moment and said, 'By God, you're right Martin.'

Jenny, drying the dishes in the kitchen, didn't know of her brothers' decision, but she hoped that they wouldn't let Linda down. Though she had to admit it had been a classic performance on her mother's part. Oh God, sometimes she hated that woman! The boys had certainly seen a new side of Norah tonight and they'd been profoundly shocked. However, she'd seen a change in both boys since they'd been away anyway, Martin more than Francis, but then as the second eldest, he was thirty-four now, not a boy any longer and had never been as compliant as Francis or Seamus. Anthony hadn't been compliant at all: he'd give the impression of heeding his mother's every word and then would go his own way.

Oh, how Jenny wished he was still alive, that he'd walk through the door one day, with his kit bag on his shoulder and the smile he reserved only for her. He would talk to her about this evening and assure her it would blow over, her mother would forgive and forget. And Jenny would believe him, even while she knew it wasn't true. Norah O'Leary never forgot or forgave; it wasn't in her nature to do so.

But it wasn't just this night she was worried about, for whatever Francis and Martin decided to do, they'd be away and out of it in another twenty-four hours. It was the nights and the days after, and how they'd all live together again that worried Jenny. They might have stood a chance if Linda hadn't retaliated, but then the girl was almost sixteen and Jenny couldn't blame her. She'd taken more insults and vindictive rudeness than many as she grew; she couldn't be expected to just sit and take it all the time.

Oh, what was the use of worrying, she asked herself crossly. Did it help, and did wishing

Anthony hadn't died bring him back to life? She resolved to take each day as it came and the first thing to find out was how many people were going to the concert with her and Peter Sanders. She packed the crockery and cutlery away neatly and stacked the pans on the rack. She then crossed the living room without a word to her mother or grandmother, who were sitting either side of the fireplace in silence, and went upstairs to see her brothers.

Bill pulled into the Phelps's farm and stopped outside the gate leading into the cobbled yard outside the farmhouse door. He gave another anxious glance at Linda. He knew there was something wrong with the girl though he wasn't sure what. Maybe he'd find out later. He raised his voice to the others and said, 'Any of you want to get out and stretch your legs, I'd say you'd have time. Sam Phelps would be late for his own funeral.' Linda gave a tight smile knowing Bill was right and slipped out of the van after him. She stood leaning against the five-barred gate watching him stride towards the house, scattering chickens before him as he went.

Most of the others had got out too and were huddled together, laughing and smoking, but Linda made no move to join them. She was no company for anyone tonight, though she was glad of the cool breeze on her face which was still crimson and burning hot from the evening's confrontation.

Bill hadn't quite reached the farmhouse door when it was wrenched open from the inside and

Sam Phelps's children, six-year-old Sally and five-year-old Charlie burst through it, calling, 'Linda, Linda!'

Linda waved and the children tore across to her and flung themselves on to the other side of the gate. 'Come on,' Charlie urged, 'we got something to show you.'

'What?'

'Molly's had her pups,' the more serious Sally said. 'They're ever so sweet, come and see.'

'I can't. Your father...'

'He'll be hours yet,' Charlie said airily. 'He ain't even shaved.'

'Yes,' Sally agreed with a giggle. 'His face is all over soap, like Father Christmas.'

'And it won't take a tick,' Charlie said.

'Oh, all right,' Linda said, allowing herself to be persuaded. It would, at any rate, stop her going over and over the awful row at home and how they would live together after it. Anyway, she liked the Phelps's children and they seemed to like her, as most children did. Funny that, she thought. It had been difficult to relate to any children in the beginning after she'd got out of hospital, but she found the more she did with them, the easier it got.

She clambered over the gate, as it was easier than opening it and then, with a hand in each of the children's, she ran across the yard. Linda knew where the sheep dog would be, in the special whelping box Sam had prepared for her in the barn, just behind the farmhouse. He bred good sheep dogs, did Sam, and always got a fair price for Molly's pups. Jenny knew he'd been as

281

anxious to get the birth over as the children.

'How many pups has she had?' Linda asked Charlie as they turned the corner.

'Five,' Charlie said, and Linda had her head turned to him as they rounded the corner. She didn't notice the man, until she almost cannoned into him. 'Oh, I'm sorry.'

'No, no. It is I who is the sorry one,' the man said. He was a stranger to Jenny, though he wore blue dungarees and carried a shovel so he was obviously a worker on the farm. His accent was even stranger. He had a squarish face with eyes the colour of a tawny owl and a firm square chin and an unruly mop of brown hair on his head.

To Linda's utter amazement, he gave a small bow and tried to click his heels together, not easy to do wearing wellingtons, thought Linda, hiding a smile. The children beside her giggled.

'That's our prisoner,' Charlie told Linda dismissively. 'He always does that. His name is Max Schulz and he's German.'

In all her life Linda had ever met a real live German. She'd talked about them, sung about them, even sworn about them, but she'd never met one. She'd never met a prisoner either, and wondered if she should shake hands or merely ignore the man. But innate good manners came to the fore, she couldn't just ignore someone – it was what Jenny's mother and grandmother did to her often – and so she held out her hand with a smile.

'How do you do, Mr Schulz,' she said slowly, accentuating every word.

'I do very well,' Max Schulz said. 'Do you also?'

'Yes,' Linda said, with a slight laugh.

'My English is not good at times,' Max said. 'But, it gets better.'

'It's heaps better than my German.'

'Heaps?' Max said with a puzzled frown. 'What is heaps?'

'It doesn't matter,' Linda said as Sally urged, 'Come on, Linda. They'll be calling you in a minute and you won't have seen the pups.'

'Yes, yes,' Linda said. 'I must go, Mr Schulz.'

'Yes, I see. Goodbye, Linda.'

Her name sounded funny in Max Schulz's strange accent and she found herself smiling at him again before being hurried away by the children. She admired the tiny blind puppies suckling at Molly's teats, while the sheep dog lay with a self-satisfied smile on her face as she whined a greeting at them.

'Daddy said we mustn't touch them until their eyes are open or Molly may bite,' Sally said.

'And we've not got to forget Molly and make a fuss of her too,' Charlie put in.

'Quite right too,' Linda said, kneeling beside the box and stroking the sheep dog gently. 'You're a good girlie, aren't you, Molly? Clever girl,' and Molly licked Linda's hand softly while her tail began to wag.

'Linda?' came the shout, and she got to her feet and dusted off her clothes.

'Got to run,' she said.

'Come and see them in a few days,' Sally said. 'Dad says they'll be more fun when they can run around a bit.'

'They will,' Linda said, as they began to walk

quickly back to the van.

'Thought we'd lost you,' Bill said, helping her up.

'I was admiring newborn puppies,' Linda explained.

'Oh, ah,' Sam said, 'they've been dying to show them off to you, the nippers.'

Bill began backing the van down the farm-track, no easy task as it was so narrow, and he growled, 'Never mind bloody pups. All this way and you're never bloody ready.'

'Well, I haven't got a nine to five job like some,' Sam protested. 'And there's a powerful lot of work to get through these light spring evenings. There's still cows to be milked, stock to feed, and late sowing to do. Least you townies haven't the farm Ags breathing down your neck, telling you how much and what to grow in your own damn land.'

'Heard you got one of the POWs from the camp in Sutton Park?'

'You heard right,' Sam said. 'I only had the one Land Girl Ruby, after young Cynthia went off and got married. Mind you, Max is worth two of the girls. He's stronger for one thing and he knows what's what. Seems he had a farm in Germany.'

'Are you not worried about being murdered in your beds?' one of the Irish step-dancers asked.

'Don't be so bloody daft,' Sam said. 'Old Max is quite a decent bloke and he likes the chance of being out in the open air again. Anyway, he doesn't sleep in the house. They round them up in Army trucks and take them back to camp every night. He isn't the only POW helping us farmers out, you know?'

'Well, I still wouldn't feel safe.'

'They're just like us. If you met them, you'd find that out for yourself,' Sam went on.

'Not in my book they aren't.'

But Linda knew what Sam meant. She was glad she'd had the opportunity of meeting the German Max Schulz, and finding him not the monster she'd previously imagined all Germans to be.

The hall was packed, Linda saw from her place in the wings as she was waiting to go on. It was a good crowd, with many Americans. She'd spotted Peter and Jenny at the back, with Francis and Martin beside them. She swelled with pride that they'd come to see her after all Norah had tried to do to stop them. She hoped they were enjoying the show. Bill Fletcher had opened it and softened the audience up with a collection of his ribald jokes. Mindful of the words with different meanings on the two sides of the Atlantic, he made a play on those first in his broadest Brummie accent and soon had the audience laughing.

Then it was Sam's turn. He enjoyed audience participation and had a host of willing helpers up on stage, hoping to catch Sam out, but his sleight of hand was amazing. The act became more and more elaborate and almost unbelievable until the audience were open-mouthed with admiration, as indeed Linda herself often was when she watched his act.

After that, Bill thought the audience needed

285

some light relief, so the step-dancers came on with their Irish jigs and reels. The audience could stamp and clap to those, and they did both. A series of sketches followed. By this time, the audience were well warmed up and then Linda stepped on to the stage. Bill introduced her as usual as 'Our very own nightingale, Miss Linda Lennox'. The applause was perfunctory as Linda crossed the stage. She saw the look of pride on Jenny's face and all fear and nervousness left her and she smiled.

Always she opened her spot with the song that had given her the nickname, 'A Nightingale Sang in Berkeley Square'. For Jenny it brought back the terrifying ordeal they both had gone through in the bombed house, and she felt tears prick her eyes. The American and British boys were stunned into silence, but as Linda's voice rose, they remembered the girls they'd loved and left behind. Linda followed on with 'I'll Be Seeing You' and finished with 'You Are My Sunshine'.

When she left the stage, there were howls of disappointment and Bill Fletcher had a job calming the audience. Wisely, he cut his act short and brought on Flora McMillan, who without further ado gave them a rendering of 'Green-sleeves' followed by 'There'll Always Be An England'.

Linda had thought Flora's second song to be a mistake as most of the audience were American, but Flora was the recognised star of the show and a law unto herself as well as terribly jealous over Linda's success, so she'd felt it sensible to keep her mouth shut. The commotion began when

Flora attempted to sing 'Three Coins in the Fountain'.

It began with catcalls for Flora to get off, answered by others that demanded the return of Linda Lennox. Some didn't remember her name and called her 'The Little Nightingale', but the sentiments were the same. Flora faltered at the noise from the hall, but continued as any true professional might. However her voice was eventually drowned by first the slow handclap, closely followed by the drumming of many feet on the floor.

Knowing how an unhappy audience could turn into an unruly one, Bill was dismayed and undecided about what to do. 'Put the kid back on,' Sam suggested.

'What? And put Flora's back up further? Are you mad?'

'Do you need her?'

'We might not, but that's another issue,' Bill reminded him. 'Any road, Linda won't go on if it's going to upset Flora.'

The noise rose steadily in the hall and the audience began making missiles of their programmes and throwing them on stage, Bill thought he'd have to risk annoying Flora. He went backstage and tapped on the door. 'It's you they want, duck,' he told Linda. 'Would you do another few numbers?'

Linda hesitated. She knew how much it mattered to Flora to succeed in this. It was all the woman had, for God's sake. Seeing her dilemma, Sam broke in 'Can you sing accompanied, Linda?'

'Of course.' That's how all the lessons had finished at Francesca's, with Linda singing to her accompaniment – and even now when Linda visited as a friend they often did it just for fun.

'Well then, why don't you sing and let Flora play?' Sam suggested. 'She's a good pianist.'

The noise and disruption from the hall had reached crescendo level. 'Oh God, who's going to tell them?' Bill said. 'And will they listen?'

Linda felt suddenly angry with the unruly hordes. 'I'll tell them,' she said, her voice as cold as steel. 'And they'll listen.'

Before Bill, Sam or anyone else could say a word to stop her, she strode onto the stage, which was littered with crumpled programmes and anything else the audience had to hand. They were booing and catcalling; many had upended seats, others were stamping and clapping. The noise and general upheaval were horrendous. Linda felt her stomach contract in fear, though no one would have known as she strode over to the mike and said quietly, but firmly, 'Would you please kindly resume your seats?'

The very softness of her voice cut through the general cacophony of noise and there was a lessening of it, but not enough for Linda's liking. 'I said,' she repeated, raising her voice, 'would you resume your seats?'

She had everyone's attention now, including Flora's, who'd at first attempted to carry on and then had given up in despair. 'You want some songs, right?' Linda said, raising her hand for silence. 'Well, that's no way to get any.' She indicated to Flora at the piano and went on,

'Miss McMillan will not play for louts and I will not sing for them. Resume your seats and have better manners and we'll see what we can do.'

All of Linda's adopted family and Peter Sanders had watched Linda walk alone on to the stage. She looked small by herself and terribly young to face such a rowdy raucous audience. Jenny had been incensed. Where, she wondered, were Bill and Sam, who'd promised her faithfully they'd look after Linda? This was a fine way of doing it! She'd have something to say to them both afterwards. Martin and Francis had risen to their feet. 'What the bloody hell are they thinking of?' Francis said. 'Fancy letting a kid face that on her own.'

He began pushing past them to the aisle as he spoke. His intention was to get Linda off the stage, bodily if necessary, and knock the head off those responsible for sending her out there. But her clear voice asking people to sit down stopped him in his tracks and when she repeated it, he returned to his seat and watched the men, shamefacedly righting the chairs and rearranging them in rows as Linda told them off good and proper.

'By God, that's telling 'em,' Martin said quietly in open admiration.

'And how,' Francis agreed.

Peter had not been so amazed; he'd had a little experience of Linda's courage and determination before, but he saw how distressed Jenny had been. He longed to put his arm around her or cover her small hand with his own, but knew he could do neither, so he turned his attention to

289

the stage again.

Bill and the rest of the cast watched open-mouthed. As the servicemen set the hall to rights, Linda went over and had a quiet word with Flora. The older woman was upset and a little distraught, but faced the fact that her days as a singer-performer were over. She'd had catcalls and boos in many locations, hence her initial jealousy of Linda, but never so many as tonight. Now Linda had given her a way of redeeming herself and still remaining a useful contributor to the group. When Linda approached the mike again, it was to say, 'Right are you all ready? We're beginning with "We'll Meet again". I don't want any blighter here not to sing it, and I want to *hear* you doing it. So let's go, Miss McMillan! When you're ready.'

She had the audience eating out of her hand. She went on to sing, 'Kiss Me Goodnight, Sergeant Major', 'White Cliffs of Dover', 'Lili Marlene', 'Somewhere Over the Rainbow' and finished off with 'Bless 'Em All'.

Before she started the last song, Linda said, 'After this, the concert is over and the concert party is going home to bed. So, I'd like you all to sing your bloody hearts out and then leave quietly, so we can all go home to be fit and healthy to play and sing another day. Now, are you ready?'

Before they could recover from her speech, she was into 'Bless 'Em All' and everyone sang along with her; the noise the audience made threatened to lift the roof. Afterwards, while they applauded as loudly and wildly as before they seemed to accept it was the end of the concert and began collecting their belongings and filing out in almost a reverent silence.

'You have summat special,' Bill said to Linda later. 'I don't just mean singing solo, but dealing with unruly crowds.'

'They weren't that bad,' Linda said, embarrassed by his praise.

'Don't belittle yourself,' said Flora McMillan. 'You do have a special gift both in dealing with people and singing, which I don't have.' She laid a hand on Linda's arm and said, 'You and I could make a great team.'

That night, Linda had also realised that, good as her voice was, alone and unaccompanied, she could go so far and no further. She smiled at Flora McMillan and said, 'You could be right.'

She was dropped off later that night in Bill Fletcher's van, glad that Martin and Francis were there with Jenny and the two older women had gone to bed. The boys were loud in their praise of her performance that night, and Jenny was as proud as punch. She told Linda how delighted Peter had been too.

However in bed that night, for all the excitement of the evening, the exhilaration she'd experienced at controlling the servicemen, and the acclaim she'd received from the rest of the cast because of it, the fact that floated in Linda's mind when she closed her eyes was that of the German POW at the Phelps's farm. She remembered how deepset his eyes were, and how his eyebrows were bushy and met across the bridge of his nose. When he spoke, his teeth were even and very white.

She recalled his square hands on the handle of the shovel and the sprinkling of brown hairs on the back of them, and his firm, well-muscled arms in the short-sleeved checked shirt he wore under the faded blue dungarees.

Linda couldn't understand herself. She was pretty enough to arouse the interest of the boys around her home, though there were precious few about over the age of eighteen. Since she'd started with the concert-party, she'd had to repel many advances. Nice though some of them appeared, she had no interest in them. Why then was she so interested in Max Schulz? She'd only met him for a brief time that evening, and hadn't spoken much more than a dozen words to him. Just before she dropped off to sleep, she told herself it was because he was different, not the usual type of lad she was used to meeting. He was German for one thing and a prisoner for another. If I met him again, I'd probably have as little interest in him as any other lad, she told herself, and held that thought in her head as she drifted off to sleep.

Chapter Sixteen

Over the next few days, the atmosphere in the
O'Leary house was more strained than ever,
especially after the men left. Norah and Eileen
didn't speak to Linda at all and not much more
to Jenny, and while both girls preferred this to
verbal abuse, the silences were awkward. After
the tea things had been washed and put away,
Jenny and Linda went down to Maureen's. However on Tuesday evening when Jenny was on duty
at the warden post, Linda didn't dare leave the
house, feeling sure the two women would take
great delight in locking her out so instead she
went up to her room where she lay on the bed
and read *Jane Eyre*.

The following day was her sixteenth birthday,
and although she knew she might get a present
from Jenny, the main celebration for it was going
to be on Saturday at Gran O'Leary's house,
where she was going to have a little party.

Surprisingly, however, there was a pile of cards
on the mat. Norah was flabbergasted and very
annoyed that both Martin and Francis had
remembered Linda's birthday, but Jenny was
pleased. She was glad, too that Beattie hadn't
forgotten her, nor had Francesca Masters. Jan,
Seamus's wife, had also sent a card and so had
Geraldine, and Jenny was glad she had reminded
them all about it. Linda was pleased she had so

many cards, for in the house her birthday might as well not have existed, except for the card and present of a wrist-watch she got from Jenny and the hug she'd given her as she said. 'Happy Birthday, Linda, and I really do mean you to have one.'

All the cards she'd received were taken down to Maureen's house on the Saturday morning where they were arranged along the mantelpiece. They made a lovely splash of colour, and Linda began looking forward to her bit of a 'do' that evening.

In the event, it was almost overshadowed by war news. For more than a month there had been rumours and wild speculation about things happening on the south coast. 'There must be something in it,' Jenny said. 'We have a girl works in our office – got married recently because her fiancé had a week's unexpected leave – embark-ation leave. She said it's got to be something big because the only time he had a week off before was just before he left for Dunkirk.'

'Could be right. Didn't your own brothers get unexpected leave too?' Maureen said.

'Yes,' Jenny said thoughtfully. 'And Bob wrote to me yesterday, saying from now, all leave has been cancelled indefinitely. You know how he was supposed to be getting off in the middle of June?'

'Something's up right enough.'

'Yes, but wait till you hear,' Jenny went on. 'The girl that was to be married fancied a few days in Brighton for a bit of a honeymoon, but they were told the South Coast was out of bounds to civilians.'

The adults looked at one another, remembering the rumours they'd heard: whole villages commandeered, huge camps of men and women waiting about, ports blocked with troops, tanks, barges, landing craft and roads impassable with Army trucks and jeeps, troop carriers and staff cars.

'This is it then, isn't it?' Maureen said sombrely. 'Let's hope it isn't another bloody massacre.'

'Well, at least we only have the Germans to beat now,' Peggy put in.

'What about the Japs?' Jenny said.

'Well, that's not our war is it, the Japs?' Maureen said. 'Though I suppose I shouldn't say that, with so many of our men dead or captured by the brutes. No, I was thinking of the Eyeties. Good job they surrendered last year.'

'Mrs Masters said they never wanted to fight, but they were made to,' Linda put in.

'Aye, no stomach for fighting, Eyeties,' Maureen said. 'Different altogether from the Germans and the bloody awful Japs.'

'I met a German last week,' Linda told everyone. 'He was working at the Phelps's farm. I saw him when we called in for Sam.'

'He'd be one of the prisoners-of-war from the camp in Sutton Park,' Gerry nodded. 'I heard they'd been loaned out to the farmers.'

'Can't say as I'd like it,' Beattie said. 'Could be dangerous, I'd say.'

'I don't think so,' Gerry said. 'They wouldn't allow out any they considered dangerous, and they go back to the camp at night. They don't sleep out.'

'Even so...' Peggy began, but Maureen burst in with, 'What d'you mean, if they're considered dangerous! They're *all* bloody dangerous! We've been fighting them for five long years. In my book, that says they're dangerous.'

'This one seemed all right, Gran,' said Linda 'And he spoke good English.'

'D'you mean to say you spoke to him?'

'Well, yes ... sort of. Sam's children introduced me.'

'What sort of a fool is this man Phelps to let his children near brutes like that anyway?' Maureen said.

'Gran, I'm sure he's all right.'

''Course he isn't all right, girl,' Maureen burst out. 'They are sly conniving bastards, the Germans. Started two bloody world wars, no less. And you don't have to talk polite to no German, he don't deserve it.'

'Oh come on, Mammy, don't be giving out to the girl and on her birthday too,' Gerry complained.

'Sure, and it's for her own good I'm talking,' Maureen said hotly.

Linda understood a little of how Maureen felt, because before she'd met Max Schulz, she had an image in her mind of Germans being murdering butchers, incapable of normal feelings. Yet the farmhand had seemed so normal and so very, very young. She wondered how she could ever reconcile what she knew the Germans to be capable of, with the polite young man working on the Phelps's farm.

Little Dermot toddled past Linda at this point

and Linda picked him up and held him close, comforting herself rather than the child as Maureen pronounced, 'The only good German is a dead one. Mark my words, Linda, and take heed.'

In the early evening of 5 June, two days after the party, they heard the planes going overhead, so many of them that Linda and Jenny went out into the garden to watch. Many of the neighbours had done the same, she noticed. 'We're for it now all right,' one commented. 'Make or break, this is.'

Jenny and Linda knew he was right, as wave after wave of planes flew above them heading south. It went on all evening, and even when the girls went to bed they heard them in the distance. It was as if every aerodrome in the whole of the country was emptying, as indeed they probably were. 'Stands to reason Jenny,' Mr Patterson had said. 'If an invasion is on the cards, the bombers will be needed to smash the German defences and the fighters to protect our blokes. Then there'll be the giant transport planes dropping paratroopers behind the lines. Mark my words, summat big's happening.'

The next morning, 6 June 1944, there was a feeling of expectancy in the air. At work, despite the posters urging people to *Keep Mum*, and others explaining that *Careless Talk Costs Lives*, all the conversation in Jenny's and Peggy's offices were about the strange happenings. In Linda's place of work, talking was discouraged, but nothing in the world would have stopped them that day.

Then, that evening, clustered around the wireless, people heard the news from the Reuters News Agency.

'*An Official Communiqué States – Under the Command of General Eisenhower, Allied Naval Forces, supported by strong Air Forces began landing Allied Armies this morning on the Northern Coast of France.*'

It was the culmination of people's hopes and fears. The hopes that it would bring a speedy end to the war that had dragged on and claimed so many lives; the fear of failure – that the invasion would turn into another Dunkirk – and the fear of the human cost of it all, for it was hardly likely the Germans would stand on the French beaches and welcome the invaders with open arms.

Later, the gigantic scale of the whole operation became known. D-Day, or Operation Overlord, used 487 squadrons of the International Air Force, marshalling 11,500 planes. Mr Patterson had been right. A third of the planes had been from Bomber Command and a sizeable number were Hercules Transporters, to drop para-troopers behind the lines. The rest were fighters to keep the Luftwaffe at bay while the vast ranks of servicemen scrambled off the 4,000 barges and landing craft in order to secure the Cherbourg-Havre area. In one of those fighter planes was Bob Masters. Jenny knew it and Linda knew it – and both were frightened to death for him.

It was about this time, a few days after D-Day, that Jenny first noticed that her grandmother Eileen's appetite had diminished. She took little notice at the time, for she was desperately worried about Bob; she hadn't heard from him for some time, although letters had been received from all the others. Jenny did wonder if her grandmother was playing up to get attention, or to make her and Linda feel guilty. And that she refused to do. Living at home had become like living in a battlefield, where shots had been fired, but where now an uneasy truce prevailed. But daily she awaited the snipers' bullets and for battle to recommence. Her nerves, already drawn taut, had become even more frayed and she knew Linda was suffering almost as much as she was.

The relief she felt when Bob's letter eventually fell on the mat was immense. He told her none of the dangers he'd been in, though she could have a good guess as he described the massive onslaught on the French beaches and the tremendous number of men, machines and equipment and supplies that had to be off-loaded. He described the Mulberrys which were, he said, a staggering invention.

Think of it Jen, four miles of piers and six of roadways towed in sections and assembled for fifteen pier heads. From the air the sight was tremendous and I'll never forget it.

He didn't tell her of the beaches he'd seen littered with bodies, young men in their prime massacred, but he didn't have to say – everyone knew.

Just the next day after Bob's letter on 13 June, a pilotless rocket landed in Kent. It did little

299

damage and most people didn't realise at first how dangerous it was. It was Hitler's revenge weapon. V-1 rockets were 25 foot long, carried 1 ton of explosive in the nose, and were capable of flying 155 miles. Most of them reached London, which was just recovering from the Blitz. The V-1s had a distinctive high-pitched buzzing noise – and hearing it stop and waiting for the inevitable crash played havoc with people's nerves. They were an instrument of terror. Very soon the people of the capital had christened the bombs 'doodlebugs' and many were leaving the city in droves to get away from them.

The Allies continued to go further into France and people began plotting their course according to the news reports. Maps of Europe began appearing in offices, schools and people's homes. For almost the first time, the British nation was feeling hopeful about the future and wanted to join the Allies' successes.

It was July before Jenny realised that her grandmother might really be ill. She still wasn't eating much at all and Jenny had to recognise that it wasn't being done to get attention or to punish her and Linda. The skin on her face had become saggy and putty-coloured and the whites of her eyes had a yellowish tinge to them.

Finally, Jenny thought she had to ask her and at tea one day she said, 'Are you feeling all right, Grandmother?'

'Perfectly.'

'You don't seem to be eating much.'

'One doesn't as one gets older.'

'Even so, maybe you should see the doctor.'

'Doctors? What good are they?' Norah scoffed. 'Don't pretend you have any consideration for your grandmother now, my girl. It's a bit late in the day for that.'

Jenny knew her mother had no time for most doctors. That was one of the reasons she'd been so surprised by her attitude to Peter Sanders, because before his arrival, she hadn't let a doctor near her or her children for years. It's a good job we were such a healthy bunch, Jenny often thought, for any doctoring they had was done over the chemist's counter. And if her father's collapse hadn't been severe enough to need hospital attention, he would probably have received none at all. Norah would more than likely have assumed he had a bad attack of indigestion and that he'd feel better after a night's rest.

Linda couldn't understand why Jenny should concern herself so much about the old lady. She did look ill, but then why wouldn't she, with all the badness inside of her? Linda's mother had always told her, you could look as pretty as you liked, but if all you had in your head was bad thoughts, they would come out in the end and make you look as ugly as sin. Well, the old lady looked ugly and unwell, and Linda didn't care, and she hoped Jenny didn't expect her to. She wasn't going to be a hypocrite because she knew if both she and Jenny were on fire in the gutter, neither of the two old misery-guts would have spat on them.

Jenny saw Linda's set face and guessed at the thoughts tumbling around in her head. She knew

Linda was a little out of sorts anyway, because following the last concert, they'd had no further work. She knew why. Most of the Forces had been ferried down to the South Coast to take part in D-Day – but that was no help to her, and Jenny knew she missed singing.

By the middle of July however, Linda was back in business again, for some of the lads had got their Blightys – their injury passes home – and Linda and her concert-party were asked to provide evenings of entertainment in the hospitals around the city. They all got together and worked out a programme.

When Bill Fletcher's old van pulled into Phelps's farm on Saturday 22 July for their concert in Selly Oak Hospital, Linda automatically looked for Max, but there were only the children waiting for her in the yard. 'Come and see, Linda,' Charlie urged. 'Daddy said we can have one of the puppies for our own. Come and help us choose.'

'We haven't time, Charlie,' Linda said. After Maureen O'Leary's warnings, she had no desire to get out of the car and come face to face with the German again.

'Oh, we can spare a few minutes,' Bill said. 'Go on. After all, Sam's not out yet.'

There was nothing for it, because to make a fuss would only draw attention to herself and confuse the children. Linda got out, climbed the gate and took the children's hands, thinking she'd take a quick look at the puppies and be back in the van in no time, probably without catching even a glimpse of the man.

302

But Max was already in the barn playing with the puppies when she arrived. They were now fluffy black and white bundles of fun and mischief, and Max had his hand covered with a rag which the puppies were attacking and worrying voraciously. Their mother Molly looked on contentedly, glad someone else was entertaining her brood for once, to stop them plaguing the life out of her.

Max stood up as he heard the children approach. His eyes lit up as they alighted on Linda, and despite her resolve, she smiled back at him. 'Ah Linda,' he said. 'Soon this war will be over for us all, I think.'

Linda lifted her chin. What was she doing smiling at a German after all Maureen O'Leary had said about them? 'Yes,' she snapped. 'And *we're* going to win.'

She was ashamed as soon as the words left her lips. She felt that outburst had been childish. The expression on Max's face was sober as he said, 'It is as you say. Then maybe I will go home again.'

'Do you miss your home?' Linda felt compelled to ask after her earlier comment.

'I would miss my family more than my home,' Max said and he shrugged and went on, 'but now they are all dead, my parents and my brother.'

'Oh, I'm sorry.'

'So am I, Linda, but in war people die. Many have died here too.'

'Linda!' Charlie's aggrieved voice said. 'You were supposed to be here to look at the puppies.'

'I'm sorry,' Linda said, and both she and Max bent down. The puppies were tugging the rag

303

Max had dropped in the box, growling and snapping at it with their needle-sharp teeth and Linda and Max were as enchanted as the children.

'Which one shall we keep?' Sally asked. 'Daddy said they're ready to leave Molly now and he's found homes for three already.'

'What about this one?' Linda said, picking up one of the squirming pups. It was very fluffy and mainly white, but with some black spots on its back and a patch over one eye.

'I liked him best,' Sally declared. 'From the beginning I liked him, but what about you, Charlie?'

'S'alright, I suppose. What is it, a boy or a girl?'

Linda was at a loss, but not so Max. He turned the puppy expertly on its back and said, 'It is a girl dog,' and at the scowling expression on Charlie's face he went on, 'It's good. Bitches make good pets.'

'I wanted a boy dog.'

'Molly is a girl,' Max reminded him.

'With a girl we can have lots more puppies,' Sally said, and Linda hid her smile. She didn't think Sam Phelps would be too keen on 'lots more puppies', but that was a problem for the future and Charlie was almost won over.

'OK,' he said at last. 'But if you've chosen the dog, I get to choose the name.'

'Have you got one in mind?' Linda asked.

'Yeah, Patch.'

'Patch is a boy's name,' Sally protested.

'No, it ain't.'

'Yes, it is,' Sally said. 'I want Susie.'

'Susie! I ain't having no dopey name like that.'

Linda, realising that this argument could go on for ever, stepped in. 'Sally,' she said, 'Patch is rather a nice name. Look at the patch over the puppy's eye, and it is as much a girl's name as a boy's.'

Sally took the puppy from Linda and examined it critically. 'What d'you think, Max?' she said.

'I think Patch. Ah yes, it is a lovely name,' Max said.

That seemed to settle it. 'OK,' Sally said, and she kissed the puppy's nose. 'Hello, Patch.'

Again Linda's eyes met those of Max's over the children's heads and they smiled. Linda felt as if her heart had done a somersault.

She got to her feet feeling flustered, and was almost glad to hear Bill calling her. 'I've got to go,' she said.

'When will you be back?' Sally asked. 'You haven't been for weeks.'

'Well, you know why that was,' Linda said, making her way to the door.

She didn't want to say any more in front of Max, but the Phelps's children had no such constraint. 'Yeah, course we do. It was 'cos of D-Day,' Charlie said.

They leapt each side of her as she walked across the yard to the van, like a pair of overgrown puppies themselves, Linda thought with a wry grin. Max, she was relieved to see, had stayed in the barn.

Suddenly Sally said, 'If we win the war like everyone says we will, Max won't be a prisoner any more, will he?'

'I suppose not,' Linda said.

'Maybe he'll stay here,' Sally mused.

'Oh, I don't think so. He'll have his own home to go to.'

'Dad would like him to stay here,' Charlie put in. 'He says he's the best bloody farmhand he's ever had.'

'Ah,' said Sally, 'You shouldn't say bloody.'

'Dad does.'

'Well, you shouldn't.'

'I can if I want.'

'Can't.'

'Can.'

Linda broke in, 'See you next Saturday because we're going to give another concert at one of the hospitals,' she said. The children stopped quarrelling long enough to wave to her as she settled herself in the vehicle beside their father, then they began again, their heads bobbing at one another.

'Look at those two, at it hammer and tongs again,' Sam Phelps said. 'Need their bloody heads knocked together, the pair of them.'

'They were arguing about whether Charlie should be able to say bloody or not,' Linda said with a laugh. 'Apparently you do and he thinks he should too.'

'He's a little bugger that Charlie,' Sam Phelps said, though Linda noticed his voice had a hint of pride in it. 'I'll "bloody" him when I get home.'

'No, don't,' Linda said. 'He'll be down on me for telling tales.'

'Well, what was it all about anyway?'

'He was telling me you thought Max a bloody good farmhand.'

'And I do,' Sam said. 'Maybe I should have expressed it a bit better, certainly in His Lordship's hearing. I tell you, my missus will be after me if she hears him. She's always telling me to watch my mouth around the kids.'

'He'll hear worse before he's much older,' Bill remarked.

'Anyway,' Sam said, 'however it was expressed, that Max is a godsend.'

'Funny word to use for a bloody German,' sniffed one of the dancers.

'He can't help his government, no more than we can help ours,' Sam said. 'It's politicians start wars, not the people, and he reckons Hitler's mad. He had no desire to go to war any more than the rest of us did. His family had a farm to the north-west of Germany – that's all gone now. After his brother died on the Russian Front and his father was killed in an air raid, he said his mother lost all will to live and died just before he got his call-up papers. So you see, he's had his own share of sorrow.'

'Don't you be feeling sorry for him,' the accordion player said gruffly. 'He seems to be having a good enough life here.'

'Well, he is a born farmer,' Sam said. 'He has a feel for the land and is able to grow almost anything. The beasts seem to feel it too and he can get as much milk out of my cows as I do. I'll tell you, I couldn't escape from the farm as often as I do, especially these light summer days if it wasn't for Max. He sleeps in the room above the barn now.'

'Really?' Linda said. 'I thought the POWs had

307

to return to the camp every night.'

'He did at first,' Sam said. 'But I needed him there for early milking and then again in the evening, so I stood surety for him. I mean, where would he go if he did escape?'

'Still, you're taking a risk, man,' said someone from the back.

'I don't think so.'

'I do, and I wouldn't let my kids near him.'

'My kids like him.'

'I don't care, they need protection. They're only nippers. What do they know?'

'You can't tar everyone with the same brush.'

'And you can't expect the British people to like Germans!' someone else said heatedly, and there was a murmur of agreement.

Poor Max, thought Linda. Nothing for him at home and only antagonism here. Really, there was little future for him anywhere. But she wasn't going to stick up for him. He was, after all, only a German when all was said and done.

The war went on apace and the concert-party was still in great demand, mainly in hospitals. There was a new batch of American recruits taken into Whittington Barracks in the summer, and the group was asked to give a little concert for them too. They were appreciative and receptive. Linda was now the acknowledged star, who closed every concert with Flora belting out old favourites on the piano, leading the men in well-known songs and choruses.

Linda had wondered where the new American recruits were heading for, and she found out when she read later of the second D-Day, led by the Americans and French on 15 August. They landed in the south of France around Marseilles and, scattering German Resistance, they went racing up the Rhine valley to meet up with General Patton's troops in Central France.

Linda just hoped the second invasion had been achieved with as little loss of life as possible. She remembered the soldiers, some just young lads not much older than she was, to whom she'd sung only days before. She was used to servicemen clustering around her after concerts, and used to declining any dates, and she seldom had to call on the services of Bill or Sam to help her out. Of all servicemen, she found the Americans to be the most persistent; they just couldn't seem to understand why she didn't find them irresistible. Certain ones stuck in her mind, which was only natural, but she wished them *all* well when she read of their exploits in France later.

She remembered particularly Lieutenant Bradshaw, who'd visited her as she was changing in one of the little rooms at the back of the hall. His knock startled her, but she presumed it to be one of the cast and she slipped her dress over her petticoat and shouted, 'Come in.' In he came, twisting his hat between his hands and wetting his lips nervously.

No member of the audience had ever come backstage before, and Linda was annoyed at the intrusion, but not in any way alarmed because she knew she'd only have to yell and folk would come running. Also, the man before her didn't look dangerous.

'I'm sure sorry to bother you, ma'am,' he'd said politely.

'That's all right,' Linda said a bit sharply. 'What is it you want?'

'I don't want anything, ma'am,' the GI said. 'Except to say what a beautiful voice you have. It's how I'd imagine an angel would sing, and that's the truth.'

'Well, thank you very much, Mr ... Lieutenant...?'

'Bradshaw, ma'am. Louis Bradshaw. Point is, ma'am, before I was called up, I was in broadcasting.'

Linda smiled. 'I thought I'd heard every chat-up line in the book, Lieutenant Bradshaw,' she said, 'but I must say this one takes the biscuit. Thank you anyway.'

'This ain't no chat-up line, ma'am. No sir, I really think your voice is something else.'

'Thank you.'

'No, listen ma'am, God, if they could only hear you in Hollywood. Your voice could take you places. I've never heard anything like it.'

Linda had been praised before, but it always made her feel uncomfortable and embarrassed. and she was glad when she heard Bill's shouts asking her if she was ready. 'Thank you once again, Lieutenant,' she said in dismissal. 'Now, if you'd excuse me?'

'Of course,' Louis Bradshaw said. He passed her a piece of paper. 'This is my address and phone number back home in the States,' he said. 'And that of the company where I have some influence. When this blessed war is eventually finished for good, I intend to try and make a break into films. Maybe you could give me a call and we could talk some more about your career? No commitment, no sweat, honest,' and he held up his hands. 'This is straight up.'

Linda took the paper and though she put it in her handbag she didn't look at it, and when she heard of the second invasion she hoped Louis Bradshaw was safe. Not because she had any intention of phoning him, but because she sensed he was a straight and honest man who'd barely begun his life.

Jenny was finding the finishing of the war a tedious business. Everyone knew they were winning, but it seemed to take an age. When Bob came home on a forty-eight-hour pass at the end of August, she clung to him. Letters were all very well, but there was no substitute for holding a real live man in your arms. She pushed her concerns for the future to the back of her mind and held Bob tight.

At that moment she cared about no one, certainly not her mother and grandmother; even Linda ceased to take priority. 'Things are going well, Jen,' Bob told her. 'Better than anyone imagined. The Allies have nearly reached the western borders of Germany, and Stalin is only a few miles from Warsaw. It's run like clockwork, pet, but Hitler took time to conquer Europe so we can't liberate it in three months. Mind, we're having a damn good try.'

Jenny held him close. 'Let's not talk war any more,' she murmured. 'Let's try and forget it, for a while at least.'

But of course it was on everyone's mind. Jenny was glad to visit Bob's mother and chat about other matters. Francesca was always so interested in people; she always asked Jenny about her job and her family, remembering people's names and events from weeks before. Linda still visited her from time to time, though not every week, and kept her up-to-date with the doings of the O'Learys. Despite that, Jenny was a little taken aback when Francesca suddenly said, 'Linda told me your grandmother hasn't been well lately?'

'That's right,' Jenny said, surprised Linda had been bothered enough to mention it to anyone. 'She's been off her food for weeks and has lost weight. Her clothes hang on her and she's tired all the time.'

'What does the doctor say?'

'She won't see the doctor.'

'How ridiculous! Why ever not?'

'Oh, I don't know. She just won't.'

'Why don't you ask your friend to look at her?' Francesca suggested. 'You know, the doctor who seems to take such an interest in you all. Peter something, Linda talks about him sometimes.'

Jenny didn't see much of Peter now, and he didn't ever call – why should he? But she knew where his surgery was. He was popular on the Estate, not least because he didn't press for payment when families were in distress.

Maybe he was the one man who could overcome Norah and Eileen's dislike of doctors. After all, they had met him once or twice and seemed to have taken to him.

Later, Bob and Jenny went for a walk, and although the evening was still pleasantly warm, summer was nearly over, and autumn on its way. Jenny wondered if it would be the last summer of wartime and hoped so. She snuggled close to Bob and he put his arm around her.

There was no doubt in her mind now that she loved Bob. She ached for him, and in their stolen moments together, she wanted more than mere kisses. But always, as their passion rose, the disapproving faces of her mother and grandmother would rise before her, and she would push Bob away, as she did that evening. The thought of possibly having to admit to them that she was pregnant was nearly enough to put her off sex altogether. 'But you wouldn't be,' Bob assured her the first time it happened. 'I'd make sure you'd be all right.'

She didn't ask him how. Really, she wasn't sure she wanted to know. She only knew other girls had been given the same assurances, but still the unthinkable happened. One had married, but the other was on her own after her boy had been killed in action before he had known he was about to become a father.

Bob didn't press her, because though he wanted her badly, he understood her fears. Never mind, he consoled himself, it couldn't be long now. By December, they'd be engaged. Jenny had agreed to that at last and as soon as this damn war was over he was marrying her. He was sure they'd be able to sort something out for her mother and grandmother, even if it was only some sort of rota between her and her sister seeing to them both. Jenny deserved some life of her own, and she belonged with him, because he loved her so dearly.

But he wouldn't spoil his short leave by talking about it. Talking about their future always upset Jenny as she saw it beset by problems. As for the other, well, he wouldn't argue about that either. He could put a rein on his feelings; he wasn't a bloody animal.

'I'm sorry,' Jenny said. 'I just can't. You see'

'It's all right,' Bob said. 'I admire you for it.'

Jenny leaned against him contentedly. She felt relieved, for many girls were pressured into saying yes when they didn't really want to. 'I love you, Bob,' she said.

'And I love you. Stop looking so worried,' Bob said, and he took her in his arms and kissed her and she responded with all her being, secure in the knowledge that he would ask for little more than that.

Chapter Seventeen

By the end of August the Germans had lost 450,000 men. People were jubilant, although they considered the cost high as nearly 40,000 Allies also lost their lives.

British morale was lifted further when the blackout was officially over by 6 September. Although the street-lights were still not allowed, now lights could be lit inside without having to put up the blackout shutters or pull the black curtains closed across the windows. Most people had hated the blackout as much as the bombing raids and for a long time Jenny had thought them unnecessary. Apart from the doodlebugs in the south, which fell indiscriminately, blackout or no blackout, there had been no raids for a couple of years.

Towards the end of September, the concert-party was asked to entertain some Londoners who'd arrived in Birmingham to escape the V-1s and the V-2s, which were pilotless like the doodlebugs, but chillingly silent. The visitors were housed in a church hall in Yardley.

Linda was angry about the new menace facing Londoners and angry with the German soldiers who, defeated and almost certainly on the run, were attacking civilian populations indiscriminately. She decided, when the van drew up at the farmhouse that evening – to collect Sam for the concert for the dispossessed families – she wouldn't get out.

She didn't want to see or speak to Max. And to think, she said to herself, only a few weeks ago I felt sorry for him! She resolved to do it no more. The Germans had started the bloody war: they deserved everything they got.

The nights were drawing in and it was dusky when they drew up at the farm. The children, watching out for the van, were perched on top of the gate. Behind them, in the evening gloom, Max was sweeping up the yard with a large broom. Linda wondered what he was doing there. Surely with the evening milking over, he should have returned to his own quarters?

Charlie jumped off the gate and said, 'Linda, come and see Patch.'

'Not now, Charlie. I'm tired.'

Charlie looked at Linda, as if he couldn't believe his ears. 'Don't be so bloody daft.'

'Less of that, young man,' Bill Fletcher said sharply. He looked over at Linda and wondered why she didn't get out of the van as she usually did. Maybe she *was* tired. She looked a bit peaky; the colour had suddenly drained from her face. Still, he knew young women, having had daughters of his own, and they had 'off' days at times. And if it was that time of the month, the last thing she wanted was Charlie Phelps tormenting the life out of her. He turned to the young lad and said, 'Make yourself useful. Go and tell your dad we're sick and tired waiting for him.'

Charlie's lip stuck out obstinately. 'Why should I?'

'Because if you don't, my lad, you'll find the toe of my boot at the seat of your pants,' Bill said sternly. 'Now scat, the pair of you. Leave Linda alone.'

Linda watched Charlie climb back over the gate and make for the house with Sally trailing behind him. Max pulled his arm as he passed and said something to him, then he leaned on the yard brush and let his eyes stray to the van. He fixed his gaze on Linda and she seemed to be unable to tear her eyes away from his. She felt the heat of embarrassment flow through her body; she knew he'd be aware she was making excuses. Well, she thought, let him. I don't give a damn what he thinks. He's nothing to me.

And then he smiled and it felt as if her heart had turned over. She was annoyed with herself and furious with him. What the hell has he got to smile about? She thought. His country's on the run and thousands of his fellow Germans are being slaughtered. They're not bloody normal. Gran's right, however nice he appears, he's a bloody monster like all the rest and the sooner this war is won and he's shipped back home, the better.

A week after the concert in Yardley, Eileen at last agreed to see Peter Sanders. She had refused to be talked into it by either of her granddaughters, or even by Norah, who'd eventually recognised that her mother was ill. In the end, it was pain that drove Eileen Gillespie to her bed, and she finally told Jenny she could ask the doctor to call. 'And when he comes,' she said, 'I'll talk to him on my own. I don't want any of you fussing around me.'

'Nothing wrong with her temper at any rate,' Jenny commented to Geraldine, as they despatched Linda for the doctor.

Geraldine smiled at her younger sister and said, 'No. I think your Dr Sanders will have his work cut out.'

But he didn't. Eileen received him quite cordially and shooed Geraldine, who'd shown the doctor up, out of the room.

Peter walked towards the bed, shocked by the old lady's wizened appearance. He noticed the yellowish whites of her eyes and his heart sank. 'Now what's this?' he said in his best bedside manner.

'You can cut out all that hale and hearty chat,' Eileen said dismissively. 'I know what's the matter with me, and I know how long I've had it. I nursed my mother through the same thing. What I want to know is, can you give me something for the pain, and some indication of how long I've got?'

Peter studied the woman under narrowed lids. He didn't like her and never would, but he couldn't help but admire her courage. However, he couldn't answer her questions just like that. 'I need to examine you,' he said.

'Go ahead,' Eileen told him. 'You'll find it is as I said.'

And so it was. As far as Peter could ascertain, a large tumour was lodged in Eileen Gillespie's stomach. He pulled the covers back over her shrunken body, sat on the chair beside the bed and said, 'I can certainly prescribe morphine for the pain. As for how advanced it is, a surgeon could tell you better than I could. I could arrange for you to visit hospital…'

'No doctor, no hospital.' Eileen said firmly. 'I want to die in my own bed.'

'You will require nursing,' Peter said.

'I know that, but Geraldine can do that in the day. She has little to do now her children are both at school and Jenny can take over in the evening. It might even do my daughter good to have to put someone else's needs before her own. She's never had to do that, you know, and I suppose I've encouraged her, but I shall not be here much longer. She'll have to learn to stand on her own two feet before very long.'

'Mrs Gillespie, without a thorough examination by a qualified surgeon, I have no idea how long you've got,' Peter said, and added, 'it could be months.'

'It won't be, Doctor. I know it and you know it,' Eileen said. She spoke matter-of-factly, without a trace of self-pity. 'I doubt I'll be here by Christmas.'

Peter doubted it too, but he didn't say so. Instead he said, 'Do you want me to tell the family?'

'You can do,' Eileen said. 'But explain I want no wailing and weeping around me. I have no time for it, and before you go – can you give me something for the pain?'

Peter thanked his lucky stars he'd thought to pack phials of morphine. He administered an injection to give the old lady some relief and went

319

downstairs to break the news to the family and write out a prescription.

Norah refused to believe it at first. Her mother had never had a day's illness in her life. Surely, she asked, there was *something* the doctor could do, some treatment he could try? Peter explained patiently that even if the old lady had agreed to go to hospital, there was little that could be done for her. 'She's known about it for some time apparently,' he said. 'But she chose not to call me in earlier because she didn't want treatment. She doesn't now. She just wants relief from pain.'

'She's monstrously selfish,' Norah burst out. 'She owes it to me to try everything!'

Jenny was the least shocked by the doctor's diagnosis. She'd seen how her grandmother's body had seemed to waste away over the last weeks; her face had pouches of skin beneath her eyes, and her chin, and her proud neck had sunk into folds of sagging flesh. She didn't doubt anything Peter said and she asked the question both her mother and sister wanted to ask, but lacked the courage to do so. 'How long has she got?'

'It's impossible to be accurate.'

'Weeks, months, a year?' Norah snapped out. 'You must have some idea.'

'Weeks,' the doctor said.

'Weeks?' Norah repeated, and faced the fact that her mother, who'd shared her home and her bedroom for the last four years and who'd been her confidante and friend for as far back as she cared to remember, would soon be there no more. An immeasurable sadness took hold of her, for she knew none of her children would make up for the loss of her mother.

'I'm sorry,' Peter said. 'It's the worst news a doctor can give.'

'Thank you, Doctor, at least for your honesty,' Jenny said, when it was obvious neither her mother nor sister seemed able to say anything.

'I'll call tomorrow,' Peter said and Jenny saw him to the door. 'I'm sorry,' he said again.

Jenny shrugged. She couldn't feel too sorry for the old lady, but she'd seen her mother's stricken face and said, 'Is she in any pain?'

'No, not now. We'll be able to keep her virtually pain-free with morphine,' Peter promised. 'I'll be along tomorrow and I'll try and arrange a nurse to call daily. She seems to think you and your sister will cope with the rest.'

'We will,' Jenny said. 'We'll have to.'

'Now, don't you go running yourself ragged,' the doctor warned.

'I won't,' Jenny promised. 'I'll have to give the warden's post up, but we're not so necessary now and everything's winding down anyway. It's all right, I'll go down tomorrow and explain.'

However, the doctor was still worried for Jenny. She had her work cut out with a full-time job and the house to run, besides nursing one terminally ill person and another who'd willed herself into disability.

That night he remembered Doctor McKenzie's theory about hypochondria. By morning he thought he had a solution of sorts. Norah O'Leary trusted him as she trusted no one else in the medical profession and she'd seen no doctor

321

for years. If he were to introduce some pills to her now, just standard painkillers, and tell her about the new breakthrough in pain relief for arthritis sufferers she might believe him, if she wanted to. It was worth a try. If she only agreed to do a few things for herself and relieve the load from Jenny's shoulders, that would be a help. He did wonder if it was a truly ethical thing to do, but he pushed such concerns aside.

Geraldine was upstairs when he knocked the next morning and she came down looking flustered. 'I didn't think you'd be so early,' she said. 'Grandmother hasn't long finished her breakfast and I haven't washed her or anything. She won't want to see you just yet.'

'It's all right,' Peter said. 'I'm in no hurry.' He was in fact rushed off his feet, but he kept that to himself and went on, 'I'll sit with your mother for a minute.'

Geraldine gratefully bustled back upstairs and Peter Sanders let himself into the living room.

Norah was bored enough to welcome the doctor. She missed her mother's company and Geraldine's too, for her daughter spent most of her time in the bedroom. So she smiled at Peter and said, 'Hello, Doctor. Isn't my mother ready for you?'

'Not yet,' Peter said. 'But that's all to the good, because really I wanted a word with you anyway.'

Norah was sceptical about the tablets as he explained, but he fully expected her to be. She stared at the young man with the beard and moustache looking at her with concerned eyes. She could have told him she could get up and

322

walk if she wanted to, almost as well as anyone else, but she didn't. What she said was, 'I've had painkillers for years, Doctor. They don't work.'

'These are specially formulated for arthritis,' Peter said. 'They're still in the experimental stages, but the result of the trials have been excellent.'

'I don't want to be a guinea pig for some drug company.'

'Oh, you won't be that,' Peter assured her. 'Don't worry. It's just that they're not yet available over the chemist's counter. I've been sent a small supply to try on selected patients, and I thought of you immediately.'

Norah like the sound of that – as if she was a special customer. Peter pressed home this advantage. 'Would you try them and tell me what you think? You'd be doing me an enormous favour.'

'You're sure they're safe?'

'Absolutely.'

'And how much will this wonder drug cost? You know with Mother's medication there isn't a lot to spare to spend on anyone else.'

'As I said, it's experimental,' Peter said. 'So at the moment it's absolutely free.'

'Oh well, in that case.' Norah weighed the small glass bottle in her hand and then opened it and spilled the white tablets into the palm of her hand. 'They don't look very miraculous, do they?' she said. 'Just like aspirins really.'

'Ah, but what matters is the ingredients,' Peter said, and wondered if he'd always been so good at lying. He was mightily glad when Geraldine

323

opened the hall door at that minute, a bowl of water in her hand and a towel draped over her arm. 'Grandmother's ready for you now,' she said.

'Ah Geraldine,' Norah cried out. 'Fetch me a glass of water, there's a good girl. I've some tablets here the doctor wants me to try and I must have a drink to help them down,' and Peter escaped upstairs as Norah was explaining the tablets to her daughter.

Jenny wasn't aware what Peter had done for her mother and he didn't confide in her. Geraldine only told her that he'd given their mother some new pills to try. She therefore didn't expect a miracle cure and wasn't disappointed when there wasn't one.

Anyway, all her energy and that of her sister, went on their grandmother. Eileen had never been easy and now pain and frustration made her querulous and quarrelsome. She was quite capable of administering a ringing slap if you did something wrong and inadvertently hurt her; occasionally she even threw things. Jenny tried to be patient, knowing that she hated having to stay in bed and have someone help her with most things, even the most personal ones. Also, time hung heavy on her hands and she missed the chats she enjoyed with her daughter. Geraldine was all right, but not much of a talker. Besides, she was always in a hurry taking the children to school or fetching them and making meals as well as helping both her mother and grandmother. And Eileen had never had much to say to Jenny.

Downstairs Norah was just as miserable. One day, just over a week after her mother had taken to her bed, she felt particularly lonely and neglected and sorry for herself. Geraldine had left the house just after dinner as she said she wanted to do a bit of shopping in Erdington village before collecting the children from school. She suddenly realised with a slight shock that she'd not spoken a word to her mother for three days, though she slept in the divan bed just three feet from her own, for Eileen was usually asleep when Norah was helped to bed at night and down again in the morning. In fact, if she didn't make the effort to see her, she might never speak to her again, for no one knew how long she had.

She pushed the rug off her knees and, grasping the chair arms, she pulled herself to her feet and stood for a moment. Her head swam a little so she stayed still until the dizziness passed off. There was also a little pain in her knees and she was stiff, but nothing like the other few times when she'd walked around the room. The tablets of Dr Sanders were very good, she decided.

She walked slowly across the room holding on to the back of the armchair and the sideboard, and out to the small hall where she looked at the stairs with some trepidation. Walking around a room was one thing, tackling the stairs alone was quite another. But if you don't, said a little voice inside her, you haven't a hope of spending any time with your mother, for she knew Eileen would never leave her bed again. Using the banister as leverage, she pulled herself up one step at a time, until slowly but surely she stood at the top, out of breath at the unaccustomed exercise.

Eileen was waiting for her, as she'd heard her laboured approach, but her smile of welcome turned into a grimace of pain, 'Oh Mother,' Norah cried.

'Don't fuss,' Eileen said sharply, 'I can't bear it and never could.' She gazed at her daughter and said, 'So you made it up at last, on your own.'

'It's the new tablets that doctor gave me – they're marvellous, Mother.'

Eileen gazed at her daughter. She knew there was little wrong with her, but she also knew why she'd pretended all this time and it centred on Dermot and what he'd put her through. If only Eileen hadn't become ill after her own husband died, she would have prevented her daughter marrying that common oaf Dermot O'Leary. Despite the lack of money, they could have made something of life, either through an advantageous marriage for Norah, or perhaps running a small business somewhere together. They'd had friends who would have helped them, but when she married out of her class, they'd been ostracised.

It had nearly sent her to the asylum when her darling sent for her and she found her beautiful daughter reduced to a drudge. In no time, she had three children and was pregnant with another while her husband was preparing for war, and all he'd provided her with was some hovel that for some reason he'd seemed ridiculously proud of.

Then there was the dreadful business of the

riots and uprisings in 1916 and he wasn't even there to protect Norah and his family from the mob that threatened to burn them in their beds. They were forced to take refuge with Maureen O'Leary. That had been a terrible time. Eileen, Norah and the children lay night after night on hard pallets, pressed in among other bodies, and never had quite enough to eat and their clothes were in rags. Eileen Gillespie knew she would hate Dermot O'Leary till the end of her days, and daily she expected him to arrive back in Ireland and take them out of the nightmare.

But when he did come, she found he had his family hanging to his coat-tails and he had to see to them too and not just his own wife and children. When they eventually sailed to England, they went together and lived together too while Dermot got work with his uncle. He worked all the hours God sent, but not to lift just his wife from the mire, but in order to care for his mother, sisters and young brother. Oh God, how she'd hated him at times and begrudged every penny he gave to his mother, but she could do nothing.

Nor could she do anything about the other two children Norah had after Dermot had forced himself upon her daughter. The first of those children, Jenny, was the spit of the O'Learys – and from day one, she'd belonged to her father. The moment she could toddle she was after him everywhere, and her first word was 'Dada'. He even took her down to Maureen O'Leary's, where Norah had forbidden the others to go. Dermot at least didn't go against her wishes there, but then he hardly knew the older ones. Jenny had been his one consolation; he hadn't bargained on another child, but two years later Anthony was born. Eileen told her daughter to put her foot down then and she had. Anthony was to be the last and she'd made it plain.

Eileen knew Norah had been hard on Jenny, but she couldn't blame her for her resentment. When Norah shouted at Jenny, or slapped or shook her, Eileen knew she was getting back at all the O'Learys, but in particular Dermot, who'd trapped her into marriage with him.

'I'm glad you came,' she said to Norah and her wizened hand clasped her daughter's.

'Oh Mother,' Norah said, and tears squeezed from her eyes as she laid her head on her mother's breast.

'Geraldine said she came round and found her in the bedroom with no sticks or anything,' Jenny told her Gran O'Leary. 'And she's been up since and more than once. I mean, I'm not saying she leaps up and down like a spring chicken, but she does go up. They eat their breakfast together and then Mother often helps Grandmother wash and they spend much of the day together. She also takes herself to the bathroom for a wash unaided and to the toilet outside.'

'And how did she explain this miracle?' Maureen said. 'Or didn't she even bother?'

'Oh yes, she bothered. She put it down to the latest pills Peter Sanders gave her,' Jenny said. 'He certainly gave her pills, but I would say they had little to do with anything.'

'Who cares what the story of it is? Lord, child, it'll lift the load off your back.'

Jenny knew that. She hoped the improvement might continue and possibly she wouldn't then feel so tied to Norah. Perhaps she and Bob could have a future of sorts.

'Of course, she might go downhill when Eileen Gillespie dies,' Maureen said.

'I know. I worry about that,' Jenny admitted. 'I've talked it over with Geraldine. She says we must make sure she doesn't, but it isn't that easy.'

'No indeed it isn't, for Norah has depended and leant on her mother for years,' Maureen said and Jenny went home with a heavy heart.

Eileen Gillespie died on 3 November and Norah was by her bedside, holding her hand, when she breathed her last. The priest had administered the last rites and then she'd asked the assembled family to leave so that she should be alone with her mother. Geraldine popped in later and saw her mother sprawled over the still figure of her grandmother.

Norah was inconsolable and even Geraldine and Jenny seemed steeped in gloom. Linda was glad it was over well before Christmas and tried not to show how pleased she was. They had shows booked for Christmas and New Year and she really hoped Jenny was not going to be hypocritical and stuffy and insist on a mourning period of a year, but it was hardly something she could ask before her grandmother was even buried, so she bided her time.

'We'll have to let the boys know,' Geraldine said one night as they sat before the fire. Geraldine had moved in for a few days and between them they'd encouraged Norah to go up to bed, using one of the boys' beds, while Geraldine said she would sleep in the other with the children.

'Not, of course,' Geraldine went on, 'that they can do anything.'

'No,' Jenny agreed. 'They probably don't even know she's ill, though I wrote and told them.'

She wondered if they'd got the letters, especially when none had mentioned it in the sparse missives they'd last sent. She imagined delivering the post was not considered as important as liberating towns and cities and fighting Germans. And anyway, how would they find them, spread across the face of Europe as they were?

'It might help Mother if they wrote to her,' Geraldine said.

Jenny knew it would, but none of the men had written by the time the funeral was arranged, though all the rest of the family and many neighbours were there.

Linda was surprised, but supposed they'd come to support Jenny. Maureen had, she knew, and so had Peggy. Norah, supported by her daughters, was also surprised at the turnout. Neighbours she hardly knew and had never spoken to, thronged the church and some stood with their heads bowed. But Norah kept her head lowered and refused to acknowledge any of them.

When Norah saw her mother-in-law standing with a woman she didn't know, she supposed it was the girl Peggy that Jenny had spoken of and she stopped dead still while her daughters stood each side of her. From her pew, Linda watched. 'I'm sorry for your loss, Norah,' Maureen said, stepping into the aisle as she spoke.

Norah looked at the woman she'd always considered a thorn in her flesh, the link with the husband who had let her down and exposed her to tyranny and hardship, and she turned from her without a word. Embarrassed by her mother's behaviour, Geraldine led her away, but Jenny turned to her gran and saw her face was flushed. She felt a flash of anger at her mother, who despite her grief, could have at least had the good manners to reply to her gran's words. She gave Maureen a hug. 'Oh Gran, I'm so glad you've come,' she said, and Maureen patted her granddaughter, and whispered, 'Don't worry, cutie. It's like water off a duck's back.'

Linda was furious. She glared at Norah and wondered if she thought everyone had come to honour her or the other battleaxe she'd taken over from. She glanced at the coffin at the front of the church, draped with a black cloth and scattered with Mass cards amongst the wreaths, and wondered how many Masses it would take and how many prayers said to get Eileen Gillespie into Heaven. A good few she decided. If it wasn't for Jenny she wouldn't have gone to the funeral and pretended to be all pious and sad about the old lady dying. She'd have waited till the old harridan was in the ground and then danced on her grave. Still, she supposed, now she was dead, Eileen would turn into a saint like

331

most people did. A man could be the biggest bastard under the sun, alive but once he died everyone would go around saying what a fine fellow he'd been. Well, she wouldn't play that game. She'd hated Eileen Gillespie living and she still hated her. She was glad she was dead and wished Norah would die soon too – and give Jenny some life.

Chapter Eighteen

The weeks after Eileen's death were very grim indeed. Norah was determined on a decent period of mourning and Jenny began to wonder if Christmas, when it arrived, would be celebrated at all. Linda was glad of her three pre-Christmas concerts planned for the hospitals; she felt she was doing something useful and, after all, there was precious little festive cheer at home.

Jenny hadn't made any objections to her taking part, despite the fact that the first concert was just five weeks after Eileen Gillespie's death. She too felt that bringing the concert-party to the hospital was a good thing and was bound to cheer the patients. Norah said plenty, of course – all of it caustic and unhelpful – but Jenny just said it was wartime and everyone needed to do their bit. 'It's also nearly Christmas,' she added, 'the season of goodwill, Mother. Surely it can't be wrong for Linda to bring some pleasure to people who are ill and in pain, especially when they can't get home for Christmas?'

Linda had to smile at that. She thought of the brightly decorated wards and the genuine warmth and concern that the doctors and nurses showed their patients. She'd prefer their festivities any day, to spending time in Norah O'Leary's presence.

However, she said none of this to Jenny, who

was hoping against hope that Bob would make it home. She knew Jenny had agreed to get engaged this Christmas and thought it was about bloody time, after four years of courting. She also knew Jenny had hesitated for so long because she thought she'd be tied to her mother for years to come. But now things were different and Norah could certainly cope around the house. In a way, Linda thought, she should be grateful to Eileen Gillespie for dying when she did, for it was Eileen's illness or at least her bedridden state before her death, that had caused Norah O'Leary to put aside her own imagined disability and get to her feet. No pills alone would have caused her to rise up from her chair the way she did, however good they were and regardless of any recommendation.

Surely that was Jenny's passport to freedom? Surely, now Norah could cope on her own, Jenny could marry Bob and be rid of her mother's dominance? When the war was finally over and she'd moved away and was living with Jenny and Bob, maybe then she'd get over the strange feelings she had for the German POW. When they called at the Phelps's farm to pick up Sam Phelps for their first Christmas concert in mid-December, Linda hadn't been near the place for weeks. Now it was black night when they drove into the farmyard, and there was no one in sight.

'You getting out to give him a call or shall I?' Bill asked.

'I will if you like,' Linda said. She jumped down from the van almost defiantly. She would not hide herself away as if she was afraid, she decided. Anyway, it was hardly likely Max would be around. He'd probably be tucked up in his own quarters in the barn.

'Tell him to get a move on will you?' Bill Fletcher said irritably. 'Before we all freeze to death.'

Linda gave a wave of acknowledgement as she scaled the gate and made her way across the farmyard. Above her, a full moon shone down and the stars twinkled. It was a clear night, and a cold one, with a heavy frost for the morning and Linda's feet slid on the icy cobbles. She gave a tap on the kitchen door and opened it, calling out, 'Only me,' as she did so. She was surprised and then put out to see Max sitting on the settee beside Ruby, the Land Girl, warming himself by the fire, like a valued member of the family. Charlie and Sally had obviously both had baths and were dressed in pyjamas, slippers and dressing gowns, and Sarah Phelps, Sam's wife, was brushing Sally's hair which shone in the light of the flickering fire.

Everyone turned as Linda walked in, and the children immediately ran to her, with a cry. But over their heads, she had eyes for only Max. 'That Sam,' Sarah said exasperatedly, 'he'd be late for his own funeral. Here Sally, run up and tell your dad they're waiting on him.'

Sally, unwilling to leave the warm room, complained, 'Oh Mom, he'll be here in a minute.'

'Do as you're told.'

Reluctantly, Sally dropped her hand that was holding Linda's, and Sarah said, 'Come up to the fire, pet, and get a warm. Sam won't be long.'

'Oh no, it's all right,' Linda said. Now she was here, only yards from Max, her insides seemed to have turned to jelly. She wasn't at all sure she could walk and was quite sure it was not a good idea to move any nearer.

'Oh come on, he could be ages yet, you know what he is,' Sarah said. 'You might as well get a warm while you have the chance.' And, with Charlie tugging on her hand, Linda felt herself pulled forward, and Ruby moved to the end of the settee making a space for Linda to sit beside Max.

Afterwards she wasn't at all sure what she'd said in answer to Sarah's questions about herself and her family. She must have made the right responses, but really, all she was aware of was the nearness of Max and the electricity that existed between them. When Sam appeared, one half of her was relieved and the other disappointed. All the way to the van, she silently told herself off for allowing a man to arouse her in such a way.

Knowing how she felt about Max, though she could confide in no one, she could understand Jenny's feelings for Bob, and hoped for her sake that he would get away to see her over Christmas.

He did, although he'd had to travel all through the night, and arrived on their doorstep in the early hours of Christmas Day. Roused from the bed she'd just tumbled into, Jenny ran down to let him in, pleased that no one else seemed to have been woken. She took one look at his face, which was grey with fatigue, and drew him indoors and into her arms.

She insisted he eat before sleeping, though Bob

found it hard to keep his eyes open over the scrambled eggs Jenny made from the tin of dried egg in the cupboard, wishing she had something more festive to give the man she loved. But the meal revived him a little and he stood up from the table and drew Jenny into his arms and kissed her. Later when she tucked him up on the settee, with extra blankets she'd brought down from the top of her wardrobe, he held onto her arm. 'I love you, Jenny O'Leary,' he said. 'All the way here I've thought about nothing but you,' and he drew her down to sit beside him.

'I'm so glad you made it,' she whispered.

'I had to,' Bob said. 'You see, I have something rather special to give you,' and he pulled a ring box from his pocket and opened it to show Jenny the diamond solitaire ring that glinted out at her.

'Oh Bob, it's beautiful!' she breathed.

'You will do me the honour of becoming my wife?' Bob said, and Jenny threw her arms around him. She'd agreed to become engaged at Christmas, but somehow hadn't expected a ring.

'Yes. Oh yes!' She cried, and their kiss was like an awakening in Jenny. She was engaged to Bob, she belonged with him and when he slipped from under the blanket and they lay before the fire on the rug together, she forgot her mother in the room above her and the condemnation of the priest in the confessional box, and she wanted Bob to make love to her. 'Go on, go on,' she panted as his fingers caressed her breasts. He'd opened the buttons of the dressing gown and nightdress and she lay naked before him. He gasped at the beauty of her, and trailed his fingers down her belly and followed it with his lips.

'Oh God, Jenny,' he groaned.

'Go on. Oh please!'

Bob's senses were reeling and yet he pulled away and Jenny looked at him puzzled and frustrated, her insides crying for relief. 'What is it?' she asked.

'Jenny, it wouldn't be right, not yet.'

'Don't you want to?'

'Don't I want to?' Bob cried. 'Of course I want to! I've wanted you from the first day we met, and each time we've been together my love has increased, but I don't want to love you this way, with your mother and Linda asleep upstairs.' He cupped her face between his hands and said, 'When I make love to you, darling, it will be a beautiful experience for us both and then you will be my wife. As soon as the war is over, we will be married.'

'But Bob...'

'Darling, we've waited so long. Surely we can wait a little longer?'

Jenny wanted to cry, but she knew that what Bob said was true. She pulled her clothes around her and said, half-jokingly, 'Why are you so bloody sensible?'

'Because I love you, Mrs Masters-to-be, that's why,' he said comfortably. 'And now you'd better go to bed, before everyone has to get up again.'

She returned the ring box and said, 'Let's tell Mother and Linda at breakfast. Keep it till then.'

'Are you going to Mass?'

'We went to the one at midnight,' Jenny

338

yawned. 'I waited all evening for you to arrive. I really thought you weren't going to come after all. Mother stayed up, so I know if you'd arrived you'd have got in, for though I told you she's much better, she's not ventured outside yet. I think the walk to church would probably be beyond her yet awhile.'

'How is she in herself?'

'Oh, still missing Grandmother and making everyone else suffer for it. Geraldine less than Linda and me,' Jenny said. 'But we cope.'

'Will she mind my being here?'

'She minds everything, Bob,' Jenny said, knowing her mother would be furious that her permission had not been asked before Jenny invited Bob to bed down on her settee.

'Would it be best if I left? I could always knock my mother up at home and come back later today.'

'No, it wouldn't be best,' Jenny said hotly. 'Not for me it wouldn't. Mother's not the only one in the house to be considered, you know.'

'It was only a suggestion.'

'Well, it was a very bad one,' Jenny said. 'Now, go to sleep for heaven's sake, before the whole house is awake.'

She left him then with a chaste and prudent peck on the cheek and made her stealthy way up the stairs, hoping she'd get in a few hours' sleep before having to face her mother's bad temper.

'How dare you invite someone into the house at the dead of night without asking me?' Norah shouted, almost incoherent with rage.

'He isn't someone, Mother. He's Bob, and you've known him for years,' Jenny said, her voice low and controlled. 'I did tell you he was going to try and make it for Christmas Day, and when he did arrive, it was the early hours of the morning. You were asleep.'

'That signifies nothing. You go behind my back, allowing him to stay the night without a word.'

Jenny wondered how Bob was feeling hearing them row about him, for although they were both in her mother's bedroom, she knew every word, certainly those her mother spat out, would be audible to him. She'd come straight into her mother's room that morning, to explain what Bob was doing on the settee downstairs, to save her mother the shock of just finding him there. Maybe she should have said nothing. Good manners might have kept her mother quiet, at least until Bob had gone.

Jenny swallowed down her irritation. It was Christmas Day and Bob was waiting for her downstairs. Now was not the time to engage in a slanging match with her mother.

If Anthony hadn't died, and there wasn't a day gone by she didn't miss him, she might never have met Bob and learned to love him. She went cold at the thought that she might never have known the lovely man who filled her with such intense desire. But now was not the time to say all this to her mother. Maybe the time would never be right; maybe she should just let her rant away and not answer back. It only prolonged things. Left to herself, even her mother would eventually run out of things to say. 'I'll go and make breakfast then, shall I?' she asked, hoping to placate her mother.

Norah glared at her. 'Go then!' she spat out. 'I haven't had a hint of an apology from you, nor have you bothered to enquire if *I* need a hand to get dressed!'

Norah had been dressing herself for weeks now, with no help at all, and Jenny wondered with a heavy heart if she was sinking back into dependency again.

'Not that I want *your* help, miss,' Norah went on self-righteously. 'You've made it quite clear that you consider me a burden, so I will struggle on alone.'

Jenny felt so angry that her body burned with it, but she damped it down inside her, knowing that it would destroy the day and upset Bob if she were to unleash it at her mother. So without a word, she turned and left the room, without slamming the door, and went down to Bob.

Bob looked at her as she entered the room. She crossed to him, put her arms around him and buried her head in his chest. 'Darling, you're shaking,' he said gently.

'I know. It's how she gets me,' Jenny choked.

'I can understand it,' Bob said with feeling. 'I heard everything she said, and it isn't just that, but how she says things.'

Personally, he thought Jenny was a saint to put up with it, day in and day out. He'd been going out with Jenny four years now, and much of the anger and nastiness in the house had been glossed over when he'd been present, though he'd sensed it simmering under the surface. The sooner he got Jenny away from here the better, he decided.

Jenny lifted her head and tried to calm herself down. She wouldn't let herself cry, it would only upset Bob further. She saw his face working and knew he was angry, and so she said lightly, 'Fold up the blankets, Bob, I'll take them upstairs and then I'll rustle us up some breakfast.' She nudged him and went on, 'I've got a bit of "under the counter" sausage as a treat, and by the way,' and at this she stood on tiptoe and kissed his lips lightly, 'Happy Christmas!' she said.

Norah started again at the breakfast-table when Bob and Jenny explained about the engagement and Jenny showed her the ring. Linda was awed by it glistening on Jenny's finger and terribly happy for the two of them. She congratulated them both sincerely. Jenny knew if her mother hadn't been at the table, as she'd taken to doing every day now, Linda would have probably thrown her arms around the two of them, but she was always constrained by Norah's presence.

Mrs O'Leary's face was drawn into a thin line and two angry spots of colour appeared on her cheeks as she snapped. 'So that's the way it is now? You become engaged without seeking approval or permission?' She'd never thought anyone would want to *marry* Jenny. She wouldn't stand for it either, she decided. Just because she was better able to move around, Jenny imagined she could leave her to cope. Well, she thought, Jenny can think again. Her duty is to look after me. 'She's not going to swan off anywhere with anyone and leave me on my own,' Norah muttered to herself. 'And if that means I have to have a relapse and become helpless again, so be it.'

Bob tried to pour oil on troubled waters, chatting pleasantly to Norah about this and that, and Norah allowed herself to be mollified. Once the young man had gone, she'd work on Jenny and show her plainly where her duty lay. Jenny was just glad her mother seemed to have accepted it at last. Geraldine said she should be more understanding, but Geraldine hadn't got it to put up with day after day. So she listened to Bob soothing her mother's ruffled feathers and blessed him for it. Later, helping her wash up the breakfast dishes, he confessed it had been walking through a minefield.

'You're better at it than me at any rate,' Jenny said. 'It wears me down.'

'I can well understand it,' Bob said. He kissed the nape of her neck as she bent over the bowl and she shivered in delicious anticipation.

'Oh Bob. I'm so lucky to have you here today,' she said. 'Some of the girls at work haven't seen their husbands for years.'

'I know,' Bob agreed. 'But I'm not going to spend my precious leave arguing with your mother, or allowing you to, or skirting around every topic as if we're avoiding an unexploded bomb. After dinner we're out of this. We're expected at my mother's for tea, but first we'll have some time on our own.

'We're engaged,' he said, catching her round the waist, 'and it's Christmas, the season of goodwill to all men. I've seen precious little of any goodwill you have towards me.'

Jenny snuggled against him and said, 'Let's go somewhere private and I'll show you as much goodwill as you like.'

'Oh promises promises Jenny O'Leary,' Bob said, but he took her hand and headed towards Pype Hayes Park.

On Boxing Day, for Bob had only managed a twenty-four-hour pass, Jenny and Linda went down to Maureen O'Leary's. Linda had told them of the engagement the day before, but both Maureen and Peggy were keen to see the ring, which they both admired. 'He's begun making plans for after the war too,' Jenny said proudly. 'He knows now it's only a matter of time till peace is declared and he's written to the firm of architects he worked for before the war to see if his job has been kept open for him.'

'And has it?'

'Yes.'

'Why then, it's all fair sailing for you.'

'Yes, yes it is. And now Bob wants me to keep an eye out for suitable houses in the Sutton Coldfield or Erdington area,' Jenny said.

'We'll have to start planning your wedding pretty soon then,' Peggy said. 'I should think there'll be a host of postwar weddings and you might have to get in quick.'

'If you ask me, there's altogether too much fuss made of a wedding,' Gerry put in. 'And far too much money spent on them.'

'Will you listen to him?' Maureen said. 'Who

asked you?' The laughter swelled around the kitchen as Peggy gave her husband a push.

It was Saturday 30 December and Linda was changing beds and cleaning bedrooms, while Jenny was tackling a big wash in the kitchen. Geraldine came around later on Saturdays, with Linda and Jenny both at home, and Jenny could hardly begrudge her a break. She'd received a letter that morning from Bob and was in the happy mood his letters usually induced, because while she heard from him, she knew he was safe. She really needed to hear from him because since Bob had left after Christmas Day, her mother had gone on and on about a daughter's duty to her mother and especially an unmarried daughter. Jenny knew what she was going on about and it was hard to take. She was affected by it and guilt had begun to stab at her, though Linda had told her not to be so stupid.

She wondered if she should go up and see Francesca that afternoon with Linda. She seldom went unless Bob was home, and felt bad about it. She'd been sure, at first, that his mother might have someone else in mind for her son, someone more in his social class, but Francesca seemed so genuinely pleased that they'd become engaged and had admired the ring over the tea-table at Christmas Day.

Francesca could have told Jenny, she wanted nothing for her children but happiness. She could have told her of the stiff opposition both she and her husband had endured when they expressed a wish to marry. Malcolm's parents

345

had threatened to cast him out of the family, while Francesca, who'd met Malcolm while visiting England with her parents, had a fiancé back home, chosen for her by her father. The autocratic opposition only stiffened the young people's resolve and they'd had a long and happy marriage: Francesca wanted the same for her own son and daughter.

But neither Linda nor Jenny did get to Francesca's that afternoon, nor did Linda get the bedrooms finished, for just as she was tucking in the sheets on Norah's bed, her eye was taken by the sight of Geraldine running down the road towards them. She was out in the raw winter's day without a hat or coat on, and she had slippers on her feet. Jamie was in her arms similarly clad and little Rosemarie was galloping along by her side. In Geraldine's hand was clutched a buff-coloured piece of paper.

Linda wondered if she should run down to the kitchen to warn Jenny, but then, she wondered, how did you prepare anyone for news like that? She knew only too well what the buff paper would say, that Geraldine's husband Dan was either *Killed in Action*, or *Missing Believed Killed*, and when all was said and done, it usually meant the bloody same thing. She left the bedroom and made for the stairs.

Jenny, garbed in a coarse heavy apron, was in the process of hauling the clothes from the boiler into the sink using wooden tongs. The kitchen was full of steam and smelt of damp washing and soap flakes and she was startled when Geraldine pushed her way in through the back door. As

346

soon as she took in her older sister's dishevelled state and the crumpled telegram in her hand, she cried: 'Oh, no! Not Dan?'

Geraldine didn't answer. Jenny realised she probably couldn't speak, but she ignored Jenny's outstretched arms and rushed instead into the living room and her mother. Unmindful of her wet arms and damp front, Jenny gathered the frightened tearful children to her, and through the open door she watched her sister sobbing in her mother's arms. Norah rocked her daughter and chanted. 'There, my lamb, there, there. Don't upset yourself like this. There, there.'

Never, Jenny thought, had her mother spoken to her in that soft loving tone, and never had she been held in her arms like that. Even as she comforted Dan's children she felt an aching loss for her own mother's love that had been withheld from her since the day of her birth.

She was glad to see Linda come in from the stairs. For a start it stopped her feeling sorry for herself, when really she should be feeling for her sister now without her husband and the children without a father. Dan had been a lovely man, a good husband and a loving father, and he would be sorely missed. Often Jenny had thought his personality was such that he'd prevented Geraldine becoming quite as bad as her mother and grandmother. When Geraldine talked things over with him, using her mother's opinions, which she adopted as her own, he'd been able to make her see how unreasonable some of them were. Jenny had thought Dan had been very good for her sister and besides that, she'd liked him

347

very much. Sudden hatred for the Germans who had ended Dan's life rose up in her.

Linda's eyes met those of Jenny's above the children's heads, and she mouthed the question, 'Dan?' though she knew it could be nothing else which could cause such distress.

Jenny gave a brief nod and indicating the children said, 'Will you keep an eye on them? I'll pop around and see Peter at the surgery. I think Geraldine could do with something to calm her.' Geraldine's gasping sobs and heartrending moans were frightening the shocked children, causing them to weep more too. 'She'll be ill if she carries on like this.'

'Go on,' Linda said. 'The kids will be all right with me.'

Jenny knew they would because they both adored Linda, but as Jenny hurried along to the surgery, for it shut at twelve o'clock on Saturday, Linda took the children into the garden. It did no good, she thought, for them to witness their mother's total collapse. Once outside she led them into the shed because the weather was fierce and, not knowing if Geraldine had explained anything to them, she told them gently of their daddy's death while she held them both tight.

She continued to hold them till their tears were spent and then answered the questions Rosemarie asked. She understood the child's anger and confusion. 'We prayed to God every night for Daddy's safety,' she said in a tight little voice. 'Me and Mammy and Jamie all together, and God didn't even blinking well listen.'

'It wasn't God killed your daddy,' Linda said. 'It was another German soldier.'

'It was God let him *be* killed.'

Linda was sketchy on theology, but she said she didn't think God could have stopped it. He made people with a free will so that they chose their actions.

Rosemarie, like her cousin Eddie, was nine years old and had been in a Catholic school for four years, so she knew all about free will. 'I know that,' she said impatiently and went on, 'but the priest said God is everywhere and can do anything, even move mountains – so why can't He stop wars and keep my daddy safe? If He's not going to listen to prayers, what's the point of them?'

Linda was in water too deep for her. 'God Rosemarie, I don't know the answer to all those questions,' she said. 'You must ask your priest.'

But Rosemarie knew she wouldn't. The priest would be shocked and would probably tell her mother, and then she'd be for it. It was no use asking her mother either; she'd only say Rosemarie should show obedience and not question the Mother Church, like she always did whenever Rosemarie asked her a question she couldn't answer. She knew it was one of those questions she'd just have to file away to find out about when she was older.

But she knew now that she wouldn't see her beloved daddy any more and neither would Jamie and he was only six. Normally her little brother drove her mad, but at that moment she felt a wave of tenderness for him and for her mother who cried in her grandmother's arms as if she were a baby. She straightened her shoulders and said, 'I think we'd better go back to the house now, Linda. It's cold in here and I'm worried about Mammy.'

Heavily sedated, Geraldine lay on one of the beds in the boys' old room. Jenny went to tell Maureen O'Leary what had happened and Linda took the children with her to tell Jan the bad news. Everyone was upset over it and wanted to know what they could do. Jan asked if she should have the children, but both Rosemarie and Jamie seemed loath to leave Linda's side and Linda said it was probably best to leave it for now.

That evening it began to snow; the children were excited by it despite their sadness, but for the grown-ups it was another nuisance to put up with. 'It probably won't lie,' Norah said.

But it did, and by the next morning, there were quite a few inches of firm snow underfoot and it was still coming down. Jenny was tired, she and Linda had talked long into the night and she had no great desire to rise early, but she'd heard Rosemarie and Jamie wake up and she crept into the room they were sharing with their mother. She needn't have worried; Geraldine still lay sprawled on one bed in a drugged sleep while Rosemarie and Jamie lay whispering on the other.

She took them downstairs for breakfast, closely followed by Linda. They'd decided the previous night not to take the children to Mass; Linda would look after them while Jenny went. The priest had to be told anyway and Masses offered for the repose of Dan's soul. Jenny kept going at home because of the children, but when she stepped out into the crisp winter's morning she felt very depressed. It had been six months since the fantastic achievement of D-Day, considered a success despite the thousands killed or seriously injured, and yet they seemed no further forward and the death toll continued to rise.

She felt better when she got to church and let the genuine sympathy of her fellow parishioners wash over her. Geraldine, like her mother and grandmother before her, had not had much to do with the neighbours, but Dan had been friendly enough and everyone who knew him was saddened by his death. The priest promised to pop up and see Geraldine as soon as possible.

Back home the fire was lit and her breakfast almost ready. When Norah had got up, Linda had gone across to Geraldine's house to fetch more clothes and the children's Christmas presents, and Jamie lay on the mat before the hearth laying out his lead soldiers, while his sister was reading *Black Beauty*. The whole scene looked homely and welcoming, Jenny thought as she kicked the snow from her boots.

'It's still coming down then?' Linda said.

''Fraid so.'

At her words, Jamie left his soldiers and crossed to the window. The lawn was covered in white and the snow lay thick on the privet hedge like icing on a cake. It covered the house roofs, the roads and pavements, and gilded the bare trees. Little of the snow was churned up, for as yet few

351

people had stirred from their houses into the swirling storm. There was a muffled silence over everything. 'We could make a snowman,' Jamie said in a small voice.

'Of course we can,' Jenny said, forcing enthusiasm into her voice. 'As soon as I've had breakfast.'

'Snowman!' Norah scorned from the chair by the fire. She glared at Jamie and snapped, 'You talk of snowmen with your father barely cold?'

Jenny glared at her mother and then glanced across at Jamie whose eyes now brimmed with tears. She could have cheerfully strangled Norah, but she ignored her and spoke to Jamie. 'It's all right,' she said. 'I don't think your daddy would mind at all. We'll see if we can find a carrot for his nose, shall we?'

Jamie's bottom lip trembled. 'It doesn't matter,' he said dully and went back to his soldiers.

Over Jamie's head Jenny's eyes met those of Rosemarie as she raised them from her book to listen to the conversation. Jenny wondered what the child was thinking and she smiled at her, but Rosemarie didn't smile back or say anything. She stared at her for a moment and lowered her head again.

Jenny went into the kitchen without another word and ate the breakfast Linda had ready for her. 'Have you been up to check on Geraldine?' she asked.

'Yes, she's sort of awake. Still groggy,' Linda said. 'I got her to have a cup of tea, but that's all.'

'I'll go up and see her later,' Jenny promised.

But before she was able to, there was a knock

352

on the door and when she opened it Peter was on the doorstep with his doctor's bag in his hand. 'Hello,' Jenny said, delighted to see him. 'Did you say you'd call today?'

'I didn't know I would be,' Peter said. 'But I was called to Phelps's farm where their Land Girl, Ruby, has slashed her leg quite badly and I thought I'd pop in and see your sister.'

'I haven't seen her since early morning,' Jenny said. 'Linda says she's still pretty dopey.'

'Good, good. Shall I go on up?'

'I'll come with you.'

'There's no need,' Peter said. 'I know the way, but in this weather I could murder a cup of tea.'

'OK,' Jenny said, smiling at him. 'I'll see to it.'

It was a few minutes later when he joined them in the kitchen having exchanged a few words with Norah and the children as he passed through the living room. Norah had sniffed her disapproval at Jenny making tea for the doctor at all and then to offer it to him in the kitchen, which she said was the height of bad manners, but Jenny ignored her and Peter seemed remarkably at ease as he sat at the kitchen table and Jenny put his tea in front of him.

Actually he was glad to be in the kitchen for he wanted to know how the children were coping. 'Well, on the whole,' Jenny said, 'they're quiet. I mean, quieter than they once were, but they're all right.'

'And they haven't cried since yesterday,' Linda said. 'Not that I've seen, any road, but they've been very near to it sometimes.'

'You want to take their minds off it, if you can,'

Peter suggested. 'The snow's a nuisance for me, but kids love it. Have a snowball fight, or help them build a snowman.'

'We would have done that,' Jenny said bitterly, 'but Mother said it wasn't decent. I would have ignored her, but the children were upset.'

'I might have expected a retort like that,' Peter said angrily. 'What good will it do those children to skulk around the house? They'll have to learn to live without their father like many more, and it's hard for them both, but they're still children and all children love snow.'

Peter remembered how, at the Phelps's farm, Sally and Charlie had been snowball-fighting when he arrived, together with the young German prisoner they seemed so fond of – and the contrast between the happy smiling faces of those children and the youngsters in this house, their pale faces pinched, was marked.

'Sarah Phelps was asking about you all,' Peter said at last. 'She was very upset when I told her about Dan. She was at school with Geraldine, apparently.'

Neither Jenny nor Linda said anything; there was nothing to say. 'She asked if you'd like to take the youngsters up to the farm today?' he said. Sarah hadn't exactly said that, but she did ask the doctor to find out if there was anything she could do to help and she said she'd be happy to look after the children any time.

'I can't possibly.'

'The Phelps's children tell me they're going to make the biggest snowman in the world.'

Jenny remembered Jamie's wistful face at the

window. She'd love to take them up to the farm or anywhere out of the house, but it was impossible.

'I couldn't, I'm sorry,' she said again. 'I wish I could, but there's Geraldine to see to now, as well as Mother.'

'Think about it,' Peter urged. 'The snow could be gone by next week and if you could get ready now, I could run you all up.

Jenny turned to Linda and said, 'You could go up with them.'

'Me?'

'Yes, go on – you know how they love you.' But Linda wasn't worried about the children, she was worried about a young German who had the power to turn her legs to jelly. She was frightened of being with him for the whole day, even while she longed for it, and she couldn't understand herself. 'No, no I couldn't,' she stammered.

Jenny's eyes narrowed. 'Yes you could,' she said, puzzled. 'Go on, Linda. Those children need to be got away from Mother at least for today. I would have thought you'd be more sympathetic. After all, you've had more than a taste of it.'

There was nothing Linda could say in her defence. Afterwards she often thought that even if she'd blurted out the truth there and then, Jenny would have told her not to be so silly. She gave a sigh and said, 'I'll tell the children to wrap up warm,' and her dejected figure left the room.

'What's the matter with Linda?' Peter asked.

Jenny shrugged her shoulders. 'I don't know. Something's upset her, but I don't know what,' she confessed. 'But I do know she liked Dan, so

355

she's maybe missing him too. Perhaps Mother had a go at her when I was at Mass earlier this morning. She didn't say she had, but then she often doesn't tell me things like that.'

'Well, in that case it will do her good to get away for the day too,' Peter said. 'Geraldine will carry on sleeping, possibly to mid-afternoon. Try to get something inside her then – soup if she'll take nothing else – and I'll be along to see her tomorrow.'

'Thank you,' Jenny said. 'You're very kind.'

'And you're very strong, Jenny.' Peter leaned across the table and gave her hand a squeeze. 'Which is a good job, for now there's another one reliant on you.'

And Jenny gave a sigh, knowing he was right.

Chapter Nineteen

'Have you been sledging before, Linda?' Sam asked.

'Hardly, unless you count riding a tin tray on a slope in Pype Hayes Park, and that was only on the couple of times it snowed enough to sledge on at all.'

But this was different. The sledge Max had built for the children from scrap wood was a masterpiece, built to carry two or even three people, if the riders were children. It had a slatted seat raised up from the runners that shone like steel and the sledge went like the wind over the tightly packed icy snow on the incline at the very edge of the farm that led down to the stream.

'In my country in winter there is always much snow,' Max said. 'And the rivers and lakes freeze so hard people skate on them.'

'It's hardly ever that cold here, I'm glad to say,' Sarah shivered. 'I'm blinking perished as it is and I'm going back to my warm kitchen soon.'

'You can't go yet,' Charlie said. 'Linda hasn't even had a go.'

He was right. Linda had watched all the children go down with either Sam or Max, and now there was just her. She was nervous, there was no denying it, for she'd never even sat on a sledge before and the bottom of the hill looked an awfully long way off; what's more, she'd seen

357

how fast the sledge went.

'I will go down with you,' Max said, seeing Linda chewing at her lip.

'No, no it's all right,' Linda said quickly.

'I would take up his offer, Linda,' Sarah urged. 'I was glad to have Sam at my back, I can tell you. I was frightened to death.'

'Aw, Mom,' Charlie said in disgust.

'You can "Aw Mom" all you like,' Sarah said. 'I daresay I wasn't frightened when I was your age, but I am now.'

'I bet Linda isn't scared.'

Oh, I am, Linda thought, but not just about the ride on the sledge.

Before she had a chance to answer, Sarah gave a shiver and said, 'I'm away in, anyway. You lot will be frozen stiff. I'll stoke up the fire and make some soup to warm you all up.'

'Ah, wait till Linda has a go,' Sally said. 'It's not fair else, 'cos she watched you.'

'Oh, I won't bother,' Linda said. 'I'll go back to the house and help your mom.' It was what she'd done ever since she'd arrived at the farm – use the excuse of helping Sarah to keep out of Max's way. That was why she'd not taken a hand in building the biggest snowman in the world. Then she'd found Max hadn't been there either, but in the barn making a sledge, when he'd found out the Phelps children didn't possess one. And then, after a wonderful casserole made with pork, that Linda hadn't tasted in a long while, with rhubarb crumble to follow, the whole family had gone to try the sledge out.

But she didn't really want to go back to the

farm. Nervous as she was, she wanted to try out the sledge as all the others had; if Max hadn't been there, she'd not have hesitated.

There was a collective groan of disappointment from the children. 'I'd never have said you were a scaredy cat,' Charlie said scathingly.

'Well, now you know.'

Sam cuffed his small son lightly and said, 'Less of your cheek, young man.'

'Go on, Linda.' Even Rosemarie and Jamie were urging and for their sake, to see them animated about anything, she decided she would go for it.

'I'll go down behind you,' Sam offered, and Linda felt relieved. She had no worries going down with Sam, but before she could accept his offer, Charlie jumped in. 'It's Max's turn,' he said. 'You went down with Mom.'

'And he did make it, Dad,' Sally put in.

What else could she do? To keep protesting would appear off and also Max might guess why she was so anxious. He might think she was afraid of him, and that was nonsense. But she made one more attempt. 'There's no need for anyone to go with me, I can go down by myself.'

'It runs better and faster with two,' Max declared. 'It's made that way.'

With a sigh Linda gave in and climbed on to the sledge in front of Max, who held the guiding ropes. With a push they were off. They flew fast over the ground polished to glistening ice, with the wind pulling at their clothes and slapping at their faces. Exhilaration flowed through Linda, both from the speed at which they were travelling and from the nearness of Max pressed tight against her. He held the ropes down low, so that his hands brushed her waist and sent little shivers of alarm through her, even while she acknowledged she was enjoying it.

She saw the snowdrift they were heading for before he did. She screamed his name in warning, but the sound was snatched away by the wind. Too late – Max tried to swerve and then they were in the middle of it. Snow – soft, brilliant white and icy cold – covered Linda's face and clothes. It plastered her nose and mouth and even her eyelashes, and dampened the hair poking out from the woolly hat she had on, and she lay in it, half buried in the drift. She put a snow-crusted glove up to wipe her face, aware of the snow that had got through the turned-up collar and the scarf, and that was now trickling in icy rivulets down her neck.

Max, his face full of concern, was reaching for her, pulling her out, but when he realised she was laughing not crying, he smiled too. 'You're not hurt?'

'No, just wet,' Linda giggled. 'Though I'm glad of the trousers and wellingtons Sarah found for me, but I think the wellies at least are full of snow now too.'

She struggled to her feet as she spoke and with the help of Max's hands tugging at her, suddenly she was upright, and she and Max were inches apart. They gazed at each other, the hilarity wiped from their faces and Linda had a great longing for Max to grab her closer and kiss her. Max, had she but known it, had the same desire, but knew he could do nothing. Nevertheless her name came out unbidden and slightly husky. 'Linda, oh Linda,' he whispered.

'Are you all right?'

The words shouted by Sam from the top of the hill broke the spell and Linda called back, 'Fine,' knowing that her voice was cracked and false-sounding and not able to do anything about it.

'Linda, we must talk,' Max said, as they began the ascent together, dragging the sledge behind them.

Linda was glad Max could not see the trembling of her legs, nor the thudding of her heart against her ribs. She licked her lips and willed her voice not to let her down as she said as casually as she could trying to pretend nothing unusual had happened between them. 'Go on then, talk away.'

'Not here, not now,' Max said. 'If you could come to the barn later...'

Linda stared at him, feeling confused and mixed up. He was a German, and therefore off-limits to her – surely he understood that! He was a prisoner, for heaven's sake! She'd deliberately held herself aloof from boyfriends while the war raged. She'd seen friends and workmates who had loved men who had later been reported dead or missing, and she saw Jenny worrying daily over Bob. But soon it would be over, everyone knew it was just a matter of time now, and then she'd meet some nice British boy who would mean something special to her – for she'd have no truck with any Yank either – and Max Schulz would be returned to his own country.

Max watched the girl he'd loved from the first moment he'd seen her. Thoughts of her got between him and his sleep, and lately she'd filled his daylight hours too. He'd quizzed the Phelps's children about her mercilessly, and being the type of children they were, they knew everything there was to know about Linda. When Max heard of the tragedy in her life, he'd bowed his head in shame, certain she'd hate all Germans with a passion. But she hadn't seemed to, at least not all the time; sometimes she'd been quite nice. He'd not known for sure what she'd felt about him until the moment, seconds before, when they'd gazed at each other and he'd seen the longing in her face that he knew mirrored his own.

But whatever he'd said had angered her, for there was no longing on her face now as she turned to him, only barely concealed contempt.

'No, I will *not* come to the barn. What sort of girl d'you think I am, to go sneaking off into barns? If you've anything to say, then say it now openly and if you haven't then be silent.'

She dropped her side of the rope and leaving Max to fumble for it, strode away from him. Sarah saw her eyes smouldering with anger as she drew close. She alone had witnessed the scene at the foot of the hill and the altercation that had followed it, for Sam, once he'd established Linda was unhurt, had taken the children a little way back to show them how to make snow angels. Sarah could have sworn there was something between Max and Linda when she'd seen them together. But Max must have said something to annoy the girl. She didn't wonder at the

362

attraction between them, for both were young and she saw nothing wrong in two young people having feelings for one another, no matter that one was a German. But she knew this wouldn't be the view of all people, so maybe Linda would be wise to nip it in the bud.

And Linda, unaware of Sarah's scrutiny, kept out of Max's way until darkness and the cold drew them all back to the big farmhouse kitchen. They were all glad of the warmth that hit them as soon as they entered, and the tantalising smell of the broth Sarah was ready to dish up the minute they'd peeled off their wet clothes and left them steaming over the guard, across the fire.

Much later, after a more than substantial tea, during which Max had constantly tried to catch Linda's eye and she'd determinedly ignored his efforts, she sat before the fire and watched the flames dancing in the hearth and decided she'd have to have it out with Max. He had to realise that she would be polite with him as good manners dictated, but no more than that, and that would have to stand, however he felt, and indeed however she felt herself, because there could be no future for them. Not of course that she'd admit she had feelings for him. That would be madness.

Nor would she go to any secret assignment in a barn or any other place. She wondered with a grim smile how he thought that could have been achieved anyway. Didn't he think it would have aroused comment if she'd left the comfort of the Phelps's fireside and gone into the black night for purposes of her own? Damn the man! He disturbed her more than he should and at the first opportunity she'd tell him he was to stop harassing her.

Sam and Sarah noticed Linda's preoccupation, but while Sarah had her own ideas about the girl's quietness and had watched her face as she struggled with her emotions, Sam just put it down to tiredness.

Then he reasoned, a death in the family wasn't something to make a joke of. He'd not known Dan Driscoll himself, but he was sure the man was decent enough and Linda was bound to be affected. He was glad to see that Rosemarie and Jamie, albeit tired, both looked a lot better than the whey-faced, subdued pair he'd first seen in the farmhouse after his children had nearly burst a blood vessel when they'd run into the barn crying that Linda Lennox had come, bringing two children with her.

He'd gone to welcome them and they'd stood stiffly and quiet beside Linda, their faces set and drawn. His heart had gone out to them both. Now their faces were tinged pink both with excitement and cold, and their eyes sparkled. He hoped they wouldn't be made to feel guilty about it when they got home. Sarah had told him how it was when she'd snatched a few minutes with him alone. She told him also that their arrival had been a total surprise to her too.

He reflected on this later as he drove the three visitors home. Sarah had told him Peter had just a few minutes to alert her and ask her permission for the children to stay, for as Linda had walked across the yard from the gate, Charlie, Sally and

364

Patch had besieged her and Rosemarie and Jamie had stuck to her like glue, giving Peter time to slip into the farmhouse.

Sarah had a soft spot for Linda – always had, and she'd do anything for the doctor. Sam liked him, too – most people did. Look at today, he'd come straight out when they'd sent for him and stitched their Ruby's leg up a treat, and then he'd dropped her at the station to catch a train home for a week or two until it healed, for Sam had told her there was no point hanging around the farm with a gammy leg, better let her rest it properly. And then he must have called in on the O'Learys to see how Geraldine was and brought the children back with him. He said Jenny's mother was set on making their lives a misery on top of the shock they'd both had of losing their father, and he thought them better out of the way for a while. God, some of the stories Linda had told her about Jenny's mother and grandmother were hard to credit, and if anyone other than Linda had told them she might not have believed them. But she'd never known Linda tell a lie.

'You're quiet tonight, Sam,' Linda said.

'Funny thing that,' Sam answered with a smile. 'I was just thinking the very same about you.'

'Ah well, maybe I have nothing worth saying.'

'Come on, girl,' Sam said with a chuckle. 'I've never known that to stop a woman yet.'

Linda found herself giggling and Sam went on, 'Did that job come to anything, the one Flora told you about?'

Linda shook her head. With little or no work now for the concert-party, Flora had been

365

seeking openings for her and Linda at other establishments. They were told of a pub near the city centre that had a piano and would welcome a young singer on a Saturday night, especially if she was a pretty young lady. Linda remembered with a shiver of distaste the dingy, smoke-filled pub with its filthy floor and the yellowed keys of the battered, out of tune piano that stood in the corner. She'd looked at the men clustered at the bar leering at her and the landlord with his huge stomach and brown teeth who declared her pretty as a picture. She knew if she took work on with Flora, she'd have to be careful where it was, for now there would be no Bill or Sam to keep an eye on her and ward off unwanted attention. 'No,' she said to Sam. 'I wasn't keen on it, to tell you the truth.'

'Did you talk it over with Jenny?'

'I did mention it,' Linda said. 'But I'd already made the decision not to take it anyway.'

'I'm glad of that then,' Sam said. ''Cos I heard of someplace the other day. Packington Hall – do you know it?'

'I know *of* it,' Linda said. 'Isn't it one of the big houses set in its own grounds that has been turned into a hotel? It's not that far from here, is it?'

'Yeah, that's right,' Sam said. 'Mind, part of the hotel was turned over to the military for the war, like. Now the owner wants a new look for peacetime, which everyone knows is just around the corner. As part of it, he's had the hotel restaurant made much bigger and newly decorated, very plush. You'd need money to eat

366

there, you wouldn't get the riff-raff you might get in a normal pub.'

'Yes, but Sam, they'd not need a singer in a place like that.'

'That's just it, they do,' Sam said. 'My mate Terry is a waiter there. He says the boss asked him if he knew anyone who could either play the piano or sing or both, and course he thought of you because I talk a lot about you, see? The boss told Terry it would lend a bit of class to the place.'

Linda giggled, 'Not with me it won't.'

'Don't run yourself down ducks. You'd lend class to anywhere with your voice,' Sam said. 'Anyway, why not go and size up the place. That can do no harm now, can it?'

'No,' Linda agreed. 'But things are a bit up in the air at the moment at home, you know? The minute we're all more settled, I'll go and see Flora and we'll go up together.'

'That's the spirit, bab,' Sam said affectionately. 'Life's gotta go on, see?'

'I know.'

'Are you bringing the kids back up here next weekend?' he added, lowering his voice so Rosemarie and Jamie wouldn't hear him, though Linda felt that they were both too drowsy to take any notice. 'Snow or no snow, they're better here than back there.'

'On Sunday I will,' Linda promised, because she knew the visit had done the kids good. 'But Saturday I must help Jenny. She has her work cut out trying to do everything at the best of times, and now with Geraldine it's even worse. She's already decided to take next week off work to see to the children. After that, of course, they'll be back at school.'

'Right then girl, just as you like.' Sam said. 'I'll tell Sarah to expect you for dinner, shall I?'

'If you're sure.'

''Course I'm sure. Like I said before, there's not that much doing at this time of the year,' Sam said. 'It's good for us, too. Sarah often feels a bit isolated in the winter when the weather's bad and she can't get out to shop and meet people, and the kids get fed up with their own company. As for me,' Sam grinned and said, 'I like to see a pretty face about the place. Cheers me up no end.'

'I don't know whether I should come and see you when you make remarks like that on the way home,' Linda said, in mock indignation, and Sam's bellow of laughter jerked the children awake and Linda was glad of it because they'd almost reached home.

The pavement outside the house had been cleared and the path too, but the snow still lay heavy on the privet hedges, and on the lawns it was spread out, pristine white and untouched. 'Look at all that snow,' Jamie yawned. 'We could make a brilliant snowman of our own.'

'No, we couldn't,' Rosemarie told him. 'Grandmother wouldn't let us.'

'I know,' Jamie said resignedly. 'I was only saying we could.'

Linda felt sorry for both of them, for their steps seemed slower and heavier as they reached the house and Linda wished she could protect them

368

in some way, but she was as powerless as they were. The excitement had slid from them as they opened the kitchen door, to be replaced by trepidation. But nothing could hide their glowing cheeks and the hint of a sparkle still in their eyes. For some reason, that had annoyed Norah and she'd laid into them, telling them they should be ashamed and hadn't they a thought in their head for their poor dead father, or their mother prostrate with grief? Linda was worse than them, but then she'd always been thoughtless.

Linda saw the happiness ooze out of the children and longed to tell Norah O'Leary to shut her mouth, but she knew anything she said would probably make things worse for them all. Instead, helped by Jenny, she got them ready for bed and when later, tucked up in beside Jamie, Rosemarie said to Linda in a small voice, 'Do you think we were wrong to go to the farm today?' Linda could have cried.

She remembered feeling that way herself and she also remembered her first Christmas at Jenny's house and what Maureen O'Leary had said to her. 'Why?' she asked Rosemarie. 'Because you enjoyed yourself?'

Rosemarie gave a brief nod and Linda said, 'When your daddy was alive, did he like you to be miserable?'

Rosemarie shook her head and Jamie looked at her with large solemn brown eyes. 'Well then,' Linda said, 'why would he like you to be miserable now?' And she added, 'When my mom and brothers died, I thought I'd never laugh or be happy again, and then that first Christmas I almost forgot about them for a little while – enjoyed myself and I did feel guilty for a bit. But someone told me that my mother was probably up in Heaven watching out for me, delighted that I was still able to enjoy things.'

She ran her hand over Rosemarie's hair and Jamie's and said, 'You'll always miss your daddy, and there'll be a pain whenever you think of him, but don't let anyone make you feel guilty for getting on with your life, OK?'

The children nodded and a tremulous smile touched their lips, and Linda bent down and kissed them both a loving goodnight.

Later, when Norah was in bed, Jenny sat beside the fire and Linda told her how much the children had enjoyed their visit to the farm. Jenny was glad of it and hoped Geraldine would take a grip of herself in the next day or so. It had surprised her a little, the intense grief that Geraldine had displayed on Dan's death. She knew her sister had been fond of her husband, and of course he was the children's father too, but she knew Dan hadn't been her choice of soulmate. Dan had been her mother's choice. It was Eamonn Flaherty, dashing, handsome and full of charm, who'd captured her sister's heart. Eamonn hadn't liked the influence Norah had over Geraldine. He'd wanted to marry her and take her to America to make a new life for themselves, but at the last minute, Geraldine's nerve had failed her and only Jenny knew how she used to sob herself to sleep every night after Eamonn had left.

Dan Driscoll was kind, but stolid, plodding and

predictable and didn't disturb Geraldine's senses like Eamonn. He must have known that her heart belonged to another and only a fragment of it would ever be his, and yet this was obviously enough for him. He'd always seemed content and Geraldine had settled just doors away from her mother. If Dan ever resented Norah's interference in their lives. he'd never said so and they'd lived happily enough and he'd adored his children.

However, now Geraldine's grief for Dan was real, for she'd come to care deeply for him. Now he was gone and Geraldine was frightened of facing life on her own. The burden appeared so great, it didn't seem worth even making the effort. So she didn't, even the following week when Peter reduced the tranquillising drugs that had kept her sedated, and encouraged her to get up out of bed and take up the reins of her own household again.

Geraldine either wouldn't, or wasn't able to rouse herself, nor move back to her own house, and Norah forbade Jenny to try and persuade her. 'Things will be decided later,' she said. 'It's early days yet. Leave your sister alone.'

Jenny wasn't going to argue with either of them. She had enough on her plate as it was.

The snow had continued to fall, freezing to ice in the bitterly cold nights and the school holidays had come to an end. Jenny was relieved, for then at least the children would be out of the house. Rosemarie was old enough to take herself and Jamie up to the Abbey School, especially as there were plenty of children on the Estate to walk up with.

It was one less thing to worry about, Jenny thought, and a good job too, because Geraldine didn't seem to be improving much. Jenny had the feeling her mother was glad of it, and possibly actively encouraging her to wallow in grief as it made Geraldine more dependent on her.

And Jenny was right. Though Norah would have wished no harm on Dan, his death meant her daughter had turned to her for support. She'd had a unique and deep relationship with her own mother and really would have been happy with just the one daughter. She admired her sons for their handsome features and loved them in her own way, but Geraldine was the one who'd always mattered to her. She only considered she had one daughter, for she never could stand Jenny and anyway, since her birth, Jenny had belonged to Dermot and his family.

But now, just as she'd needed her mother, so Geraldine needed her. It had gone full circle. Now Jenny could do as she pleased, Norah thought. In fact, she wanted her out of the house as soon as possible. She wished to have Geraldine totally to herself; even the children irked and annoyed her. Funny that she didn't take to them when they were Geraldine's after all but then she'd never liked children very much. She was glad when the holidays had come to an end and glad too that that sly venomous bitch Linda seemed to have a soft spot for them, and took them out at weekends.

Linda knew she wouldn't be quite so pleased if she knew where she took them sometimes. Dan had been dead two weeks when, on the way back from fetching the rations from the shops on the Tyburn Road, Linda decided to take them to Maureen O'Leary's. 'It's a secret,' she told them the first day.

'Why?' Rosemarie wanted to know.

'Because your mom and grandma don't like this person much,' Linda said. 'They wouldn't like you going to see her, but I think you should because she's your great-gran.'

'Great-gran,' Rosemarie said. She was beginning to understand relationships while Jamie still looked confused. 'D'you mean with Grandmother Gillespie being Mommy's mother, this person is our grandad's mom?'

'That's right.'

Jamie made a face and Rosemarie didn't blame him. Neither of them were too keen on grandmothers and they had no desire to meet another one. Grandmother Gillespie was always on to them for one thing and another. Rosemarie, in particular, thought she was monstrously unfair. It wasn't as if she and Jamie hadn't loved their father, and she was terribly sorry he wouldn't ever be back again. She'd cried for hours over it, and Jamie cried so much he'd made himself sick into the chamber pot underneath the bed. She needed her mother badly, they both did, but Geraldine lay sick in bed and their grandmother seemed to have the final say in everything. It was as if they'd lost both parents, not just the one, yet she wasn't old enough to put these feelings into words. But all in all, she'd had a bellyful of grandmothers and she knew her little brother felt the same. A great-gran was sure to be worse.

373

'Why didn't our mammy like her?' she asked Linda as they turned in the gate.

'Oh, I don't know, it's a long story,' Linda said, not wishing to relate the whole family history to the child.

'Maybe we won't like her.'

'I think you will,' Linda said. 'One thing I do know, you shouldn't listen to what other people say, you should always make your own mind up. Another thing is you'd be damned hard to please if either of you took a dislike to Maureen O'Leary.'

Within a few minutes of being in her company and that younger lady, Peggy, Rosemarie knew Linda was right. No one could dislike the old woman who hugged them both to her with a genuine warmth although she had tears in her eyes as she did so. She even coaxed Jamie out of his shell; he'd been far too quiet since the news of his father's death. They liked Peggy too and their great-gran's son Gerry who seemed to fill any room he was in. Jamie was particularly interested in the chubby toddler Dermot and happy to lie on the floor to build blocks for him to demolish endlessly.

It was as they sat up to a big feed in the kitchen, that out of the children's hearing, Maureen expressed her misgivings to Linda. 'It's not that I'm not glad to see them,' she said, 'don't think that. But things might be worse for them, if it got back to you-know-who.'

'It can't really get worse, Gran,' Linda said. 'She's leaping on them for something all the time, the old one that is, their mother lies like a statue. She reminds me of my mom when she got the letter from the Corporal about my stepfather and collapsed.' She smiled a little sadly and said, 'That was the first time I set eyes on Dr Sanders, when he called to see her. But even he can't seem to talk sense into Geraldine, and he has tried.'

'Ah well, to lose your man is a heavy burden to carry around,' Maureen said. 'If he was a good man, some never really get over it, I'll miss my Michael until the day I die.'

'But you got on with your life,' Linda protested.

'Like I had to.'

'She will too,' Maureen said. 'But it will take time.'

'But meanwhile the children are suffering,' Linda said. 'It's a good job they've got the farm to go to.' Linda didn't say anything else. She'd been telling herself since the first snowladen day that Max Schulz meant nothing to her, but every time she thought of him since, her heart had seemed to skip a beat. She could say none of this to Maureen O'Leary who'd expressed her views on the whole German nation so bitterly and not that long ago either.

'How do you get over there?' she asked.

'Sam Phelps comes to fetch us,' Linda said. 'He says Sarah likes my company, especially in weather like this when she can't get out much, and the children get on well and more importantly can be children again. Rosemarie and Jamie are able to forget for a little while at least, what has happened to their daddy.'

Just at that moment, Jamie let out a squeal of laughter at some tomfoolery Gerry was doing to put the children at their ease. Immediately, he clapped his hand across his mouth, while tears squeezed out of his eyes and ran down his cheeks. 'Sorry,' he whispered.

'You see how she has them?' Linda hissed angrily. 'Scared to laugh. Scared to bloody well live.'

Dear God, Maureen thought, but to the child she said with a smile, 'Sorry, boy? Nothing to be sorry about,' and then added in mock severity. 'but you'll be sorry in a minute, if you don't eat that last piece of soda bread. I'm just after having made it only this morning. Come on now, get it down you.'

Jamie scrubbed the tears from his eyes with his sleeve and looked at his new great-grandmother he couldn't remember ever having met before. She was buttering and putting jam on a slice of the nicest bread he'd ever tasted. He'd never seen anyone like the woman with a body so fat it shook when she laughed. Her face was lined and she had two chins one behind the other, but her hazel eyes were the kindest he'd ever seen and her mouth seemed to be made to smile. He gave a small sigh and tucked into the soda bread, and Rosemarie met her new great-grandmother's eyes and flashed her a smile of gratitude.

Later, going home, Linda said, 'I wouldn't mention where we'd been today if I were you. You wouldn't want to upset your mother and grand-mother, I'm sure.' Neither child wanted to upset their mother further, but if they'd been honest both would have had to say, it was the threat of their grandmother's angry tantrums, which

376

they'd witnessed just a few times, but which they were terrified of, which would still their tongues. Without being told they also knew if they were to breathe a word of where they'd been, they'd never be allowed to go there again. So Rosemarie knew she spoke for both of them when she said, 'You needn't worry, Linda, we won't say a word.'

Chapter Twenty

'I think you have an admirer,' Jenny said.

'Don't be daft.' But though Linda dismissed Jenny's words, she'd felt the man's eyes boring into her all evening. It bothered and embarrassed her. She wasn't used to such admiration. The servicemen she'd sung to had often jostled around her after the performance and vied for her attention, and some had pleaded with her to go out with them. But very few had just stared at her like this man had done, and yet he'd made no move to speak to her, even now when she was on her break.

Not that she'd have wanted him to; he wasn't her sort – a proper toff, that's what – and she had no time for them.

Why then, she wondered, had she agreed to sing at Packington Hall? Didn't she know the place would be full of toffs? Only the rich could afford to eat in the plush and opulent restaurant set up alongside the hotel where the waiters were dressed up to look like penguins. Linda had never seen a place like it.

Feet sank in the thick pile carpets and snow-white cloths covered the tables, there was so much cutlery beside the plates, Linda knew she wouldn't know which to use. The wine glasses sparkled in the light from the dazzling chandeliers and they had red napkins arranged like fans inside them; fresh flowers graced every table.

Even the chairs the waiter pulled out from the table for the diners were padded, and some had arms too – polished so hard they shone. The men all wore suits and ties and some had funny clothes on that were similar, at least to Linda's unaccustomed eyes, to the waiters' outfits. Jenny told her they were dinner suits. The women's dresses fair took Linda's breath away, for they were so beautiful, though she was shocked that some of them had no back at all. Others were cut so low at the front they showed their bosoms and some had slits so high, you could see much more than a flash of thigh. Linda remembered the drab clothes in the shops and knew most people couldn't even afford those because they hadn't enough coupons, and she wondered how these rich women had come by their wonderful clothes. Some shimmered in the chandelier's lights, others sparkled and rustled as they walked. They wore strappy shoes despite the winter weather, and sheer silk stockings, and had fur stoles around their shoulders. Their necks were hung with jewellery and there were even decorations in their hair. 'D'you think they know there's a war on?' Linda whispered to Jenny.

'There isn't for them, I shouldn't think,' Jenny said. 'Money talks.'

And Linda knew it did, because the car park was full of cars and not just ordinary ones either, but big flashy cars. It was a strange sight for Linda. Precious few people she knew owned cars and those that did, couldn't use them if they wanted to, with the petrol rationing being so strict, unless of course they were a farmer like Sam, or a doctor like Peter.

But still it was no good her moaning, for Packington Hall paid good money for her and Flora to sing and play to their guests. At first, Linda had been loath to accept the job, as things were still dicey at home with Geraldine still installed in the boys' bedroom, two weeks after she'd received the fateful telegram. But Sam told her if she didn't soon make up her mind, the manager would get someone else and then where would she be? When Jenny heard that, she insisted Linda should at least go for the audition. The result of that was that by the third week in January, Linda and Flora were engaged for Friday nights. If they proved popular, the manager said, perhaps Saturday nights would be offered at a later date. In addition to their wages, they had their taxi fares paid both ways. Linda had insisted on that, knowing no trams would go near Packington Hall and she had no wish to traverse the winter nights in her satin gown and soft slippers. This was her debut night after spending the week rehearsing with Flora and that first Friday night, the medley they put together proved very popular indeed.

Jenny had come along on the first night, both to give Linda encouragement and to check out the place for her as Linda was not yet seventeen. She was impressed by the restaurant itself and the clientèle they got, and thought Linda had done rather well for herself. She approved of the arrangements for a taxi there and back that

Linda had negotiated, and realised that the girl was well able to look after herself.

But she was unnerved by the distinguished man who was so obviously impressed by Linda. Why hadn't he come over to speak to her in the normal way? She'd made a joke about it, but really it was no laughing matter. What if he made a nuisance of himself? She imagined Linda would give him short shrift, but how would that go down in a place like this? Linda and Flora could be out on their ear before they'd really begun.

Linda had scarcely been aware of the man's scrutiny in the first half, but after Jenny's comment, she became embarrassed by it as the evening drew on. She wondered what he was after; for a man in his position was usually after something. He probably thought she was some easy piece. Well, he'd soon find out his mistake if he said anything suggestive or offensive to her. She'd clock him one and the job could go to blazes.

In fact, Charles Haversham thought he'd never seen anyone quite like Linda. She was so beautiful and vulnerable-looking, and her voice had a haunting quality about it that mesmerised him. The older men at his table had barely noticed the entertainment. They'd commented briefly on the singer being a pretty little thing with a damned good voice, but then they'd returned to their general conversation and attacked their meals with gusto. Charles thought they had no soul. But he noticed others around the room who had been affected like himself; women as well as men

381

were enthralled by the girl and when she finished the evening with 'We'll Meet Again', he noticed many people dabbing at damp eyes.

Linda saw the reaction and was glad they'd agreed to include the old wartime favourite, for everyone knew it and most liked it and it was appropriate, for the last song of the night. She listened to the applause and so did the restaurant manager. The little girl was a find, all right, he decided – a regular little gold mine she might turn out to be. Still, it wouldn't do to show her he was too pleased, he couldn't risk her getting above herself and asking for more money, but he'd let her know that he was moderately satisfied.

A fortnight later, Flora and Linda were working on Saturday night as well as Friday. It meant a lot of work for them both as they needed time to rehearse two evenings' work, though the money was useful. Linda had wanted Jenny to take a good share of it, but she wouldn't. She said Linda already gave her most of her wages and she would take no more. Linda argued with her, but to no avail. There was little to buy in the shops, for even if you had the money you seldom had the points needed and she had opened a Post Office account where she put any money she had left at the end of the week. Now all she earned at Packington Hall was deposited in there too. Things were much easier for Jenny too these days, with Linda's wages contributing to the household expenses; together with the rises she herself had had over the years, it meant she had been able to save a little to buy things for her bottom drawer after the war when there might be more about.

'What are you saving for, girl?' Maureen had asked Linda with a sly grin one Saturday morning.

'Nothing really,' Linda said. 'I'm just saving. What d'you mean?'

'There's not a young man in the offing?'

'Some bloody chance,' Linda scoffed. 'If I ever had a young man, when the hell would I get to see him?' But she did see him, of course, and at the farm, though she made sure all she did was see him. She spoke to him only when necessary and usually when someone else was present too.

Maureen supposed Linda was right. It was a bleak time for many young women. She decided to change the subject. 'How are things up at the house now?' she asked.

'Doesn't Jenny tell you?'

'Jenny wraps things up so as not to worry me,' Maureen said. 'Now you are another like myself, who says things straight out.'

'Well, yes I do,' Linda admitted. 'But really Gran, there's not much to tell you. I mean, Geraldine's getting about more. At least she's not lying in bed all bloody day like she was.'

'So now she sees to her own wee ones?' Maureen asked. 'And about time too, for it's better to keep busy and Jenny has enough to do.'

In truth, Geraldine still didn't seem to do a great deal. All she seemed to want to do was to sit before the fire with her mother and drink cup after cup of their precious tea ration and talk

383

about Dan for hours. It got on Linda's nerves. It was so bloody depressing and although she was sad Dan had died, for she'd liked him too, she knew it did no good to keep going on about it. It wouldn't help Geraldine get over it quicker, nor would it help the children.

Since that first awful day when the telegram arrived, neither Geraldine nor her mother seemed to care where Linda went at the weekend. On Saturday after the rations had been collected, she, Jenny and the children usually went to Maureen's or Jan's, and they were welcome in both houses, but on Sundays they always wanted to head for the farm. They liked the feel of open space and all the animals.

Both children were fascinated by the large fat pink and black sow. She was so fat, her skin lay in rolls and she lay supine on the pigsty floor, while thirteen baby piglets crawled squealing over her body. 'Can she walk?' Rosemarie has asked one day. 'I mean, she looks so fat.'

'She can walk,' Sally had told her. 'Only there's no great place to go, is there? I mean, she's got to stay in the sty.'

'And her teats would probably hang on the ground,' Charlie had put in.

Rosemarie had turned beetroot red and said, 'You shouldn't say that, it's a bad word.'

'What is?'

'That word you said.'

'What word?' Charlie was genuinely puzzled and Rosemarie wasn't going to enlighten him about it.

It was Sally who'd cried out, 'It's teat, isn't it?

You think it's a bad word. That's a daft idea. It's what mothers feed their babies with, their teats.'

Her face aflame, Rosemarie felt shame seep through her and she said with some venom, 'That's wicked talk.'

'No, it isn't,' Sally cried, and she appealed to Max who was crossing the yard at the time. 'It isn't wicked to say "teat" is it, Max?'

Rosemarie had told Linda this as she'd tucked her into bed that same night. 'And what did Max say?' Linda asked.

'He said it wasn't wicked, Sally was right.'

'And so she was,' Linda said. 'But don't you go shouting the word around the tea-table now, or wicked or not, you'll get your bottom skelped.'

Rosemarie raised her eyes to the ceiling and said, 'And don't I just know it?'

Linda smiled at the child's woebegone expression, but her mind was on Max – as it so often was. The children loved him, that much was obvious. Didn't that make him out as a decent person? Wasn't it said that animals and children had a sort of sixth sense where people were concerned, and were not fazed by a veneer of respectability or charm, but saw the real person beneath? She wasn't sure if it was true or not, but if it was, what then? It just meant whatever Germany had done, he was an all-right human being. What did it matter, anyway? He'd soon be gone and out of her life for good, and the sooner the better.

She was surprised with the children liking the man so much, that neither mentioned Max at home, although they actually said little of what they did at the farm and neither their mother or grandmother seemed the least bit interested. She wasn't going to ask them not to talk about Max, for that would have made him seem important – important enough for them to be secretive about him. She didn't want that, and yet in the beginning she braced herself for the row to come. But it didn't come, for the children seemed to have another sixth sense regarding what to say at home and what not to say. Max's name never passed their lips, for never would they give their mother or grandmother ammunition to stop them going to the Phelps's farm.

'Don't you just love it there?' Sally asked Linda one Sunday night as she'd gone upstairs to say goodnight.

And Linda had to admit she did, and knew why, and though every sensible bone in her body said she should not go near the place, she still went, longing for the sight of Max Schulz so much, she was often unable to sleep on the Saturday night.

The tide had turned in the war and now it was time for the German cities to be pounded. Most British people thought it about bloody time, especially after the Russian troops reached Auschwitz concentration camp in late January. The conditions of the 2,819 inmates, with their shaven heads and skeletal bodies, had shocked the world, as did the stories of the gas chambers and mass graves and the smell of death that hung over the whole place.

However, the incendiary raid on Dresden,

which left 350,000 people dead, stunned many people with its ferocity. Churchill, for the first time, expressed doubts and concern as he said, 'The destruction of Dresden remains a serious query against the conduct of Allied bombing.'

Many people were still talking about it when Linda and Flora were at Packington Hall the following Friday evening. They sat at the bar during their break and listened to the rights and wrongs of the case, but neither took any part in the discussion.

Suddenly Flora nudged Linda in the ribs and whispered, 'He's coming over.' Linda saw the man Jenny had described as her admirer some weeks before, get up from the table and make his way towards them. Linda couldn't understand him.

This was her fourth week at Packington Hall, and since the first night the man had come every night she performed and had never spoken a word to her. He'd given her the creeps, and if it hadn't been for her needing the money – and the venue at Packington Hall being such a safe place to gain experience – she'd have jacked it in long before.

She had plenty of time to observe him as he approached, for she held her head up to show she was not afraid, and saw he was very handsome. His skin was fairly dark and yet his hair so light it was almost blond, his eyes were deep set, his nose fairly long and his lips thin and perfectly formed, and he had high cheekbones and a chiselled chin. He wore an extremely smart dark blue suit with a pristine white shirt and a tie which matched the handkerchief poking out of his top pocket. The cuffs peeping out from the sleeves of his jacket were fastened with gold studs.

The man smiled when he saw Linda scrutinising him and it transformed his whole face. Despite herself, Linda found herself smiling back, 'Good evening,' he said, and his voice was pleasant on the ear. And when he went on to say, 'I must compliment you ladies on your beautiful performance,' Linda realised he had no accent at all.

'Thank you,' she said.

Flora simpered a little and said, 'How kind of you to say so.'

'Can I buy you both a drink?'

'No thanks,' Linda said bluntly. 'I'm fine.'

'Are you sure?'

'I don't mind if I do,' Flora put in.

'And what is your poison?'

'Gin and It, please,' Flora said, and she eyed Linda's empty glass. 'I'm sure Linda would like another orange.'

'Just an orange?'

'Yes,' Linda said, annoyed at Flora deciding things for her. 'Alcohol doesn't help my voice for one thing,' she snapped, 'and for another, I'm not seventeen yet.'

'Ah, so young and so wise,' the man said. 'While I am almost twice your age and quite stupid.'

'Oh, I wouldn't call you stupid, Mr...?'

'Haversham. Charles Haversham,' the man said. 'And you are?'

'Flora McMillan,' Flora said, shaking the hand

the man extended.

He turned to Linda and said, 'I know your name. It is Linda Lennox, though I always think of you as "the little nightingale". And now I will buy you both a drink.'

'Please don't trouble yourself,' Linda said. 'Our break is almost up and we'll have no time to enjoy extra drinks.'

'Oh, but Linda...'

Linda slipped from the stool and, cutting across what Flora was saying, she went on, 'And, if you will both excuse me, I must go and powder my nose,' and so saying, she walked away from them.

She was surprised how angry she felt at the man Charles Haversham. Just being the type of man he was annoyed her, and Flora was playing up to him, expecting her to do the same. Linda peered at herself in the mirror. She had no illusions about herself – she was slim and pretty enough, but she considered her only truly beautiful attribute was her voice. She looked her age and her accent betrayed her as a Brummie, and she had no idea what Charles Haversham was doing, bothering with her and Flora. If he'd liked her voice, why hadn't he come over the first night and said so casually? Lots of people had done just that, but he'd had to make a drama of it, to sit staring for weeks and then approach her as he might walk across a stage in a play.

She was annoyed with herself for even thinking about the man at all, and for her display of bad manners; that probably showed him she was disturbed. She decided she'd go back in and be polite, but no more, proving that she thought him no more important than any other patron of the restaurant.

And it really seemed as if it was going to work. She walked up to Flora, still talking to Charles Haversham and sipping at her second gin and It and said, 'Are you ready, Flora?'

Flora took one look at Linda's angry eyes and quickly gulped down the rest of her drink. As Linda sang, the agitation left her and it wasn't until the end of the evening that it surfaced again tenfold.

The taxi that brought them in the early evening came to fetch them around twelve o'clock when the taxi driver parked in the car park and called in to the restaurant to pick up the two ladies. But that night, no taxi arrived. Linda was peering into the black night to see if she could see a sign of it, and didn't notice Charles with Flora's and Linda's coats over his arm until her attention was drawn to it.

'I took the liberty of cancelling your taxi,' Charles said smoothly. 'I have my car outside and would consider it an honour to take you both home.

'You what?' Linda said, her voice almost a shout.

'Miss McMillan was quite amenable. I asked her at the break. I thought she would have mentioned it when you returned.'

'Oh, did you? Well, she didn't,' Linda cried. She glared at Charles and then said, 'Would you excuse me a minute? I have to speak to my friend.'

'Of course.'

390

Linda barely waited till he was out of earshot before she rounded on Flora. 'How could you be so stupid? We know nothing about this man.'

'I do. I asked the manager. He's a millionaire, Linda.'

'Yeah, well he could still be a mass murderer.'

'Don't be silly.'

'Me being silly? That's a laugh,' Linda cried. '*You're* being plain stupid.'

'I'm not.' Flora had gone red. 'They know him well here, the manager said so.'

'Bully for them, but we don't.'

'Oh, please Linda. He's a really nice person, a gentleman. He owns a factory in Aston that makes parts for guns, he was telling me about it and because of that, he was exempt from active service.'

'Oh yeah. So he wangled that as well,' Linda said scathingly.

'It wasn't his fault,' Flora said placatingly. 'Our armies couldn't fight without guns and that, could they?' Linda didn't answer and Flora went on, 'Oh, go on, Linda. Say yes? He's got a Rolls and I've never ridden in a Rolls in my life.'

Neither had Linda. Indeed, she thought, neither had most of the nation. In fact, a ride in any type of car was a novelty, but a Rolls...

'And after all, he's cancelled the taxi now.'

'Rather high-handed of him, don't you think?'

'He asked me,' Flora said. 'I said it was all right. I forgot to mention it, that's all. If you're cross with anyone it should be me.'

'It *is* you. I'm so flaming mad I could clout you,' Linda said.

She wondered what she should do now, accept the man's offer or insist the manager order another taxi. He wouldn't like that, especially if Charles was as well-heeled as Flora said. He was certainly a regular at the restaurant and if she refused, then it might make things awkward. Also, time was getting on and if she had to wait for another taxi to be sent out, it would be very late when she got home and Jenny waited up. Then of course, she'd have given her eye teeth for a chance for a ride in a Rolls. 'OK,' she said. 'Just this once. Don't do anything like this again and I'll tell you now, if he tries any funny business, I'll slap his bleeding face for him.'

Charles drove well, although before the war he'd actually driven very little, for his chauffeur Grimes had taken him everywhere. But Grimes had enlisted as soon as war had been declared, and Charles was surprised to find how much he enjoyed driving himself.

He glanced across at Linda, struck again by the uncanny resemblance she had to his late mother. Not, of course, the way his mother had looked just before she'd died six short months before. Then she'd become wizened with the weight she'd lost, and her skin had a yellowish tinge to it, but before that Charles had spent hours looking at the photographs of her as a girl and a young woman, and Linda Lennox could have been her double.

Charles had adored his mother. His father hadn't needed to ask him to look after her as he lay dying on a hospital bed when Charles was in his early teens. From the moment his father had breathed his last, he'd refused to return to his boarding school. Instead, he'd gone into the factory daily, learning the business that he would one day be in charge of. His Uncle Reginald, brought in to oversee the factory until Charles was old enough to take up the reins himself, was astounded at the young boy's dedication to follow in his father's footsteps, both in business and in caring for his mother.

Girls had never interested Charles. At his school he'd had relationships with a couple of boys, but those encounters hadn't really done anything for him either. Sex was unimportant to him. His mother was pleased to have such an attentive and devoted son and had no desire for any woman, however suitable, to take Charles's attention from her; she said so often. Charles told her not to worry; he had no wish to go out with anyone, let alone marry.

He was surprised how lonely he'd felt since his mother had died. There was no one waiting for him when he walked in the door in the evening, to mix him a drink and listen to him talking of the events of the day. He had few true friends, but money and privilege ensured he had many acquaintances and of course business colleagues, but their company could not make up for the loss of his mother and he mourned her deeply and sincerely.

At first, he had no desire to leave the house. It was comfortable for him with the daily help they had to clean the place. Amy Sallenger had been his mother's companion and she now ran the house in place of her mistress. Amy saw to the laundry, talked over the menu with old Bessie the cook and saw to Charles's clothes herself, starching his collars and cuffs and pressing his suits.

So Charles had little to do when he returned home in the evening but mix his own drink. Later, he would eat the meal Bessie would cook, always alone for though he'd asked Amy many times to sit at the table with him, she never would. It wouldn't be right, she said, and she was happier in the kitchen. Charles was sure she was, but he would have welcomed another face across the table some nights.

In the end, crushing boredom had sent him to Packington Hall with a small crowd of business associates to try out the restaurant, and from the moment he saw Linda Lennox, he was almost transfixed. It was as if his mother had returned to him and all night he'd been unable to keep his eyes off her; when she began to sing, he was bewitched. The uncanny likeness to his mother made it imperative that he speak to her.

However, his nerve had failed him, though he was there every time she sang. That evening at home, while he had his pre-dinner drink, he'd got out his mother's photograph albums again. She'd been born while Queen Victoria was on the throne, but had grown up in the elegant Edwardian era, and he saw photographs of her at summer picnics in her long flowing dresses and the parasol and bonnet to protect her pretty skin from the sun's rays. He saw her being rowed in a punt by a young man in a striped blazer, and at parties and gatherings of young people together

394

and eventually, she and her handsome husband were photographed on their wedding day. Linda's floor-length dress of apricot satin that she still wore while she sang, made the similarity between her and Charles's mother even more marked, and that evening he knew he *must* speak to her.

And he had. And now he was taking her home, although he'd sensed her hostility to him. Even while he didn't understand it, he told himself to tread carefully. He behaved impeccably, and Linda, unaware of his thoughts, was able to enjoy the sensation of being carried along in a car that just purred its way forward. Both women sat in the back on the plush leather seats and felt like royalty.

Charles took them both home again the following Saturday evening. While they were waiting for Flora to fetch her coat, he asked Linda for a date, and she politely refused. 'The management at Packington Hall wouldn't like me to have relationships with the patrons of the place,' she'd said in explanation.

'I'm sure I could get them to stretch a point in my case,' Charles had replied.

Linda thought maybe he could. Certainly the management would do little to antagonise a man so influential or so wealthy, and she sought about for another reason.

'Linda, do you like me?' Charles had asked earnestly.

'Mr Haversham, I hardly know you.'

'My name is Charles and I thought that was the purpose of a date – to get to know one another,'

Charles had said.

'Yes, but...'

'Is there someone else in your life?'

'No,' Linda said. 'Of course not. I'm not ready for any sort of relationship yet, that's all.'

Charles was bemused, for he knew Linda wasn't telling him the truth. There probably *was* someone, but whoever he was, he was not making her happy. Indeed, maybe he didn't know of her love for him. But he did not press her. One thing he'd learned was patience and he would bide his time. He knew now he wanted Linda in his life, in his home. He wanted to dress her in silks and satins similar to those his mother had worn, so that she could be a fitting hostess to the people he would invite to their home, and when she sang for them, they would know what a lucky man he was. In short, Charles Haversham wanted to marry Linda Lennox and give her a life she could only dream of. She could have anything she desired, for he was generous as well as rich. He was sure she wouldn't mind his lack of sexual response; she was such a child still, it couldn't be important to her. She would be grateful to him and would have plenty of pleasurable amusements and pastimes to fill her days.

However, he said none of this to Linda. The time wasn't right yet, but one day, he would have her. Whoever the man was she imagined herself in love with, he would not be able to give Linda half as good a life as he could. Of that he was certain.

Linda watched his face and was glad he hadn't pressed the point of her going out with him, for nice as he was, it would have been ridiculous. Charles Haversham seemed even older than his thirty-four years, and though he appeared pleasant enough, Linda thought it would be like going out with her father. So when Charles pulled up at her gate, she thanked him politely as she got out of the car and went up the path without a backward glance.

Chapter Twenty-One

The following Sunday afternoon, Linda recounted some of the conversation she'd had with Charles Haversham to Sarah Phelps, as they sat before the fire. She'd gone alone knowing the Phelps children would be away. Jenny had taken Geraldine's children out for a walk on her own for a change, saying it was time Linda had a break. She was glad of it, for she needed to talk to Sarah Phelps.

'And why did you refuse him, lovely?' Sarah asked. 'A man like that could give you a good time.'

Linda stared at her, and then said, 'I wasn't born yesterday, Sarah. I know what a man like that wants with a girl like me, and I'm not that kind of girl.'

'What d'you mean, a girl like you?' Sarah demanded. 'Ain't you as good as anyone?'

'No. No, I ain't. Not to people like him,' Linda said. 'You should see them. Proper toffs they are. They don't marry the likes of us. They just like to have fun with us. Only trouble is, it's not them that has to pay for the fun, it's the girl every time, and it ain't a game that I want to play. Any road,' she went on, 'he's much too old for me.'

'How old is he then?'

'Thirty-four.'

Sarah Phelps thought a bit about that. She

knew Linda had a point and hated the thought of someone playing with her affection. But Linda wasn't stupid and seemed to be able to see rogues a mile off. This man certainly sounded like a rogue. Old enough almost to be Linda's father and asking her for a date like a young lad! Linda seemed to think he was after one thing and she could well be right. So he was a toff. Did that matter after six long years of war that surely would have turned the class system on its head?

'Is that the whole reason?' Sarah asked.

'What d'you mean?'

'Is the total reason you rejected him because he's older than you and because he's rich and you're not?' Sarah said.

Linda flushed and said, 'Course. What other reason could there be?'

'You could have your eye on someone else?'

'Well, I haven't,' Linda said.

It was said so definitely that Sarah thought she'd probably been mistaken about the incident she'd observed in the snow between Linda and Max. It had happened weeks before anyway, and since then she'd seen nothing to make her think Linda even liked the young German. She was polite and that was all. Of course, she was a sensible girl and would know it was no good starting anything with someone who could be whisked back to Germany any day soon.

Linda sat and darned socks and the silence stretched out between herself and Sarah while she tried to analyse her feelings about Max, but she found it almost impossible to do so. In the first place, she had denied to herself and others that she felt anything for the tall handsome German. She hated his race with a passion, a view that, at that time, most British people shared. She knew Maureen did and Beattie, and now even Jenny and Geraldine. Yet, on a personal level, she couldn't even dislike Max. She was ashamed of her passionate feelings about him. She wanted to feel his arms around her, his lips on hers. Sometimes her dreams of Max and what she wanted him to do disturbed her sleep and remembering them later disturbed her daylight hours as well, but never ever, she thought, had she betrayed herself. Maybe, she thought with a sigh, it's time to get it all out of my system. Maybe I should talk to Max and probably find he's just an ordinary man who has no more fascination for me than any other. Maybe it will get rid of the madness of my mind and body that is causing me to lose sleep and concentration.

Sarah saw the doubts and fears flooding over Linda's face, but she didn't speak. She wondered what was going through her mind, for she was a complex person. Eventually Linda said, 'Where's Max today?'

She could have kicked herself as soon as she said it. She knew Ruby had gone to visit friends in the village and Sam had taken his children off to an auction of farm machinery, and presumed Max had either gone with him or stayed at the camp all day, for she imagined prisoners had to be under the jurisdiction of someone.

But apparently Max was still here because Sarah said. 'He's in the top field. In fact, you'd do me a favour if you'd take him some tea up. I'll

400

make up a flask and some sandwiches, for he'll not take the time to come down because the sheep broke through the fence in the bottom field last week. They ate up all the vegetation to be seen in the vicarage garden and defiled many of the graves. I tell you Linda, our names were mud at the meeting of the parish council.' Sarah giggled and went on, 'We made sincere and abject apologies to all and sundry, and Sam, Max and Ruby made an inspection of the fields and repaired any holes or other potential escape routes. The only trouble is, Sam will be turning the sheep out into the top field soon, which he does once the lambing season is over. Max said the fencing is so bad, battered as it is by winter gales, it will all have to be either replaced or strengthened, and he's at it now. Mind you,' she went on, listening to the wind howling around the house, 'the weather doesn't get any warmer. God, here we are in March and it's colder than December.'

'And will Max welcome me breaking in on such important war work?' Linda asked.

'God, girl, he'll probably think you're a miracle itself,' Sarah said. 'With the wind and cold up there, he needs some sustenance.' She glanced slyly at Linda and gave her a dig in the ribs. 'Even if he is a German and as such our mortal enemy?'

Linda didn't really want to go, but she could hardly refuse and anyway, it would give her a chance to talk to Max. She didn't know if she wanted to talk or not, but if she decided not to once she got there, she could just put the snack down in front of him and walk away.

'Come and give me a hand then?' Sarah said, jumping to her feet. 'We have to feed our captives well.'

And laughing alongside Sarah, Linda went into the farm kitchen and helped prepare a feast for Max Schulz.

'I've brought you up your tea,' Linda said.

Max straightened his back from where he'd been bending over, strengthening the fencing, and smiled. He took the small parcel from her hands. 'You have saved my life,' he said.

The top field caught the full blast from the north wind, thought Linda as she watched Max unwrap the sandwiches. Small wonder indeed that the fences were blown over. She knew that Sam would only judge the field to be suitable for his sheep when the harshness of winter, with its ice-bound ground and frosty fields, was at an end – whenever that was. Sarah was right – the cold was intense and you'd hardly believe it was very nearly spring. It was making her breath escape in little puff balls from her throat, while the wind whistled about her head and set her ears throbbing and her teeth chattering.

'Thank you,' Max said. 'You will share with me, yes?'

'No,' Linda said. 'It's for you. I'll get mine at the house.'

'A little only?' Max said. 'Please?'

'Just a bit then,' Linda said, thinking it was sensible to wait and take the things back to the house. Max led the way behind the hedge skirting one side of the field. It offered quite considerable shelter from the wind and she sat on the edge of a hummock and Max sat beside her on another, the parcels of food and the flask between them.

Max smiled at her and the smile turned her insides to jelly. 'Ah Linda,' he said.

Linda took a deep breath and struggled to control her voice and said as casually as she could, 'What?'

'You know what.'

Linda couldn't look at Max: she knew she'd be lost if she did that.

In answer he picked up her hand, and held it.

'Oh, Max please. Stop all this. It's madness.'

Max gently lifted her chin and gazed deeply into her eyes and Linda felt her knees tremble. He knew he'd loved her from the moment she'd bumped into him that first evening. He'd sensed her unease when she'd learned he was not only a prisoner-of-war but also a German. He'd loved her, though he'd sensed her reluctance. He'd sensed her fear and trepidation, and he'd wanted to tell her she need never be afraid of him. God, anything but. Given a free choice, he'd have laid down his life for her. But his life wasn't his own and he had no right to do what he wanted with it. He was a German and had no right at all to love anyone and certainly not an English girl, but he couldn't help himself. He'd tried to put her out of his mind, but she'd invaded his dreams even though he'd only seen her for moments at a time.

And then came that snowy blustery day at the end of December, when she'd arrived un-

403

announced, flanked by two children so silent and white they might have been walking corpses.

He'd seen them arrive from the barn where he was making a sledge for the young ones. Sam had filled him in later as to who the children were and what had happened to them. Max felt bad that the family had been deprived of a husband and father. But there were so many families like them in Germany, and all over Europe. God, the carnage was terrible.

He recalled how he'd taken Linda down the slope on the sledge and as a consequence had virtually half buried her in a snowdrift. God, how he'd panicked, digging frantically to release her until he'd pulled her free and held her in his arms for the first time. Then he knew he wanted Linda and only Linda in his life for ever. At twenty-one, he was no virgin though he'd been celibate since his capture the previous year, but no knowledge could have prepared him for the gut-wrenching sensation he'd felt as he held the young girl tight against him.

He wanted to talk about how he felt, and yet when he tried, Linda had become angry, and for weeks afterwards she'd remained remote. She seldom spoke to him and then only when there were others about, and she purposely averted her eyes from his. Yet here she was bringing him some tea and sandwiches. They were alone, in a deserted field.

Knowing he might never have another chance, Max looked into her eyes said earnestly, 'Linda, I think I love you.'

'Don't be silly,' she said crossly.

'It is not silly to love.'

'Yes, it is. You are a German. We're enemies.'

'Our countries perhaps,' Max said. 'Please listen, Linda. I didn't plan to love you. It would be better that I didn't.' He took her hands again and she allowed him to, as he asked, 'What do you feel for me?'

What did she feel? Linda knew she should tell him he meant nothing to her. She tried, but she couldn't get the words out and so she said nothing.

Gently Max released Linda's hands and, cupping her face, he kissed her lips. Linda gave a gasp. She had never been kissed before and was surprised how much she enjoyed it. And when Max kissed her again she was in his arms, kissing him back with an intensity that took her by surprise, and moaning with pleasure. It gave him the answer she'd refuse to voice.

Max moved his hands over Linda's body and she pulled herself from his arms and unbuttoned her coat, but as she was about to remove it, Max protested, 'No, no. You'll get cold.'

Linda took no notice. Get cold? She felt as if she was on fire! Max kissed her neck and throat and she moaned again and his own desire mounted. He took off his jacket and laid it on the grass of the field that had been rimed with frost that morning and he pushed Linda gently down on top of it.

Heedless of the icy wind, Max slipped his hand inside Linda's jumper and she wriggled beneath him as he cupped her firm breasts. In all her young life, Linda had never felt such passion.

Boys had never been a feature in her life and even the servicemen she'd played to, had never touched her heart in the slightest. Max had captured it totally and he guided Linda's hands and moaned with desire to match her own. For a brief moment, Linda remembered the fumbling of her stepfather, but she firmly shut that image out of her mind and responded to Max.

But he pulled back, as Linda was reaching her peak of excitement, 'No,' she cried.

'Linda, we cannot. We must not,' Max said. His breath was coming in great gasps and he drew away with difficulty, frightened for Linda, who he was sure was a virgin.

But Linda couldn't bear the emotions charging through her body and she refused to let him go and pulled him down on top of her and held him tight. 'Oh, love me Max,' she cried desperately. 'For God's sake love me.'

For a moment, Linda felt a sharp stabbing pain and then a sensation so exquisite, that she cried out again and again as her rapturous pleasure rose higher and higher in waves.

And when it was over, the tears came, squeezing from her eyes and trailing down her cheeks. Max was alarmed, 'What is it? Oh, my darling. Don't cry, ah my love.'

Linda continued to weep as Max kissed the tears from her eyes. He pulled her clothes around her and wrapped her in his arms. Eventually, she lay quiet and Max said, 'I'm sorry.'

'Don't be.'

'You are not sad?'

'No, Max you dope,' Linda said and she

thought, so that's what all the fuss is about, what everyone talks about and hints at. She had no idea it could be so lovely and feel so good. No one had ever mentioned that.

But Max thought of the possible consequences and hoped there would be none. He held Linda close to him and wished he could say he'd look after her, but he couldn't and he castigated himself for possibly endangering her in any way.

'Put your coat on,' he advised and she did so, beginning to feel the cold seeping into her bones again.

Max's own jacket was soaked from the grass but he put it on anyway. 'Now,' he said. 'We will eat the food and drink the hot tea. We have much to talk about.' He put his arm around Linda and went on. 'Not how much I love you, for that you know already. We need to discuss the future.'

Linda had settled herself back in the shelter of the hedge and accepted a sandwich before she spoke and then she said regretfully, 'There's no future for us, Max.'

'Ah. This is rubbish,' Max said. 'We are two people in love. We belong together.'

Linda shook her head. 'Max, I can't even tell my family about you, never mind discuss a future together,' she said. 'No one knows about you at home. I made the mistake of mentioning you once the first time I saw you, and that was enough. They hate Germans.'

'All Germans?'

Linda nodded.

'But, this is crazy.'

'It's how it is, Max,' Linda said. 'I can't tell

407

Jenny, with her brother, brother-in-law and friend killed, and her fiancé in constant danger. She'd never agree. And I love her too much and owe her too much to go against her.'

'Even if your heart tells you otherwise?'

'Even that.'

'But why? If this Jenny loves you...'

'There's no if about it,' Linda said firmly. 'I'm sorry, Max.'

Max looked so sombre, Linda felt for him. 'What we have experienced today,' she said, 'will probably have to last us a lifetime. Soon the war will be over and you will go home, and that will be that, anyway.'

'I don't intend to stay in Germany,' Max said. 'There is nothing there for me any more.'

He was silent for a moment. Linda opened the flask and poured them both tea, and handed Max a cup before she asked, 'So what will you do? If my family think like the rest of the country, and I believe they do, you won't be welcomed back here after the war.'

'I know that too and I also know I have to be sent back to Germany first. Then I will apply to emigrate to America.'

'America?'

'New York,' Max said. 'At least at first. I have a cousin called Werner there who will sponsor me. He is many years my senior. Werner got out of Germany years before the war. He told my mother and father what was coming. Not, of course, that he foresaw the true cost of human life and six years of war, but he knew when the Nazi Party got in, a little of what it would mean,'

Max said. 'He asked Mother to send Joseph and myself, even if they couldn't go too at that time, but my father refused to separate the family.'

'Your lives might have been totally different if your father had agreed,' Linda said, gulping at the hot tea, glad of the warmth of it seeping through her body.

'But yes,' Max said. 'I would be an all-American boy right now, fighting the Japanese.'

'Do you wish you'd gone?'

'Sometimes. I didn't like the things the Nazis did to the Jews. Many of my friends disappeared from school. Our family doctor was a Jew. We didn't know. I mean, as far as we knew, he was German – he had a German name. But one day we arrived for an appointment and he just wasn't there.'

'Why didn't you do something about it?' Linda cried angrily. 'I can't imagine that happening here.'

'We didn't know they were being killed,' Max said. 'I still find it hard to believe, but Auschwitz is not a lie told by the Russian Army. I know this. We were told the Jewish people were being resettled. I remember asking my mother where my friend Rudi was going to be resettled, because he considered himself a German rather than a Jew, and my mother told me to hush. It was better not to ask questions. Children were encouraged to inform on parents and school-teachers who didn't toe the line. Our teacher turned Hitler's picture to the wall one day – there was one in every classroom, you see. She said it put her off teaching to see that evil man's face, and then one day she just disappeared. We were told she was a bad woman and an enemy of the state.'

'That's terrible!'

'That's how it was. People were frightened all the time. You said nothing, not even to your family or your friends,' Max said.

Linda listened, horrified. Germany sounded a dreadful place to live, even for the non-Jewish people, a place where you'd be fearful of speaking against anything or anyone and where you could trust nobody.

No wonder Max had no burning desire to return to his homeland. Wherever he went she would wish him well, but it was not her concern. She took the empty flask cups, folded up the greaseproof paper and stood up brushing the crumbs from her skirt. 'I must go back,' she said. 'Sarah will be worrying.'

'I know,' Max said, getting to his feet too and holding Linda in a tight embrace.

She responded to his kiss with passionate intensity but allowed it to go no further, and with a wave was off back to the farmhouse. She wondered what she should say to Sarah, but the farmer's wife only had to look at Linda and see the glow in her pink-tinged face and the look in her eyes, to know that something had happened between the two young people and she was surprised and a little alarmed.

But Linda said nothing to her and Sarah felt she had no right to ask.

Later in bed, she told Sam she thought Linda and Max fancied themselves sweet on each other.

Sam was outraged and far too perturbed to sleep. Max was there on trust, to work on the farm. He was not there to make eyes, or worse, at young innocent British girls.

He didn't blame Linda. He knew she was a healthy girl with normal needs, who was growing in a world sadly lacking in boys near her own age. Max, he had to admit, was a handsome, well-set-up chap and probably the fact that he was a German and a prisoner at that, lent a romanticism to the whole thing.

He knew any relationship between them – if Sarah had got it right, and she usually had – must have been instigated by Max. Linda could have gone out with any number of servicemen, but she never agreed to, nor encouraged them, nor had her head turned by the attention, as many others would have done. So in his opinion, she'd been taken advantage of and he'd have something to say to the chap about it in the morning.

The next day, Max was surprised to find an angry Sam waiting for him in the cowshed. He didn't try to defend himself as Sam tore a strip off him for encouraging Linda's affection, when he had nothing but heartache to offer her, nor did he deny it. When Sam's fists shot out, the first blow blackening his left eye and the second causing his nose and lip to spurt with blood, he didn't retaliate. He staggered but didn't fall from the power of the blows and faced Sam unafraid, and Sam felt ashamed of himself. Whatever Max had done, he knew he shouldn't have hit him, for if the camp were to find out, he'd be in big trouble. Max thought the treatment quite

411

justified; he knew he should never have allowed himself to have got so carried away. Linda was little more than a girl and a virgin, and all night he'd worried about it. He felt better when his eyes throbbed and his lip and nose smarted and stung.

'I'm sorry,' Sam said. 'I shouldn't have done that.'

'You had a right.'

'I had no bloody right!' Sam cried. 'Don't you see? Oh, what's the use. Look, go down to the house and get yourself tidied up.'

'The milking...?'

'One of your eyes is closing up, man,' Sam growled. 'And I don't want you dripping blood into the milk. I left Ruby having breakfast, she'll be along shortly.'

Max left him without a word and as he neared the farmhouse, Ruby came out of the door. She stared at him for a moment or two, but when she gave a grin and said 'God, Max. What did the other feller look like?' he walked straight past her without a word.

Ruby went on to the cowshed and wondered why Sam Phelps had hit his German farmhand, for that's what had so obviously happened. She'd never known anything like it before. Sam was the most easygoing of men and so, she would have said, was Max – yet they must have had words, and strong words for it to come to blows.

Yet she noted Sam's face had not a mark on it, though it was set. His mouth was a thin angry line and his brow puckered, and Ruby knew it was no good asking him any questions. He glowered at her and almost snarled, 'You took your time.' She bent her head to the task in hand, knowing that Sam wasn't really mad with her, but if she wasn't very careful, she knew he might snap the head off her.

Later that night he said he'd decided to send Max back to the camp. 'You can't,' Sarah complained. 'Look, blame me if you like. I asked Linda to go and take him his tea and told her where she'd find him.'

'Don't talk so bloody daft,' Sam snapped. 'Taking his tea is one thing, but taking advantage is another. God, Sarah, it doesn't matter whose bloody fault it was.'

'You care, and you're blaming Max.'

'I'm not,' Sam said, and more truthfully admitted, 'all right then, maybe I am. I think it's all his bloody fault, if you must know.'

'Sam,' Sarah said, 'we're coming up to the busiest months on the farm. You'll miss Max.'

'I'll get another prisoner.'

'Not like Max, you won't,' Sarah said. She laid a hand on her husband's arm and said, 'I'll talk to Linda. 'They're young, they fancy themselves in love. It will pass, they'll get over it.'

'Oh yeah?' Sam snapped, shaking off his wife's hand. 'And what if Linda's left with a bleeding broken heart and, God forbid, something worse – a German bastard to bring up before they get over it. What then?'

Charlie and Sally sobbed bitterly when Sam told them Max must leave. 'But why?' they cried and Sam could not give them an answer.

But in the end Max didn't go, because Sam

couldn't think what reason to give the camp for his return. Not the truth certainly, for he'd really be for the high jump, and what else could he say? Sarah was right, it was the busiest time of the year in farming, excluding the harvest, and so he couldn't say he no longer needed him; they'd know that to be a lie.

So, the next day he told Sarah that if she wasn't to actually forbid Linda to visit the farm again, she was to make absolutely sure she and Max were never to spend time alone again. And Sarah assured him she would.

Chapter Twenty-Two

All through the next week, Linda went over the events of that day. She couldn't believe what she had done – and with Max, of all people! She'd never even kissed a man before, and had a horror of appearing fast and some of the exploits the girls at work boasted of, had shocked her to the core. Now she was no better than them. In fact, she was worse and she couldn't understand why she'd let Max take such liberties or to kiss her in the first place, never mind run his hands down her body the way he had. God, she must have been mad! And what if there were repercussions? All week, that thought had been with her, but it was on Saturday that she realised that she was safe.

She didn't want to go to the farm the following week, and certainly didn't want to see Max; she'd be too ashamed to look at him. But she could think of no excuse for either her or the children, and Sam came to fetch them as usual. Normally, he'd laugh and joke with the children and chaff her a bit – for after all, he'd known Linda some time. But that Saturday he was silent, not a laugh or joke out of him and when Linda, in an attempt to open up a conversation spoke to him, his answers were brusque.

She didn't associate Sam's behaviour with what had happened to her the previous Sunday; she simply presumed that he and Sarah had had words. However, she hadn't been at the farm half an hour, when she knew that wasn't so. There was an atmosphere about the place. She didn't see Max till dinnertime because he'd kept working well away from the house, and then he seemed very awkward. She was embarrassed too and glad when the meal was over and he was sent to work again. She was more than ever convinced that the tension running through everyone was somehow connected to Max and possibly herself. Max's injuries had healed and Ruby might have let on what had happened if Sarah hadn't cautioned her that Sam would get into big trouble if the news leaked out. Ruby knew he would, and she also knew Sam to be a mild-mannered man. If he'd hit someone, she reckoned he must have deserved it and she agreed to say nothing about Sam's little mis-understanding with Max.

Linda was hurt and confused, and for the first time felt unwelcome at the farm, though nothing was actually said because Sarah couldn't think how to broach the subject. Eventually Linda asked Sarah if she'd done something to offend her, but Sarah, embarrassed, told her she hadn't because she didn't know what else to say.

Linda knew Sarah wasn't speaking the truth. Somehow she had guessed that there was something between her and Max, and she went hot with embarrassment at the thought that she might find out how far it had gone. She knew there was only one thing to do. 'I don't think I'll come up to the farm for a little while,' she said.

'The children are a lot better now and I'll find other things to do with them.'

Sarah was relieved. It would take a great worry off her mind, though she said, 'I'll miss you.'

Linda heard the relief in her voice and knew that what she'd guessed was right. 'I'll miss you too,' she said. 'But we can't rely on you all the time and anyway, it's coming to the busiest time of year on the farm and we'd just be in the way.'

What she really wanted to do was to cry out, *'I love Max Schulz with all my heart. I know it isn't sensible and in fact, it's the stupidest thing in the world, but there it is.'* She wanted Sarah to put her arms around her and say she understood, because no one else would. But now, she wasn't even sure of Sarah's reaction.

Sarah saw the sadness in Linda's eyes and could have cried for her. She wished Linda had had a normal peacetime adolescence because then this feeling she had for Max would be put into perspective. She wanted to say she'd probably fall in and out of love many times before she had to settle down, but she couldn't. She didn't want to start any sort of conversation about Max Schulz. One thing she was sure of – Linda had to forget him and as quickly as possible.

She remembered the man Charles, whom Linda had once mentioned, and she said, 'What about What's-his-name at the restaurant?'

'Charles Haversham?' Linda said with a sigh. 'Oh, he's still there.'

'Still asking you out?' Sarah asked, and Linda nodded mutely. 'Why don't you go, pet?' she urged.

417

'I told you...'

'No, listen,' Sarah insisted. 'Do you like this Charles?'

'He's all right.' Linda was noncommittal.

'You don't dislike him, or think there's anything odd about him?'

'No, not really.'

'He's not made a pass at you or anything?'

'No never,' Linda said. 'I can say that. He's been a perfect gentleman.'

'Then go to the theatre, or out to dinner, or anywhere else he wants to take you,' Sarah suggested. 'Soon all our lads will be home and the place will be flooded with men. Now though, they're in short supply, but you can practise on your Charles.'

'I'll think about it,' Linda said.

One of the hardest things, Linda found, was that having made her decision not to visit the farm and Max again, she could tell no one of the heartache she was suffering. No one knew she'd loved a German prisoner and had let him make love to her in an icy muddy field, and no one knew he'd taken her heart. Her normal confidantes Jenny, Peggy, Maureen and even Beattie would have had no sympathy for her plight at all, and would have been totally shocked at her behaviour, but as the weeks passed, most of the family became aware that Linda had lost her sparkle.

Jenny noticed her malaise, but put it down to the tedium of the last few weeks of the war. They knew they'd almost won, the outcome was in no doubt, but it dragged on and on. She was too worried about Bob to have much energy left for Linda, because she hadn't seen her fiancé for months and though he wrote regularly, it wasn't quite the same. In every letter she sent him she begged him to take care, for Hitler always seemed to have something up his sleeve.

So Linda struggled on desperately, feeling very alone. Rosemarie and Jamie didn't make it easier because disappointment made them play up when Linda told them they'd not be going to the farm for a few weeks. Linda could have done without the tears and tantrums, but she held firm and said the Phelps were very busy in the springtime, there was a lot to do and they'd only be in the way.

They eventually accepted it, as children do, and after a week or two no longer spoke of the farm and Linda was grateful. She knew it would fade from their minds in the end and remain just a pleasant memory.

The third week away from the farm, she decided to visit her mother's grave. She was grateful to Beattie who had been keeping it tidy for her while she'd been dealing with the children at weekends. She hadn't intended to take Jamie and Rosemarie with her, partly as she was going fairly early on Saturday morning – it being a busy day – and partly because she thought it might upset them. Jenny said if they went it might make them realise they were not the only ones to lose loved ones and to take them if they wanted to go.

Rosemarie had been a little girl, four years before, when Linda had lost her mother, but now

419

she read the headstone with horror – a little boy of three and another twelve months and their mother. All of Linda's family had been wiped out, because she remembered Jenny telling her of her father dying from TB and her stepfather at Dunkirk.

It seemed a terrible shame and Linda was so nice and kind. Rosemarie helped her tidy up the grave and arrange the flowers she'd brought in the pot that Mabel Sanders had given her years before. She wished she had a grave to tend for her daddy, it would be the best-kept one in the cemetery, but still, she reminded herself, a grave was all Linda had.

By the time they'd got back on the bus, Rosemarie was deep in thought. She'd always miss her daddy, like Linda must miss her mammy and wee brothers, but the older girl was brave and strong and had managed to live her life without them. Rosemarie decided that she would have to do the same and help Jamie, for he was still only a wee boy and maybe wasn't quite up to it yet.

Jenny could see the change in her niece right away and thought it a pity Linda hadn't taken Geraldine up there too, for the constant melancholy was getting to her. Also, her mother had been in a funny mood from the post arriving that morning when she'd retrieved a letter from the mat.

Norah was standing in the living room when Linda went in with the children, pink-cheeked and windblown from the fresh air and laughing together over something. She was holding a letter in her hand and fair shaking with temper. 'I'm glad you're back,' she snapped. 'It will save me having to tell the news twice.'

'What is it, Mother?' Jenny said impatiently. 'You've been going on all morning and told me nothing.'

'Well, I'll tell you now, miss, you and that brazen hussy you foisted on me years ago. It's over, do you hear? You're out, the pair of you.'

Jenny and Linda looked at Norah as if she'd gone mad and she went on, 'I'm giving up the tenancy of this house and moving into Geraldine's.'

'Moving into Geraldine's,' Jenny repeated. 'But the boys...?'

Norah flapped the letter she'd been holding in front of her face furiously. 'The boys are not coming home,' she said. 'Francis has written to tell me that Martin is going to marry a most unsuitable girl called Dora as soon as the war is over. He presumed Martin had already told me, but he's not said a word. But the best bit is, the girl is in the Salvation Army. Can you believe it – and him brought up a good Catholic boy? Well, that's the finish for me, he's no son of mine.'

'Oh, Mother.'

'Don't you "Oh Mother" me,' Norah cried, turning on Jenny savagely. 'You've probably encouraged him.'

'I know nothing about it,' Jenny said truthfully. 'But he's well old enough to marry.'

'Yes, a good Catholic girl,' Norah snapped. 'Francis said they'll be staying down south where her parents live. Well, he can stay where he likes for I'll never see him again.'

Jenny hoped she'd get over the shock of Martin marrying given time, but doubted it; her mother's memory was long and she bore grudges for years. She wondered why Martin hadn't written to tell his mother himself. Maybe then she'd have been less upset, but looking at Norah's outraged face she knew nothing could lessen the shock, not of Martin marrying, but marrying someone in the Salvation Army. 'I'd rather see him dead than that,' Norah said emphatically.

'What about Francis?' Jenny said.

'Oh, Francis doesn't want to come back to Birmingham either,' Norah said. 'Not good enough for either of them, it seems. He wants to go into partnership with another soldier and buy a boat between them.'

'A boat!'

'You heard – a boat. This man comes from Folkestone and he said after the war people will want to go out from Folkestone and cruise around the coast and they'll take them. Stupid idea! It will never work, of course.'

Jenny hoped it would. She hoped both her brothers' lives would change for the better. They deserved it, all the servicemen deserved it and she wished them well.

'And you, miss, can take that smirk off your face,' Norah said. 'Because I'm giving up the tenancy of this place next week and you'd better have somewhere to live by then or you'll be out on the street, and it will give me great pleasure to see the pair of you there!'

Afterwards Jenny was to say to her Gran, 'It shook me up a bit and Linda too of course, because she is so much younger, but in a way my mother did us both a favour. Francesca Masters took us in without a qualm, and now I can do what Bob was always urging me to do and start looking seriously for a house. Geraldine and Mother can look after each other. The only ones I really feel sorry for are the children.'

Linda felt for them too, especially as Norah was not as keen as she had been for Linda to take them out at weekends. She'd assumed full control of Geraldine and her children as well as the house. Linda told Jenny it was almost as though Geraldine had slipped back into child-hood, letting her mother decide everything. Jenny said it had always been that way. Linda was now an unwelcome visitor. Norah had eventually got her from under her roof, and she certainly didn't want her calling round. She said Linda had allowed the children undue licence, had let them run almost wild and it was about time some discipline was instilled.

The children's sorrowful faces smote Linda and she wondered if she'd been wise to take them about with her in the first place. 'They haven't even got a bolthole,' she complained to Jenny. 'Not like you and I did. I mean, they can't run to Gran, and you know your mother will never let her near.'

However, there was nothing they could do about any of it, but Linda was depressed enough about everything to eventually agree to go out one evening with Charles Haversham.

He was delighted. 'Where would you like to go, my dear?' he said. 'The theatre, the opera?'

Linda shook her head. 'I haven't the proper clothes for places like that.'

'I have plenty of things,' Charles said. 'Things of my mother's I'll have altered for you.'

'Charles, if you want to take me out, you must take me as I am. I'll go out in what I have, not in borrowed clothes.'

'I've offended you.'

'Not at all. I just thought we'd get things straight from the start.'

Jenny hoped Linda knew what she was doing, going out with a much older man and one of a different social class. 'Why worry,' Francesca said when Jenny expressed concern. 'Linda is a sensible girl and nearly seventeen years old, and really she's had little enjoyment in her life so far.'

'I suppose it has been a bit dull for her,' Jenny agreed. 'And that's probably what's been the matter with her these last few weeks.'

'I would say that's probably so,' Francesca said. 'After all, in normal times she would be able to dress as well as she could afford and be off with friends in the evening, and boyfriends would be part of it.'

'There's not so many men about now,' Jenny commented.

'That is why I say let her have her head now. Let her enjoy herself.'

And she did enjoy herself. Charles picked her up from the door in his Rolls and presented Jenny, who opened it for him, with a big bunch of flowers. For Linda, there were chocolates on the seat. His mother's favourites, though he didn't tell her that.

He could hardly believe Linda had at last agreed to come out with him, and he wanted nothing to spoil the night. And nothing did. Linda, who'd sat so rigid beside him for the first half-hour, eventually began to relax as she realised he only wanted to hold her hand. In the restaurant afterwards, she found Charles was good company and very amusing.

He didn't ask any personal questions and Linda was glad. She had no desire to open her heart to Charles Haversham. Charles didn't care about Linda's past or even about her background; he wanted her on his terms and that was that. He was used to always getting his own way, but in pursuit of it, he could be charming, generous and very attentive. When he delivered Linda back to the door that night and gave her a chaste kiss on the lips, she realised she hadn't enjoyed herself so much for a long time, and readily agreed to go out with him again.

She wasn't ashamed of Charles and yet she didn't mention him to Maureen; it was Jenny who did so after Linda had been out with him for the third time. When Linda went down to Maureen's the following weekend, they were all waiting for her, even Beattie who had popped along for a chat. 'Well, girl?' Maureen said.

'Well, what?'

'Get away out of that,' Maureen scoffed. 'We've all heard about the new man in your life.'

'What's this?' Beattie said, for she'd not heard the news.

'It's nothing,' Linda said. She tried to be nonchalant though her face burned crimson. 'It's just someone I've gone out with a couple of times.'

'From that fancy place where she sings in the evening,' Peggy put in and added with a smile, 'And not a waiter or barman you understand, but a customer.'

'I thought it was a toffs' place.'

'And so it is.' Linda said.

'Oh Gawd girl, you'll be joining the snobs' club next.'

'No I won't.'

'And voting bloody Conservative,' Beattie chuckled. 'And talking all lah-di-dah.'

'Beattie, I've only been out with him a few times,' Linda cried in exasperation.

'Come on and tell us all about him then,' Peggy urged.

'Not if you're going to poke fun,' Linda said mutinously and they promised they wouldn't, though Beattie hooted a bit when Linda said he owned a factory in Aston and a large house in Four Oaks, Sutton Coldfield. She didn't say that she'd been introduced to Bessie the cook, or Amy Sallenger who was a sort of housekeeper. For one thing, she knew they'd all find that hard to take and for another she'd been uncomfortable herself. She knew her nervousness showed and not only that, neither woman had taken to her, she could tell. Amy in particular had an almost proprietorial air towards Charles, treating him almost as a mother might. She had cast Linda a scornful look and gave an expressive sniff of disapproval when the girl was introduced to her.

Linda's face had flushed, but it was with anger

426

not embarrassment. She'd lifted her head high and extended her hand. 'Pleased to meet you,' she said.

Too late, she remembered Jenny's warning: 'Always say "How do you do",' she cautioned. 'Never "Pleased to meet you".'

'Why not?'

'That's just the way it is.'

'You mean "Pleased to meet you" is common?'

'Sort of.'

Ah well, Linda thought, now at least we know where we stand, but I'm just dating Charles not marrying him. She didn't really know why she'd been taken to his house and introduced to the two women; he wasn't the sort to show off. But now she had met them she didn't much care for them, and was glad she would see so little of them in the future.

But she couldn't say any of this to her friends and so she missed out that part of it and Beattie's only comment when she'd finished was, 'Fancy our Linda going out with a bleeding toff.' She glanced over at Linda and said, 'Hope you know what you're a-doing of, girl?'

'Course I do,' Linda said irritably. 'I ain't stupid.'

She could have gone on to say 'like your Vera's Vicky,' for the girl, only a year older than Linda, was seven months pregnant and the American father, unaware of his responsibilities, was busy liberating Europe. What Beattie had prophesied had indeed happened, and though Vicky knew the child's father was American, she'd tearfully confessed to her parents, when her condition

427

could be hidden no longer, that she wasn't sure which one of the many she'd slept with was responsible.

'Well, I'm just saying, lass,' Beattie said gently.

'I know, but there's no need.'

Jenny had already had a talk to Linda, knowing how easily feelings can overwhelm a couple. Linda could have laughed. She knew only too well. She was no longer a virgin and had given herself freely to a German prisoner in a field, but Jenny didn't know that and must never know, so she listened politely and said she needn't worry. Charles was a perfect gentleman.

And he was. He'd hold hands or link arms as if they were an old married couple and kiss Linda on the lips, but very chastely and only at the end of the evening. Linda supposed it was because he was older than her that he had such control of his feelings. Anyway, she didn't know what she'd allow him to do if he tried anything on, so it was probably better that he had decided to act so courteously while she made up her mind what she thought of him.

'And how's Jenny's house-hunting going?' Maureen asked Linda.

Linda was glad to change the conversation. 'Fine,' she said. 'She has a few she's viewing this weekend, all in the Erdington area, though some of them are on the Sutton Coldfield boundary. Francesca told her there's no rush. I think she likes having us there.'

'Well, you're company, I expect.'

'Yes, she says the war's not finished yet and Bob won't necessarily be demobbed immediately,'

Linda said. 'Still, Jenny is anxious to have everything ready for him.' She shrugged. 'I don't care. I'm glad she's got something to do. It keeps her from fretting about Bob every minute of the day.'

'Ah you can't blame her, cutie dear,' Maureen said. 'For doesn't she love that man with all her heart and soul?'

By 11 April 1945, the Allies had reached the Buchenwald concentration camp and released over 25,000 people of all nationalities. Four days later, they opened the gates of the Belsen camp, liberating 40,000, but inside were 10,000 unburied bodies.

The horror of that, and the tales coming out of those places, shocked the world. Newsreels showed pictures of the skeletal people who were often too weak, ill and undernourished to survive their release. Soldiers were visibly moved by the poor inmates of these torture camps, shambling around in inadequate clothing and often barefoot. They spoke of their deadened eyes and the lice-ridden stubble covering their shaved heads, of the smell of burning that hung in the air and the grey ash film that clung to everyone.

Linda had read the newspapers and listened to the wireless and was upset and angry, but when Charles took her to the cinema and she saw the footage on Pathé News, she wept in his arms and she wasn't the only one either. People were right, she thought, as her tears dampened Charles's jacket. The Germans *were* monsters, inhuman barbaric monsters, and they were all tarred with the same brush.

After that display of emotion where Charles had supported her, Linda's feelings for him changed somewhat. She liked the way he looked after her, the way he held her close and made her feel cherished and precious. Now he collected Linda every Friday and Saturday evening and drove her to Packington Hall. Flora made her own way there, but Charles always took them both home. He was also waiting for Linda when she came offstage for a break, with drinks for her and Flora. And far from being annoyed at her going out with one of the customers, the owner of the restaurant was delighted. It wouldn't do to antagonise Charles Haversham and he thought Linda a canny little girl for understanding it.

Life for Linda and Jenny was very peaceful during that time. It was lovely to go home in the evening and know you'd be greeted pleasantly, and over the tea-table, you could talk about your day easily, without any feeling of constraint. The three women got on very well together and each day they waited for the news that Germany had surrendered.

And then it really seemed as if it was all over at long last, for on Monday 1 May, Hitler's body was found in a German bunker, along with that of his wife, Eva Braun. He'd been dressed in a new Nazi uniform, complete with medals and they'd both taken poison. The Russians broke into the bunker and poured petrol over their bodies and burned them. Goebbels and his wife killed themselves and their six children the same day. Very few in the world were unhappy about Hitler's death and most of the British were ecstatic.

But Germany hadn't officially surrendered and the next day, the bombers took off to attack Kiel, a seaport in Northern Germany. It was to be the last raid of the war and Bob Masters flew one of the fighters that accompanied the bombers.

This time, Bob didn't return. They'd met heavier opposition than they'd expected and Bob's plane was badly hit, the fuel tank soon ablaze. Many of his squadron saw him leap from his burning plane as they crossed over France, but his parachute failed to open and they saw him plummeting to the ground.

The next day, the telegram was delivered to Francesca Masters's house before Jenny had left for work. Washing the breakfast dishes in the sink, she heard an anguished cry and ran into the hall to see Francesca clutching the telegram. 'Oh let it be Juliana – please, please,' Jenny prayed silently, but she knew, when she saw Francesca's pain-filled eyes turn on her that it was Bob who was dead. Her Bob, her wonderful fiancé, the man she loved above all others. 'Oh Christ no!' she cried in denial and fell to the floor in a dead faint.

Chapter Twenty-Three

Linda took all the holiday she was entitled to in order to support both Jenny and Francesca Masters, and even took two weeks off from her job at Packington Hall. She was pleased when Francesca's husband, whose job was officially over now, was released early to be with his wife, while her daughter Juliana was given compassionate leave. Linda had met Juliana a couple of times, but the white-faced girl she opened the door to, bore no resemblance to the lively girl she'd met when she'd been home on leave. A young naval officer she introduced as Paul, had an arm protectively around her and Linda thought he looked solid and dependable and was glad they were both there. She recognised Malcolm from the photographs around the place. The man was bowed down with grief, but determined to support his wife and show a typical British stiff upper lip.

Jenny felt as if her limbs were not connected to her at all, and her legs shook when she tried to stand. When she'd recovered from her faint, she found Peter Sanders sitting by her bed, holding her hand. The tears squeezed out of her eyes, but Peter didn't urge her not to cry; he seemed to think it was good for her to let go and grieve like that.

Five days after the telegram had been delivered,

Linda heard the sound of street parties outside to celebrate VE Day. She went into the bedroom to see Jenny at the windows looking out at the chattering happy people, stringing bunting across the wide road. Jenny's eyes were like pools of sadness in her white face and Linda wished she could shut out the sounds of the celebration from outside. It was like a mockery.

Suddenly, Jenny's hand came into contact with the mizpah Bob had given her for her twenty-first birthday. She'd worn it every day, since Bob had put it around her neck and had thought it was like a talisman, a pact with God to keep him safe.

The Lord watch between thee and me while we are absent from one another.

Well, God had let her down, hadn't He? He hadn't watched over Bob at all. Some bloody good it was, making any sort of deal with Him! In despair, she yanked the mizpah with such force, the chain scored two lines in her neck before snapping in two, and she turned and flung it across the room.

Linda didn't say a word, but later when Jenny had left the room, she picked up the mizpah and wrapped it in a bit of tissue paper and tucked it into her underwear drawer, under the lining paper. She didn't know why she did it, but thought that Jenny might regret throwing it away one day and want it back, for it was, after all, a present from Bob.

Malcolm Masters had made further enquiries about his son's death, and when he was told that Bob's mutilated remains had been buried by the French farmer who'd found him, he arranged for

433

his son's body to be brought home for a proper burial.

Jenny was glad that she'd at least have a grave to visit and tend. Everyone could pay their respects then. She hadn't been able to take the condolences of the family and friends who'd called; though she appreciated their sympathy, she was too upset to see and speak to any of them.

Jenny didn't know if she'd be able to make it to the church for the funeral; it was to be held at the Abbey as that was the Masters's parish church. She was incredibly weak and her head swam when she tried to stand. The loss of Bob was like a gut-wrenching pain inside her.

Peter said he'd drive them. 'I've agreed to pick your mother up already,' he said.

'My mother!' she cried for, despite Norah's improvement, Jenny knew she'd seldom left the house. In fact, she believed the last time had been to visit her in hospital.

'Geraldine wanted to pay her respects,' Peter said. 'And apparently your mother is insisting on coming with her.' He made a face and went on. 'I could hardly refuse.' He'd wanted to. He knew how she felt about Jenny and hoped she wasn't out to make mischief for her.

Many people, it seemed, wanted to pay their respects, for the Abbey was packed. Jenny, leaning heavily on Linda's arm, almost staggered when she saw the mahogany coffin that Malcolm Masters had ordered for his son, drawn up before the altar. It had Mass cards amongst the wreaths

434

and Jenny found it hard to come to terms with the fact that all that remained of the man she loved was in there, and would soon be put in a hole in the earth and covered up.

She noticed her mother glaring at her and Geraldine beside her with her eyes full of sympathy. She turned away from them both and directed her gaze to the front of the church and put her energies into reaching it without falling into a heap on the floor.

She made it, but all through the Requiem Mass, she felt her mother's malevolent eyes boring into her back. Linda was aware of it too and wished she could put her arms around Jenny and protect her from further hurt. Peter wished he could do the same; all around her, people were crying, but she stayed dry-eyed throughout the service. Peter watched her and knew inside she was dying and he was filled with respect for the girl he'd loved for years.

The clods of earth landed on the coffin with a dull thud and as Jenny turned away from the grave, she came face to face with her mother. Linda saw the older woman's eyes narrow and knew she was unmoved by the grief etched on her daughter's white face, though Geraldine's eyes were full of tears. Norah had a gloating look on her face as she hissed, 'So your great plans have come to nothing. Well, don't think you can come running to *my* door, because I'll slam it in your face and take delight in doing so.'

Linda heard gasps of shock from those who'd been near enough to hear what Norah had said.

435

But she was neither shocked nor surprised. She was just blisteringly angry, and she turned to the old woman and spat out, 'Get out of here! Come to pay your respects, my eye. You wouldn't know respect if it leapt up and hit you on the nose. You're a mean, malicious bugger and you always have been. So now you know.'

Francesca, seeing Linda's agitation, came forward, but Linda said, 'See to Jenny. I'm all right.' And she strode towards Peter standing well to the back of the group of mourners. 'Get her out of here,' she said to Peter quietly. 'And now – before I do something to that vicious old bitch. I don't know why you brought her here in the first place.'

Peter had witnessed the scene at the graveside and although he hadn't heard the words, he'd seen the angry satisfaction in Norah's eyes and the resulting fury in Linda's. 'I'm sorry,' he said in a whisper. 'I shouldn't have.'

'No, you bloody well shouldn't,' Linda raged. 'That old crow has done her level best to destroy Jenny all her life. And,' she added, 'she's doing a grand job today too.'

Peter watched Jenny being helped into one of the funeral cars and a wave of pity washed over him, followed by one of guilt. He knew what a malicious creature Norah O'Leary was. He should have refused to take her. 'I'll see to it,' he promised Linda.

Linda gave a brief nod, but before she turned away, she looked towards Norah O'Leary and could have sworn Geraldine was having a go at her mother. The people passing in front of her cut off her line of vision, and she decided she must have been imagining it.

Many hours later, after the funeral tea, when all the mourners had gone, Linda was in the kitchen making some supper. Francesca came in. Jenny had gone to bed, but Linda saw the woman glance around the kitchen as if making sure. 'I think you'd better have this,' she said to Linda. 'I don't want to upset Jenny.'

Linda opened the package and found the other half of Jenny's mizpah – Bob's half – and her mouth dropped in surprise.

'The farmer had it,' Francesca said chokily, 'the one who buried Roberto. He removed all his papers. He thought later when conditions in France had settled down, he could probably find out who the young airman was, and when he saw the mizpah around his neck, he removed that too. It came back with all his effects and I thought Jenny might like it, but she's too upset now. You give it to her when you think the time is right.'

Linda didn't tell Francesca how Jenny had torn the other half of the mizpah from her neck just days before. Instead, she thanked her and embraced her, and wrapped the mizpah up in the same tissue as the other one that night before she climbed into bed.

But sleep didn't come, for Norah's hate-filled words came back to her and she did wonder where she and Jenny were going to live now that the war was over. It had been all right temporarily lodging with the Masters while Bob waited for his demob, but Linda was sure Francesca wasn't looking for permanent house guests. It was no good worrying Jenny about it;

she had enough on her plate. It would be up to her to find somewhere for the two of them, and as soon as possible. But just before Linda drifted off to sleep, she wondered where she would find suitable accommodation in a city ravaged by war, where all the housing stock was in shorter supply than ever.

A month later, Linda was no further forward in the house-hunting. Jenny was much better, back at work and coping – at least on the surface. She was quieter and thinner than ever, but a lot better than she had been. The weather was balmy and warm despite the fact it was only early summer, and Linda was glad of it for as Maureen said, 'Everything looks better when the sun shines on it.'

Francesca told Linda she was in no hurry for them to move, but Linda knew Malcolm found their presence irksome, though nothing was ever said. Also, she knew Juliana was getting married after her demob and coming home to live for a while. 'Just while they take stock,' Francesca said. 'And Paul must find work, of course.'

Linda guessed that Francesca would like her daughter on hand, for a while. The family needed to be together again after their years of separation, and the tragedy of losing a son and brother in the closing days of a war that had dragged on for six long years. She knew that she and Jenny would be in the way. Every night sleep eluded her, as she wrestled with the problem.

She'd neglected Charles shamefully during this time; although she'd seen him at the restaurant, she'd always resisted his offers to go out anywhere. She was beginning to feel guilty about it. Charles had been so very patient, so when he arrived one evening unannounced, she did at last agree to go out with him again.

They went to a restaurant they'd been to before, but Linda's appetite was poor and she was so preoccupied by her problems that even Charles, not the most astute of men, noticed. He watched her move the succulent roast beef around her plate and placed his hands over hers. 'What is it?' he said gently. 'Are you still worried about Jenny?'

'No,' Linda said, and added, 'I mean yes. To be honest, the thing that's worrying me most is where we're going to live now.'

'What's wrong with where you are?'

'Oh Charles, we can't stay there, not indefinitely,' Linda said. 'It was always meant to be a temporary arrangement. Anyway, I feel Francesca's husband resents us. You can understand it. After all, he was away years and now he wants his wife to himself. Then their daughter is going to live there for a time after her marriage, so there will be even less room.'

Charles rubbed Linda's fingers with his own and said, 'I could solve your problems for you, it you'd allow me to.'

'How?'

'You could marry me,' he said quietly.

'Marry you!' Linda's voice was high in surprise.

'Surely you must realise how fond I am of you?'

Did she? Linda thought. No, she didn't. Charles's lovemaking had never proceeded past holding her hand, or giving her cheek or lips a chaste kiss when he delivered her home. 'I didn't know you felt that way about me.'

'What way?' Charles said and added quickly, 'I'm not into a silly romance here. I like you well enough to share my life with you. You'll have a beautiful home that you'll be mistress of, plenty of money, and nothing to do but spend it.'

It wasn't the proposal Linda had dreamed of, but it was a solution of sorts and the only solution she could think of.

'Do you love him?' Jenny asked, when Linda told her the news.

'No,' Linda admitted. 'But I like him and that's a start, isn't it?'

'I suppose,' Jenny said. 'But are you sure about this?'

'I'm sure about the fact that we have to find somewhere to live and soon,' Linda said. 'I know Charles will be kind to me and generous. What more do I want?' But Linda knew well what she wanted. She knew what it was to love and feel passionate desire for a man, and how it felt to make love together. But Max was in the past and she didn't believe she would feel the same about any man again, and yet she had her life before her. She had to forget her German lover.

'You're so young,' Jenny said.

'What's the alternative?' Linda asked and Jenny shook her head helplessly. She had no solution to offer, but she hated to see Linda sacrifice her life. And yet, wasn't she being a little melodramatic about it? Charles was charming, rich and influential. Linda's life with him would probably

440

be satisfactory to both of them, even if it didn't match the relationship she'd shared with Bob. Maybe, she thought bleakly, it's better not to love someone so much.

'Well, if that's what you want Linda,' she said, 'you have my blessing.'

The ring, a diamond cluster, was bought by Charles. Linda complained she could have got it cost price working for a jeweller as she did, but Charles was affronted at the very idea. 'It's stupid,' Linda said privately to Jenny. 'Mr Tollit said he could have arranged it. It would be just as nice as the one Charles bought and at two-thirds the price.'

'Price doesn't bother him though, does it?'

'Apparently not. But I still think it's mad.'

Charles said he didn't want Linda working after they were married. It wasn't fitting for his wife, and there was no need for it. He was quite adamant about it.

'But what would I do all day if I didn't work?' Linda asked him.

Charles wasn't sure, but his mother had never seemed bored. 'You could plan the menus with Bessie,' he said. 'Discuss the household tasks with Amy, or perhaps visit people.'

'I visit my family and friends at weekends.'

'I don't mean those sort of people, my dear,' Charles said chidingly. 'I mean friends of mine – formal visits – and I'm sure they'll come calling on you. Then of course, there's shopping.'

'For what? There's hardly anything in the shops. Anyway, shopping's not much fun on your own.'

'I'm sure Amy Sallenger would go with you,' Charles said. 'She always accompanied Mother.'

Linda, forthright as ever, said exactly what was in her mind. 'I'm sorry, Charles, but it sounds terribly dreary, talking to Bessie about meals I know little about, when she's been cooking them for years. She'd resent my interference.'

'She would not,' Charles said emphatically. 'Bessie always has my best interests at heart.'

'But not mine,' Linda said. 'And Amy knows how to run the house far better than me who haven't a clue. I'd do well to let them both get on with it by themselves. As for visiting people I don't know and might actively dislike, I'm not keen on that at all, and I only shop if I need something. I've got out of the habit of shopping somehow.' She saw Charles was displeased and she was sorry for him. It was, after all, the way he'd been brought up. Surely she could agree, at least for a little while, and see how it went? She put a hand on his arm and said, 'All right, Charles, if that's how you want it. Anyway, I'll probably have plenty to do when the babies start arriving.'

She didn't see the expression of horror flit across Charles's face. To get off the subject quickly, for he definitely didn't want children cluttering up his life, and had no intention of having anything to do with the messy business of creating them, he put his arms around Linda and said, 'Thank you, darling, I knew you'd see it my way in the end.' Linda smiled and gave him a kiss on the cheek and thought how easy he was to please.

The wedding was planned for mid-September. 'Before the real cold weather comes,' as Charles put it. The honeymoon was a bit more difficult, with practically the whole world recovering from war. 'Maybe we'll just have a week now?' Charles suggested. 'And then have a month in Europe later, perhaps on the anniversary of our wedding. What d'you say?'

Linda was flabbergasted, but no more than her family. 'God, girl, me and Bert had a couple of days in Blackpool and I was made up.' Beattie said. 'Thought I was the bee's knees, I did.'

Maureen had had no honeymoon at all, and the war and finances had put a damper on Peggy's few days and though all three were envious, they were pleased for Linda. Linda, true to her roots and her background, had taken Charles to meet them all as soon as the engagement was official. Charles was fond of Linda in his fashion, and wishing to please her, he went out of his way to charm them all, even the awful old woman Beattie. After they were married, he'd make sure she saw much less of them; they were *not* the sort of people he'd wish his wife to associate with. But that was for the future.

Norah, when the news reached her, was incensed. 'A dirty little trollop,' she called her.

Geraldine was finding it a strain, living with her mother. She'd forgotten the tantrums she used to have. And as for what she had said to poor Jenny at the cemetery – well, it was despicable!

'Mother, calm yourself,' she said sharply.

But Norah couldn't be calm. How had the brazen hussy dragged herself from the gutter to

443

become engaged to a gentleman such as Charles Faversham, while she, the daughter of gentry, was only able to marry a common working man? Her screams of rage frightened the children and could be heard clearly halfway down the street.

Linda neither knew nor cared for Norah's opinion and went on blithely planning her wedding. Peggy's mother offered to make the dress, but material was the problem until Charles brought out one of his mother's ball gowns from the wardrobe. Peggy's mother sat fingering the glorious material and said she'd adapt it to make Linda a beautiful bride. Linda was hesitant to accept Charles's offer at first. She'd always instinctively refused to have anything to do with Charles's mother's clothes. But in the end, common sense and Peggy's mother prevailed, and reluctantly she agreed. Charles was ecstatic. He remembered his mother wearing the ivory silk dress trimmed with lace with the layers and layers of soft underskirts, the top layer caught up at intervals and fastened with rosebuds of peach and blue to match those decorating the modest neckline.

'Oh it's beautiful,' Linda exclaimed, remembering for a moment the beautiful Shirley Temple dress given to her by Beattie's niece Vicky, that she'd worn at the hospital concert. Never had she had such a beautiful dress since, but still she shook her head. 'I couldn't wear it Charles, not as it is, anyway.'

'And why not?'

'Don't you think it will look a bit silly wearing a dress like this for a register office wedding?' she asked. 'I'd be overdressed, to say the least.'

'Nonsense.'

But the family agreed with Linda although Peggy'd said she was sure she could make something more suitable using the material.

Linda found she couldn't get terribly excited about her wedding day. In her heart of hearts she knew she was using Charles. She didn't love him and he'd never said he loved her either; in fact, he'd used few terms of endearment. She didn't know what he was getting out of it, but she was marrying him for convenience, basically to get a good home for her and Jenny and in a way she felt bad about it.

But she could confide in no one and certainly not in Jenny. She hardly ever mentioned anything to her about Charles, sure she was probably upset enough seeing Linda planning a wedding that by rights should have been her own, but neither of them discussed it at all.

In mid-July, Sam Phelps brought a letter for Linda. 'It's been around a bit,' he said as she looked at it, puzzled. 'It went first to Whittington Barracks, addressed as you can see to "The Little Nightingale" and "The Brummagem Beauties". Eventually, after kicking around the office, someone gave it in to Bill Fletcher, but he couldn't find you. Went to the old address and the new people said they didn't know where you'd gone, so he brought it to me.'

Linda, who'd been tearing open the envelope as Sam spoke cried, 'It's from Lieutenant Louis Bradshaw!'

445

'Who's he when he's at home?'

'He was just one of the American boys at the camp,' she said. 'He works in broadcasting in New York and said I'd be a sensation over there. He wanted me to go over for an audition after the war.'

'What's he say in the letter?'

'Much of the same,' Linda said. 'Says he hasn't forgotten me and he'll sort something out as soon as he gets back home.' She flashed her ring at Sam and said, 'That letter has come too late. My dear husband-to-be says I must give up the job I have now, so I don't think he'd be mad keen on me nipping over to the States.'

'What about you?'

'It was a dream, that's all, and not one I really believed in,' Linda said quietly.

'Oh,' Sam said. He seemed strangely ill at ease.

'What's up?' Linda asked.

'Nothing much. Just someone else is going home tomorrow afternoon and he'd like to say goodbye.'

'Max?' Linda said. She'd assumed he'd gone ages ago. She shook her head. 'I don't think that would be a good idea, do you?'

'Look, Linda,' Sam said. 'The man's gone on you. He was never the same after you stopped coming over.' He held up a hand to still Linda's protests as she was about to interrupt. 'I know there's no future in it as much as you do, but Max refuses to accept that. Come and see him, convince him it's over. Show him your ring and say goodbye, that's all I'm suggesting.'

Linda could see the logic of it. Surely when

Max saw her engagement ring, he'd know finally that whatever had been between them was dead – dead and buried. She smiled at Sam and said, 'OK then. It's a good job tomorrow is Saturday. I don't think my boss would take kindly to my having time off to say goodbye to a German POW, do you?'

The farm was dusty now rather than muddy, but hens still pecked at the ground relentlessly and she had the same welcome from the children; their arms and legs were bare and a brownish colour from the sun, while their faces were pink and Charlie's freckles more prominent than ever.

Peter's car pulled up alongside Sam's in the farmyard and before Sam could say a word he said, 'Got a call just a few minutes ago. Sarah said your Ruby had cut herself on the scythe.'

Sam raised his eyes to heaven. 'She's a good girl that,' he whispered to Linda. 'But clumsy isn't in it. If there's anything to be knocked over, Ruby will oblige, and anything to be spilt, she'll be the one to do it. As for cuts and bumps and bruises – she's an expert. A Land Girl was a bad choice for her. She'd have been better off working for the Red Cross rolling bandages instead of continually wearing them.'

But for all Sam's flippancy, he was very concerned for Ruby, who sat in the kitchen with her arm raised under Sarah's direction. The blood had stopped running, but thick lines of it had crusted on her arm. 'Um – nasty,' Peter said. 'I think it needs a stitch or two in that.'

'Can we watch?' Charlie and Sally said

447

together, and Peter smiled grimly and said, 'If Ruby doesn't mind.'

But Ruby had had a shock and wasn't up to saying much, and Sarah whispered to Linda, 'This is your chance to say goodbye finally to Max while my little ghouls are being entertained. He's in the barn.'

And Linda knew it was her last chance once and for all to make Max realise that whatever had been between them was over and done with. She had moved on and so must he. He had his back to her when she entered and she saw he wore his overalls with nothing underneath; the ripple of his muscles as he forked the hay into the troughs made her stomach do a somersault. 'Steady,' she cautioned herself, and very softly she said, 'Max.'

He turned slowly as if he hadn't really been sure he'd heard right; his face was red and running with sweat and brown hairs from his chest peeped above the bib of his overalls. His mouth fell open in astonishment. 'Linda?'

She'd forgotten how her name on his lips made her feel, and when he crossed the ground in three easy strides, tossing the fork to one side as he did so and held her tight in his arms, she made no move to stop him. Nor did she stop his lips that descended on hers. In fact, she wound her arms around his neck and pulled his head down and when eventually Max released her, she felt as if she were on fire. She told herself she was stupid. It was madness!

She stood slightly breathless staring at him as he said, 'Oh my darling, how I have longed for just the sight of you.' His hands held her shoulders as he went on, 'Soon I shall be a free man, Linda. I will go home and find out how rich or poor I am, then I will come back for you.'

'No, no,' Linda cried. 'I came just to say goodbye.'

Max shook his head. 'You do not kiss goodbye the way we did,' he said. 'That is a kiss you keep for the one you love. I love you now and I will do so till the day I die.'

'Max, please listen to me.' Linda said. 'We haven't long. I'm ... I'm getting married,' and as if to prove it, she showed him the ring.

'What is this nonsense – getting *married*?'

'It's not nonsense,' Linda said. 'Please believe me. I'm getting married to a man called Charles Haversham.'

Max stared at her in shock. His face had gone a ghastly grey colour. 'And do you love this Charles Haversham?'

The slight hesitation was Linda's undoing and Max pounced on it. 'So, I see you do not,' he said triumphantly. 'And does this Charles Haversham know what a fool you are making of him? Does he know your heart belongs to another – to me?'

Linda realised Max was angry: she'd never seen him angry before. His eyes flashed and his brow was puckered. She put a hand on his arm placatingly and said, 'I'm sorry Max, truly sorry, but it's better this way.'

Max shook her hand off. 'Better this way!' he repeated sarcastically. 'You break my heart, but it's better this way. How? Explain it to me. How is it better this way?'

'Max, it would never work for us,' Linda said.

449

She was desperately near to tears. 'We don't belong to each other, you must see.'

'Because I am German and you are British,' Max said. 'But hearts do not care which country you come from, and our hearts are bound together and have been from the first day we met.'

'Oh Max.'

Max took Linda in his arms again and kissed her eyes gently and tasted the tears on his lips. 'You're crying?' he said.

'Not really. I'm just upset for what might have been.'

'Don't talk like that.'

'I must Max, for there's no future for us. I told you this a long time ago,' Linda said. 'Please, let us part as friends. Let's remember the love we shared and then put it behind us.'

In answer Max's lips descended on Linda's again and as she kissed him back she forgot all her resolutions. This was here and now, and all that mattered. She had no thought for Jenny and the rest of the family and their disapproval. She felt Max's strong shoulders and as his tongue probed her mouth, shafts of desire went shooting through her body. She waited to feel Max's hands on her body and when they slid over her bottom, she sighed in contentment.

'Don't let me interrupt or anything!' The sharp voice jerked them apart and Linda turned to see Peter framed in the doorway. He ignored Max totally and said coldly to Linda, 'I came to find you.'

Guilt caused Linda's face to flame. She cared

about Peter's opinion. What did he think of her? He didn't know about Max. How could he? Did he feel she'd just go around kissing anyone?'

'And you,' Peter said, casting his eyes at Max, who stood defiant with his head up, wondering what right he had to speak to Linda that way, 'you're wanted in the fields.'

He still stood and Peter barked, 'Did you hear what I said?'

'Yes. I heard,' Max said and he put his hand out to Linda.

She pulled back from it as if she'd been stung. 'You'd better go,' she said.

Max's eyes clouded over and Linda could have cried at the hurt expression in them. He gazed at her for a moment longer and then, squaring his shoulders, he walked out of the barn without looking back. Linda had the urge, regardless of Peter and his opinion, to lie on the floor and howl like an animal, for she knew she loved Max Schulz with a love deeper than she'd ever felt for anyone else, and she knew equally she'd never see him again.

All the way home Peter let rip and Linda cried. She cried because everything Peter said was related to how it would affect Jenny. Had Linda no thought to the grievous loss she was still coming to terms with? He demanded. Had she thought of the shame of it all for Jenny, Linda carrying on with a German of all people? He said 'German' as if it was something venomous that slithered across the floor; that you'd like to put your foot on.

'Haven't the German nation done enough to you, too?' Peter said angrily. 'They took your whole family and Jenny offered you a home after her own brother had been killed. God, Linda, hasn't she suffered enough? If she'd witnessed what I interrupted at the farm, I dread to think of the consequences. Girl, what were you thinking of, throwing yourself at that fellow like that? It's even worse now that you have another man's ring on your finger. I hope you're thoroughly ashamed of yourself.'

And Linda was. She was mortified. She should never have gone near Max, she knew that now. She'd forgotten the power he had over her. Peter glanced at her. The tears had stopped, but dry sobs were still escaping from her and his anger began to evaporate. She was, after all, he reminded himself, still very young and Sam had treated the young German like a member of the family. Sleeping in the house no less, as Sam had said the barn was too cold for him in the winter, and he sat at the table to eat with the family and the Land Girl, Ruby. Little wonder he had got ideas above himself.

Linda, like many other girls of her age, had lived in a world without men for a long, long time. True, she'd sung to hordes of them, but that wasn't the same as courtship with one special boy, holding hands at the pictures and walks in the park, getting to know one another. That's what Jenny was worried about in this engagement with Charles Haversham. 'She's known no one, Peter,' she'd said. 'No boys, I mean – not that that's her fault, for after all, there's not been

452

many around. But then she chooses a man nearly old enough to be her father. I'm sure she's doing it for me, you know. It's like a payback, isn't it? It's just the way Linda's mind would work. I offered her a home when she needed one and now the tables are turned, she has the chance of doing the same for me and has taken it.'

Remembering that conversation now, Peter was almost certain Jenny was right. You couldn't kiss someone with the type of intensity he'd witnessed, if you loved another man enough to marry him. Not that he was totally happy about Charles Haversham anyway. There was something strange about the man – but he couldn't put his finger on it. But then it wasn't his business. More gently he said, 'You can't go in like that, Linda. Jenny will know you've been crying. Have you anything with you to try and repair the damage?'

Linda drew her compact from her bag and looked into the mirror. Peter was right, her nose was bright pink, her cheeks stained with tears and her eyes red-rimmed. She could do nothing about the eyes, but she dabbed the powder puff over her face and pulled a brush through her hair tousled by Max. And as she tidied herself, she felt she had to tell Peter how it had been.

'I do know Max and whatever you saw, or think, it wasn't meant to be that way. I've known him since I was in the concert-party, but I really got to know him when I came up with the kids after Dan was killed. And,' she added accusingly, 'that was *your* idea.'

She shrugged. 'There was something between

us from the start. I didn't encourage it, I tried to pretend it wasn't happening at first. But it was no good. You can't help loving someone, even if they're unsuitable or don't love you back. You of all people must know that.'

Oh yes, Peter knew that, all right. He didn't deny it. For five long years he'd loved Jenny. Linda went on, 'We just talked at first. I'd never spoken to a German person before. They were always held up as bogeymen, like the baddies in the stories I used to tell Rosemarie and Jamie. But Max wasn't like that and it gave me a shock. But don't worry,' she said with a sigh. 'He leaves in the morning, and I know however much we love each other, we can't do anything about it. And,' she added resentfully, 'you don't have to tell me how much I owe Jenny. I'd never do anything to hurt her.'

'I know,' Peter said. 'I'm sorry I yelled. It was just...'

'It's all right,' Linda said tiredly. 'I'm glad you roared at us in the barn. It brought me to my senses. I was behaving like a prize idiot.' Then as the car was just about to turn into Grange Road, she said, 'I'm not going home, Peter. Jenny will want to know what has brought me back so soon.'

Peter knew that was true. His anger and Linda's mortification had been so acute that neither of them could have stayed to make polite conversation after the confrontation in the barn.

All in all, Linda had only been away just over half an hour, and Jenny was bound to ask her why. 'I'll go to Gran's,' she said. 'She didn't know

I was even going to the farm today so she won't ask any awkward questions. Drop me in Pype Hayes Road and I'll walk around.'

'Yes, miss,' Peter said sarcastically, and was thankful to see the ghost of a smile at last playing around Linda's mouth.

'Sorry,' she said. 'And thanks for the lift and the lecture.'

'I'm sure you didn't appreciate both?' Peter said.

'Yes, I did,' she told him. 'It's nice to know someone cares at least.'

Peter drew up in Pype Hayes Road and Linda got out and waved her hand as he drove off. Then she stood for a moment to compose herself, before walking round to Westmead Crescent.

Chapter Twenty-Four

It was hard for the people of Britain during the first summer of peace to remember that the war was still going on in Japan. It was brought sharply to their attention on 7 August 1945, when they heard that the previous day, an atomic bomb had been dropped on Hiroshima. Jenny and Linda were in the sitting room with Francesca and Malcolm, as they listened to the details on the wireless. No one knew how many had died that day, but official US estimates put the number at 78,000.

'How can so many people be killed with one bomb?' Linda had asked. 'It's unbelievable.'

Malcolm, who knew more about the capabilities of atomic warfare than the others, commented, 'Seventy-eight thousand is just the number who died today. The death toll will go on for years, believe me.'

But no one believed him, not really. What they did want to believe was that this highly destructive bomb might shorten the war. A second atomic bomb was dropped on a smaller city called Nagasaki on 9 August, where it was estimated 35,000 people died.

But even after the atomic bombs had been released, there was still no sign of surrender. Then on 13 August, 1,600 Allied aircraft attacked Tokyo. The Japanese surrendered unconditionally the following day, and VJ Day was declared on 15 August 1945. To most people in Britain, VJ Day meant little, although everyone was glad the war on all fronts was finally at an end.

'So many dead,' Jenny said morosely, one evening just after VJ Day. She became very depressed when she considered all the people killed, not just in the Japanese cities but worldwide. And every time she thought of the wedding, she felt sick. If it had been anyone else's but Linda's, far from being a bridesmaid and helping her celebrate the damn thing, she would have turned tail and run away somewhere until it was all over. Peggy's mother had fashioned a beautiful dress for Linda, and had enough material over to make a dress for Jenny, too. But though she thanked her, she didn't care what she wore. She still felt an incredible sense of loss. The sorrow of it all invaded her dreams when she did eventually drop off to sleep at night. She woke every morning with a leaden weight in her heart but said nothing to anyone; it did no good.

Everyone except her had something to look forward to, Jenny thought in a moment of self-pity. Gerry was talking about buying a house. 'He has a wee bit put away.' Maureen said. 'You know, with all the overtime he worked in the war, and Peggy's money that she's saved as well.'

'Do you want to move, Gran?' Jenny asked anxiously.

'Well, it's not a question of wanting to, is it?' Maureen said. 'With Peggy on again, we'd be best looking for a bigger place before all the men

457

come back. Gerry says houses will be in short supply then.'

Jenny supposed he was right, it made sense, but she didn't know how she'd cope without her gran just down the road. She'd miss Peggy too, for she'd become a good friend, the only friend Jenny had ever really had, except for Linda, who was as close as a sister and much closer than Geraldine had ever been.

Gerry came in then and put his arms around his wife, and a stab of sheer envy pierced Jenny. The love between Gerry and Peggy was deep and strong. She knew whatever life threw at them they'd weather it as long as they were together. She could hardly bear to look at them and had the urge to put her head on her gran's shoulder and cry her eyes out. It wouldn't do, this feeling sorry for herself. She had to begin to get over Bob's death. She wasn't the only one to suffer like this, but that fact hardly made it easier to bear.

Even Beattie was looking forward. 'I've put my name down for one of those new prefabs,' she said when she came to visit. 'With my Alan and young Bert expected back any day, I had to get something organised. They could hardly come and live at our Vera's. She always stuck up her nose at my kids. Even when the lads came home on leave she never made them welcome.' She gave a sniff and went on, 'Well, now she ain't got nothing to be proud of. My girl at least never got her belly full before the ring was on her finger.'

'How is the baby?' Linda felt compelled to ask.

'Well enough, I suppose,' Beattie said. 'I mean,

I was a bit worried it might come out coffee coloured, 'cos some of those Yanks were as black as coal, weren't they?'

They were, and a bit of an eye-opener for the people of Birmingham, who hadn't really had any dealings with black people before then. 'Turn-up for the book that one, wouldn't it have been?' Beattie chuckled. 'But he weren't, and all in all he ain't a bad babby. But my sister and her husband… Well, you'd think there'd never been one born before him, and it's not as though he has a father to take him about. Nowt to be that proud about, if you ask me. And fancy calling him Hank! What sort of a name is that for a babby? I told our Vicky it makes him sound like a bleeding ball of wool.'

Linda roared. Oh, Beattie was marvellous, a real tonic. She hadn't had a good laugh for ages. 'So,' she said, 'you'll be moving into a prefab?'

'I might be,' Beattie said. 'Then again, they might be keeping them for people with children. Mind, I quite like those flats in the Lyndhurst Estate as well, and if we move there and my Bert misses his garden, he can always take an allotment on. Any road, I ain't going far away. I've lived in Pype Hayes too long and I want to come back. To be honest I think I've been a bloody saint, putting up with our Vera all this time and living in snobby Sutton Coldfield. Any road, I can't sit here all day,' she said, getting to her feet. 'I ain't collected my rations yet.'

Linda saw Beattie to the door. She had called at the Masters's house before, when Jenny first had news about Bob's death, but she didn't make a

459

habit of it and Linda knew she felt uncomfortable in the large house. 'Jenny ain't much better, is she?' she whispered in the hall, for Jenny had sat virtually silent during Beattie's visit.

Linda gave a sigh. 'I don't think all the talk about weddings is helping,' she said. 'She'll be better when we're away from here on our own and the wedding's over and done with.'

'And your Charles knows that Jenny's going to live with you, does he?'

''Course. He's known that from the start.'

'And he don't mind?'

'Why would he mind? Beattie, you should see the place. Compared to where we used to live it's a mansion, even when you compare it to this place. It's not as if we'd be falling over each other.'

It was after Beattie had gone that Linda realised Charles had never indicated which room Jenny would have. He'd shown her hers and his own. She'd pulled a face at that and said she'd never imagined sleeping in another bed from her husband, never mind another room. Charles had laughed at her and said that was how it was. His parents had always had separate rooms.

But Linda didn't laugh. She wondered how they were going to have sex together if they slept in separate rooms. Did you have to make an appointment? Maybe discuss it over dinner? She thought the whole thing stupid.

But there was something else worrying her, and that was about sex too. Once you were engaged, you could allow your man to be more amorous; you didn't have to put the brakes on quite so soon. In fact, Linda had looked forward to more intimacy, hoping it would drive from her mind the vision of her lying like a wanton in the arms of her German lover.

Charles, however, didn't seem to see it like that. He was a kind and considerate man, and very generous, and all her family thought her a lucky girl. But he never seemed to want to go further than tame kisses on the cheek or lips, or holding hands. He'd hold her tight and tell her she was a lovely girl, but it was how Linda imagined a big brother might be. Once, when she'd forced his lips open with her tongue, he'd jumped away from her as if he'd been shot. She'd been too embarrassed to ask him what was wrong, and he never volunteered the information. Another time she had opened her coat and taking his hands, had placed them on her body. He'd just removed them with an embarrassed laugh and advised her to do her coat up as the summer nights could suddenly turn very chilly.

His reaction made Linda's blood run cold and she wondered if he found sex distasteful, and whether if he did, it mattered to her. In her experience many women put up with their husband's often excessive demands for years. Linda told herself not to be daft, she was going to live in luxury, she and Jenny. It was just payment for what Jenny had done for her, years before.

As long as Charles got over his distaste enough to give her a child, Linda thought she'd cope. She could probably do without sex, but she longed for children. These would be the children of peace who'd have the chance to grow up strong and healthy and not be crushed to death by a bomb blast.

Funny they'd never talked about it, nor where Jenny's bedroom was going to be, Linda thought, and she decided to remedy that the next time she met Charles. She'd like Jenny's room as close to hers as possible. Charles would probably know that. It would help Jenny too, for she knew the talk of the wedding depressed her; she might cheer up on learning where her room would be in Linda's house. She could begin to plan how she'd like it decorated. Linda was sure Charles wouldn't mind spending a bit of money on it. It would be Jenny's own, for as long as she wanted it. Eventually, with Linda's help, she'd get over Bob's death and begin to live again, and with these thoughts in her head, she returned to Jenny with a smile on her face.

Two days later, Jenny noticed some letters lying on the mat. She picked them up and glanced idly through them. Now that the condolence cards had stopped arriving, the bulk of the post was usually for the Masters household. And so it was that morning, except for one letter addressed to Linda in a hand she didn't recognise and with a German stamp on it.

She stood with it in her hand wondering who it could possibly be from. A soldier she'd sung to perhaps, but she knew most of the soldiers were back now, except those on peace-keeping duties. It was mainly relief agencies in Germany at the moment, dispersing aid to the destitute, and Jenny was sure Linda knew none of them. Of

462

course she might have done, she didn't know her every move. She took the letter up to their room and placed it on Linda's bed. She didn't want the Masters to be asking questions about it. She also resolved to think no more about it herself. Linda, she was sure, would clear up the mystery as soon as she came home from work.

Jenny wasn't even surprised to see Peter waiting for her by the tram stop outside the Dunlops' that evening. She'd come out of work with Peggy, who only had a week to go before she had to leave, as it was less than two months before her new baby was due. Peggy was more grateful than Jenny to have the comfort of a car to bring her to the door rather than cope with the rattling, uncomfortable trams and then struggle up the road afterwards. She knew though, it wasn't for her benefit that Peter Sanders came, and couldn't understand how Jenny didn't see that he was crazy about her. But then it was early days, and she wasn't really over Bob's death yet.

Maureen was well aware of it. 'It's been like that from the start,' she said. 'Linda told me. But Jenny ... I think she sees him as a friend and that's all. She might be a one-man girl, you know. I couldn't have looked at another when my Michael was killed.'

'Och, Mammy, don't be saying that,' Peggy was shocked. 'Sure, she has her life in front of her.'

'Aye, but we are what we are,' Maureen replied. 'Still, if that Dr Sanders has patience, in the end he might get somewhere.'

And Peter had patience, as well as terrific

compassion for Jenny. He knew how much she'd loved Bob and he himself doubted she'd ever love so deeply again. He'd settle for a small slice of her heart, but it was far too early to tell her so and he had no idea of her feelings for him.

Jenny, though unaware of how he felt, had come to depend on him somewhat in the weeks since Bob's death. She didn't analyse her feelings any further than that. She felt, at any rate, she had little to give anyone. There was a numbness in her that frightened her a bit and she did wonder sometimes if she'd ever feel true emotion again.

She slipped into the front seat of the car that evening while Peggy settled herself happily in the back with a grateful sigh. Jenny said, 'Thanks, Peter. It's great of you giving us a lift most evenings, especially for Peggy.'

'Are you finding life hard going?' Peter asked, glancing in the back.

'Sure the job's fine, and aren't I sitting down all day?' Peggy said. 'No, the heat gets to me a bit and then my wee imp Dermot is one body's work. He was born with mischief built into him.'

'I thought they all were,' Peter said with a smile.

'Him more than most,' Peggy said emphatically. 'I bless Mammy for coping with him all the day. But I tell you, if her hair hadn't been grey before, he'd have turned it that way. Now the wee devil's starting waking up at night and after him sleeping fine for two years. He says he's lonely and doesn't want to be by himself.'

'You'll have to kick Gerry out and make him take a turn.'

'Huh,' Peggy said. 'I'd have less trouble waking up a corpse than rousing Gerry.'

Peter laughed and Peggy gave a grin, but Jenny's face stayed fixed. She glanced across at Peter and saw that despite his laughter he was watching her closely.

In an attempt to change the subject Peter said, 'How's Linda? I bet she's getting excited now.' Almost at once, he realised that it probably wasn't tactful to talk about Linda's wedding, but it was too late, the words were out.

'No, no she isn't,' Jenny said flatly. 'Not really. Is she, Peggy?'

'Not so you'd notice anyway,' Peggy agreed.

'I'd feel happier if she was getting excited,' Jenny said. 'It's not natural.'

"Oh, she's probably nervous,' Peggy answered. 'Anyway,' she went on as the car drew up outside her gate, 'you'll see, she'll get better about it as the day grows nearer. Don't worry. See you tomorrow, Jenny.'

'Yes. Bye Peg,' Jenny said.

As the car drew away Peter said, 'What exactly are you worried about, Jenny?'

'I don't know,' Jenny confessed. 'But there's something wrong somewhere.'

'Do you like her husband-to-be?'

'I don't exactly dislike Charles Haversham,' Jenny said. 'It's just a feeling, that's all.'

'Is it his age that's bothering you?' Peter suggested.

'Not just that. Though that's another factor against him, if you like.'

'You don't think Linda might be searching for

a father figure?' Peter said. 'After all, she's never really had one, has she? Her own father died when she was little more than a baby, she told me, and her stepfather didn't make it past Dunkirk.'

'No,' Jenny said and she thought back to what Linda had told her about her stepfather when they'd been trapped in the tunnel together. That was not for any ears but her own and she couldn't share it with Peter, but maybe he was right: that was possibly what Linda was searching for. If she was sure she'd found a man to love her and care for her in Charles Haversham she'd be happy, but she still wasn't sure. 'It's more than that.' She shrugged. 'But it's Linda's choice.'

'You're right there. And Peggy's right, too – you mustn't worry so much.'

'Is that your professional opinion?' Jenny asked, the ghost of a smile playing on her lips. 'Have you any anti-worrying pills in your black bag?'

'Not today,' Peter said, returning her smile. 'I'll see what I can do for next week.'

There was silence for a minute or two and then Peter said, 'Has she sent the invitations out yet for the reception?'

'No,' Jenny said. 'There was a bit of an argument about where it was to be. Charles wanted it at the house, but Linda said Four Oaks was too far for people to travel to. I mean, not many people we know have cars. So Linda is having it at the Social Club on Tyburn Road. I should imagine Charles would have turned his nose up at that, at least to start with, but she dug her heels in. Time's getting on. I said only the other day she should get cracking.'

Thinking of the invitations brought to mind the odd letter Linda had received that morning and she said, 'She had a most peculiar thing through the post this morning though.'

'What was that?'

'A letter from Germany.'

'Germany!' Peter exclaimed. 'Who from?'

Jenny shrugged. 'I don't know,' she said. 'She'd gone to work before the post came, but I'm intrigued. As far as I know, she knows nobody in Germany.'

Unbidden there came into Peter's mind the sight of Linda clasped in the arms of the POW on the Phelps's farm. He said nothing, but his face was troubled and as he drove down Jenny's road, she said, 'What is it? Do you know someone who could be writing to our Linda from Germany?'

'No. How would I?'

'I don't know how,' Jenny said. 'But you know something. Come on, tell me. She'll be home soon and I'll find out anyway.'

'That's best,' Peter said. 'Let her tell you herself.'

'Peter?'

He sighed. If he was right, then maybe it was better to prepare Jenny a little, give her time to get over the shock – for a shock it would be. He drew up outside her gate, turned off the engine and swung around to look at her. 'Look, Jenny,' he said. 'I might have totally the wrong idea. The letter could be from someone totally different, but I know Linda was friendly with a POW on the Phelps's farm.'

467

Jenny's face seemed to collapse as she repeated, 'A POW? You mean a German?'

'Yes, he was a German.'

'And she was friendly with him? Friendly with one of the people who killed her family, my brother, my brother-in-law and fiancé? Peter, how could she?'

'I don't know,' Peter said helplessly. 'She's young.'

'That's no excuse,' Jenny snapped. 'And, anyway, how friendly is friendly?'

Peter couldn't tell her of the clinch he'd broken apart when Linda and Max appeared oblivious to everything and everybody else, nor of the passion he'd seen flowing between them even when they were not touching each other. But before he had a chance to frame a lie, Jenny broke in, 'It doesn't matter, Peter. They must have been friendly enough for him to write to her now.'

'It might not be him,' Peter protested.

But Jenny knew it was. Who else could it be, and how else would they know where she lived? Look at the letter Louis Bradshaw had sent – it went around the wrekin before it got to Linda. No, this man had her address because she'd given it to him.

After Bob's death, she'd believed herself incapable of any sort of emotion ever again. But now anger coursed through her veins and a great heat filled her body. With the briefest of thanks to Peter, she left his car, ran up the path and into the house. She met no one and for that she was glad as she galloped up the stairs and retrieved the letter.

She had to decide what to do with it, and for that she had to know what was in it. She knew she was going to do something she'd never done before, and that was steam open the letter to see if Peter's suspicions were right. But how to do it was the problem, for Francesca cooked the meal every evening. She said it was the least she could do for the workers in the house and it would be hard to find time alone before Linda came in from work. She slipped the letter into the zipped pocket of her handbag and went down to the kitchen to see if Francesca wanted a hand with anything, vowing to deal with the letter later.

Jenny had been in a funny mood all evening, Linda thought. She'd snapped at her a few times and Linda couldn't understand what was the matter with her. Francesca asked Linda if they'd had a row, but they hadn't and Linda couldn't think of anything she'd said or done to upset her. She supposed Jenny was tormented by the wedding talk, which made her more determined than ever to tackle Charles about where Jenny's room was to be. So when he collected her later that night, she suggested they drive across to the house.

Bessie and Amy were flustered by their unexpected arrival. 'Don't worry,' Charles said.

'But if you'd let me know I could have made dinner,' Bessie complained.

'We've eaten,' Charles assured her, and then to smooth her ruffled feathers he added, 'A pot of tea would be nice, though.'

As the slightly mollified woman left the room,

Charles said to Linda, 'So what is it you wanted to talk to me about?'

Being Linda she plunged straight in. 'I'd like to get the question of Jenny's room sorted out,' she said. 'Where it is to be, I mean. I feel if she could get started planning her room, it might make her feel better about the wedding. I'd like it fairly near to mine, especially as yours is at the other end of the corridor.'

Charles didn't speak, and Linda didn't notice the expression on his face. 'But then,' she went on, 'when we eventually have children, I'd want their room right next to mine, I suppose.' She laid her hand on Charles's arm and said, 'I know this is strange to you, you probably were brought up by nursemaids, but I don't want that. I want to bring my children up myself.'

'Linda,' Charles said, but whatever he was going to say was interrupted by Bessie tapping on the door and bringing in a tray on which stood a pot of tea, two cups and a plate of homemade biscuits.

'Thank you, Bessie,' Charles said, and he waited till the woman had left and closed the door before he leaned forward and took Linda's hand in his own.

'Linda,' he said again. 'Jenny will not be living with us.'

Linda snatched her hands away. 'What do you mean? What are you talking about?'

'I'm marrying you, my dear, not Jenny.'

'Jenny's my friend – my dear, dear friend,' Linda cried. 'I owe my life to her.'

'I know,' Charles said. 'But that is in the past.

470

Now we need to go forward.'

'Charles, what's the matter with you? This is a huge house. What's one bedroom?'

'The bedroom is not in question, my dear.'

'But you like Jenny,' Linda cried desperately. 'I know you do. Look how good you were to her after Bob died.'

'Calm yourself, my dear,' Charles said patronisingly, patting her hand. He leaned forward and poured the tea into two cups and handed one to her. 'Drink this.'

Linda took the cup; she was so shaken, the cup rattled in its saucer. She looked at Charles through narrowed lids. She couldn't understand him. This was Charles – the charming, considerate and very generous man she'd agreed to marry. 'Look, Charles, I can't just leave her,' Linda said, feeling sure she could make him see how impossible that was. 'And what's more, I don't *want* to leave her! You know she has nowhere else to go.' They'd been together for so long now, Linda knew she'd feel bereft without her. If Bob had lived, Linda would have been given a home with them. Also, Linda didn't know how she could manage the household without Jenny's advice and support.

'Jenny wouldn't fit in here,' Charles said. 'Surely you can see that?'

'No, I don't see that. I don't see it at all,' Linda said. 'And if you think that about Jenny, how well do I fit in?'

Charles smiled. 'You're young, my dear,' he said. 'You'll learn.'

'Learn? I don't bloody well want to learn!'

Linda cried angrily. 'I think I'm all right as I am and so is Jenny, and I want her to live here when we're married.'

'And I do not.'

Linda was bemused. He was acting as he did when she said she wanted to continue working. He seem immovable. And he was immovable. He wanted none of Linda's relations around while he was training her in his ways. He'd make sure she'd sever all ties with them eventually. He had far more suitable people he wanted her to cultivate, ones who could be an asset to him in his business. On her own, he felt sure Linda would succumb in the end to his demands, but with Jenny beside her, it would be more difficult, he knew.

'What about children?' Linda's tone was hectoring now. 'Let's get it all out in the open at once. We've never discussed starting a family. Odd, don't you think, when we're getting married? Not,' she spat out, 'that you've ever come anywhere near doing anything the remotest bit intimate.'

'Linda!'

Linda placed her untouched cup of tea on the table and said, 'Upset your sensitivities, have I? Well, I don't give a monkey's. Now tell me – what do you feel about children?'

Charles shook his head. 'I don't want children,' he admitted.

The words were like hammer blows to Linda. 'Not want children?' she repeated, aghast. 'What the bloody hell do you want to get married for then?'

Charles shook his head.

'What's in it for me, Charles?' Linda cried. 'Here I'd live in a house bigger than I've ever seen in my life. I'd have someone to keep it clean, someone to cook my meals and organise my days. But I can't have my friend, who is closer than any sister, to live with me, though you know she has no other place to go. What's next, Charles? You won't want me seeing Gran, or Peggy, or Beattie, or even Francesca?'

She saw by Charles's face that she'd hit the nail on the head. She went on, 'And then to cap it all, this mansion of a place is not to be filled with children as I'd hoped. I need children, Charles. I can't live a sham of a marriage without family or friends and without children.'

Charles, angered at last, snapped back, 'What do you get, you ask? Always you, you, *you!* What do I get? You agreed to marry me because you needed a home and that's all. There is nothing between us but convenience.'

'Is that what you really think?' Linda said in an appalled whisper. 'What do you really feel for me?'

'What do you mean?'

'Do you desire me? Do you imagine yourself making love to me?'

'Linda, please.'

'Why does that shock you, Charles?' Linda asked. 'We are to be married. It's what married people do.'

When Charles gave an involuntary shiver of distaste, Linda saw suddenly what sort of life she'd have if she married him. She'd be pampered and privileged and indulged, but inside she would shrivel up and die. 'Charles,' she said, 'are you a nancy boy?'

'No! I'm not!'

His denial was so emphatic, Linda didn't doubt it, but she knew there was something wrong. The worst mistake she could make was to marry him. She took off the admired diamond cluster and said, 'I think it's best if we break it off now.'

Hurt, Charles cried out, 'Break off our engagement just because I won't have my house filled with your common friends and family? Don't be so foolish, girl. Look at what you're giving up!'

'I'm not foolish,' Linda said steadily. 'So don't say I am. Who are you anyway, to call me names? Bloody hell, Charles, at least I'm normal. It's you that has the problem. You want to make me something else, something I'm not.'

'What if I am?' Charles said with a sneer. 'What have you got to hang on to? You were born in a slum of a house and dragged up on a disgusting council estate, and your friends that you lay such store by, are only those like yourself – even your precious Jenny. I was going to show you a better life and I would have taught you and groomed you. In the end, you would have had no further use for those you now claim as friends. I would have bought you beautiful clothes and expensive jewellery. I would have wined and dined you at the best places with rich and influential people. In time you would have forgotten your humble beginnings.'

'How dare you talk about my family and friends in that way,' Linda exclaimed furiously.

'They're worth much more than yours any day of the week.' She leapt to her feet almost upsetting the small table and cried out, 'You don't want a wife. I'd be like a bird kept in a luxurious and gilded cage, but not allowed to fly. I'd have everything with you, except a life.'

'Of course you'd have a life,' Charles said. 'Don't be so melodramatic.'

'What sort of life? Your sort? The sort you chose for me?'

Linda's face was crimson with temper and her eyes too were sparkling. Charles looked at her with distaste. His mother would never have lost control in that way. He hoped Bessie and Amy couldn't hear Linda's high indignant voice, for she was making no attempt to lower it.

'Not even a normal married life would be mine,' Linda went on. 'Because that, all that goes with it, bleeding well embarrasses the arse off you.'

'Linda, please!'

'Embarrassed by my language now, are you?' Linda cried, too angry to care what she said. 'Well, I ain't speaking any lies. There's something wrong with you, Charles. You say you're not a nancy boy, but you've got a problem all right.'

'Keep your voice down,' Charles hissed desperately.

'Oh, I'll keep my voice down, all right,' Linda said. 'Right down, because I'm going back to my common friends and family, so you won't have to listen any more.' She looked at Charles and shook her head as she went on more quietly, 'I know what I'm doing. I'd never be happy with you and you wouldn't be happy with me. In time

475

we'd make each other miserable.'

And Charles realised Linda was right. She resembled his mother in looks only. In temperament and personality they were completely different. He'd never heard his mother even raise her voice, never mind use coarse language. For him too, the bubble had burst.

Linda placed the engagement ring on the table and said, 'I'm sorry, Charles. But really, it's better this way.'

Charles didn't speak. He sat with his head in his hands, for he saw a lonely, frustrated life in front of him. But Linda had no time to waste pity on him. She wrenched open the door and surprised the figure of Amy Sallenger, who'd been listening at it intently. They spoke not a word to each other as Linda retrieved her coat from the cloakroom and went out the front door. She had no idea how to get home, but she'd find out; she wasn't helpless. As she walked out into the summer's night the tears coursed down her cheeks.

At the same time as Linda was trying to find her way back home, Jenny was steaming open Linda's letter, hoping no one thought it a good time to make a cup of tea that evening while she was in there bending over the kettle. She scalded her hand and found steaming envelopes open wasn't as easy as she'd imagined. But as last, there it was.

My darling, darling Linda,
Sarah Phelps gave me your address. She did not want to do this, but I tell her you will like to know

476

what happens to me now. It is bad here – worse even than I thought. My farm is destroyed. There is nothing for me here. I will leave as soon as I am allowed. I know we may never meet again, but I will write to you until the day you tell me you are married, then I will stop. But still you must know you have my love now and always, darling Linda.

Max. xx

How dare a German write to Linda in such a way, Jenny thought savagely. What right had he? She was gratified to know that Linda at least hadn't given him her address, he'd got that from Sarah Phelps. Therefore, she thought, Linda hadn't given him leave to write to her and she'd never expect to get a letter from him.

Yet from the tone of the letter, she knew their relationship had gone beyond mere friendship, and anger and resentment against Linda fizzed sourly inside her. Linda had no self-respect, she decided. No consideration for anyone but herself. Fine gratitude she shows for all I did for her, Jenny thought. Once she'd told Jen she didn't want gratitude, but now she expected a measure of it. She was going to save Linda from herself, for she didn't know how she'd react if she saw this letter. So Jenny decided she wouldn't see it. No one but Peter knew it had come and he'd say nothing if she asked him not to. She'd burn it and say nothing to Linda at all.

Linda walked all the way to Sutton town centre where she eventually found a bus to take her along to the Pype Hayes Estate. From there she walked to Grange Road. When she arrived home, footsore, weary and dispirited, even Jenny couldn't help feeling sorry for her, though she still felt anger against her, and it was hard for her to act naturally. She was brusque and rather remote at first, and Linda, expecting sympathy, was both hurt and mystified.

They went into the kitchen and Francesca left her husband snoozing behind his paper and came in too, to see what had happened. Linda was glad of her company because she didn't know what was up with Jenny. Linda told them that her relationship with Charles was over; the engagement at an end. She didn't think she was ready for marriage and not at all sure she'd be happy in the big house managing servants and everything. But Jenny knew that wasn't all. Linda was watching Jenny and trying to decide if she'd recovered from her ill-humour. She hoped she'd tell her what it was all about eventually. Anyway, she didn't think it would help for her to say that Jenny didn't feature in their married life together. Eventually, she said, 'The end came really when he said he didn't want a family.'

'Not ever?'

'Maybe he thinks you're too young,' Francesca said.

'I think,' said Linda wearily, 'there's more to it than that.'

'What d'you mean?'

'Well, he doesn't … he's never…' Linda didn't know how to explain, not in front of Francesca anyway.

'He hasn't tried anything on?' Jenny said.

life. There was her family, of course, but she'd never been that close to Geraldine. Martin and Francis were on the South Coast and in the spring Jan and Seamus were moving to Northfield, totally the other side of the city, where Seamus had got a job in a firm making cars. She would miss her gran, but though she always made time for Jenny, Maureen's life was full now with Dermot and little Niamh. Francesca Masters would be glad to get rid of them, though good manners would prevent her from ever saying so.

All night Jenny tossed and turned as her thoughts tumbled about her head. At last she slept and dreamt of Peter Sanders. She was on the train pulling out of New Street Station and he was running beside it, begging her not to go.

She woke with a cry of distress and told herself not to be so silly. Peter was a friend, no more and no less. But sleep evaded her for the rest of the winter's night and when the alarm clock woke Linda, she told her to find out about passports and visas and any other documentation they'd need for the two of them to travel to the States.

When Jenny and Linda announced their plans for a new future, not everyone was enthusiastic. Both their bosses thought the two girls were totally irresponsible. Linda felt sorry for Mr Tollit, who told her over and over that she could be a first-class jeweller in time. She knew he'd taken trouble to teach her, and thought she had real talent. Once, to work in the jewellery quarter, making beautiful pieces of jewellery, had

483

been the limit of her ambition. Now, new horizons had opened up for her. The audition might come to nothing, but Linda would regret it for ever if she didn't go, and would always wonder if she might have made it, had she taken the opportunity.

The personnel officer at the Dunlop had a heart-to-heart chat with Jenny, to try and talk her round. Jobs were going to be hard to get with all the men returning to Civvy Street, she said. It wasn't the best time in the world to leave her job. Jenny refrained from saying she thought few returning servicemen would take up typing and accounts, and anyway, her mind was made up.

Meanwhile, Linda wrote long letters to Louis Bradshaw and sorted out passports for herself and Jenny while he sorted out visas and work permits and made arrangements for their accommodation. Just before Christmas, Malcolm and Francesca Masters travelled to Portsmouth to watch their daughter become Mrs Paul Talbot, and in the New Year, Martin finally married his Dora. Jenny and Linda went down and Jenny watched him wed the girl not much bigger than herself, with the slightly dumpy figure and the laughing kindly eyes, and knew she would be good for her brother. Neither Martin nor Francis blamed her or Linda for leaving Britain and grasping new opportunities. 'The world's shrinking anyway, sis,' Francis said to Jenny. 'And you can always come back if it doesn't work out.' Jenny and Linda were both ︙red by the boys' positive outlook and put ︙doubts aside.

While the girls were away at Martin's wedding, there was an incident at Geraldine's house that caused her to examine her relationship with her mother properly for the first time. According to what Geraldine told Peter, Norah had gone berserk. She actually danced with delight when she heard that Linda's engagement was off, but when the news filtered through about Linda and Jenny going to America and why, she'd become hysterical. 'She was screaming fit to burst, Doctor,' Geraldine had said tearfully. 'I was trying to calm her, but she was beside herself and calling Linda dreadful names – you wouldn't believe... I mean, I never thought to hear such things from my own mother's lips.'

Peter was kneeling by Rosemarie, who was unconscious and ominously still, while an agitated Geraldine twisted her hands together and tried not to cry. The child was white-faced, but for a scarlet handprint and Peter, looking up said, 'And what happened next?'

'Rosemarie argued with Mother,' Geraldine said. 'And then she slapped her.'

'Some slap!'

'She knocked her off the chair she was sitting on in the kitchen, and she hit her head on the sink,' Geraldine said and added on a firmer note, 'but you needn't worry, Doctor. It will never happen again.'

'It had better not,' Peter said grimly. 'You must assert yourself, at least for your children's sake.'

'I know,' Geraldine said. And she did know, but it was hard after a lifetime's obedience and deference to her mother, to stand up for herself.

She watched the doctor go up the stairs and a sudden memory flashed into her mind that she hadn't thought about in years.

It was the word 'America' that did it, and she remembered the dashing Eamonn Flaherty who'd wanted to take her there once. She refused him because her mother had wanted her to, and had married Dan Driscoll for the same reason. She'd been contented enough with Dan and she loved her children, but in the early years of her marriage she'd often wondered what her life would have been like, if she'd followed her heart.

Now her sister had the chance to go, although her reasons were different, for Jenny was going to try and rebuild her shattered life. Good luck to her, thought Geraldine. I think it's about time I took charge of mine.

In the bedroom Peter looked with some dislike at Norah O'Leary, who'd taken to her bed, leaving Geraldine to deal with the child she'd injured and her hysterical brother. One day, he thought, she'd probably collapse in a seizure brought on by her own bad temper. Even now, her blood pressure was dangerously high. Norah made no attempt to talk to Peter and he was glad of it. He'd sent for an ambulance for Rosemarie, hoping it was just concussion she was suffering from. He was disgusted by Norah's actions.

Norah wasn't one whit sorry for what she'd done, for she thought Rosemarie had deserved to be chastised. She reminded her of Jenny as a young girl, and she wondered how her compliant beautiful daughter had given birth to such a child. And after the doctor had gone, Geraldine had looked at her in a way she never had before, and said coldly that she was never to lay a hand on her children again. Really, it was not to be borne.

Peter didn't know what had happened between Geraldine and her mother, and he never told Jenny and Linda what had happened to Rosemarie. He was just glad they were both out of the way.

He continued to support them, glad that Jenny appeared to need him after Bob's untimely death. He'd felt sorry for Linda too after her cancelled wedding plans, not that he'd have wanted her to marry the man. Haversham had made his skin crawl.

Linda was not heartbroken, but she was bored after she'd told Charles it would be better for them to part. She'd given in her notice at Packington Hall. Flora had been furious with her at first but the manager made it obvious that if she hadn't, she'd have been given the sack. Charles Haversham was too rich and influential to made a fool of, and the restaurant couldn't risk making an enemy of him.

Peter often wondered if she'd received any more letters from the POW, but felt sure she'd have mentioned it if she had. He didn't ask Jenny because they'd had a blistering row after the first letter arrived; Jenny had admitted to steaming it open, and then throwing it away, not even letting the girl see it. Jenny had claimed she'd been protecting her from herself. 'She's naïve,' she'd said.

'She's not that naïve,' Peter protested. 'And I

487

think you should have let her see the letter and decide for herself whether or not to answer it.'

'Don't you think she owes me something, after all I've done for her?' Jenny had asked.

'No, I bloody well don't!' Peter had thundered. 'Is that the reason you went back into that bombed house, to have Linda in thrall to you for the rest of her life?'

The anger in Peter's voice had reduced Jenny to tears, which melted his rage. He pulled her into his arms where she'd clung to him and wept. Peter longed to kiss her trembling lips, but instead he said gently, 'You gave Linda her life in a way. Now you must let her live it as she sees fit.'

Jenny said nothing but, though she knew Peter had a point, when the next letter came from Max Schulz, she wouldn't take a chance. She opened it, read it and burned it. They came regularly, and in the end she stopped reading them and burned them unread. But since the New Year, there had only been a couple and by the middle of February, she realised there had been none for weeks. She assumed the German had got fed up when he received no answers. She was glad she hadn't mentioned the matter to Linda and upset her for nothing. There was no place for an ex-prisoner-of-war in their plans for the future.

However, for a time, it looked as if those plans would come to nothing. Most of the ships trawling the Atlantic route were either still troopships, or hadn't yet been refitted for Civvy Street. Desperate to get Linda over in time for the audition, they booked a cabin on the *Queen Mary* for Saturday 30 March. This ship was operating between Southampton and New York primarily to transport British wives to American servicemen, but it also carried ordinary passengers. Southampton was the devil of a long way to travel from Birmingham, but, as Linda said, when you're already going thousands of miles to another continent, what did a couple of hundred miles further matter? Anyway, there was no other way to reach New York, so they had to put up with it and Linda wrote to Louis Bradshaw giving him details of when they would both arrive.

Peter was plunged into gloom again; he hadn't been sure they were serious. When Jenny and Linda had first mentioned going to America he'd thought it was a dream that would never become reality. Now it was fact, and the girl he'd loved for years would be thousands of miles away. But maybe that was better by far than seeing her regularly and not being able to admit how he felt about her.

Linda was glad she would not be there during the last week to witness Peter's distress, for the following morning she was travelling to her aunt's new house in Basingstoke. The small house she had been evacuated to in 1939 had been attacked by a doodlebug in 1944, and eventually she'd been re-housed with her family in a four-bedroomed council house in the same town.

Linda had kept up a correspondence with her Aunt Lily since the accident, because she knew her mother would have liked her to do so. Aunt

Lily was delighted to get her news, and when she wrote and told her of her plans to travel to New York, she replied immediately inviting her to come and stay with them for a few days beforehand so they could get to know one another better.

I never thought I'd be happy away from 'the Smoke' and it took some getting used to, I can tell you, but I got to like the place. My Sid settled in and got a job straight away and now with the three eldest working too, we're in clover. And the house is lovely, Linda. I don't know I'm born with all this space and a proper bathroom, and we'd all love to see you. You could catch a train from here to Southampton in time to meet your Jenny the day before you sail.

Linda really wanted to see her aunt, for she was a true blood relative, her mother's oldest sister, and she'd also like to meet Lily's husband and sons, her cousins, for nice and friendly though Jenny's family were, they were not her own.

And so it was arranged. Linda was to travel to Basingstoke the following morning after the party Maureen had planned to wish them all Godspeed. A week later, she would meet up with Jenny at the Metropole Hotel in Southampton. 'Might as well splash out for once in our lives.' Jenny had said. 'Then, after a good night's sleep and a decent breakfast, we'll take a taxi to the docks.'

'Let's hope the crossing is smooth so that the breakfasts stay in our stomachs long enough to do us some good,' Linda had said, looking with

490

horror at the price list in the information pack Jenny had sent for. 'Otherwise, I'd think it an awful waste of money.'

They'd both been horrified to find that even to travel third class on the *Queen Mary* cost fifty-nine pounds. Louis Bradshaw had wanted to pay for their tickets, but Jenny had said that, although it was quite all right for him to send the cost of Linda's fare, she couldn't possibly ask him to fund hers too. But she didn't see how she'd manage to raise that amount of money. She had some saved; she'd been putting something aside for her bottom drawer. Linda had a little more, but it would leave them dangerously low on funds and Jenny was worried about going so far with so little money.

Salvation came in the shape of Francesca Masters who presented Jenny with a gift of £300. Jenny was aghast and loath to accept it, but Francesca explained that her son would have come into this money on his wedding anyway under the terms of his grandfather's will. But as soon as Jenny had become engaged to Bob, he had made a will gifting the money to her if anything happened to him. The will had only recently come to light, however, for the man he'd entrusted it to had also died in action. The Masters family had all agreed that Bob's wishes should be adhered to.

Jenny was astounded by the family's generosity, and enormously grateful. Never had she had so much money before! Now nothing could stop her and Linda and their future was assured.

Both girls were all set to enjoy the party

Maureen O'Leary had put on for them that evening. However, when the house was packed with friends. neighbours, and family, Linda was sorry that she hadn't asked Sarah Phelps. She hadn't seen her since Peter had driven her away from the farm in disgrace the previous summer.

She could have claimed she was busy, and in a way it was true: Jenny had needed a lot of support after Bob's death, certainly in the beginning; then there was her own marriage to arrange, and at first she was still singing in the evenings and working full-time. But, really, she was embarrassed to meet Sarah and the more time that passed, the harder it was to turn up at the farm casually and uninvited one weekend.

Still, Linda thought, she should have asked Sarah to the party, or at least written and told her about going to America. She might have done, had she not received a letter from her two weeks before.

Haven't seen you in ages. Hope Christmas was good for you and things are OK generally. Please get in touch soon. I have news about Max.

Max! It was a bolt from the blue and a most unwelcome bolt at that. She'd taken a long time to get over Max, but now she was getting on with making a new life for herself. She wanted no reminder of a wartime romance to mess anything up. She'd accepted the fact she'd never see him again, and she had no intention of sailing to America upset and unsettled because of any news Sarah Phelps wanted to tell her about Max Schulz.

Jenny was quite concerned about her sister at the party that night. She thought she looked unwell and there were lines of strain on her face that had never been there before. However, Geraldine assured Jenny she was fine. It was Jenny and Linda's night and there was no way she was going to spoil it with grim tales of her life. She'd made the decision to stand up for herself and her children the day her mother had smacked Rosemarie, but she was finding that arguing with and defying her mother was harder work than she had ever imagined.

She caught Peter Sanders' eye across the room and smiled at him. She liked the doctor; he had no illusions about her mother and could be very helpful when she was at the end of her tether. Peter didn't return her smile and Geraldine realised he wasn't looking at her, but at Jenny – and looking at her as if... Well, as if he was gone on her. Jenny seemed unaware of it and Geraldine wondered why no one had put her wise.

Gerry had noticed Peter's preoccupation with his niece, too, and had watched him morosely knocking back the beer all night. He followed him into the kitchen as he headed for yet another refill. 'Tell her how you feel man,' he advised, watching Peter fill his tankard to the brim.

'Tell who?'

'Jenny! God, man, I'm not blind!'

'Jenny appears to be – at least where I'm concerned.'

'Well, that's women for you,' Gerry said. 'But tell her. If you let her go without telling her, you'll regret it.'

'She doesn't want me. She doesn't see me that way.'

'How do you know?'

'I just do,' Peter said, knowing his heart would break when Jenny walked out of his life for ever.

'I'll tell her for you.'

'No you bloody won't,' Peter said. 'She has to realise it herself.'

'What are you going to do?'

'Tonight?' Peter asked, and waved his glass in Gerry's direction. 'Tonight, I'm going to get very drunk.'

Gerry gave a sigh and left Peter to get on with it, wondering how Jenny could not see what was in front of her.

Every time Jenny thought of the party the following day she was upset and troubled. She'd been enjoying herself until almost the end of the night, when she'd stepped into the garden for a breath of air. The room had been stuffy and full of smoke and eventually the weepy remembrances of her gran and Beattie had succeeded in making her feel very emotional.

She'd noticed Peter at the party and thought him in a mood, for he'd barely spoken to her and had taken himself out into the kitchen where he'd stayed most of the evening. So she was surprised when he stepped into the garden after her, but pleased too because she'd known him for years now and welcomed the chance to have a few words alone. 'Hello, Jenny O'Leary,' Peter said and Jenny realised that he was quite drunk.

Never ever had she seen him in that state before, or anywhere near it. But, she told herself, it was the man's own time and a party, after all. 'Hello, Peter.'

'Will you miss us all then, all your wonderful friends?'

'Of course I will.'

'You have lots of friends, don't you, Jenny O'Leary?' he asked. 'I'm a friend, am I not?'

'Of course,' she said again, and added, 'an old and valued friend.'

'An old and valued friend,' Peter repeated and gave a laugh. 'And what would you say, Jenny, if I said I had no wish to be your friend, however old and valued?'

Jenny was lost for words. 'Well, I'd... It would be...'

'What would you say, Jenny, if I said that I set out to get drunk tonight, because I wanted to tell you something I could never tell you sober?' Jenny didn't answer. She just stared at him and Peter went on, 'I might never have the courage to say this again.' He took one of Jenny's hands and looked into her eyes and said, 'Jenny, I love you with all my heart. I think I've loved you since you came out of that hellhole of a tunnel. You were encrusted with filth, dripping with blood and your clothes hung in tatters around you. You went for me like a tiger, you remember?'

Oh, she remembered. For years she'd had nightmares about being buried alive from her experiences in that tunnel. But what was alarming her was what Peter had said about loving her.

She nodded her head, 'I remember.'

'Well, from that day, that moment, I've loved you and over the years it's got worse. I know you loved Bob and I tried not to mind. I knew Bob would have made you happy. And now that Bob is dead, you are making a new life for yourself. I don't blame you, but I didn't want you to go before I told you that I love you – and probably always will.'

Before Jenny was able to say a word, Peter dropped her hand and put his arms around her, pulled her towards him and kissed her.

Jenny was astounded by the kiss. How in God's name had she been so blind to this good, kind and thoughtful man? The kiss wasn't the kiss of an old and valued friend. Peter gently parted Jenny's lips and she responded to him, giving a little moan of pleasure; desire she thought extinguished for ever at Bob's death, rose in her again.

Abruptly, Peter released her and lurched back into the house and Jenny staggered back against the wall while tears streamed from her eyes and coursed down her cheeks. When eventually she was composed enough to go back into the house, it was to find him gone. 'I think he had a skinful on him and that's the truth,' Maureen had said.

Jenny knew that better than anyone, but she also knew he'd meant every word he'd said. Her gran was fond of saying, 'What's in the heart sober, comes out drunk,' and she knew that that was true.

The next day, Peter called round and apologised

to Jenny if he'd said or done anything embarrassing. 'I'd drunk more than normal,' he said. 'And I'm afraid I remember very little about it all.'

Jenny looked into his eyes and knew he was lying; he could remember every word, but she assured him he'd said nothing offensive.

'Oh Peggy, Gran – what am I to do?' she cried later that same night, when she'd fled to them for advice.

'God Jenny, the man is eating his heart out for you,' Peggy said. 'Do you love him?'

Did she love him? She'd loved Bob. Could you love more than one person? She'd never thought of love except as between one friend and another in connection with Peter Sanders. But when he'd kissed her the previous night... 'I think I do,' she said.

'Then, tell him how you feel.'

'I'm going to America in five days,' Jenny said. 'How can I? It would be best if Peter forgets all about me.'

'You should talk to the man at least,' Maureen advised. 'Surely you owe him that much?'

Jenny shook her head sorrowfully. 'No, Gran.' she said. 'What good would it do?'

Maureen shook her head, certain Jenny was making a mistake, but recognising that Jenny's mind was made up.

'She's answered none of your letters?' Sarah Phelps asked the tall German striding agitatedly around her kitchen. 'It's not like her, not Linda.'

She hadn't answered Sarah's letter either, but it

wouldn't help to say that. 'And you say you wrote often?'

'I wrote every fortnight or so, until six weeks ago,' Max said, sitting down at last. 'I tell her how bad things are there, and how long everything takes. For some time I have little money and I am fed by the Red Cross. But always I find money for a stamp and I beg the paper and envelope.

'In the end I wrote to my uncle in America and he sent me some money – American dollars, they are prized in Germany, and in time I may get compensation for my farm. I took a labouring job while I wait for permission to join my uncle in America where he has a job for me in the factory he owns. For now he says I will lodge with him, but soon I will move to my own place. No one will care there that I'm a German. They have already many nationalities in New York.'

'I believe so,' Sam said. 'I should say it's the place to go, right enough.'

'But without Linda my life is meaningless,' Max said. 'I told her I would write until she told me she was married and then I would stop. But she never wrote back once and now you say she never got married.'

'It's what Sam heard,' Sarah said. 'I don't know what happened. I haven't seen Linda myself for some time.'

'I must know,' Max said. 'I must see her.'

'Do you think that's wise?' Sam said. 'If she didn't write back, she was perhaps trying to tell you that that part of her life was over. Maybe she doesn't still feel the same about you.'

'Maybe she doesn't, but I have to know from

her lips,' Max said. 'Oh, I have nothing to offer her at the moment. I just want to know that she'll wait for me. When I have much money and a fine house, I will send for her if she will have me.'

He leapt to his feet again and began to pace the room afresh. 'I must see her,' he said. 'I purposely broke my journey to come here and I'll not go until I see her with my own eyes.' Sam and Sarah's eyes met. They didn't know whether that was a good idea or not, but it seemed clear that Max would not be dissuaded.

Jenny was alone in the house, sorting out the things she and Linda were to take with them and those they could leave behind when the doorbell rang. She opened the door to find a stranger on the doorstep. He wore a threadbare overcoat and his shoes, she noticed, were well worn, his trousers thin and shapeless. He was the picture of faded respectability, but not so very different from most of the post-war people about, really. His face was a handsome one, the chin chiselled and firm and the tawny-coloured eyes penetrating, but his cheeks were hollowed out and his face thin almost to gauntness as if he'd not had enough to eat, or perhaps suffered greatly. There were many penniless, or almost penniless refugees in Britain at that time, so Jenny asked gently. 'Can I help you?'

The man clicked his heels together at her words, gave a small bow and said, 'I wish to see Linda Lennox. My name is Max Schulz.'

Max Schulz! The name burned into her brain. The German POW who'd written to Linda not once, but many times! She wondered what the hell he was doing in England. She was glad she was the only one home; she'd have hated Francesca and her family to think they had German friends. She was also glad Linda was away and safe from this man. 'Linda's not here,' she said.

'She has left?'

'Yes.'

'But where is she? I must see her.' Max said.

'I'm afraid I don't know.'

'What do you mean you don't know?' the man cried. 'Did she give you no word, no address?'

'No. No she didn't,' Jenny said. 'Now if you'd excuse me, I'm rather busy.' She moved as if to close the door, but Max was too quick for her and his foot shot out.

He looked into Jenny's eyes and said, 'Are you the one Linda calls Jenny?'

Jenny was taken aback. 'Well, yes.'

'Then,' said Max, 'you are lying to me. Linda would never, ever go away without letting you know where she went.'

'She did! I tell you she did,' Jenny cried wildly.

Max shook his head. His smile was maddening. 'Jenny,' he said, 'have you ever been in love?'

'How dare you!' Jenny said angrily. 'That's a very personal question. Don't you Germans understand even basic good manners?'

Max ignored the question. Instead he said, 'I love Linda with all my heart and soul, and I think she loves me. She did once. But I must see her, hear from her own lips how she feels about me, and then I believe it.'

'It's too late,' Jenny said, desperately, 'She's married.'

Max shook his head. 'She *was* to be married,' he said. 'She even showed me the ring, but the marriage did not take place. Please, Jenny, think about what I've said. I love Linda more than anything in the world. I'll never do anything to hurt her. Soon I set sail for America. I want to know that Linda will wait until I can send for her, and then do me the honour of becoming my wife.'

The sincerity of Max's words finally got to Jenny and she had to remind herself the man was a German in order to keep the fixed look on her face. 'I'll return tomorrow at four-thirty,' Max said. 'Maybe then you will tell me where Linda lives,' and he bowed once more and went back down the path.

Confused, upset and not at all sure what to do next, Jenny went to Peter's house as he was the only one who knew of the POW and the only one who knew she'd read and destroyed Max's letters. Peter led Jenny into the room downstairs that he used as a study, away from his mother's prying eyes and interference. Mabel had let Jenny in with barely concealed curiosity and had taken herself off to the kitchen as Peter firmly shut the study door. She'd make tea, she decided, and take it in, in a moment or two. It would be a good excuse to catch any snippets of gossip.

'He says – this man, this German – he says he loves Linda,' Jenny said sitting down in the black leather chair Peter indicated. 'He says he knows she was to be married. He saw the ring, but he also knows the marriage was cancelled.'

'He did see the ring,' Peter said sitting in the chair beside her. 'Linda went up to the farm and he would have seen it.'

'Why did she go?'

'The man was moving out,' Peter said, and went on with a sigh, 'you may as well know, when I surprised them in the barn, they were kissing. I mean, really kissing, you know? And the way it was – well, I shouldn't have thought it was the first time.'

'She can't love him,' Jenny declared. 'Not a German.'

'Of course she can,' Peter said impatiently. 'People don't always love wisely. I know that to my cost.'

'I'm sorry, Peter.'

'Don't worry about it,' Peter said, and added, 'isn't that what old and valued friends are for?'

Jenny saw the pain behind his eyes and knew that whatever she told her gran, she couldn't walk out of Peter's life until she'd found out how he really felt about her, now she'd had time to examine her own feelings. 'I'm sorry' she said. 'I've hurt you.'

'No, it's me,' Peter said. 'You can't pretend what isn't there.'

Jenny hesitated and bit on her bottom lip nervously. Peter didn't know her feelings for him had changed. He didn't know she was almost sure she loved him, but was scared to say so in case her gran was wrong and Peter's drunken outburst at the party was just that; something to

502

be regretted in the cold light of day.

Seeing Jenny's discomfort, but not knowing the reason for it Peter said, 'Sorry, Jenny, I didn't mean to embarrass you. Look, if you're worried about what I said the other night, I was a bloody fool. I was drunk and no drunk speaks sense.'

'So you didn't mean it?' Jenny cried.

Peter gave a grim laugh, but it didn't take the bleak look from his face as he repeated, 'Like I said, I was drunk.'

He hadn't answered the question, so Jenny tried another. 'Why did you get so drunk, Peter?'

'It was a party, for God's sake,' he retorted. 'People get drunk at parties.'

'But you said you got drunk for a reason.' Jenny persisted. 'You said you needed it to give you the courage to tell me something.'

'Don't analyse it, Jen,' he said. 'I told you, I don't remember.'

'I think you do.'

'What is this?'

Jenny faced him and said, 'I need to hear you say those things to me again, now that you're stone cold sober.'

'Bloody hell, Jenny, are you some kind of sadist?' Peter cried. 'You want me to pour out my heart to you so you can kick me in the guts by telling me you just want to be my friend?'

Jenny reached for Peter's hands and held them tight between her own and looked into his deep brown eyes and said, 'Peter, I've known you for years. You've always been there when I've needed you and you've become a good friend to me. All that time, I've taken you for granted and never thought that you cared for me in any sort of intimate way.'

'You don't have to go on with this,' Peter said. He was embarrassed and tried to pull his hands away, but Jenny held on tight.

'I do,' she insisted. 'Please listen. I loved Bob and I'll never pretend otherwise. Had he lived, I wouldn't be having this conversation with you. But Bob didn't live. I didn't think I could ever love another man, but when you kissed me at the party...'

'I'm sorry,' Peter said. 'That was wrong of me.'

'No, it wasn't,' Jenny contradicted. 'This is what I'm trying to say. I responded to you. I wanted you Peter, like I never thought I would. I mean, I thought feelings like that had died with Bob.'

'I believe you,' Peter said. 'God, I felt you respond, but that doesn't necessarily mean anything.'

'How can you say that?'

'Because you are a normal young woman with normal sexual feelings,' he explained. 'Just because you enjoyed the kiss and all it engendered doesn't mean– What I'm saying is, don't confuse it with love.'

'God, Peter, aren't you pig-headed?' Jenny said grinning. She released his hands and leapt to her feet. 'Do I have to spell it out for you?' she cried. *'I love you!* I probably have done for ages, but you were so much part of my life already, I sort of couldn't see the wood for the trees.'

Outside the door, Mabel stood with a tray of tea and heard Jenny's declaration. About bloody time, she thought. Maybe now Peter can do something about getting his life together. She'd seen him moon after Jenny O'Leary for years and, though he'd gone out with other girls, Mabel knew they'd meant nothing to him. She took the tray back to the kitchen guessing that, at that moment, an intrusion wouldn't be helpful or welcomed.

Peter had got to his feet too and was staring at Jenny as if he couldn't believe his ears. 'You love me?' he asked incredulously.

Jenny nodded.

'I mean as a lover? As a husband, not just a friend?'

Jenny looked into Peter's eyes. The love she saw shining there brought tears to her own, and any doubts she might have had about the depth of love *she* felt for the man before her, flew away.

She put her arms around his neck and kissed him. Peter did nothing for a second and then his arms encircled her, pulling her to him. She felt her knees feel suddenly weak and her lips opened as Peter's tongue probed her mouth. When it was eventually over, she leant against him with a groan of desire. 'Is that answer enough?' she said, when at last she could speak.

Peter could only gaze at her with wonder. 'God, Jenny, I've loved you for so long,' he said, hoarsely. 'I never thought you would be mine.'

'Well, I am. Yours for ever.'

'You will marry me?' Peter said. 'And just as soon as it can be arranged?'

'Yes, I will. But first there's Linda and America, and this bloody POW.'

'Oh God,' Peter cried. 'I almost forgot all about that. What time is he coming?'

'Half four,' Jenny said. 'If I hadn't already have given in my notice at work, he wouldn't have found me in today.' She looked at Peter and said, 'I don't want to meet him, Peter.'

'We'll meet him,' Peter said. 'But together,' and he gave Jenny a kiss and said, 'Don't worry, darling, it will be all right. Let's go and give Mother the good news about us.'

'Will she mind?'

'Mind?' Peter said. 'She'll be delighted. She's known for ages the only girl I'd ever settle down with was you.'

Jenny took the hand that Peter held out to her, and her heart almost burst with happiness. She wondered how she'd been so blind for so long.

Chapter Twenty-Six

Peter and Jenny decided to take Max Schulz to Peter's house to talk to him, for as Jenny said, they could hardly evict the Masters family from their home to entertain a German visitor and it would be totally unsuitable to take him to her bedroom.

Jenny had had to confess to Peter before the meeting with Max what she'd done with the many letters he had sent to Linda. He was furious. 'I can't believe you,' he'd said, deeply shocked. 'Especially after the row we had when you destroyed the first one. Please don't try telling me you did it for Linda's good.'

'But I did.'

'Don't kid yourself,' Peter said roughly. 'You decided to play God. Max obviously believes Linda got his letters and ignored them. You'll have to tell him what you did with them.'

'I know.' Jenny's voice was a mere whisper.

Peter sighed. 'Jenny, you have to accept that Linda is grown-up,' he said. 'She has to make her own decisions and her own mistakes. If she'd had the opportunity to write back to this Max, maybe they might have begun a relationship.' He caught sight of Jenny's face and snapped, 'Don't look like that. The man's a German, not someone from Outer Space. Anyway, this whole thing must be Linda's choice.' He wondered what the

507

man was like. He'd had just a glimpse, not enough to judge his character especially as he'd been so angry with Linda at the time, he hadn't taken that much notice. Anyway, he'd soon see and judge for himself.

And Peter liked what he saw. His mother was unashamedly curious about the man he introduced as simply Max, a friend of Linda's. Mabel would have been quite happy to have sat and chatted all day, but Peter cut her off. 'Mother, I have evening surgery soon,' he said. 'And we have things to discuss.' He ushered both Jenny and Max into the living room and asked them to sit down as he shut the door firmly.

And there followed the most uncomfortable half-hour of Jenny's life. Max was just as angry as Peter had been at the destruction of the letters he'd sent Linda. 'Well, what can you offer her?' Jenny cried out at last.

'At this moment, nothing,' Max admitted. 'But, I want Linda to wait for me. I will send for her when I have something to offer.'

'So, you expect her to moulder away here, while you make your fortune?' Jenny said sarcastically.

Max leapt to his feet. 'You mock me,' he said. 'My Uncle Werner has a factory in New York, which one day will be mine. He says I must start at the bottom and work up. This is what I tell to Linda in my letters,' he said, glaring at Jenny.

She had the grace to feel ashamed. 'I'm sorry,' she said. 'But really, Linda might not wish to marry you, or anyone. She has the chance of a big audition, a part in a musical. She might not want to give that up for marriage.'

'Why should she have to?' Max said. 'I want what Linda wants, because I wish her to be happy. I should be proud if she did this thing.'

'When do you sail?' Peter asked.

Max answered, 'In a week's time. When Linda didn't answer my letters, I think I might need a week to convince her that we belong together.'

'Do you love Linda, Max?'

'With all my heart.'

'And does she love you?'

'She does,' Max said. 'At least, she did once. This man she was marrying, she was making a mistake. It is good that she realised it before the wedding.'

'She never loved him,' Jenny said. 'That I do know. But there were good reasons why she was going to marry him, and even better reasons why she didn't, but that's really Linda's story to tell.'

Max sat down opposite Jenny and said, 'Where is she?'

'Basingstoke,' Jenny answered. 'She's visiting an aunt of hers.' She shook her head at him and said, 'It's too late, you see.'

'What's too late?'

'Max, we sail for America in two days' time,' Jenny said. 'That's where the audition is. In New York.'

'*Mein Gott!*' Max exclaimed, and slapped his forehead with the flat of his hand. Jenny again felt deeply ashamed of what she had done. Linda might not have felt the need to sail to America if she'd known Max was returning to England. Peter was right, whatever she felt personally, Linda should have had the chance of getting to know the young German, who truly seemed to love her dearly. How she wished she could turn back the clock. 'Oh God,' she cried. 'I'm so sorry, but it's just too late.'

'Not necessarily,' Peter said.

Linda was so excited when she arrived in Southampton that it was only the risk of being run into the local mental home that kept her feet on the floor. Just hours before, she kissed the aunt and uncle she'd got to know well in their week together. Their sons had been self-conscious with their little Brummie cousin at first and then began to enjoy her company.

She'd been sorry to leave them, but America and all it promised was a great lure. Louis Bradshaw was meeting them in New York and his family were putting them both up till they got the feel of the place. Jenny had spoken to them on the telephone and seemed a little happier. They sounded decent people, she said. Louis told her that when they felt the time was right, he'd find them a nice apartment they could afford.

It was all so strange and yet exhilarating. Even the opulence of the Metropole Hotel, where she had arranged to meet Jenny, could not dampen down the excitement that flowed through Linda every time she thought about the next day. She crossed the room with a level of confidence she was far from feeling. 'Linda Lennox,' she said. 'We have a reservation in the name of Jenny O'Leary.'

'Ah yes,' said the man behind the desk, who spoke as if he'd swallowed a bag of marbles. 'Miss

510

O'Leary has sent a telegram for you.'

For years telegrams had meant bad news and Linda opened hers with trembling fingers: *Unavoidably delayed. STOP. Cannot make hotel. STOP. Meet you on board tomorrow. STOP. See you soon. STOP. Love Jenny. STOP.*

'Oh,' said Linda, feeling lonely and abandoned. She'd been looking forward to seeing Jenny to tell her all about her relations and discussing their plans for the sea voyage and what they intended to do in the great city itself.

Now all that had gone flat. She gazed into the dining room, hesitant to eat there alone, but she could hardly wander through the streets of an unfamiliar city looking for a chip shop. She sat at a table by the door and felt conspicuous and out of place.

She didn't enjoy her dinner much and finished it in record time, and then wondered what to do with herself. Newspapers were provided, so she took one up to her room, but was too excited to read it. She listened to the wireless and wished she'd thought to bring a book. Far too early she went to bed and tossed and turned, wishing Jenny was in the other bed in the room. She wondered what had held her up. It had to be something major, and she hoped it wasn't anything too dreadful.

Just before dawn she fell asleep only to be woken by the alarm call she'd requested. She stumbled about the room, had a wash and was hungry enough, after her small dinner of the previous evening, to eat a sizeable breakfast.

Then, at last, it was time to call a taxi to the

docks. She was glad she'd kept her own ticket. She had asked Jenny if she wanted to hold on to them both, but Jenny had said you never knew what might happen, and they each should keep their own. Linda felt excitement grip her as the taxi driver drove her along; she saw the gulls wheeling and screeching overhead and knew the docks were near at hand.

She'd never seen a liner before, except in a book, and as the taxi turned into the quayside, the enormous size of it took her breath away. Deck upon deck rose before her, all of them thronged with people, and funnels spouted grey smoke into the dank air. She felt a sense of awe to be going aboard such a wonderful ship. 'All right, miss?' the taxi driver asked as she sat entranced in the cab and made no move to get out.

'Oh yes. Yes, I'm sorry,' she said, fumbling with the door handle.

The man smiled at her eagerness and he left his side of the cab and opened the door for her. 'Is it America you're bound for?'

'Yes. New York.'

'On your own?' he said, and frowned a little for he would not be happy to think of such a young girl going all that way on her own.

'No, my friend is going with me,' Linda said, watching the taxi driver deposit her luggage on the cobblestones on the quayside. 'She's my guardian really, I suppose. I lived with her after I was bombed out and my family killed.'

'Ah well, plenty had that happen to them,' the taxi driver said sympathetically. He felt a sense of

512

protection towards the girl and he looked about the busy bustling quay. 'Where are you meeting?'

'On the ship.'

'That's best,' said the driver. The place was teeming with people. 'She's probably already aboard. You stay here now, and don't move. I'll get you someone to help with your luggage. You'll never manage it by yourself.'

He was away before Linda could express her thanks and she was grateful for his kindness, for she'd not realised the amount of luggage she'd accumulated, for though she'd only taken one case to her auntie's, the rest had been sent on to the hotel.

The taxi driver was soon back, with a tall broad-shouldered man, who wore a uniform of sorts, so Linda knew he was part of the crew on board the ship. He picked up the cases as if they weighed nothing and was off, leaving Linda to pay the kind taxi driver and pick up her hand luggage and scurry after him. And scurry she did, desperate not to lose sight of the man who seemed to stride away from her so effortlessly.

He hardly seemed to notice the crowds of people and thrust his way through them with Linda striving to follow, muttering apologies that she knew would probably not be heard, for the noise was almost deafening. When she eventually reached the gangplank, she noticed the thick grey ropes coiled around the bollards on the quayside that were anchoring the ship. The ropes looked coarse and greasy and were as thick as a man's forearm.

But Linda had no time to stare. Already, the

man with her luggage had reached the deck and the gangplank was before her. It had wooden ridges at intervals along its length and the sides were not solid wood, but in a criss-cross design, and she gave a deep sigh of contentment as she breathed in the salty tangy air, and stepped on board.

The steward, or whoever he was, pointed her to a man who crossed her name off the passenger list and then led her to the little cabin Jenny had booked for them both. She'd wanted to ask if Jenny was aboard yet and whether her name had been deleted, but there was no time in the rush and noise of the place. However, when she got to the cabin there was no sight of Jenny or any of her belongings. There were four bunk beds in the room with a locker, set of drawers and a tall cupboard beside each set of beds. The other two women in the room had finished putting their belongings away and were chatting to one another.

'Thank you,' Linda said to the man who dumped her cases on the lower bunk bed. She wondered if she should tip him, but he didn't seem to expect it. 'My pleasure,' he said, the first words she'd heard him speak, then he touched his hat and was gone.

Linda nodded to the two women she'd be sharing her cabin with for the next five or six days, but felt shy speaking to them and instead, began to empty her cases, leaving plenty of space for Jenny's things. She turned to look out of the porthole. The sea was grey and choppy and she hoped the crossing wouldn't be too rough.

Already her stomach was churning, but she didn't know whether it was from excitement or fear. She glanced at her watch and wished Jenny was here.

'We set off too late,' Jenny said crossly to Peter. 'We shouldn't have left it to the last minute.'

'Relax,' Peter told her. 'We'll get there, don't worry It was that accident forcing us to take a detour that held us up. God, we couldn't have set off any earlier – it was nearly the middle of the night as it was.'

Jenny knew that was true, but she was too jumpy to be reasonable. They'd been on the road since half-past five that morning. Out of the corner of her eye, she could see Max sitting in the back seat of Peter's car and though he sat perfectly still, Jenny could almost feel the tension flowing through him. She wished she knew if she was doing the right thing; it had seemed such a good idea when Peter explained it all to her in his mother's front room two days before.

In an effort to change the subject and to stop herself looking at her watch for the hundredth time, she said, 'Are you sure your mother is all right about me moving in?'

'She's delighted,' Peter said with a smile. 'In fact, when I told her, she said it was about time.'

Jenny sincerely hoped that her move and the news of their impending marriage might take the heat off Linda, for she knew the family would never understand – God, she hadn't understood herself and if she was honest, still didn't. 'They'll crucify her,' she'd cried at Peter. 'You don't know.'

515

'Of course they won't.'

'They will,' she said firmly. 'They hate Germans.'

'Jenny, the war is over,' Peter had replied. 'We can't keep harking back. In time the war will be a distant memory. Never totally forgotten, because of the thousands who gave their lives to give us all freedom. But most of those who died would, I'm sure, hate us to wallow in bitterness against a whole nation for the decisions of its government.' He'd crossed the room as he spoke and held Jenny tight at that point and went on, 'Wait till we tell them they have a wedding to prepare for and at double-quick speed too. They'll have no time then to worry over Linda.'

'I'll still worry,' Jenny had said resignedly. 'It's a habit I've got into. Anyway,' she added, 'what exactly do you mean by a double-quick wedding?'

'I mean one that takes place as quickly as it can be reasonably arranged,' Peter had said. 'I've waited more years that I care to remember for you. I refuse to wait one day more than is necessary.' He loved Jenny dearly and always had. He wished she'd not destroyed the letters Max had sent to Linda because then they might have some measure of the young girl's feelings for him. If she was sure Linda would be happy, she would not fret so much.

Jenny also wished she could have the time back again and deal with it differently. Linda had never confided in her about her love for the young German at the Phelps's farm, and she thought she knew why. It was because she was afraid of upsetting her. Jenny had often said how she felt about the German people and she knew Linda wouldn't knowingly do anything to hurt her. Linda knew just how much she owed Jenny and she carried a heavy weight of guilt around because of it. God, she had even been willing to marry someone she didn't love to provide her and Jenny with a home together! A girl like that would kiss her German goodbye, not because she didn't love him, but because to admit to her love would give Jenny pain. She shifted uncomfortably in the car seat. She wished they were there at the quayside already. She wanted to have some time with Linda before the boat sailed, and hold her in her arms and see for herself how she was with Max. Then she would know, whatever Linda said. She would know.

They reached the docks in record time considering the tortuous journey and delays and diversions they'd endured, but Jenny didn't breathe easily until, after leaving the car in a back street, they hurried to the quayside and Jenny saw the liner still in port. 'Now, you know what you must do?' she said to Max. 'Keep out of the way at first. Give me time to talk to her.'

Max nodded reluctantly. He didn't totally trust Jenny, she'd tried to part him from Linda once before, but he knew the doctor was straight, he was sure of that. He made his way through the crowds on the quayside and up the gangplank after Jenny and Peter, and then mingled with the crowds on the lower deck while Jenny went in search of Linda.

Linda had left the cabin and gone out on deck

where the wind took her rather by surprise. She was glad she'd kept her coat on, but it whipped her scarf about her face and threatened to lift the woolly hat off her head altogether. She held on to the rail as the wind buffeted from side to side.

Around her she could see clusters of people clutching one another. Some were in tears and from the snatches of conversations she over-heard, Linda knew many of those on board were the wives of American GIs travelling to a new life, and a new land and bidding a tearful farewell to their loved ones. She felt lonely suddenly and wished Jenny would appear.

And then, as if her mind had conjured her up, she saw her there across the deck. Peter was by her side and she ran towards her, her arms opened wide. And though they didn't hug each other on a regular basis, Linda went into Jenny's arms as if it was the most natural thing in the world. She met Peter's eyes over Jenny's head and was surprised to see a twinkle in them and even more surprised when he gave her a broad wink. She presumed he'd brought Jenny to the ship because whatever had delayed her the previous day had meant there hadn't been a train suitable for this hour in the morning and Peter, as usual, had obliged. But she hardly expected him to be happy over it. Even if he'd accepted the fact that Jenny thought of him as a friend and nothing else, she hardly thought he'd be smiling about it and winking at her as if they shared some secret, when in just a few minutes more Jenny would be sailing to another continent entirely.

Linda drew out of Jenny's embrace and saw her

eyes wet with tears. 'What is it?' she cried and then looked around and demanded, 'Where is your luggage? Have you taken it straight to the cabin?'

Jenny shook her head, too full of emotion to speak and pressed a small tissue-wrapped bundle into Linda's hand. The younger girl knew what it was, for she'd wrapped the two halves of the mizpah in the crinkly paper herself. She unwrapped it carefully and saw just one half lying in her palm.

'I found them in your drawer,' Jenny said brokenly. 'I was packing your things to send to the Metropole.' She pulled the scarf away from her neck as she spoke and unbuttoned her coat, and Linda saw the other part of the mizpah resting in the hollow of Jenny's neck. 'I mended the chain,' she said.

Linda didn't answer. She didn't need the other half to know what the inscription said. *The Lord watch between me and thee while we are absent from one another.*

Suddenly, she knew what Jenny had come to tell her. She took a step back and said, her voice both in surprise and fear: 'You're not coming with me, are you? That's why you've given me this.'

The tears coursed down Jenny's cheeks and she was unable to speak, but Peter intervened, 'Linda, there is someone I want you to meet.'

And then Max stepped out from the crush of people on deck behind whom he'd hidden himself. Linda's mouth dropped open with surprise. 'Max?' Her lips formed the word, but no sound came out and Max strode across the deck and took Linda in his arms as if they'd never been apart. Her mind bounced with questions and slight annoyance too, that the man who had disappeared from her life nine months before and not communicated one word since, held her in his arms as if he had a right. And there was Jenny, watching it all as if she thought it was OK. What the hell did it all mean, she thought bemusedly.

But when she looked into Max's deep brown eyes, it was as if nothing else mattered. No one else even existed. She felt the familiar tremble in her legs and her whole body seemed loose and fluid, as if all the parts were unconnected. She did nothing to stop Max's lips descending on hers and her longing for him was so great, she barely suppressed a groan of sheer desire.

Jenny watched and clutched Peter's hand for support and knew that German or not, he was the man for the child who had grown into a woman in her care. She was so glad she'd given him her ticket. So glad to have had a chance to make reparation. She remembered the trouble they'd had to go to, to get it changed into Max's name. And then to ensure that there was a bed for him in the men's cabins, because he wouldn't be allowed to share with Linda as Jenny had intended to do.

Not knowing any of this, Linda had pulled away from Max and now faced him angrily. 'What the bloody hell are you doing here?' she exploded. 'Don't think you can come waltzing back into my life when you haven't bothered to get in touch with me all these months, because you can't. I'm not that sort of girl.'

Max glanced across at Jenny and she realised it was up to her. She was scared to tell Linda what she had done, terrified that she'd see disbelief, disdain and perhaps even hatred in those large eyes. She tried to swallow the lump in her throat and said, in a voice that shook: 'Max did write, Linda, and regularly. But I ... I burned his letters.'

The 'Why?' was on Linda's lips, but she didn't utter it. She knew why. When she looked at Jenny, she didn't see a woman who'd prevented her from receiving letters from her lover, she saw a girl not much older than herself, who'd crawled back into a dangerous house and risked her life to fulfil a promise made to a terrified and badly wounded child. She saw someone who'd swallowed her own fear to help Linda cope, who'd talked to her for hours to keep her conscious and then defied the two harridans she'd lived with to offer Linda a home.

She owed her life to Jenny and nothing mattered beside that. Besides, she remembered the cryptic message Sarah Phelps had written weeks before, mentioning 'news of Max'. Why hadn't she contacted her and asked what she meant? Because she was pig-headed, that's why. She put her arms around her friend's heaving shoulders.

'I'm sorry, I'm sorry,' Jenny said through her sobs.

'Hush, hush,' Linda said soothingly. 'It doesn't matter.'

Jenny could hardly believe her ears. 'You forgive me?' she asked incredulously.

Linda shrugged. 'Nothing to forgive,' she said, and she gave Max the mizpah, taking the scarf from her neck as she did so. 'Will you put it on?' she asked.

Max did what she asked as the call came for those not travelling to disembark, and Jenny said to Linda, 'Louis Bradshaw and his parents are meeting you at the other end – it's all arranged.'

Linda knew that Jenny was saying that if it *didn't* work out with Max, if at the end of the trip she decided she hated the sight of him, she still would have friends in New York. She felt warmed by her concern, but felt it to be unnecessary, for she knew her future lay with the tall handsome German, although she was determined also to appear at the audition Louis had arranged for her. She gazed at Jenny and said, 'It's all right,' and Jenny pressed Linda's hands, knowing she understood.

But there were other things Linda did *not* understand. She looked from Peter to Jenny. For years she'd been aware of Peter's devotion and before she sailed away, she had to be sure she wasn't leaving Jenny alone and bereft. 'Are you and Peter... I mean, did you... Oh God, have you...'

Peter smiled and put Linda out of her misery. 'Jenny and I have discovered we love each other,' he said.

That was no news to Linda from Peter's point of view, but she glanced at Jenny for confirmation and she smiled back at her. 'Don't worry about

522

us, Linda. Peter and I are getting married.'

Linda hadn't been aware she'd been holding her breath, but it escaped in a large sigh of sheer relief. There was no more time to discuss it, people were streaming past them disembarking from the ship and Peter said, 'We'll have to go, Jenny, otherwise we'll be carried to New York with this pair.'

Linda and Max accompanied them to the gangplank and it was as Jenny and Linda embraced for the last time that the tears started in Linda's eyes and she realised she'd miss Jenny so very, very much. She watched her walk down the gangplank with Peter holding her arm and she gave a sniff. Max turned Linda to face him and kissed the tears from her cheeks and held her close. 'Don't cry, my Linda,' he said.

'I'm not,' Linda said untruthfully in a voice that wobbled with emotion. 'It's the wind making my eyes water.'

Max ignored Linda's explanation and went on, 'You will have no reason to cry ever again. I love you more than life itself. My life is nothing without you.'

Linda saw the love for her shining in his eyes and knew, whatever anyone thought, that Max Schulz was the man for her for the rest of her life, and she sighed contentedly as she leant against him.

On the quayside just below them, Jenny and Peter, entwined together, watched the gangplank being raised and the hawser ropes unwound. Jenny turned to Peter and said, 'I can't help worrying about her, you know?'

'I do know,' Peter said. 'But you've done all you could. You've spoken to the young soldier's parents and sister and the Lieutenant himself, and said they sounded genuine people.'

'They did,' Jenny agreed. 'And Max was right about being his Uncle Werner's heir. The man told me himself on the phone. Really, he said, there's no one else left. But it does mean Linda will be set up for life if she marries him.' She looked at Peter and said, 'D'you think Linda will make it?'

'What, as the wife of Max, or as a singer?'

'Well – both, I suppose,' Jenny said and her heart gave a lurch as there was an enormous screech from the hooter and the smoke billowed out more fiercely – black against the pearly grey sky. Slowly she watched as the huge ship pulled away and she fingered the mizpah on her own neck and said a prayer for a safe journey and a good life for the two young people aboard.

'I don't know whether it will work out for them or not,' Peter said eventually. 'Only time will tell. What I do know is, she had to try for this audition or she'd have wondered about it all her life and as for Max,' he shrugged, 'Let's face it Jenny they're made for each other.' Jenny nodded, agreeing with him and he gave her shoulder a squeeze and said, 'Let's go home and break the news.'

'Not yet,' Jenny said. She had her eyes fixed on the two young people on the ship and she waved and shouted with all the rest and not until the ship was far away on the horizon did she turn and say, 'OK.'

Peter saw she was tearful and to cheer her up he said, 'I meant exactly what I said about getting married soon. It'll probably upset everyone, but I don't see why these things have to be planned a year in advance.'

'You know what people will think if we have such a hasty marriage?' Jenny teased provocatively, a smile on her face.

'Will you mind that?'

'I won't give a damn,' Jenny said firmly.

'Good girl,' Peter said. 'And, if you're very lucky, young lady, we might just take our honeymoon in New York. We'll go over and see how Linda is and have a look at the set-up for ourselves.'

'Oh Peter,' Jenny cried. She threw her arms around him and gave him a long, lingering and very ardent kiss.

This Large Print Book for the partially sighted, who cannot read normal print, is published under the auspices of

THE ULVERSCROFT FOUNDATION